PRAISE FOR

Mademoiselle Eiffel

“For anyone who has ever admired the Eiffel Tow[illegible] at-
ing tale of a woman ahead of her [illegible] ur
heart, in much the same way [illegible] n
the world.”

—Kristin Harmel, [illegible] hor
[illegible] *Paris Daughter*

“Atmospheric, immersive, and brimming with fascinating details surrounding the construction of the Eiffel Tower, Aimie Runyan’s *Mademoiselle Eiffel* will delight historical fiction lovers. A powerful tribute to the incredible life and legacy of Claire Eiffel!”

—Chanel Cleeton, *New York Times* and
USA Today bestselling author

“The story of one of the most iconic landmarks in the world is entwined not only with its architects but with the families of those who built it. Its creation is due in large part to the efforts and support of Claire Eiffel, a young woman forced to grow up too soon but who rose to the challenge. *Mademoiselle Eiffel* shines a glorious light on an unseen woman from history.”

—Erika Robuck, nationally bestselling author
of *The Last Twelve Miles*

“*Mademoiselle Eiffel* is a charming and affecting portrait of a young woman caught between the long arm of grief and her own hopes for her future, who is thrust into adulthood before her time and yet builds a life worthy of the tower that bears her family’s name. Comme la tour Eiffel, c’est magnifique!”

—Bryn Turnbull, internationally bestselling author

MADEMOISELLE *Eiffel*

Also by Aimie K. Runyan

The Wandering Season (forthcoming)
The Memory of Lavender and Sage
A Bakery in Paris
The School for German Brides
Across the Winding River
Girls on the Line
Daughters of the Night Sky
Duty to the Crown
Promised to the Crown

With J'nell Ciesielski and Rachel McMillan

The Liberty Scarf (forthcoming)
The Castle Keepers

MADEMOISELLE

A Novel

AIMIE K. RUNYAN

wm
WILLIAM MORROW
An Imprint of HarperCollins*Publishers*

This book is a work of fiction. References to real people, events, establishments, organizations, or locales are intended only to provide a sense of authenticity, and are used fictitiously. All other characters, and all incidents and dialogue, are drawn from the author's imagination and are not to be construed as real.

HarperCollins books may be purchased for educational, business, or sales promotional use. For information, please email the Special Markets Department at SPsales@harpercollins.com.

FIRST EDITION

Interior text design by Diahann Sturge-Campbell

Eiffel Tower art © wajan/Shutterstock

Library of Congress Cataloging-in-Publication Data has been applied for.

ISBN 978-0-06-332928-7

24 25 26 27 28 LBC 5 4 3 2 1

For my parents, Wayne and Kathleen Trumbly,
who never questioned that I was the author of my own story

Chapter One

September 7, 1891
1, rue Rabelais, Paris

Damn the brutes." Papa muttered an uncharacteristic curse as he surveyed the wreckage of his office. He lingered over a pile of white plaster shards that had once been a likeness of some Greek goddess or another, shaking his head. "That statue belonged to my mother."

My lips turned up at the memory of my grandmother, the great Bonne Maman Eiffel. Were she still with us, I liked to imagine she would have fended off the intruders with the power of her steely gaze alone. Where lesser mortals might have needed a blade or a firearm, her fittingly Gorgon-esque stare would have been enough to terrify a workaday thief into a life so virtuous they'd be fit for the Vatican.

"She gave it to you and Maman because she hated it, if it's any consolation." She'd muttered as much one day when she'd seen it in Papa's office and didn't realize I could overhear. She thought the neoclassical phase, with all the scantily clad Greek deities, was an unmistakable sign that civilization had irrevocably teetered over the precipice of decline. The statue must have been a gift from someone significant enough that it couldn't be disposed of, no matter how discreetly, but passed along to young newlyweds who so desperately needed to feather their new nest.

She was always a clever one, especially when it served her own interests.

Or those of the Eiffel family name.

"Have the brigands taken anything?" Adolphe stepped gingerly around some strewn papers; sketches of a bridge in some remote corner of the Orient that Papa had been engaged to build some years back. There were dozens of detailed plans for the ambitious projects of the company papering the floor so that the thick Turkish rug was hardly visible beneath them. "Was there anything of value in here?"

My hand fluttered to the ruby collar at my throat. Another expensive token of Papa's affection and appreciation. And there were many others in the case upstairs. The cool bands of metal felt as though they might constrict around my windpipe. As extravagant as the bespoke silk gown I wore for an evening at the opera and a decadent meal beforehand at the Café de la Paix.

"These weren't robbers coming after my diamond ear bobs, Adolphe." My husband crossed his arms, awaiting my explanation. I went to the sideboard for a snifter of cognac before sating his curiosity. "They were looking for evidence to use against Papa and the company."

With my free hand I gestured to the forest of ledgers that covered the entire surface of Papa's mammoth desk, all of them open, though nothing ripped or damaged. Those documents were treated with a modicum of care. The looters had been reading them and searching for the evidence to prove their case against the Compagnie Eiffel.

I sipped my cognac. "I'd wager Maman's rosary that there are several volumes of ledgers missing: 1886 to 1889, when the canal project folded. Even those since then, if they wanted to be thorough."

Adolphe crossed to the desk and examined the leather tomes for himself. "Every ledger since 1886 up through last year. They didn't get this year's because it's locked in my desk upstairs. For trained police, they treated your father's property with no more respect than common thieves, whatever you say."

I nodded. "They acted like thugs, I won't deny it. The staff were scared out of their wits. I'm only glad they didn't try to interfere with the search and get themselves in trouble to protect us. The police had their warrant and I'm certain they planned it deliberately for an evening we'd be away so we wouldn't have the chance to hide anything."

"I can only imagine how they must have felt. A miserable business, the lot of it." Papa flung himself into his chair and rubbed his eyes in exhaustion.

I placed a hand on his shoulder. "You'll have to speak to them all in the morning. Don't just assure them that you in no way hold them responsible for the actions of a few zealous detectives, but rather thank them for their cooperation with the authorities in a manner that corroborates the innocence of the Eiffel name and your company."

Adolphe stifled a growl at the idea of his father-in-law, employer, and mentor having to smooth over such a thing with the staff, but Papa understood what had to be done. "Quite right, I'm sure."

"You know I am," I said, my eyes fixed on my husband rather than my father. "But I'd very much like to know one thing."

"And what's that?" Adolphe said in a tone that betrayed that he was more than a little frightened of what query I would pose.

"Will they find what they're looking for?"

Adolphe and Papa exchanged glances that confessed the truth they were loath to speak. The accusations against Papa and the company might be overblown, but they weren't baseless.

I fought against the urge to hurl the snifter against the brick of the fireplace but restrained myself. The time might come when we'd regret the loss of expensive crystal that could fetch a price. I gripped the mantel and gritted my teeth.

It might not be my face that had been plastered across every scandal rag from Cherbourg to Marseille. It wasn't my name that would be sullied. But it might as well have been.

I'd sworn an oath to Papa years ago, and I hadn't faltered a single step in that time. I would not fail him in his hour of greatest need. The sacrifices had been too great to stumble now.

But try though I might, it might not be enough to save that which mattered most to him.

His legacy.

Chapter Two

September 1877
Levallois-Perret, Hauts-de-Seine, Île-de-France, France

As was often the case after a long day, and this had been the longest of my life, my eyes trailed to the massive tapestry on the far wall of the sitting room. I'd stared at it so often that even the smallest detail was burned into my memory. It was a quaint pastoral scene that had been woven a hundred years before by Papa's family when they settled in Paris. The grass was composed of a dozen shades of green; the sky was a melody of countless blues. Even the shepherdess's dress spanned every nuance of pink available to the imagination. Each strand of thread had been chosen with careful deliberation to make the scene seem as realistic as if it had been committed to canvas with the brush of a master painter. I imagined my great-to-the-third-degree grandfather overseeing the work on this very tapestry, perfectly content to have a seamstress remove hours' worth of stitches if the colors weren't precisely right. Papa had to have come by his exacting nature somehow, and it served him well. In architecture, there was even less room for imperfection. One botched calculation could cost untold lives.

"At least the worst is over."

My head—and the thoughts inside it—pivoted to where Bonne Maman Eiffel rested on a plush fauteuil. She was a formidable woman with a solemn face and shrewd eyes that were not tempered with kindness like Papa's. She leaned forward in her seat, her hand gripping the ball of her cane, and sighed as though the black dress she wore were made of iron instead of crêpe.

A heavy silence weighed on the room. We all looked at her in disbelief. The *funeral* was over, yes. The last stragglers from the throng of visitors who had come to pay their respects to my much-lamented mother had left, and we now regained some solitude in the house. Only my aunt, uncle, and grandparents remained in addition to our little family of six, and I could admit I was glad for some quiet.

But was the worst of it over? No. Not by half.

The funeral was indeed an ordeal. It involved planning and organization and a generous measure of grace and poise. Things the Eiffel family possessed in spades. But now that the work of the services was over, we didn't have anything to distract us from the real task at hand: learning how to rebuild our lives without Maman.

Papa seemed as if he wanted to dole out a rebuke to his mother but swallowed back his censure. "Quite" was all he could muster.

"Papa, you should have some coffee." I leapt from the settee and crossed the room to pour him a cup from the service on the sideboard before he could object. The maids had, on my orders, kept it filled with coffee, tea, and platters of simple food throughout the gathering that afternoon. Strong coffee, I'd insisted, the sort that might peel the enamel from your teeth, just as Papa liked it. I added a couple of his favorite butter biscuits in a wordless plea for him to eat something. He'd only picked at meals, and I was certain from the dark circles under his eyes that sleep was no friend to him.

I expected him to refuse as I approached his seat with the coffee and pastry, but his eyes met mine for a moment and he gave a small smile of appreciation as he accepted them. I felt the muscles loosen in my shoulders as he took a sip from the cup and absentmindedly dipped the edge of a biscuit in the strong brew. It was an improvement. I couldn't bear the thought of him growing weak and falling ill as Maman had done. He had a far stronger constitution than she had, but it wasn't a chance I was willing to take.

"I suppose your father is the only one who merits such attentions?" Bonne Maman chided. Of course, no one else could be doted upon in her presence if she were not included.

"My apologies," I mumbled, rising to fetch her a cup and some biscuits of her own.

"No, I can't drink coffee after luncheon, or I won't sleep a wink. It's the principle of the thing, Claire."

Papa made no attempt to hide the rolling of his eyes.

Bonne Maman and Bon Papa would return to Dijon next week, which would be a loss and a relief in almost equal measure. Tante Marie and Oncle Albert lived close enough that they would return home after the supper that none of us would likely touch. I wished they would stay to help divert Bonne Maman's attention, but I wouldn't impose it on them.

"Dearest Marguerite," Tante Marie said. "It won't be the same without her laugh."

"Such an affable, sweet woman," Bonne Maman said, for once in agreement with her daughter. And it was true.

Maman hadn't been as vibrant as Tante Marie or as sharp-witted as Bonne Maman, but her presence had been soothing in a way no one else's was. No one else's could be.

I felt, for perhaps the millionth time, the tears burning at the corners of my eyes, begging to be released in a torrent. I kept the dam from bursting, but a few errant tears slid down my cheeks.

"Not now, child. We mustn't upset the little ones. They've lost their mother." Bonne Maman clucked her tongue in reproach. Little Valentine, seven years old, and the most beautiful girl in all of France in my view, was playing despondently in a corner with the baby, little Albert, who was only four. If they noticed my tears, it would be through a veil of their own.

Albert didn't fully understand what was going on but could read our sadness like words on a page. Valentine understood better and pined for her *maman* with heartbreaking candor.

Laure, who was only a year my junior at the age of thirteen, sat beside the spot I'd vacated on the settee. She looked like a miniature version of Maman, and was every bit as elegant. She had daintily dabbed her own tears with a lacy handkerchief throughout the day. Édouard, just eleven and on leave from school for the funeral, tried to manfully keep his tears from surfacing, but he hadn't been entirely successful.

Tante Marie turned to her mother. "As did Claire." Her tone was low and soft as velvet but laced with venom.

Bonne Maman shot Tante Marie one of her famous withering glares. She didn't speak a word, but her meaning was clear enough: *It isn't the same. She's older and must be mistress of herself for their sakes.*

She wasn't entirely wrong. Valentine, and especially little Albert, would only have dim memories, faded around the edges, to cling to. I'd had fourteen years with her. It was far more than they would have. But that didn't mean it was anything like enough.

It was never supposed to be this way. Maman was supposed to live decades longer, and I was supposed to have a mother for many years after I had children of my own. I had questions. About growing into a woman, about marriage and babies, about running a house. All those chapters of my life lay ahead of me, and I knew nothing about how to take them on.

I had spent so much time trying to be Papa's shadow, I'd never taken the time to be Maman's. To learn all the lessons she had to teach.

Bonne Maman? She'd tell me I was an Eiffel and clever enough to figure it out on my own and to, for heaven's sake, stop pestering her.

Tante Marie would be more helpful, but she had her own house to manage and enough to get on with without having me as an added concern. She never had children of her own, and I sensed she enjoyed the freedoms her childless state afforded her.

Maman was only three years older than I was now when she married Papa. When Maman was alive, it seemed like I'd have an eternity before I had to worry about adult concerns like marriage and managing a house and children. Now that she was gone, those milestones in my life would come all too soon, whether I was prepared or not.

And I was not.

A maid came to collect Valentine and Albert for their dinner in the nursery, and the rest of us went into the dining room. Bonne Maman looked askance when Édouard joined us at the table. At the age of eleven, he was a bit young to dine in company, but he was already enrolled at school and perfectly well-behaved enough for a family dinner.

The cook, Monsieur Lebec, had been at dire straits trying to prepare meals that would please us when it seemed nothing could tempt us to eat. I'd tried to reassure him that nothing was amiss with the food itself, only our appetites, but he was still peevish that so much of the food went untouched. Tonight, he set before us course after course of culinary marvels, taking extra care since Bonne Maman was in attendance. He would hear of it if she were displeased, and he knew it well. My head swirled as the canapés were followed by watercress soup. An exquisitely roasted duck in a port wine reduction, braised carrots, and green beans with butter-and-almond sauce were on their way. My stomach rolled at the thought of such richness. We would have to sit through the main course, cheeses, and then *poires Belle Hélène*—pears poached in sugar, drizzled with chocolate, and served with vanilla ice cream. The dessert was Bonne Maman's favorite, so I ordered it especially to please her. And while most of us merely sampled our food, Bonne Maman, Bon Papa, and Oncle Albert ate heartily. At least Monsieur Lebec would be mollified that our guests were pleased.

The conversation had been muted through the appetizers, but it seemed Bonne Maman could not let the soup course come to completion without getting down to the business at hand.

"Now that poor Marguerite is laid to rest, your work will require your attention again, Gustave. Even in such sorrowful circumstances, you cannot allow mistakes to happen when the company bears the Eiffel name." She thunked her spoon down next to the bowl, which sounded as definite as the hammering of a gavel.

"Maman, I hardly think this is the time—" Tante Marie interjected.

"If not now, when, Marie? Gustave cannot afford to stain the reputation of a company in its infancy. No one will much care that he is mourning for his wife if one of his bridges collapses or a building tumbles over." Bonne Maman's expression dared anyone to contradict her.

"Gustave knows better than anyone the value of reputation in this business, and he doesn't need you to remind him of it, woman." Bon Papa spoke for the first time since arriving beyond "hello," "goodbye," and general pleasantries with the guests that afternoon.

"Thank you," Papa said, his voice several degrees lower and huskier than I was used to. He sat up taller in his seat and directed his gaze toward Bonne Maman. "I'm getting daily reports from the workshops and regular reports from our projects abroad. I'm keeping an eye on all of it, even now."

"That is all well and good, Son. But your clients need to see you with feet on the ground overseeing things," she pressed.

"In due time, Maman," Papa said.

"Gustave, I really must insist—"

Papa, for perhaps the first time in his life, put up a hand to silence her.

She glowered at her son's directive. He was a grown man in his own home, and she owed him some measure of deference there, but it was evident she loathed it. "Very well, but your father and I are resolved to take Claire and Laure back to Dijon with us when we leave. You don't need added distractions here. Édouard is occupied with school, and I trust Marguerite had adequate help for the little ones. But the girls will need more looking after than you should devote time to."

I bit my tongue. Never once had Papa acted as though the time he spent with us was in any way a distraction for more important duties. He'd be mortified if we'd ever thought such a thing.

"Claire stays with me," Papa insisted. "Laure may go for a visit if she wishes, but we will depend on having her home for Christmas. Her tutoring will resume here in the new year."

"Gustave—"

"The younger children will need Claire's attentions. Hired help cannot replace a mother."

"Neither can a girl barely free from her leading strings," Bonne Maman countered.

Papa slammed a hand down on the table, causing the china to rattle. "On this, I will not yield, Maman. I lost my wife, but I will not be separated from Claire."

Bonne Maman's face was pinched as she sat taller and rounded on Papa. "I insist—"

"Insist all you wish, Maman. Claire's place is with me. I cannot run a home and a business alone, and I cannot depend on staff to do it. I will have no more conversation on the matter."

Bonne Maman opened her mouth to protest, but closed it just as soon, looking oddly like a fish gasping for breath. It was a day that would be etched in my memory, not only because it was the day we'd laid my beloved mother to rest, but because it was the first time anyone had seen Bonne Maman Eiffel at a loss for words.

Chapter Three

"You call that proper stitching, do you?" Bonne Maman asked, appearing out of nowhere and peering over my shoulder to examine the sampler I'd been embroidering.

I'd chosen to fuss with my embroidery that morning, knowing it was an activity Bonne Maman deemed suitable for a young lady, but she had managed to find fault even with this. "Your mother should have taken more pains with your education," Bonne Maman said, clucking her tongue.

"She was ill, if you remember," I said through clenched teeth. I'd regret my cheek later, but I found it too irresistible in the moment.

Bonne Maman glowered. "That will be quite enough of your impudence. I know full well that your mother was of a weak constitution for quite some time, but if she was unequal to oversee your training, she ought to have engaged the staff to see to it in her stead."

"I can read and speak three languages fluently, have earned highest marks from my tutors in French composition, and have long since outstripped Édouard in mathematics. I am proficient at the pianoforte and amuse myself by reading many of the great works in Papa's library. I apologize if you feel my needlework isn't up to snuff, but Maman occupied my time with more serious pursuits."

In truth, Maman *had* lamented over my mediocre needlework and knitting but had always been supportive of my weightier academic interests. As I wasn't permitted to attend a proper school like Édouard did and little Bébert soon would, Maman had always engaged tutors of the first order. And it wasn't that I found no enjoyment in these ladylike arts; it was that I simply had no natural talent for them and had taken too little time to improve myself in them. Maman had understood.

"And she's a brilliant artist," Laure supplied, shooting me a supportive glance. She meant well, but I doubted Bonne Maman would respond graciously to her defense of me and my education. Maman had found numerous art tutors for us over the years, and it was the diversion I loved best in the world.

"Don't be boastful," Bonne Maman snapped. "All the Greek and Latin in the world won't find you a suitable husband. Quite the contrary, men don't like their wives to be smarter than they are. They look for wives to be decorative, obedient, and sweet. Not clever."

"Were you not instrumental in furthering Bon Papa's career?"

I wished instantly I could swallow the words back into my mouth. Papa had spoken with deep admiration of how his mother had pushed his father to greater heights.

"Of course I was," she replied. "But I had the good sense never to let him know it. Now rip out that last row and try again. Pay attention and keep your work tidy. I'll be inspecting it later."

She padded out of the room, whether to pester the children or Bon Papa, I didn't know. "She is so awful," I muttered when I was certain she was out of earshot.

"You shouldn't say that," Laure whispered, her eyes darting about the room as though she expected Bonne Maman had stationed hidden informants throughout the house. "She's merely trying to help."

"We buried Maman yesterday, yet she insists on finding fault with everyone and everything. No, Laure. That isn't trying to help. She's an overbearing witch."

"Who's that?" Papa asked, entering the room with a thick book in his left hand. The dark circles under his eyes were still prominent, but he did look as though he had slept better last night.

"No one, Papa," I said hastily. "We were just discussing a novel."

"Careful with those around your grandmother," Papa said with a roll of his eyes. "She doesn't approve."

What doesn't she find wanting? I swallowed the question and found a more pressing query waiting on my tongue. "Where is she now?"

"In the library," he said.

"Didn't you tell us you were not to be disturbed there?" Laure interjected.

"Your grandmother does not respond well to such directives, so I retreated here with my book if you ladies don't mind my company. Though you have a guest in the foyer, Claire, who is quite eager to see you."

"Ursule?" I had few intimate friends, and she was the only one who was dear enough to me to drop by without an invitation.

"Indeed. Canvas in hand and ready to set to work in the gardens, I should think."

"May I go, Papa?" I asked.

He nodded. "Off you trot, little Monet. Degas is waiting. Your sister and I will make excuses for you."

I tossed my needlework aside and bounded across the room to kiss Papa's cheek before collecting my own art case and rescuing Ursule from the foyer before Bonne Maman discovered her. Ursule Blanchet, our neighbor and my closest friend, was of average height, but wiry and thin as a greyhound. She had frizzy hair that couldn't decide if it was strawberry blond or caramel brown, and the most arresting green eyes I'd ever seen. We'd been friends since we were small girls and had cultivated a love of art together. Our keenest wish was to go to art school together in the city and shock our parents by making a name for ourselves in the male-dominated world of art. Nothing would do until our work was on display at the Louvre itself.

"I hope it's all right that I came today," Ursule said. "You must feel free to send me away if you'd rather I hadn't. I wasn't sure if you would want company and diversion or if you'd prefer solitude and time with your family."

I kissed both her cheeks with gusto. "You're the most welcome sight I've seen in ages. Let's go."

We lugged our cases, replete with canvases, easels, and paints, to the farthest reaches of the gardens, where we were certain the scope for the imagination was at its best. The warm autumn sun, still clinging to the last vestiges of late summer, seemed to mock me with its cheer, though simply having Ursule nearby was such a comfort that it warmed me just as thoroughly. I knew the grief would come surging back, like a wave crashing onto the shore, but for now I could enjoy a few hours where the pain was at low tide.

Ursule had begun a fine painting of a rather charming chestnut tree and was anxious to make progress on it. My canvas was blank, as I had spent much of the summer frantically painting the flowers until they went out of season. Since many of the varietals in our gardens were going dormant for the year, I'd have to find a new subject.

I studied Ursule's canvas, admiring her talent and her patience. "You've been working on that painting for weeks and weeks. Haven't you grown tired of staring at the same tree all this time? The flowers are far more fun. You have to capture them before they wilt."

"That's where you're wrong," Ursule said. "It's never the same tree twice. I'm trying to capture all of its moods. To this tree, your flower friends are just passing through."

"What a lovely thought." I smiled at her, always happy to get a glimpse inside her brain, which was often more philosophical than my own.

"It's the beautiful thing about art. We can capture the fleeting and the eternal. A dandelion or a mountain, all as we please. Now that you've spent months on flowers, you ought to choose something that will last the winter and spend some time on it," Ursule said, her eyes already fixed on the chestnut tree she'd dubbed Hector.

And this was why I loved Ursule. She didn't just enjoy making pretty things; there was a philosophy behind all that she did. Like me, she was a passionate reader, and her parents had encouraged her education just as mine did.

I chose to paint the corner of the house that jutted into the garden. There was something pleasing about the angle as it encroached into the greenery of the out-of-doors, the way the light bounced off the gray stone, the way the vines spiderwebbed up the side of the building. I sketched outlines for some time, then I concentrated on the various hues of gray in the rock and all the greens in the vines, trying to capture the nuance of the color and the subtleties of the light.

Our habit was to chat for a while as we worked, but inevitably we'd be pulled into our work and lose ourselves in it. We simultaneously forgot the other was there and were somehow comforted by the presence of our fellow artist. There was no need for idle conversation to feel the camaraderie as we immersed ourselves in a sea of burnt sienna and viridian.

I couldn't have told a soul if we'd been at our work for an hour or six by the time I heard the slam of a door and angry footsteps rushing toward us in the garden. Bonne Maman Eiffel had discovered my escape.

"What on earth are you doing out of doors? In the sun, and without a hat too. Have you lost your senses completely, or were you never born with any?"

I fought the urge to fling paint at her with my brush and did exactly as Maman would have done. I pretended that Bonne Maman hadn't said anything beyond "Good afternoon" or "How do you do?"

I plastered on my smile that I reserved for the moments I was fighting not to lose my temper. *Always turn to manners when your anger gets the better of you,* Maman had said. "Bonne Maman, I'd like to present my dear friend Ursu—"

"I don't care who this is." Bonne Maman turned to Ursule. "Go home to your parents, child, if you have any. I don't want to see you here again."

Heat rose in my cheeks. My mother had loved Ursule and her family and always welcomed them into our home. And this harpy was insulting the one person who had thought to look after my needs when I'd run myself to the point of exhaustion taking care of everyone else's. "Bonne Maman, she's our neighbor. Her father is friends with Papa. How can you speak to her in such a way?" I tried, for Papa's sake, to keep my tone even, but wasn't entirely successful.

"How dare *you* contradict me," Bonne Maman fired back. She glanced at my painting and grabbed the canvas from the easel. "You've wasted time enough for one lifetime on childish things. You'll take your paints to the nursery for the children and spend your time profitably from now on."

I yanked the painting back from her before she could damage it, which was surely her intent. "I will not, you nasty cow. I wish you'd never come here. You're just making everything worse."

She stood slack-jawed, and I didn't wait for her to regain her composure to give me the tongue-lashing I was due. I took my easel, case, and canvas awkwardly in my arms. My pained look was an unvoiced apologetic farewell to Ursule. I marched back to the rear entryway of the house with Bonne Maman trailing in my wake, no doubt aggravated that her age kept her from matching my stride.

"Back already?" Papa asked when he saw me reenter the drawing room. I glanced to the clock and saw we'd been at our travails for two hours. There were times when we devoted five or six hours to our artwork without a pause, and today would have been an ideal day for it. To have a reprieve from the grief and a chance to be out of my own skin for just a short while.

And Bonne Maman had taken that from me.

"Do you know what your daughter has been doing, Gustave?" Bonne Maman barked as she entered the room.

"Painting with the neighbor girl," Papa said, his expression wary. "It's a thrice-weekly occurrence and hardly one that merits hysterics from you."

"Watch yourself, boy. I'm still your mother."

His eyes flashed in a rare display of anger, though his voice remained steady. "And this is my house. Claire has leave to paint with her friend when she likes."

"It's unseemly for her to be out of doors unchaperoned. Not to mention she'll grow freckled and brown out in the sun without a hat. You must take charge of her, Gustave, or she'll grow willful and disobedient."

"Oh, I should hope so," Papa said. "I can't say I value brashness in a woman, but I've an absolute horror for the overly meek ones. If I wanted that for Claire or the girls, I'd send them off to finishing school in Britain. That would suck the merriment from their lives and the color from their cheeks in short order."

"Don't speak nonsense, boy. She's nearly fifteen. She has to consider her prospects unless you want her to remain an old maid and a millstone around your neck."

Papa turned to me, mischief glinting in his eyes. "That sounds like a grand plan to me, Cherub. What do you say? Traveling to all the worksites and learning the trade with your old papa? Making sure I take my meals and don't look a fright as I leave for the office."

"That sounds lovely to me, Papa." I returned his smile and directed it back to Bonne Maman. Millstone indeed.

"It's settled. And I've given it some thought. I want you to move to your mother's rooms. If you're to help me in my endeavors, it's only right you have a space befitting the office."

Bonne Maman threw her arms up in exasperation. "You're a fool, Gustave, and that is one thing I cannot suffer. I am going to lie down."

"Ring the bell if you require anything, Bonne Maman," I said in my best "lady of the manor" voice.

When the sound of her footsteps faded into the distance, Papa and I dissolved into peals of laughter.

"Pay her no mind, Cherub. She sniffs out happiness like a hound and tries to snuff it out. She'll be gone in a few days, and we'll be able to breathe again. Do think to wear a hat out of doors when she's around, though. We can indulge her that far."

I looked to Laure, who would not escape as easily as we did.

"I'll be fine," she said, answering the unasked query. "I manage to irritate Bonne Maman less than either of you."

Papa patted her knee. "It's just as well one of us developed that talent. But I urge you to heed her lessons with skepticism. She is a woman with some very keen insights, but an equal amount of the ridiculous."

Laure nodded sagely, and I hoped, for her sake, that her time in Dijon would not be an exercise in torment.

He turned to me. "I was serious in my proposal, Claire. I do mean for you to help run things if you're willing. I cannot do it alone and I won't trust it to staff. No matter how loyal, it simply isn't the same. It's more than I should ask of one so young, but there is no one else I could trust so well."

Pride rose in my bosom. "Anything you need, Papa. If I can't do it, I'll learn how."

Papa bent and kissed my forehead. "An Eiffel through and through, and my heart's own pride and joy."

He retreated to his library, and with each step, I felt the weight of my vow like a leaden mantle on my shoulders.

Chapter Four

I sat on the edge of Maman's bed, a large gleaming walnut four-poster affair with a plush mattress and thick damask bedding in shades of soft pink and ivory, and tried, in vain, to take a proper breath. This was *her* suite of rooms and I felt like an imposter in them. True to his word, the moment he left the drawing room Papa had ordered the staff to move my things here from the nursery wing. My assortment of dresses and my small collection of girlish knickknacks hadn't taken long to transport down the hall, and so my tenure in these rooms would begin that very night.

The little porcelain cat that Papa had brought back for me from one of his many sojourns abroad had been placed on the vanity next to Maman's silver brush and comb. My modest pastel dresses, befitting a girl of gentle birth, now hung in the wardrobe next to Maman's fine embroidered silks, crisp linens, and lush velvets. Her scent now interlaced with my own. The housekeeper, Pauline, had placed my small leather jewelry case, containing only a few delicate pieces suited to my age, on Maman's mammoth chest of drawers. The little case was shadowed by Maman's far grander carved wooden box that contained years' worth of bejeweled gifts from Papa, who had been so devoted to her.

Seeing our effects commingled was disconcerting as a chartreuse sunset. I was surrounded by Maman's precious things, and Papa had made it clear that the duty of distributing them among my siblings would fall to me. I could keep the things I wanted, but I was to make sure my younger sisters, Laure and Valentine, had their remembrances of Maman to treasure, and to keep a few pieces for Édouard and Albert to give to their sweethearts one day as well.

I opened the heavy lid to the wooden jewelry box, admiring Maman's collection. Deciding who should receive Maman's belongings felt ghoulish, but accomplishing any task was better than remaining idle. Some of the decisions were easy. Valentine simply adored Maman's ruby brooch that had been a wedding gift from her parents. She could have that when she came of age. Laure had always admired the emerald ring that Papa had gifted Maman for her twenty-fifth birthday. It would be an appropriate gift when she married. As for me, I had always felt a flutter in my heart when Maman emerged into a room, dressed for a party or an important dinner with the amethyst choker she saved for special occasions. I'd reserve it for myself, but it would be many years before I would wear it in public. There were a few necklaces, quite lovely, that had been given to Maman more recently that I'd set aside for Albert's and Édouard's future brides. They would be a token of the esteem Maman would have bestowed upon the new members of the family but didn't have the sentimental attachment of some of the older pieces.

I organized the jewels, one by one, each in a separate drawer of the case, one for each recipient. Laure on top, then Valentine, then Édouard, then Albert. The things I saved for myself would remain in the bottom drawer.

I hesitated when I came across the piece Maman wore most often. It was a button necklace on a long chain that she wore around the house and on informal occasions. I could hardly picture Maman's person without seeing the necklace draped artfully at her neck. I slipped the chain on over my head and sat at Maman's vanity to admire the effect. It looked comical hanging down to my undeveloped bosom. If I were to pair it with my inky-black mourning dress, I'd look as ridiculous as a girl playing dress-up in her mother's clothes.

Like most girls my age, I wore my golden-brown curls down but pulled away from the face at the sides. I took Maman's brush and hairpins and twisted my hair into a low chignon as she used to wear. Wearing hair up was a rite of passage for women who were out properly into society and ready for courtship. That would be several years away for me yet, but now that the rooms of the lady of the house were my own, I was curious to see how I would look. I'd envisioned Maman helping me pin my hair up properly for the first time, clasping some pearls around my neck, placing her hands on my shoulders, and pronouncing me the loveliest young woman Paris ever saw. But that wasn't to be.

She was gone, her weak lungs finally breathing their last, and I was to take her place.

A knock sounded at the door. I quickly removed Maman's necklace and pulled the pins from my hair.

"Come in," I bade.

Laure emerged from the hallway, timid as though she were intruding in a shrine. "I hope it's all right that I've come to see you here." She surveyed the room, and it was clear that my presence in Maman's quarters was as unsettling to her as it was to me.

"I'm always happy to see my sister," I said, folding my hands in my lap and looking up at her. "Are you all right?"

"Fine. Well, as fine as I can hope to be," she replied. We all felt the need to qualify such statements these days.

As she stood next to my vanity, Laure looked so young, like a china doll in her flowing, white lace-trimmed nightgown, though she was thirteen and becoming more ladylike every day. In many respects, she was far more of a lady than I was. She was elegant like Maman, where there was something graceless about me.

But I could see a storm cloud lurking over her angelic face. She was troubled, and it wasn't just about Maman. "Are you sure you want to go stay with Bonne Maman and Bon Papa Eiffel? I'm sure we could make other arrangements."

Laure sighed. "I'd give anything to stay with you and Papa. But it's probably better for everyone if I go. I'll divert Bonne Maman's attention away from everyone else so you can breathe for a few moments."

I took her hand. "That's an awfully big responsibility for you to take on. She's terrifying."

"Keeping Bonne Maman happy for a month or two is a much smaller job than the one you've been handed." She gestured to the rooms and all they represented. "It's only fair I do my part."

"I just hope your time won't be too dreadful."

"I'll be fine. But how are *you* faring? I know you're delighted to help Papa, but it's a lot to be getting on with."

I squeezed the hand I'd taken in mine and tried to control my ragged breath, but I felt like my body might rend itself in two from the effort. I'd tried so hard to be strong for the children, but the undertaking was draining.

Not now, child. We mustn't upset the little ones. They've lost their mother. The words rang in my ears again.

Laure knew better. She didn't try to tell me to wipe away my tears or to put on a brave face. She simply took Maman's brush from the vanity and ran it slowly through my hair.

"I ought to be mad that you got the prettiest hair. And Valentine the prettiest face. You all left nothing for me." She tried to sound affronted by nature's oversight but failed.

"There's a simple explanation. You got the kindest heart and the rest of us must make do with consolation prizes." I patted her hand that rested on my shoulder. She was a striking beauty, like Maman, whose graceful carriage made her seem even more so. My features were most like Papa's, while the three others were a blend of both parents to varying degrees. Valentine's features were the finest, mine the least. But I had a lush head of hair I'd always considered my one claim to conventional beauty. Both girls had sweeter dispositions than I, which had endeared them to Maman, who often had little idea of what to make of a daughter who was content to silently hole up in her father's study with a book while he worked.

When Laure finished her brushing, my hair fairly glowed in the lamplight. Maman's brush was finer than my own, and I mentally added it to the list of possessions I'd keep for myself. Laure and I would get the most good from her gowns. By the time Valentine was grown, they'd be dreadfully out of fashion. But what would it be like to wear Maman's favorite lilac silk gown? To smell her scent on my skin? To see Papa's haunted look when he remembered, once again, that she was gone?

That was one of the hardest parts of grief. One moment, all would be well enough, then a small reminder of the loved one lost brought all the memories flooding back in an excruciating torrent. There were obvious things, like passing by the photograph of Maman that Papa had framed on his desk, but oftentimes the reminders were more subtle. The sight of the chair she'd favored. A flash of her favorite color—a gentle mauve that matched her tender soul. The scent of her favorite roses from the garden, even the memory of it. It was honestly easier to stay mired in the grief than to tread above its surface for a few hours only to be pulled back deeper into the chasm.

"I do worry about you," she said once more. "Papa will expect much of you. The little ones will need nurturing in a way a nanny cannot do. It's why Papa had you move into Maman's rooms. So they know her place won't remain empty."

I felt a pang at the enormity of that realization. Loving them was something I could do, to be sure. It wouldn't be the same as having Maman back with us, but it would be better than the absence of maternal affections altogether.

But Laure needed someone to finish teaching her how to be a woman. I was hardly equipped for such a task. I had so much to learn about how to run a home, how to entertain, how to present myself in public. Of all the people in our family I was worried about failing, it was Laure I worried about most. Bonne Maman was right to worry after the little ones, but I thought the loss of Maman hit Laure the hardest. They had been inseparable, Maman and Laure. Laure tried to emulate her in all things, while I had clung to Papa. I would endeavor to fill the role Maman had taken in Laure's life, but I couldn't envision that my performance would ever be sufficient.

I'd have to hope it would be at least adequate in some small way.

I rose from the vanity and kissed Laure, first on one cheek, then the other. The soft skin of her cheeks, like the rest of ours, was perpetually clammy from the tears that seemed to spring forth at the most inopportune times.

"You need rest, darling," I told her, pulling her into my arms. "It's been an exhausting time for all of us, and I don't want anyone falling ill. Papa couldn't bear the worry."

"Mother hen already," she said, a glint of playful defiance in her eyes.

"You don't resent me, do you?" I asked. "Being installed in Maman's rooms and all while you're still in the nursery? I know I'm barely older than you are."

"I'm glad Papa had you move in here. It would be worse if you didn't. It would be dreadful if he brought in another woman to take her place. Moving you into these rooms means he doesn't plan on doing such a thing anytime soon."

I shuddered at the very thought. The pain was still too fresh to even contemplate the idea of Papa moving on. Hopefully that day would be many years off, if at all. Laure was braver than I to even consider the possibility.

"I'm sure you're right" was all I could manage to say. "Off to bed with you, sweetheart. You need your wits about you with Bonne Maman here."

Laure returned my kisses and scooted out into the hallway and back to her little room down the corridor with the other children. Papa was indulgent with us in so many things, but bedtime was to be strictly observed in the nursery wing. I'd been given a bit more leeway, being the oldest, and doubted that Papa would insist on a bedtime of any sort now beyond what I deemed appropriate for myself. Perhaps the privilege of staying up later than the younger children would be extended to Laure now that she reigned over the nursery rooms. I'd hate for our bedtime chats to be eliminated because our rooms were no longer next to each other as they had been our whole lives.

I no longer heard the soft padding of Laure's steps, and found that despite feeling weary, deep in my bones, sleep was going to continue to elude me as it had done in the days since Maman's passing. I crossed over to Maman's sitting room, hoping to find a book or two that might interest me, rather than going to Papa's library and running the risk of disturbing him. She'd left a few books behind, though none of them of great interest to me. There was one, a novel by an English author I'd not yet read, with a neatly embroidered bookmark holding her place. It was a book she'd started, before she fell ill. Had she known when she closed the cover those weeks ago that she'd never read the rest of it? If she'd known she wasn't long for the world, would she have pressed on to know how it ended?

Unlikely. If she'd known how short the rest of her life was going to be, she'd have tossed the book aside and held us all close to her heart until the illness had weakened her to the point her arms could no longer keep us.

The ghastly truth was that none of us thought Maman's illness was grave enough to take her until hours before she was so ill, she didn't recognize any of us. If we'd known, how differently we would have done things. Fewer schoolroom squabbles, and more time by Maman's side asking her all the questions we'd never be able to ask.

I noticed Maman's knitting basket in its usual spot by her chair. Knitting had always been a comfort to her. Even when she was ill, which wasn't an uncommon event for her, she could knit for us. We all had hats, mittens, scarves, and blankets enough to keep the whole of the French army outfitted for winter. Maman's latest project had been a lace collar for a dress for Valentine. I was clumsy with needles, but Valentine had been looking forward to the fine dress that Maman had promised her for mass on Christmas night.

I knew how to knit and purl reasonably well. Casting on was harder, but that task was done. I had no idea how to finish the project and remove it from the needles intact, but there was enough stitching left to be done that I could save that worry for another day. But as I looked down at the intricate stitches Maman had begun, I couldn't make any sense of the pattern she'd woven. I didn't know a rose leaf from a diamond lace pattern when it came down to the anatomy of the stitches, though she'd tried to teach me more times than I cared to remember.

But when it came down to producing the beautiful lace collars we wore with our dresses? I was useless. I tried for what felt like hours to decipher Maman's stitches but was no closer to understanding it by the time my eyes grew weary, and I had to abandon the effort for bed. As I held the scrap of unfinished lace in my hands, I realized that while Papa had been engineering badges and viaducts in his study, Maman had been engineering masterpieces of her own in this sitting room. Somehow, understanding the intricacies of iron and steel seemed less daunting than deciphering this web of silken thread.

I replaced the collar in the basket, hoping it was no worse for my meddling, and retreated to the massive four-poster bed, not confident my mind would be kind enough to let me rest.

As I tried so desperately to find some respite in a bout of sleep, no matter how brief, I wondered what other incomplete tasks Maman had left behind and how I could ever hope to finish them all for her.

And, amidst completing all she'd left undone, what time might be left for me to weave some sort of a life for myself.

Chapter Five

I thought I'd help you with your correspondence this morning if you have the time to spare for it, Papa," I said as we breakfasted the following morning.

"You will be going into town with me this morning," Bonne Maman interjected.

"Oh?" I turned to her. "On what errand?"

"It isn't for you to ask questions." Bonne Maman stabbed a piece of sausage for emphasis.

"But it *is* my prerogative to do so," Papa replied. "I may have need of her help and you *will* ask me before making any engagements on her behalf."

Not for the first time since her visit, Papa was forced to use his best *I am not to be trifled with* voice and I wanted to beam at him, though it would have just incited Bonne Maman's wrath later, so I did my best to keep my expression neutral.

She bristled, but softened her tone. "It is a matter pertaining to female concerns. I will thank you to leave the issue alone for the sake of feminine delicacy."

I looked to Papa, my brow furrowed in confusion.

"I'll risk scandal." Papa put down his newspaper and glared at his mother. "Where do you propose taking my daughter?"

Bonne Maman's nostrils flared. "I will be taking her to the modiste. If she is to be allowed in public, she must have the appropriate . . . garments befitting a lady."

"Very well." Papa reclaimed his paper and opened it with a flourish. "You'll see to it the bill is sent to me."

Bonne Maman grunted something like approval. "You needn't worry on that score. I won't spend one *centime* to support how you're raising this child, but I will insist any child bearing my surname is dressed properly, whatever foolishness you get up to."

Papa rolled his eyes and rose from the table. "I hope you have a jolly time, ladies."

My eyes pleaded with him, but he shrugged, powerless against her arguments. He retreated to the solace of his library and left me in Bonne Maman's clutches.

"It's kind of you to take me, but I have plenty of dresses, Bonne Maman. Especially as I won't be out of mourning for months yet." According to custom, I'd be required to wear black clothes for three months and half-mourning—gray or violet—for another three. Papa's mourning would last twice that duration, but given the nature of men's wardrobes, it was hardly different from what he wore in normal times, though he'd miss his light gray and soft tan linen suits next summer, to be sure.

"We aren't going to buy *dresses*." Her voice was a low growl. "Fetch your cloak and let's get to town."

"My cloaks have been stored until winter." I tried and failed to keep the annoyance from lacing my words like arsenic. The sun had barely lost the intensity of summer, and I was not about to subject myself to heatstroke for her ridiculous rules of propriety. My dress was black and made of wool and would be stifling enough.

Bonne Maman gritted her teeth but didn't speak further for the duration of the carriage ride. We pulled up to a shop called Maison Léoty. But instead of dresses and fabrics in the windows, the mannequins were squeezed into corsets in a rainbow of colors.

I'd seen Maman laced into one a number of times, and always found the rigid garment curious when I embraced her. As though she were made of sterner stuff than bone and flesh. As though the steel, whalebone, and stiff cotton became a part of her. It made the loss of her all the harder to fathom.

Bonne Maman saw me admiring the window as I descended the carriage. "If your father is going to treat you like a woman, as idiotic as that might be, you must have the proper undergarments. I was bought my first corset at the age of twelve and made to sleep in it to improve my posture. That the practice has gone out of fashion is a shame. People have grown soft. But you won't. Not while you're under my sphere of influence."

Her words were meant to intimidate me, but as we entered the shop, I didn't feel cowed in the least. The shopkeeper ushered us to a fitting room as though we were expected, and we were surrounded by swatches of fabrics that were a delight for the senses.

"Lord help me now, what sort of place has your aunt recommended?" Bonne Maman despaired. "If we were in Dijon, I'd take you to my own *corsetière*. Sensibly made and built to last. No silly frills."

A young woman emerged into our little chamber, measuring tape around her neck, and smiled at me. "Ah, I expect this is the first fitting for the charming young lady." She purred rather than spoke. I nodded and returned her smile.

"Very good. I am Mademoiselle Berthillon, but you may call me Delphine."

Bonne Maman's lips pursed, but I pretended not to notice. The *corsetière* was trying to put me at ease, but Bonne Maman saw it as an untoward familiarity. That Delphine hadn't addressed her first, I suspected, was the real insult.

"Now, I am certain you will find our corsets are perfect for a young woman who is still growing into her form. They will give just enough to allow freedom of movement but restrict you enough to be effective. Once you get used to it, you'll never want to go without."

Bonne Maman bristled. "What nonsense. What good is a corset with any sort of give to it? It must stay rigid to help mold her posture."

"You would be surprised at the efficacy of our corsets, madame. Moreover, we have found it is much more healthful for the body to be able to move as God intended. Especially true for active young ladies," Delphine replied.

"*Active* and *lady* are contradictory terms," Bonne Maman snapped. "Come, Claire. I'll have your measurements taken elsewhere and order your things from Dijon, where all this new claptrap mercifully hasn't spread. Good day to you, mademoiselle."

I was on the point of capitulating out of sheer force of habit, but then turned to Bonne Maman. "No thank you. You're quite right that it's time I had the undergarments befitting a lady. I won't trouble you to order the things and have them posted when we're already here. It's the shop Tante Marie recommended, after all, and we don't want to slight her."

"Claire." Her face glowed red and she was barely equal to speech, so great was her anger. "At once."

But I turned away from her and focused on the *corsetière*. "Shall we begin?"

Bonne Maman sat in the chair Delphine offered her with arms crossed over her chest. I swore that if one looked hard enough they could see the steam coming from her ears. Delphine had me disrobe so she could get the most accurate measurements. Once I was in a dressing gown, she showed me a few of the designs but recommended the simplest of the lot for my first corset. I agreed, and even Bonne Maman didn't argue with that particular decision.

Delphine produced a sample corset in the model we'd selected. She slipped me into it and began tightening the laces like a tall boot so I could get a feel for it before placing an order. I'd expected to have difficulty breathing, but the snugness around my ribs was pleasant. It was a new sensation, certainly, but not an uncomfortable one. I admired my form, far more curvaceous than before, and I felt beautiful. And the corset itself felt like . . . armor.

I loved it.

"Now, *chérie*, you must remember that your own corset will be perfectly bespoke—made exactly to measure—so it will be even more comfortable than the garment you wear now. Tell me what you think."

"Her shape is pleasing enough, but it seems too slack," Bonne Maman offered from her green tufted throne before I could speak. "Can it be tightened?"

"There will be plenty of room to tighten for those special occasions when one wants to be . . . shall we say, particularly eye-catching. At a ball or the Opéra, for example. But it will provide all the desired benefits as it is when she needs more freedom to move. But it is always best practice to make gradual reductions in the waist as you learn to wear the corset. The results will be far better."

Bonne Maman didn't look mollified by this explanation.

I inspected my form from different angles in the mirror to admire the transformative effects of the garment. "I think it's wonderful. It's hard to imagine how even one made to measure will be able to improve on the sample, but I think this style will do marvelously."

Delphine squeezed my shoulder appreciatively, then pulled out the fabric swatches. "What colors do you like, *chérie*? You should choose something that makes you feel beautiful."

At this, Bonne Maman stood from her seat and placed herself between me and Delphine. I was surprised she didn't take the book of fabric samples and hurl it across the room. "Bleached white cotton will suffice. She's a child. No one will see her."

Delphine expertly sashayed around Bonne Maman.

"She will see herself, and that's what matters," the *corsetière* said with a conspiratorial wink. "She must choose something that will delight only her."

"A lovely idea." I opened the book and pored over the luscious fabrics. The decadent silks and brocades were enticing, but it seemed frivolous for a garment I would outgrow within a year or two. I looked to the rich cottons, and determined I would choose any color other than white to spite Bonne Maman.

"The rosebud pink is lovely and the cream with blue flowers too. What do you think?"

Delphine smiled. "You would do well to have two corsets to alternate so that one may air out while you wear the other. Why not do both?"

Both cheerful colors would feel like a deception under mourning clothes, but most of my regular wardrobe was fashioned from pastel fabrics, and the lighter choices seemed more sensible than black.

"One is enough," Bonne Maman insisted from her perch.

"Alternating between two will extend their lifespan by months," the *corsetière* said with a syrupy smile directed at Bonne Maman. "It will be more economical in the end."

I arranged for delivery of the corsets when they were ready and, obeying Papa's instructions, for the bill to be forwarded to him. And all of it without casting a glance at Bonne Maman.

"Of all the impertinent children I've met in my life, you take the prize, Claire Eiffel." Bonne Maman was in fine form, setting in before the wheels on the carriage had made a full rotation. "You didn't listen to a word I had to say."

"If I am to help Papa run the household, I will have to rely on my own opinion quite often. I see no reason not to do so now." I kept my tone away from the impudence I felt, but I would have dearly loved to release some of the cheek I was holding in so tightly I was afraid it would leak from my very pores.

"You're too young to be charged with such responsibility," Bonne Maman countered.

"Papa believes I am ready, and I am not one to argue with him." I adopted some of the *corsetière*'s feigned sweetness, hoping it might improve her mood, though I wasn't optimistic.

"Perhaps it isn't your place to question your father, but it *is* mine. If you're shouldered with such responsibility and granted such independence now, you'll be wholly unfit for marriage when the time comes. Men want young ladies who are quiet and biddable."

"Forgive me, Bonne Maman, but you're neither of those things, and yet you've been married to Bon Papa for decades."

"Like I said, impertinence." She was properly seething now. "It took years for me to earn my voice, child. You must be brought to heel before you've ruined your disposition entirely. Your mother's poor health is already one black mark against you, and you cannot afford another."

I gripped the cushion of the carriage seat and sank my nails into the supple leather. It would scar, but it was far better than the result of letting my temper fly against Bonne Maman. "My health is sound, and I have no use for the society of anyone who is small-minded enough to think me less than worthy because of her misfortune to be born with weak lungs. Especially as I myself was not."

"But you cannot be sure that your children won't be born with the same condition. These things run in families. And your father's name is prominent enough, people will have heard about how she died. Do not fool yourself into thinking it won't be a challenge for you to overcome when you enter the marriage market."

"You're quite right, Bonne Maman." I eased my grip on the carriage seat cushion.

She looked both self-satisfied and surprised in equal measure. "For once, some sense out of you."

"If indeed my prospects have been so very damaged by Maman's ill health, I might do better to tend to Papa's affairs as he's asked me to and leave marriage to others. It seems a simple enough solution."

"That isn't—" Her body fairly convulsed in exasperation. "God save me from such an obstinate child."

She heaved a sigh and looked out the left window. I followed suit, looking out the right, proud of my ability to keep the smirk off my face.

"SUCH A GROWN lady," Pauline said with a sigh as she tied the bow at the small of my back. The corsets arrived a week later, much faster than I anticipated. I wondered if Delphine had managed to pull some strings to rush the order, or if the shop was always so efficient.

I admired my form in the mirror, hugged into an hourglass by the contraption of rosebud cotton, steel, and whalebone. It did seem as though I'd traded my girlish figure for a more womanly one, almost overnight.

It wasn't just the new undergarments; my bosom was growing more ample, and I noticed small tufts of wispy of hair under my arms. It was the sort of thing that would have sent me to Maman with a torrent of questions . . . and yet each time I was bursting to rush to her rooms and pelt her with my queries, I had to remember afresh that she was gone, and her rooms were mine.

It never ceased to sting.

Pauline, who had served as Maman's lady's maid and our housekeeper, looked satisfied at the result. "Your dear *maman* would have been so proud to see you looking so ladylike. I'll have to alter some of her things to fit you once you're out of mourning. The girlish togs won't become you for much longer."

"Thank you, Pauline, I would appreciate that very much," I said, patting the hand she'd placed on my shoulder. Hers was a maternal presence, and I found myself both grateful for it and torn by memories of my own mother.

"Your mother had a superb eye for fabric and always engaged a skilled tailor. Her things will be quite fetching on you, I'm sure."

I smiled, for the pragmatic side of me was happy the gowns wouldn't go to waste. Though part of me thought it would be horribly morbid to wear her things, and I did wonder if I would ever feel at ease in them.

I noticed an envelope tucked in the elegant box lined with *peau de soie* where the two garments had been nestled and opened it with the slide of my index finger.

Courage, ma chère Claire. You are a young lady with great spirit. The world will break that spirit if you let it. Don't let others mold you to their expectations; be faithful, first and foremost, to your own. Enjoy your armor, ma belle.

Your friend,
Delphine

I was surprised for a moment. I didn't recall voicing my thoughts about "armor" aloud. Certainly, Bonne Maman would have thought me dotty. But I couldn't be the only young woman who felt stronger when she was encircled in steel and bone. It wasn't the gilded cage some people painted it as; my corset was my breastplate, and I was dressed for battle.

And every general needed a loyal bevy of officers at the ready.

"Pauline, you served Maman faithfully for years and I trust you. I know I am just a whisper of the woman she was, but I hope you will offer me your guidance as my duties here increase. I don't want to let anyone down."

"Dear girl, you have her rooms now. It's my duty to serve the mistress of this house, and you are filling that office now, no matter how young you are. You've but to ask for anything."

"It would be ever so helpful if you'd relay that to the rest of the staff. There haven't been problems, but I imagine some might be wary of taking orders from me. Papa means for me to run the house, and I don't want to trouble Papa by passing orders through him all the time. It's no way to run a household."

"No, I daresay it isn't. I'll take the staff in hand. They're to accept your orders without question, just as they would have for your dear *maman*."

"It's important you understand that directive doesn't apply to you." I turned to Pauline and took her hands in mine. "I am perfectly happy for you to question my orders if something doesn't suit. Quietly, and in private."

"Understood, mademoiselle. Very sensible, though I don't think it will take you long to master things. You've got your mother's charm and your father's wit, if you don't mind me saying it."

"Not at all. I just hope I am worthy of such lofty praise."

She smiled. "No doubt on that score. Shall I help you into your dress for dinner? It will be a treat to see how it looks over your new underpinnings."

I assented and she went to work, first dressing me, then styling my hair. "Pauline, there is one other matter I could use your assistance with."

"Anything, mademoiselle," she said.

"When Madame Eiffel is in residence, if you could remind the staff that my orders . . ."

"Take precedence over your grandmother's?" she supplied.

"Exactly. I don't mean to say that I want the staff to disregard her entirely, but if her orders contradict my own . . . it is important for me to establish myself as mistress here if I am going to do the job, is it not?"

"I know exactly what you mean, mademoiselle. And you will rest easier knowing that she is bound for Dijon tomorrow."

"That is a relief," I admitted. To have the opportunity to settle into my new role without her interference would be a delicious reprieve. But she would take poor Laure with her, and I hoped she'd be none too altered by the experience. If Bonne Maman had her way, Laure would return to us a shadow of her former self, cowed by a woman who'd had the misfortune of being born female in a time when her gifts could not be celebrated but had to be disguised as the work of a man or hidden altogether.

She was the most overbearing woman I'd ever met, but I had to admit that if she'd been born a man, she would have been one of the great men of France. Or else its most formidable tyrant.

Chapter Six

The air seemed lighter in the days after Bonne Maman and Bon Papa left, but Papa had yet to return to his workshops on the rue Fouquet. No one blamed him for taking a leave of absence, but it was hard for him to be away from his work for so long, no matter the reason. I suspected that each day that he spent without sketching, poring over diagrams, and calculating every last detail of one of his grand structures was uncomfortable to him as a burr in his shoe. There were men who loved their work, and others who let themselves be defined by it. Papa waltzed back and forth over that line with the grace of a classically trained dancer. His obsession over small details, his desire to manage every element of each project that bore the Eiffel name, warred with his desire to be a father with more than a cursory presence in our lives. Usually, to Papa's credit, we won the battle for Papa's attention, but he seemed happiest when he was free to work without the burden of us on his conscience.

I'd taken breakfast with the younger children that morning, knowing they'd been without company for some time, but soon after, Pauline summoned me to Papa's office. His inner sanctum and his haven from the bustle of the world. Papa was indulgent with us, doting in ways that many fathers—especially ones with such demanding work—were not. But if Papa was in his office, he was not to be disturbed unless the house itself were on fire. Even then, he would have appreciated us making an effort to extinguish it first before alerting him. My siblings were banned from the space altogether, though in the past two years I had been permitted entrée with the understanding that if I were to be allowed to occupy it with him, it was on the condition that I would be reading or studying silently for the entirety of my stay. Any queries about the book I read or the materials I studied would be held for later unless Papa specifically offered his guidance.

It might have seemed harsh, but I understood, perhaps better than the others, the level of concentration Papa needed. One flubbed equation, one imprecise sketch, could compromise an entire project. It could cost lives, and perhaps worse, it might damage the reputation of the Compagnie Eiffel. When one was in the business of building something as precarious as a bridge or as massive as a railway station, trust was a commodity more precious than diamonds.

I knocked on the door to Papa's office and waited for the sound of his distracted "Come in," before pushing down on the brass handle.

He was, as always, seated behind his desk, which more closely resembled a dining table. It was necessarily monstrous in size to be able to accommodate unfurled blueprints or schematic drawings in their entirety. He looked up from the whirlwind of papers that littered the massive table and proffered a small smile. The most I'd seen from him in weeks.

"How are you settling into your routine, Cherub?" He put down the paper he'd been reading and sat back in his chair. Usually he was so absorbed in his work that he only peered over the edge of whatever pressing document held his attention. The attention he bestowed with his blue gaze was almost unsettling.

"Perfectly well, Papa." I had a million questions about what duties I needed to fill, but they were jumbled in such a heap in my brain, none of them managed to reach my lips.

He laced his fingers. "I'm glad to hear it. I hope you've nothing planned this morning. I have a visitor due any moment, Monsieur Seyrig."

Papa's junior partner, and a brilliant engineer in his own right. And more importantly to Papa, he'd invested a tremendous sum of money in the company. I'd met him only a handful of times but knew his name as well as my own. "He's coming *here*?" Papa rarely had meetings with anyone of import at the house, preferring to meet them in his offices a few streets over in the Compagnie Eiffel workshops. But the last month had seen any number of unlikely—or even impossible—events transpire.

"Yes. He's been my eyes and ears on the bridge project in Portugal, and it's long past time that I hear a report."

The bridge. The Maria Pia Bridge, which would span the Douro River and connect the major city of Porto with Vila Nova de Gaia, and the railway from the capital, Lisbon, to Porto. It was Papa's biggest project to date and would be the largest iron arch bridge in the world when it was completed. Since Papa's company was so new, success of the project would determine the viability of his whole enterprise. Indeed, Papa had spoken of little else since construction began the year before.

Papa had taken several trips to Porto to keep an eye on the project. His absence from the family had worn on him, so on one occasion he brought Maman and little Valentine along with him for an extended stay near Porto. It was on this trip when Maman took ill with pneumonia, which weakened her lungs to the disastrous effect we were all still reeling from. For the past several months, Papa had to oversee the construction, as much as he was able, from his offices in Levallois with the help of his staff, who wrote or returned with status updates. Men like this Seyrig were his lifeline to Portugal.

"And you want me to ensure the children are quiet and in the nursery wing of the house before he arrives?" I asked.

"No, I've asked one of the maids to see to that. Seyrig will be giving me a report on the progress since I was last in Porto, and I want you to listen in. Take notes. I don't want to miss a single detail of what he says, and I can't do that while taking notes. Can you do this for me?" He looked at me, like an exacting tutor looking for a precise answer to his query.

"Of course, Papa. I'd be happy to." I, the dedicated pupil, knew the answer. I was less certain of being able to deliver the service he required of me up to the standard he would expect. But as I heard footsteps approaching from the corridor, I didn't have time to raise my doubts to Papa, and I thought it was just as well. He handed me paper and a fountain pen already loaded with Papa's preferred sapphire-blue ink.

The door opened and my heart lurched with the creak in the hinges.

Seyrig, a young man in his mid-thirties, fastidious in manner and dress, entered in full state. He looked prepared to address the Assemblée nationale, which probably was exactly how he felt, entering the home of his senior partner.

Papa extended his hand and Seyrig took it in a terse shake.

"What news from Porto?" Papa asked. No idle chitchat. I admired it, and I doubted a man as serious as Seyrig would have suffered idle queries about his health with much patience.

Seyrig glanced to me. "I'm sure your daughter has much to occupy herself with. Wouldn't she prefer to find amusement elsewhere?"

"Seyrig, this is my eldest daughter, Claire. She will be sitting in as my scribe today. I trust you don't mind." Papa's expression dared Seyrig to contradict him.

"Monsieur, the nature of our business is rather—"

Papa cleared his throat and leaned forward in his chair. The meaning was plain: *Get on with it, lad, or get out of my office.*

"Very well," Seyrig said in a tone that stated as clearly as the words on the blueprint on Papa's desk that my presence was an affront. He likely felt his report was too important for the delicacy of female ears. "I'll begin with the principal point: the bridge has progressed well under my supervision, but I fear it will not be completed on schedule if we do not lengthen the workday."

"A ten-hour day in construction is long as it is, Théo. Surely the king and queen won't mind a week or two delay?"

"They have plans for the inauguration. If we delay, it will cause them quite the headache," Seyrig countered.

"Then we hire more workers, if we can find some worth having." Papa had the look of a man tabulating ledgers in his head at the added labor costs.

"We're almost at budget as it is, monsieur. An added bill will not endear us to the throne." Seyrig grew, if possible, more sober at the idea of offending the crowned heads of Portugal.

"If they won't allow us to hire more laborers and they insist on their deadline, the only outcome is a hurried completion and jeopardizing the safety of their people, not to mention my workers. I cannot think a small overage in the budget or a grand party would be worth such a risk," Papa said, folding his fingers.

"The most complicated parts of the structure are built, monsieur. We're merely laying the platform. If there was a time for a bit of haste in the building process, surely this is the least problematic."

"*Just* the platform. *Only* the foundation upon which locomotives weighing thousands of pounds will traverse many times a day? My good man, there is never a good time to cut corners."

"Is pleasing the client not a chief consideration? You've said it yourself." Seyrig gripped the brim of his brown wool bowler hat to the point I was worried it would be crushed beyond repair.

"Pleasing the client, while important, is second to public safety."

Seyrig looked heavenward, as if pleading for patience. "Twelve hours a day still leaves them twelve hours to rest."

"And when will they eat? When will they see their families?" Papa countered.

"How does that concern us? They're hired to do a job. You think too much about their personal matters." I could hear Papa grit his teeth at the slight. Papa's money was new, and he couldn't bear to be thought of as too sympathetic with the working class, no matter how pragmatic his reasoning for it.

"And you think of them too little, Théo. Tired workers make mistakes. Unhappy ones don't bother to correct them. I can't have it."

"You're quibbling over two hours." Seyrig expelled a weary breath.

"We will hire more workers, Théo. I'd rather have ten fresh men work eight hours on a site than twenty exhausted ones working twelve. And it's more than that, I am quibbling over principles. The principles that the company which bears my name will adhere to."

Seyrig emitted a defeated grunt and rubbed his temples. He knew when Papa wasn't willing to entertain any further discussion. Smart man.

Seyrig then launched into a soliloquy about the more intricate points of the bridge's construction. He waxed on about materials used, the staffing, and all that was left to be completed. I didn't understand all the specific technical details but copied every word down faithfully. I made little side notes to clarify with Papa after the meeting had concluded. A few words I wasn't sure if I spelled properly, a few terms I wished to understand better for their own sake.

When Seyrig's report finally came to its conclusion, he rubbed his eyes and leaned back in his chair.

"You've done well, Seyrig. The bridge will be a marvel."

Seyrig, unused to Papa's praise, blinked in surprise. "Thank you, monsieur. I've given her all I have. It will be a joy to see her commemorated and go on to the next great thing."

"Indeed. You've taken up the slack when I—and my family—needed you most, and I thank you for it."

"And with that, I should take my leave. I've much to attend to in town before I return to Porto. I've only scheduled myself three days in Paris before going back."

"No need," Papa replied. "I'll go to Porto myself to oversee the final testing. I prefer to be on site for that myself."

"But, monsieur, I—" Seyrig began.

"You said yourself, you've given this bridge all you've got. You need to rest before we move on to, as you say, the next great thing. I can't have you exhausting yourself."

Seyrig opened his mouth to argue. Perhaps he wanted to see the commissioning of the bridge himself. Perhaps he didn't like Papa giving him orders. More likely, I suspected he didn't like the appearance of the *grand patron* coming to Porto and scooping up the credit for all his work in the final month of construction.

But Papa *had* been there. Spent months there, personally seeing to everything. Gone so long that he couldn't bear to be apart from Maman and brought her and Valentine along with him. Though if he had to make the choice again, he would have borne his solitude without complaint as the trip had weakened Maman's constitution. Seyrig failed to see what this bridge had cost our family, and worse, I wasn't sure he really cared. Nothing, no matter how precious, mattered to him more than his career. Papa, as much as he loved his work, knew that there were other things that mattered in life.

Seyrig left with a terse goodbye to Papa and not so much as a backward glance at me.

Papa turned to me and chuckled. "He hasn't changed in the months since I saw him last."

"I've never thought him very friendly," I admitted.

"No. The public face of things is not his strong suit. And if his career is to reach the heights to which he aspires, he needs to acquire those skills or else come to terms with the reality that he will have to work with someone who does."

In other words, someone like Papa.

I handed him the record of the meeting I'd taken down and he looked it over with the same meticulous attention he paid to any other work document, pausing only to answer the queries I made in the margins.

When finished, he set the report atop a stack of other papers. "Nicely done. Your eye for detail is impressive."

"I'm your daughter, am I not?"

At this, he smiled. A genuine smile for the first time in weeks.

"Can I get you anything, Papa? You must have a mountain to get through if you're to go to Porto."

"Indeed we do," he said. "I'll wire your grandparents to see if they'll keep Laure with them for a month or so longer. I trust your aunt and uncle can be persuaded to look after the little ones and the house. We're to leave in three days' time if the arrangements fall into place."

The significance of the *we* was not lost on me.

"Do you mean—?"

"Ready your bags. And mine too with Yves's help," he said,

referring to his valet, who had prepared him for more journeys than I could hope to count.

I gasped.

"You do *want* to go?" Papa asked, looking up from another document that had already captured his interest.

I rushed around to the other side of his desk and planted a kiss on his cheek by way of response.

I scurried off to Maman's rooms—my rooms—and hunted down her cases. The last time they'd been used was for her own trip to Porto, so they'd already know the way.

My mourning wardrobe was limited, so I supplemented with a few of Maman's darker garments and prayed that neither she nor Papa would object. Her clothes would be large on me, but I hoped Pauline could be persuaded to take them in before we left.

I had three days to prepare but was packed before midday. I knew nothing of Portugal but had read far too many novels to not dream of the thrill of travel and the allure of the world beyond our sweet home in Levallois.

Chapter Seven

October 1877
En route to Porto, Portugal

By the end of the week, we boarded the train for Porto. It was a long trek by train, not to mention the hired carriage to our lodgings in Vila Nova de Gaia, which required stopping for rest in Madrid in a proper hotel along the way. As the carriage trudged along the cobblestoned road, I removed my hat and allowed the welcoming sun to beat down upon my face.

Maman would have bidden me to replace my hat to save my complexion, but Papa didn't have it in him to worry over the freckles that sprang up like so many constellations over my nose if I went too long uncovered out of doors. I knew in ten years' time I might well rue the day I didn't heed Maman's warnings, but I hoped that when the day came, I'd remember how glorious it felt to feel the sunshine down on my face as we passed through the narrow streets lined with buttery-yellow houses with terra-cotta tiled roofs. The city lacked the elegance of Haussmann's Paris but spread its warmth in abundance.

The carriage took us closer to the Douro River, the one Papa was charged with conquering with his bridge. It was swift compared to the lazy waters of the Seine and filled to brimming with numerous boats. They moved quickly as the river's traffic would allow and somehow, despite being made of wood and metal, managed to look impatient. More elegant vessels that must have been for pleasure sailing and passenger trips were much fewer in number and seemed far more content to glide along with the river's current.

I wanted to laugh at the sight of exuberant children playing with their well-beloved dog, the beautiful blue-and-white ceramic tiles on the sides of the buildings, the cheerful waves from the people of the town who seemed to recognize Papa. But there was something in Papa's expression that caused me to keep my delight to myself. He was exhausted from the days of travel, to be sure, but there was more in his face than just fatigue. As he looked out the window of the carriage, there was a pain in his eyes. I guessed it was the pain of happy memories that would never be repeated. He'd been here with Maman less than a year before, and there was no doubt they'd shared some happy times here.

"What do you think of it, Cherub?" Papa asked, his eyes still gazing out the window.

"It's simply marvelous, Papa," I said, unable to temper the truth. "The colors are so vibrant. And you can smell the sea air."

"It's not far. I'm only sorry it's a bit late in the year to take you sea bathing." A wistful glance made me feel like I was intruding in his reverie.

"Not to worry, Papa. We have other things to attend to, I'm sure."

"That we do, my dear. Much to do to ensure the workers finish everything up to standard. Things can get sloppy at the end when the more challenging structures are in place. Then there is the testing of the bridge, which is the moment of truth for the whole project."

At this, Papa's face looked grim.

"Are you worried about the tests, Papa?"

"An engineer who doesn't worry about the tests is a fool. If the bridge fails, it will mean delays, costly repairs. God forbid, a major rebuild."

"Oh, Papa—"

"I don't mean to worry you, child. There's no more reason to believe this bridge will fail inspection than any other project I've worked on, but a thinking man will always be concerned until the inspectors give it their approval."

"I'll do what I can to help, Papa. I hope to be of use to you."

"Your presence means more than I can express, my dear. There will be plenty to keep you occupied, I am sure. It will be a busy month or two as we see it all completed. Perhaps longer."

A month? Two? In my joy at the prospect of travel, I hadn't asked Papa how long we were meant to stay in Porto. I was enchanted by the sun-soaked river town, but to be parted from my siblings for so long made my chest ache. Was this what it had been like for Maman when she left us behind to accompany Papa? When she died, did the weight of all her responsibilities somehow land on my shoulders?

I couldn't be sure whether the worry was a gift from her, or if I somehow chose deep within myself to take it on when she left us. But it felt like the weight of a circus elephant was on my shoulders, and for the sake of Papa and the little ones, I had to keep wading forward through the unending field of mud that stretched before me.

We arrived at the bed-and-breakfast where we would be lodging by the late morning, and my legs screamed in protest as I accepted Papa's hand and descended from the carriage.

We were ushered in by a woman, Madame Lopes, who was the matronly sort who seemed to be almost entirely made of bosom.

She alternated between Portuguese, which I could barely parse, and broken French, which I was only marginally better able to discern.

"Come, come," she urged, practically pulling us into the room that served as a lobby. It was nothing like the grand hotels of Paris but was far homier for an extended stay. "Such an honor to have you back with us, Monsieur Eiffel. You both must be simply exhausted from your travels. I'll have Iria pour baths for you this very moment and bring up some good coffee and *pão de ló* and you'll see if my sponge cake doesn't put everything to rights."

"You're an angel, Madame Lopes, really and truly."

"Think nothing of it, child," she said. "You must think of yourself at home."

The house was bright and cheery, a vibrant tableau of colorful tile work and dark stained woods that were weathered from use but polished to gleaming.

Just as soon as we were installed in our rooms, Papa suggested we visit the worksite straightaway. Many people might have taken a day of rest after three days of arduous travel, but Papa wasn't one to let the grass grow under his feet when there was almost a full afternoon ahead of us. I linked my arm in his and we walked the modest distance to the riverbanks.

The job site for the Maria Pia Bridge was order that skated perilously close to the realm of chaos. The workers moved at a frenetic pace, knowing that the deadline loomed close and there would be hell to pay if the bridge wasn't commemorated on time.

I'd been to job sites a number of times before, though not as often as one might have expected for the daughter of an engineer. Papa didn't like disrupting busy sites for the sake of amusing his children with a tour, but it was always important that we know what the company did and what he was trying to accomplish. Despite the mild weather, I felt a shiver as I saw the expansive arched bridge that spanned the sparkling waters of the Douro in the soft hues of the autumn light. I was filled with a sense of awe that man had been able to conquer nature with such a feat of engineering. And marveled at the way this structure would materially improve the lives of the people in the area. How businesses would run more efficiently without having to travel miles and miles to cross the river for deliveries.

Papa and I surveyed from a distance at first, not wanting to alert the workers to our presence just yet. There was a mesmerizing cadence to the way they lifted, carried, and coordinated their efforts. It was like a magnified colony of ants hard at work but building something far more complex than a series of dirt tunnels.

"What do you think, Cherub?"

"The bridge is a wonder. You manage to make the practical beautiful. The arch is so graceful." And it was . . . it brought to mind the curve of a ballerina's back, but I didn't utter such fanciful thoughts aloud to Papa.

"A better compliment, I can't envision. But look closer. What do you think of the men?"

I took a few moments to study them more intently. They moved with alacrity and undeniable skill, but there were slumped shoulders and, though it was hard to tell for sure from a distance, harried expressions and eyes that had grown dull under the strain of their labors. "The workers look exhausted."

"That's what I see. And it's not yet two in the afternoon," Papa observed. "If it were three or four hours later, I wouldn't be as concerned. Seyrig has been working them to the bone."

"He's paying them extra, is he not?"

"Having a few extra sous in the pocket is a good thing, but it can't buy time for sleep and leisure. He forgets that. Tired, unhappy workers aren't efficient ones, no matter how much he might wish it were so. If he wants to speed things along, he needs to engage more workers, not drive the ones that he has to exhaustion, even if it costs more."

"That makes sense, Papa."

"There isn't much for it now. We'll have to just be as thorough as we can with the safety inspections."

"We ought to ensure the men get some respite," I said. "The project may be nearing its end, but wouldn't it be better to finish strong? And for the men to finish the job with a good taste in their mouths, so to speak?"

"A grand idea," Papa said. "Quite literally too. We should host a good dinner for them."

I brightened. Papa had been one to make these sorts of gestures before and they were always well received, when accompanied by good compensation. "Yes, a show of our appreciation. A fine meal and some hours off, don't you think, Papa?"

"Shall we roll out the *nappe blanche*? Show them as fine a meal as they could find in the best restaurants in Paris?" Papa's eyes twinkled mischievously, likely thinking of the workers' reactions to some of our French delicacies.

I thought a moment. "No, I think they'd prefer a hearty meal of homespun dishes they know already. Perhaps some they don't have the opportunity to enjoy very often. A family-style party with music. Putting on an elaborate affair would just put them ill at ease, don't you think?"

"You might be right." Papa stroked his beard. "Putting on company manners would hardly be restful for them, I imagine."

"Madame Lopes would be a help discerning what they'd like, I'm certain. We should consult her." The kindly proprietress of the bed-and-breakfast seemed a ready ally in such an enterprise.

"Indeed you should." Papa used his walking stick to punctuate his words. "I say *you* because I am leaving you in charge of the whole affair."

He suggested a date for a week from the coming Saturday, and offered a budget, which I was to adhere to strictly. He made no further suggestion. It was to be my project. I would be able, and was in fact encouraged, to bring on help to organize the festivities, but Papa made it clear that the task was mine. And just like with any of his projects, any number of factors might lead the dinner to fail. But if it did, that failure would be on my shoulders. It was the same for Papa; an engineer in his office could miscalculate by a fraction of a centimeter and cause disaster. Smaller still, a poorly fixed rivet from a laborer could cost lives. Not to mention the worry of materials that appeared sound but hid fatal defects. Any of these things wouldn't have been—strictly speaking—Papa's fault. But it would have been his responsibility because, as he mentioned so often, it was the Eiffel name that was associated with each edifice and structure the company agreed to build.

I could tell he was assessing my reaction to the assignment. Would I balk at such a weighty task, or would I rise to it? I wasn't sure how well it would turn out, but I felt confident enough that I had a chance at succeeding. The stakes were, thankfully, a lot lower for hosting a meal than they would be for building a bridge. Unless the dinner was a disaster of incredible magnitude, it was unlikely anyone would die or be hurt in the course of the evening. Still, organizing a soirée for eighty men was quite an undertaking, and it was the first time I'd ever been charged with a task so adult in my entire life.

We broached the perimeter of the job site, now ready to reveal ourselves to the men who were preparing for the final, most important, and exceedingly nerve-racking process of systematically testing every inch of the bridge for weaknesses. They paused and doffed their caps at the sight of us. A foreman, one of the few men on the site who spoke French, approached and shook Papa's hand. Clearly they were acquainted from his previous trip and the man was used to serving as Papa's interpreter on the site.

Papa walked, observing, mostly wordlessly, though he occasionally paused to ask a question. Our guide, Davi, would translate Papa's French into rapid-fire Portuguese and deliver the response back to Papa in capable French. Papa's questions were, on the surface, mundane. "How many months have you been working on the job site?" "Do you know who to ask for a new tool if one breaks?" "Are your gloves in good condition?"

Papa was testing the workforce, as much as the bridge itself, for weaknesses. If all the laborers were new to the site, they would lack the benefit of experience with the specifics of the job. If they had all been on-site for months and months, there was the worry that new laborers weren't being brought on to replace those who, inevitably, went on to find other jobs. There was no such thing as a construction job of this size and duration without *some* attrition. The question about tools was testing the chain of command. Did the newest and lowest-ranking workers know who to tell if there was a problem? If they hadn't been told whom to ask for a new wrench or a hammer, they wouldn't know to whom they should report a serious problem. One of the few things workers were expected to provide was their own gloves. If they did not replace them at regular intervals, it showed discontent with the work and a desire to move on.

It wasn't that Papa was an overly sentimental man. Workplace injuries, even deaths, were a regrettable necessity in the world of construction. But Papa took them more seriously than many men in his position. On the pragmatic side of things, deaths and injuries slowed the work and dampened morale immensely. On the ethical side, if a job could be done without loss of life or serious injury, Papa believed it should be. For the good of his workers, the reputation of the company, and his own moral conscience.

For Papa, the bridge was the essential thing. That the bridge would come in under budget and on time was important, but that the bridge would last for centuries was the vital concern. He wanted people to choose Eiffel, not because they were cheap and fast, but because their work would stand for countless generations.

I listened intently as Papa interviewed the men but did not speak. I listened, as Papa did, for subtext. What was being communicated between the words the men spoke that might give me insight to perform my task, small though it was, to Papa's exacting standards? I didn't speak Portuguese well enough to follow along with their conversations and pick up intelligence on favorite foods or drink, but I listened to what they cared about when they answered Papa. And when later that afternoon I enlisted the help of Madame Lopes, I would be armed with information that, I hoped, would make the evening a success.

Chapter Eight

October 1877

Despite the date on the calendar reminding me that winter should be hard on our heels, the balmy evening felt more like the last days of summer back home as they graciously, slowly gave way to the cooler days of autumn. The perfumed air brought with it the promise of more temperate weather for months to come. Even the coldest winter days in Porto were mild compared to Paris, I'd heard. I couldn't imagine a Christmas where the chill didn't reach the marrow of your bones despite layers and layers of wool, like the ones we knew at home, but I was grateful the weather that night would be conducive to a lively party.

"You have as beautiful an evening for your party as you could hope for, *querida*." Madame Lopes looked out as the sun set in the west over the river and the sky darkened to an inky pool dotted with flickering stars. "You have worked so hard, even Mother Nature didn't want to disappoint you."

I smiled appreciatively, and turned back to survey the rented hall one last time before we were descended upon by our guests. Madame Lopes, as I suspected, was an immense help in preparing for the festivities. She had thoughts on a venue to rent, a menu, chefs to hire, and even a band for entertainment after dinner. She served as my interpreter as I engaged help and advised me about fair prices for their services.

If I'd been planning a dinner at home, I'd have asked the staff to bleach, starch, and press the white tablecloths, polish the silver, and prepare a host of complicated, delicate dishes designed to impress company. Such gestures would have only made our guests from the job site uncomfortable.

"The yellow tablecloths look stunning with the dried lavender arrangements. You have an eye for color," Madame Lopes declared. I had to agree the room looked a treat with the white plates contrasted against the sunny yellow of the tablecloths and rich purple of the flowers. It was all set off by low ivory candles of varied height that gave the room a welcoming glow.

"Thank you." Maman frequently made comments about which colors paired well together when discussing anything from new furniture to flower arrangements. I'd never paid much heed to her little lectures, likely thinking them frivolous at the time, but now I could see the utility in them. To harmonize colors could determine if a room was welcoming or forbidding; warm or austere. It was one tool in a woman's arsenal to command the spaces under her sphere of influence. "I couldn't have done any of this without you."

She waved her hand. "If you were not a stranger to Porto and more versed in our language, you'd have managed it all without the least bit of help from me. I don't know many girls of fourteen years who could have managed as well."

I held back a laugh at how easily she dismissed the importance of her invaluable guidance. Without her knowledge of the town and the language, my task would have been infinitely harder. I'd wished I hadn't had to be so reliant on her assistance, but I'd decided that if

I had to be, I'd make use of the gift and be as attentive as I could be to her coaching so that I'd bring the gifts of her shared knowledge home with me. But I appreciated that she didn't dismiss my efforts because of my age, as Bonne Maman was apt to do. She praised me for my work instead of deriding my competence as impertinence.

At long last, the hour was upon us when the guests began milling into the foyer of the beautiful hall. We formed a small receiving line and shook the eager hands of the workers and their families as they arrived, Papa affording each of them the same courtesy as a visiting dignitary. He met their gazes and shook each hand with both of his. Davi, one of the first to arrive, served as our interpreter, but Papa did his best to offer pleasantries in admirable, if imperfect, Portuguese as a sign of respect.

When everyone had arrived and was seated, we took our places at the head table with Madame Lopes and the foremen.

There were waiters hired to serve the dinner, but before they set about their task, Papa stood and clinked his fork against a water goblet. His piercing blue eyes scanned the crowd, who grew silent in anticipation.

"Gentlemen, it is my great pleasure to join with you tonight and share a meal after your many months of toil on what is, and will remain for many decades—and even centuries—to come, one of the finest railway bridges in Portugal, and indeed all of Europe. You are to be commended for your tremendous efforts. The sweat of your brow, the calluses on your hands, the blisters on your heels are all evidence of the sacrifice you, and your dear families, have made for the advancement of your nation and the fine people of Portugal. I raise a glass to all of you."

Papa gestured to waiters who were poised, ready to pass champagne to all those assembled. The one nod of the evening to our

Frenchness, but hardly one that would be objected to on such an occasion. Papa raised the flute of shimmering golden bubbles to the crowd. "*Saúde*. To your health."

"*Santé!*" the workers and their wives responded in French. Davi smiled, having anticipated the need for French lessons in the week leading up to the dinner. Papa rewarded them with a broad smile that had been so rare over the past few months, which in turn warmed my heart, to see him so genuinely pleased.

Instead of signaling the staff for the meal service to begin, Papa remained standing. "And a word of thanks to our hostess and the organizer of this evening's fine meal, to my daughter Claire."

Papa raised a glass to me, as did the rest of the room in turn. My cheeks burned to have so many eyes on me, even in praise. Like most girls of my station, at the age of fourteen, I was just now allowed out in public, so the sensation was a foreign one to me. But though the experience was new, and somewhat uncomfortable, I found it exhilarating. Beyond the pampering of my vanity, I knew my efforts had helped Papa win the hearts and minds of his workers and boost the image of the Compagnie Eiffel in Porto. In the event another project emerged in the area, Papa's name would be remembered with kindness. Even if his bid were not the lowest, his efforts in the community might win him enough goodwill that the contract would be his.

Papa gave the signal and the dinner, a veritable seafood feast, was served. The waiters brought around massive platters of expertly prepared fish caught as recently as that very morning and kept alive until they were ready to be cooked. Grilled filet of sea bream, shrimp croquettes, cod cooked in every way imaginable. Not to mention platters of vegetables in every color of the rainbow and two massive bowls domed with rice for each table.

Madame Lopes squeezed my hand in approval after she'd sampled the food, and I didn't try to conceal my pleasure. She'd guided me every step of the way, but I'd overseen every detail and put my personal touches where I could. If I had to repeat the occasion in Paris, or at some other job site in France—and I had the feeling I would—I already had ideas about how to translate what pleased the workers of Portugal to what might appeal to the workers back home. Once the dinner ended, the band I'd hired, which had been occupied playing quiet, lilting music during the meal that wouldn't overpower conversation, burst into traditional music so lively and compelling, everyone was on their feet in seconds.

"I hope you're pleased, Papa." I leaned close to him so I wouldn't be forced to shout.

"Darling girl, there's only one thing you could do to make the evening a grander success in my view," he said, finishing the last inch of red wine in his glass.

"What's that, Papa?"

"Get out with the others and dance. You worked fiendishly hard on this soirée for a week, now go on and enjoy it."

Madame Lopes waved me to the dance floor, and as soon as I stood from my place, a girl not much older than me grabbed my hand and pulled me out to the dance floor. The other girls and young women were dressed in gay colors while I still wore mourning clothes. But I whirled on the dance floor, trying to emulate steps that in no way resembled the waltzes or the quadrilles I'd learned from my instructors.

For what seemed like hours, I spun on the dance floor, not minding the steps, but doing what I could to match the rhythm of the music. I danced in groups with the girls, and other times we commingled in pairs, though it seemed that there was never a dance where anyone stayed with a partner for more than a minute or two of any given song. It seemed as though the dancing was designed so that no one felt left out—or at least not for long.

When, at last, I'd danced my fill, I rejoined Papa at the head table. I was damp with sweat, and my heart thudded against my rib cage from the excitement of the dance floor. He smiled broadly and offered me a glass of wine to quench my thirst. "It's good to see you smile, Cherub."

He raised his glass, and I clinked mine against it before taking a generous swallow. The workers and their families danced with an indefatigable lust for life that I had never seen at even the most spirited dances back at home. Later, the quiet of the carriage was almost deafening after the din of the music and boisterous conversation.

"A triumph. There wasn't a sour face in the bunch. Well done." He patted my shoulder in appreciation.

"And ten percent under budget." I handed him a ledger sheet of my expenses from my reticule. Every centime I'd spent was meticulously accounted for as if the project were under the same scrutiny as the bridge itself.

"You are an Eiffel through and through." Papa laughed as he scanned the page in the dim light that flickered in from the streetlamp. "You've made me proud tonight, Cherub. And your mother would have been too. She planned any number of these events for the company, and none would have noticeably outstripped your efforts tonight."

I leaned over and kissed his cheek. He knew he could have paid me no better compliment, and I knew he was sincere in his praise. "Thank you, Papa."

"No need for thanks. I know it's unfair of me to ask so much of you, but I'll need you to perform these duties for me now that your mother cannot. Tonight showed you're equal to the task."

"That I am, Papa," I said, summoning confidence from the energy of the evening. "You can count on me."

He patted my hand affectionately, and I found comfort that, if he could not have Maman's help and guidance when it came to matters of entertaining and hospitality, he could at least have mine.

Chapter Nine

The success of the dinner for the workers left me feeling heady, even as I woke up the following morning. I rubbed the sleep from my eyes to see the splendor of the blazing Portuguese sunrise, the color of liquid gold that turned the sparkling waters of the river into a ribbon of inky cobalt. I lay still awhile, appreciating the stillness of the morning after all the activity and commotion of the night before. I could have luxuriated in the downy covers, and the satisfaction of the previous evening's triumph, for the rest of the morning without complaint. But if I knew Papa, he was up, breakfasted, and deep into his first tasks of the workday.

Added to that, the smells of toasted ham-and-cheese sandwiches—*tosta mista*—wafted up the steps, causing my stomach to rumble in anticipation. The dish seemed an odd enough choice for a breakfast to my French palate, which would have chosen such a heavy meal for lunchtime instead, but there was no denying it was more filling than the French answer to the meal: baguette, jam, butter, and coffee. As an added treat, Madame Lopes often made her famous *pão de Deus* or "God's bread," which were perfect little round buns that had been baked with lemon zest and topped with flakes of toasted coconut and were as delectable as any pastry one could find in Paris. The *meia de leite*, coffee and hot, steamed milk served in almost equal measure, was something like café au lait, though different enough that every sip reminded me I wasn't at home. The orange juice she served, made by Madame Lopes herself from oranges grown in the region, tasted like the sunshine itself. The scents creeping up from the kitchen were the only siren song enticing enough to pull me from the warmth of my soft bed.

As I went to sit, I felt an uncomfortable heaviness at my midsection and a dampness between my legs. I flung back the covers to discover a pool of blood soaking through my nightdress and onto the sheets. I froze. Was there a cancer eating away at my core? Surely if it was this severe, there would be no saving my life, no matter how skilled the doctors might be. If the bleeding was this heavy, certainly I couldn't live much longer even with expert medical intervention within the hour.

What would this do to Papa? He was depending on me to take up the slack for Maman. Could sweet, gentle Laure manage a house at the age of thirteen?

Was I going to leave the children bereft of a mother figure a second time in a matter of months?

My hands shook, and I didn't know how to proceed. Try to clean the mess and assess how bad the bleeding was? Call for help? Scream?

Papa. I needed Papa so he would at least have the chance to say goodbye. I ached to know the children wouldn't have the chance, though the goodbyes with Maman had been so painful for the little ones especially, I wasn't sure they had been in their best interests.

No, perhaps it was best that their last memory of me was in my traveling dress, kissing their cheeks and promising them a suitcase full of gifts upon my return.

I had sworn I wouldn't leave promises unfulfilled. I would do everything in my power to make sure Maman's work was finished. But I was failing her. I was failing the children all over again.

I was failing Papa.

Maybe there was something that could be done. And I owed it to all of them to try. I would call for help.

I stood, glad that my knees didn't feel too wobbly despite the loss of blood, and wiped the tears from my face. I would not greet help looking like a coward. If I was to die, I'd be brave and stoic for Papa's sake.

I cracked the door open only a few inches, gripping it for support in case I grew faint.

"May I have some help please?" I called, trying to sound firm but not panicked. "*Ajude-me, por favor,*" I repeated in Portuguese for good measure. I wasn't sure if Papa was still in the pension or if he'd gone to the offices in town by now, but surely someone would be there who could fetch him.

I found myself breathing easier when I heard footsteps coming up the narrow staircase, Madame Lopes herself emerging after a few moments.

"What is the matter, *querida*? Are you unwell?" She blanched at seeing my terrified face at the bedroom door.

"Yes, I'm afraid I'll need a doctor. And someone to fetch Papa if he's gone."

"*Meu Deus*, my poor girl. Of course, but tell me what is wrong so I can tell the doctor."

I opened the door so she could see the state of my nightgown and the bed. "Clearly something is horribly wrong. I just hope it isn't too late for help." I had tried to keep the tears at bay but found them stinging at the corners of my eyes. "I don't want to leave Papa and the children so soon after Maman."

Madame Lopes's face split into a smile. "Oh, *querida*. You aren't going to be leaving us to be with your blessed *maman*. Not for many years. You don't need a doctor either."

I gestured to the pool of blood. "You cannot tell me there isn't something gravely wrong."

"It is as natural as flowers and sunshine, I promise you. But I will send word to your Papa that you won't be joining him at the offices this morning."

She sent word with a messenger and prepared a steaming bath. As she worked, she explained what was happening to my body and what it all meant. I had trouble deciphering some of her French, and her explanations in Portuguese were of even less help, but by the end of it, I had the gist of what it all meant.

"But I won't be ready for children for years yet. Why wouldn't it wait to start until I am married?"

"Because, *querida*, Mother Nature doesn't understand human things like marriage. All she knows is that, physically, you are a woman now and your body is behaving as such. You are fourteen years old, and it is the usual time for this to begin. Usually, the mother begins to recognize the signs and prepares her daughter for what is coming."

"My *maman* had been sick for a very long time. She was too busy trying to get well to notice such things."

My dresses had grown tight across my chest, it was true. And I had tried to ignore the patches of hair that had appeared under my arms around the time Maman died. But it had soon spread to other, more awkward, places and there was no one in whom I could confide this revolting truth. Surely other girls didn't have to deal with anything so unsightly. I'd even considered purchasing a men's razor to rid myself of the new growth but wasn't sure if it would be harmful to do so. Not to mention, it seemed that touching that area long enough to shave would be unhygienic.

"I know, may that sweet lamb rest in peace." She made the sign of the cross and then helped me into the bath and whisked away the soiled nightgown and bedsheets, with a promise of having them freshly laundered by evening. She also brought in clean rags and explained how I was to use them to keep clean for the next several days.

The water was so hot, I thought my skin would melt away, but I wouldn't have wanted it any cooler. I took in deep breaths and willed each of my tensed muscles to uncoil in the scalding copper tub. I felt the prick of embarrassment that I had been ignorant of such an important milestone in a girl's life. The prick of anger that Maman hadn't prepared me. Mad that this country had made her ill and taken her from me.

No. That wasn't fair.

I was angry that Maman hadn't been given the chance to prepare me. That she'd spent the last months of her too-short life in her sickbed, unable to be a true mother to us. And as irrational as it was, I was angry with Portugal for being the place where she contracted her final illness. If she'd stayed home, perhaps she'd still be with us. It wasn't just unfair to me; Maman had been robbed of the chance to see me through this as well. I knew she would have acquitted herself with the same kindness and grace as Madame Lopes had done.

I blessed the woman with my whole heart, not just for me, but for Maman, who would have been grateful that I'd had a kind, motherly figure to explain things to me with tenderness and understanding. I was a muddle of emotions but was able to cling to the gratitude I felt for Madame Lopes and her myriad acts of kindness that morning.

Once I was clean and dressed, she reappeared with a plate of the breakfast that had, an hour ago, smelled like the nectar and ambrosia of the gods. In addition to the usual fare, there was a large slab of dark chocolate on a small plate. The Portuguese were not known for their sweet tooth of a morning, preferring to reserve their pastries and cakes for a midmorning boost or an afternoon pick-me-up, so I looked curiously at the confection added to the tray.

"The business of being a woman can be unpleasant at times, darling girl, but you will find that a bit of good chocolate is balm for the soul in times like these."

I smiled and kissed her plump cheeks in thanks. I interspersed bites of the chocolate bar with the warm, savory sandwich and did find some comfort as the rich cocoa melted on my tongue.

I vowed to explain things to Laure the moment we returned home so that she'd be spared the same embarrassment. And Valentine, too, in a year or two. And knowing I could protect them from this was, miraculously, even more comfort than chocolate.

Chapter Ten

"It's simply been ages!" Valentine threw her arms around me. "It's been dull as a tomb around here without you!"

I kissed her cheeks and held her close in my arms. Little Bébert, hard on her heels, squeezed me around the waist. Bonne Maman rounded the corner suddenly; her face was gray and she had a mood to match. "Don't say such things, Valentine. 'Dull as a tomb'? Why, it's positively vulgar. I shall have words with your tutors if this is how you're permitted to speak." She strode into the nursery room with Laure trailing in her wake. I swallowed back a sigh. I had hoped they would be a few hours behind us, but luck was not on our side. Bonne Maman and Bon Papa had arrived from Dijon with Laure just an hour after we had done, and I'd spent every moment in a tear, doing all I could in such scant time to ensure everything was prepared for their arrival. I was just now coming to see the children and was not even permitted to have the joy of this moment go unspoiled.

We had made it back to Levallois just in time for Christmas, and though I had adored my time in Portugal, it was time to be home. I'd longed to be reunited with Laure, Valentine, and the boys, but unfortunately Bonne Maman Eiffel would be part of the bargain, along with Bon Papa, who had likely scurried off to the drawing room for cigars and to sample the port wine Papa had brought back with us.

I folded Valentine, who had shrunk at the sight of our grandmother, into my arms. "I'm sorry, Bonne Maman. I didn't know you were here."

"Never mind that, child. You ought to watch your tongue as if I were in the room at all times. It would be a better yardstick for manners than most."

I fought the urge to roll my eyes in her direction—blatantly—at her overbearing tirades. "Though the common wisdom is that young girls would often do better to listen, we should like to hear her speak *sometimes*, Bonne Maman."

"What do you mean by that?" she snapped. "I didn't tell the child to remain mute like a fool."

Lord, if only fools remained silent, the world would be a far pleasanter place. "You told her to monitor her speech as though you were in the room at all times. Such a terrifying directive would rob any sensible child of her words."

"That will be quite enough cheek from you, Claire Eiffel. Fortunately for your sake, I haven't the energy to deal with you now after all the banging and rattling on the train. I must find Pauline and have my rooms readied. I only came to the nursery to look in on the children and see they were profitably occupied for the afternoon."

I set my teeth. "Your rooms are readied, Bonne Maman." I kept my tone as smooth as lake water on a still day. I would not let her incite me to ire. "And I was on the point of speaking with the tutors to inquire on their progress and their lesson plans until the holiday." I didn't bother telling her the children were released from their tutor until the new year, as was our custom. This was the time they were permitted to read, practice their music, and learn new skills and was, to my mind, one of the more valuable parts of their education. But Bonne Maman would not have approved. She would have insisted on them working on their studies up until Christmas Eve services if she had her way.

"I would have thought your father far too busy to trouble himself with such things after his long absence." Her face betrayed her surprise. She spoke the word *absence* as though it indicated some moral failing. As though his trip to Portugal had been a wastefully extravagant vacation while the atelier and the workers sat idle. Nothing could have been further from the truth. And she was deliberately acting as though she'd forgotten I was charged with the running of the house. One of her more malicious traits.

"I saw to it myself. Practically the moment my boots crossed the threshold. Pauline had the maids ready the rooms immediately and I just inspected them myself. You'll find everything is in perfect order. And if you do not, the staff is under my orders to set it to rights. You've only to ring the bellpull if you require anything."

She looked mollified, if only slightly. "Very well. I shall lie down and recover from that horrible train before I discuss the holiday arrangements with Pauline. Though heaven knows it's terribly late to be putting on a proper Christmas with only three days' notice."

"Quite impossible, which is why I sent Pauline letters with my plans via post. I'm surprised the evergreen boughs and the baubles in the foyer escaped your keen eye."

I smiled, not out of demure servility to my grandmother, but out of pride in a job well done. Indeed, Pauline had risen to the occasion marvelously and followed each of my instructions without faltering. There was much to discuss with her now that I was back in Paris, but I would not have Bonne Maman think that there was anything left to be done or she'd snatch the entire project from my hands. Papa had asked me to make this holiday—the first without Maman—a special one for the children, and I'd not skimp on that duty or any other issued by Papa.

"It isn't suitable for a girl your age to take so much upon herself. Impertinent and too bold by half. I'll see to everything myself while I'm here and insist your father hire someone to manage the staff until he finds another wife to do the job. His foolish experiment is at an end."

Laure and I exchanged glances, remembering the fear she'd voiced that first night I'd taken up residence in Maman's rooms. Of course Bonne Maman would assume Papa would want to remarry. Running a house of any size was an onerous task, and incomparable with a career as demanding as Papa's. A wife was the logical choice for the role. A housekeeper was a part of the staff, and therefore it made her authority less absolute. She would still have to confer with Papa on any number of things, which would be an unwelcome distraction for Papa.

But Papa hadn't asked another woman to come run the house for him; he'd asked me. I'd passed any number of tests while we were in Portugal, and I myself felt equal to the task after weeks of tending to Papa's needs.

And I would not fail in this endeavor, no matter what Bonne Maman might think about the arrangement.

"If you remember, Papa is quite determined the running of the household should fall to me. I doubt you'll disabuse him of the notion." I arched a brow, daring her to spread the venom that lurked in her fangs.

"I'll talk sense into him tomorrow." She spoke with the sort of confidence I outwardly pretended to but could lay no claim to in practice. "It's not fitting. You have no idea the work involved in running a proper household. Either you'll let things slip and your father and the children will suffer for it, or you'll ruin your constitution and end up in the same sorry state as your poor mother."

I stood straighter, containing with all my might the last steel cable of restraint that held back my temper. It was frayed and liable to snap at any moment; the lashing would scar anyone who stood within a hundred meters of where I stood. Grandmother or not, I wouldn't stand to hear my mother maligned on that old crone's tongue. "My mother prepared me to keep a house just like this, or even grander, from the time I could speak. I am well aware of the incredible amount of work involved."

"Claire, I'm too tired for your insolence. I—"

"Precisely. You must be dead on your feet. Your rooms are ready. Please avail yourself of their comforts for as long as you wish. Dinner is at eight as always."

She opened her mouth, but the insults seemed to, miraculously, lodge themselves in her throat. She spun on the ball of her foot and left, presumably in the direction of her rooms, where she would do her best to find fault with them.

"Oh my goodness, Claire. How did you find the nerve to talk to Bonne Maman like that?" Valentine said in a whisper as though she feared Bonne Maman might reemerge at the mention of her name like some wicked apparition.

"She isn't mistress here. And while her age and relation require us to treat her with deference, I won't be cowed by her any longer. I've been charged with the running of the house by Papa, and even if she doesn't like it, it's his decision, not hers. And I won't allow her to treat me like a brainless twit."

"But what about your art school?" Laure chimed in. "And Bonne Maman has a point. You can't neglect your own accomplishments if you want to make a good match. Keeping house for Papa would make all those things incredibly hard, would it not?"

She, always Bonne Maman's favorite because of her biddable temper, was likely to see her view more clearly than the rest of us. "I'll find time for my studies when I can. And as for making a match, isn't the primary objective of a wife to keep a house for her husband? I should think having years of practical experience with it would be a boon, not a liability."

Laure looked dubious but said nothing.

"Why don't you two find a good book or some needlework to occupy you this afternoon? Anything constructive and reasonably quiet as Bonne Maman will presumably be napping. I'll see you both at dinner."

The pair of them exchanged a look. I couldn't tell if it was apprehension or disbelief that I was issuing orders just as Maman had done, but they scurried off without complaint.

As I exited the nursery to find Pauline to finalize the holiday plans, I permitted myself a small smile of satisfaction. If I was going to be charged with the work of lady of the house, I would insist on being treated with the same deference.

"YOU'RE A WONDER, Pauline," I said as she walked me through her plans for the festivities. She'd done the marketing and festooned the house just as well as Maman had done in her prime. It would be simply perfect.

"I hope you don't object, but I thought to substitute the potato-leek soup for a chestnut soup. They had some lovely ones at Les Halles, and I thought it would be a pleasant change to the menu."

"Potato-leek soup is Monsieur Eiffel's special favorite," a woman's voice blasted from the kitchen doors. "He would be very disappointed from any change in the menu."

"I thought you were napping, Bonne Maman."

"I told you I meant to take over the preparations for the holiday, and I am never one to speak idle nonsense." She took in a massive breath and puffed out her chest in a barely controlled rage.

"It's all managed, Bonne Maman. Pauline has done marvelous work and she and I can see it to completion now that I'm back." My tone soft as silk, daring her to raise her voice in anger.

"Listen to me, Claire. I will not—"

"Oh, there you are, Claire. I was wondering where you'd got to." Papa bounded into the kitchens.

"My point exactly. Your father feels the need to oversee your work. A house can't be run that way. Your father's mind must be free to focus on his work. He cannot spend his precious time correcting your mistakes in the kitchen. Tell her, Gustave."

"I came here to do no such thing," Papa said, as calmly as though he were commenting on the weather. "She has everything well in hand, don't you, Cherub?"

"As always, Papa." I flashed a confident smile.

"That's my girl. I've merely come to tell you that Ursule is in the foyer, and no doubt hoping you'll join her in the gardens as we're blessedly free from rain today."

"Gustave, I must insist—" Bonne Maman began.

"Come have a rest, Maman. Claire is quite capable, and I am sure Papa is lonely in the drawing room by himself. I have a few things to see to in my office and won't be able to entertain you until evening."

"If this meal is a disaster, don't blame me. Who ever heard of leaving a half-grown child in charge of a household?"

"You'd be surprised by Claire if you allowed yourself to see her properly. She's every bit the talented hostess her mother was."

Bonne Maman sniffed in wordless disbelief, a half measure shy of scorn. I refused to look in her direction.

"Papa, what say you to chestnut soup for the entrée on Christmas

Eve? You won't be too disappointed for a small variation in the usual menu, will you?"

"Not at all. Sounds like a delightful change. I confess I've never been especially fond of potato-leek soup. I've always thought it the course to endure before the delights of the others. Carry on as you wish, only make sure you see to Ursule."

"Of course, Papa."

Papa took Bonne Maman by the arm and escorted her from the kitchens, Lord bless him, though she managed to shoot me a withering look over her shoulder. I'd won this battle, but she was equipping herself for the inevitable war.

"I think we have it all well in hand, Mademoiselle Claire. Why don't you go spend some time with your friend before the real hubbub begins," Pauline suggested. I loved how she was able to speak to me in a way that was motherly but not condescending. And because she accepted my new lead in the domestic sphere, she would make the rest of the staff toe the line, which would make my job infinitely easier. I smiled in gratitude and met up with Ursule in the foyer. I gathered my case and we trundled to our favorite patch of the gardens.

"Were you able to work much when you were in Portugal?" she asked, not taking her eyes from her favorite tree as she prepared her paints.

"Not much. A few sketches. Papa needed my assistance more often than I expected. It was a lovely place though. The light was amazing."

"It's too bad you didn't have the chance to take more advantage of it." Her tone was disapproving, but she wasn't wrong. If I wanted to get into the École des Beaux-Arts, or someplace like it, I'd have to live and breathe my art. A fear bloomed in the pit of my stomach that I'd never be able to fit in the necessary time to practice with all the new duties that had fallen on my shoulders, but I couldn't consider that possibility just now. I had a few moments to paint now, and it would be a waste to spend them worrying about the moments I wouldn't have down the line.

"Well, we can get back to it now. I can pick up right where I left off." Those words, almost as soon as I uttered them, were like a curse.

I tried to focus on the corner of the house I loved so well, but the light felt wrong, and I found myself unable to re-create the grays and browns to my satisfaction. Sometimes painting sessions were like this, when I couldn't get my hands to replicate what I saw in my head. But it had been months and months since I'd had one this frustrating. Try as I might, nothing was working. And when I looked to the window, I saw Bonne Maman Eiffel glowering at me. Her meaning was clear: *Either be the lady of the house or a child. You cannot be both.*

I was sure the only reason she wasn't out here and dragging me back inside was because Papa had ordered her to leave me alone. If he hadn't issued a direct order, there was no question that she'd repeat her behavior from September. And there was no use trying to paint while she was doing her best to intimidate me from afar. Her scowl was enough to ruin the precious little time I had to work on my craft.

I wanted more than anything to hurl my brush at the canvas and to storm off in a rage, but I would not give the old woman the satisfaction of seeing me throw a childish tantrum. It might have felt satisfying in the moment, but I would regret it as soon as the outburst passed.

"Ursule, you must forgive me. I'm going to give this up as a bad job and try again later. Perhaps after my grandparents have re-turned to Dijon." I began to hastily return my supplies to their case, keeping my movements measured so that my annoyance wouldn't be seen under Bonne Maman's watchful eye.

"You can't let her get to you." Ursule had noticed the old woman's peering just as I had done.

"I'm not," I protested. "It's just that there's so much to do with the holiday approaching. I have to manage it all."

"Do you really? I'm sure your grandmother would gladly take over at the helm." Ursule tore her eyes away from her canvas at last. "Why not accept the help while you can?"

"Because Papa wants *me* to do it. Bonne Maman won't be around forever, and I must learn to do it without her." I snapped my case shut. "And what's more, she's a nasty old woman, and I don't want her ruining the holiday. She'd poison everything with her sour disposition."

"Is one holiday more important to you than painting? Art school?"

"That's an unfair question. She'll be gone soon, and I'll be able to paint in peace."

Ursule shook her head, almost imperceptibly. "You feel a sense of obligation, and I understand it. Your mother just passed, and you want to ensure the children have a merry time and all that. But you're choosing it over your art. Today it's Christmas plans, and there will be something else next week. You might be making the right choice, Claire, but I hope you realize what you're doing."

I clenched my jaw, wishing I could refute her. It was all the more infuriating because she was right. "Feel free to paint as long as you like. I'm needed inside."

"Run along, then. Your art will *always* wait for you, won't it?"

"Ursule, you have no way of understanding what we're going through. The role I've been charged with."

"Perhaps not, but I know exactly what you're going to sacrifice: your art."

I jutted my chin defiantly. "I will not. I thought you knew me better than that."

"Just be careful, Claire. One abandoned afternoon can become ten years in the space of a blink."

I wanted to throttle her for her smug pronouncement. If only she *had* been smug, it would have been easier to take. She was speaking in earnest. She was speaking the unembroidered truth. And it was more than I could bear.

I hauled my case back to the house without another word or a backward glance to Ursule or an acknowledgment of Bonne Maman when I passed her in the foyer, though she called my name to get my attention.

I retreated to the nursery with the younger children, finding that they'd heeded my instruction and were busy with their various pursuits. Valentine had made progress on a charming sampler she hoped to finish in time to gift Papa for Christmas and Laure was deep in study with her Latin. She had a list of queries for me in the absence of her tutor, and I spent the next hour attending to them. Bébert amused himself with wooden horses while the girls worked. Édouard would be home soon and I ensured his room was ready.

I tried to put Ursule's warning from my mind as I attended to the children and their studies, but her words haunted me.

One abandoned afternoon can become ten years in the space of a blink.

Chapter Eleven

May 13, 1884

I balanced a tray on my forearm and knocked on the polished walnut door that led to Laure's rooms. She was no longer in a nursery wing and had a proper bedroom and sitting room now, as a young lady of nineteen ought to have. It was one of the many benefits that the family's move to the rue de Prony had afforded us all. Though the quiet neighborhood was still in the periphery—the seventeenth arrondissement being in the far northwestern part of the city and scarcely nearer to the city center than the suburbs of Levallois—it was a mile or two closer to the beating heart of Paris, where Papa's work demanded his presence more and more.

But for more than just the practical reasons, the move was a healthy one. The walls of our home in Levallois were wallpapered with memories of Maman. Too many layers for us to peel back. And it was a relief that I wasn't occupying Maman's rooms anymore. My rooms here truly were my own. As painful as it was to leave behind the memories we'd created in that sweet house in Levallois, I could breathe more feely in rooms where Maman's perfume didn't still cling to the draperies. And as much as I'd feared Bonne Maman terrorizing our household with unplanned visits, she passed away just two months after my first Christmas as chatelaine of Papa's house. Bon Papa outlived her by less than two years. Papa was left bereft by these losses, and I felt more keenly than ever the need to ensure he was well cared for.

Laure opened the door, her expression a bit harried, and motioned for me to enter.

"A tisane and some butter cookies, Madame LeGrain?" I winked at Laure as I set the tray down on the small table in her bedroom. She had her nose in her wardrobe and was flinging clothes about and hastily folding skirts and chemises, the ones she wore most often and had waited to pack until the last moment, into the smallest of her cases. Most of the contents of her rooms had already been boxed up and were ready to go to Maurice's little pied-à-terre during the church service the next day.

"Oh, how that name will take some getting used to. And I'd love some, Mademoiselle Eiffel. How thoughtful of you."

Mademoiselle Eiffel. The title felt as permanent as Mother Superior, but the idea of retaining it indefinitely didn't give me much disquiet. Perhaps at the age of twenty, the prospect of remaining unmarried *ought* to have bothered me, but it didn't. Papa needed me too much for my attentions to be divided.

And moreover, perhaps it should have bothered me that Laure was married before I was, but it didn't.

At least, not in the way people thought it might. I didn't begrudge her happiness with Maurice. He was a good man and would provide well for her. Better still, he would endeavor to make her happy. That was of paramount importance in my eyes, as I knew she was the sort who would twist herself into knots trying to please him. She deserved a man who wouldn't take advantage of her sweetness.

No, what bothered me wasn't that she'd beaten me to the altar, but that she was leaving the nest at all.

She let out an exasperated sigh. "Where *are* my new gloves? And my good cream blouse is nowhere to be found."

"Your new gloves are in your going-away bag so you'll be able to find them after the wedding. I packed them myself. And Pauline is working to get the spot of red wine off the cuff of the cream blouse. She wanted to make sure every garment in your trousseau was flawless."

"Bless her." Laure flopped onto her green velvet side chair. "Packing is a dreadful business."

"Then leave it to her. She dotes on you and would just as soon do it all herself than see you troubled over it. Not on the day of your wedding."

She took her cup of tisane, Pauline's special blend of herbs, and took a sip. "The first of them, anyway. Odd to think I'm actually married, isn't it?"

"You aren't yet, according to Papa. You won't be married in his eyes until you're married in the eyes of the church." She was legally married now, and many couples didn't wait for the religious ceremony to begin their married lives together, but Papa was a stickler for the rules of propriety. Especially when it came to the girls and me. Édouard was given more leeway, but it hadn't come to good outcomes. He was an unmotivated scholar with a taste for mischief that cost me sleep and cost Papa . . . well, plenty. Albert was still young, and I hoped he'd prove more responsible than his brother.

She waved her hand, dismissive. "Papa's not wrong. Today was just the paperwork. Tomorrow is the real fun with the gown and cake and all the fuss."

"True enough," I agreed. Laure had worn a new, very nice blush-pink dress for the ceremony at the *mairie*, but apart from the little nosegay of roses and forget-me-nots she carried, she didn't look much like a bride. She looked like a happy young woman, to be sure, but there wasn't the same mystique that one felt when seeing a woman in a sweeping white gown with a veil.

I picked at a loose thread on my skirt as I settled into the spare chair by her bed. The one placed there for me for the very purpose of visiting her in the waning hours before sleep. It took me a moment to find my voice, and when I did, it shook. "D-do you have any questions for me?"

Laure arched a brow. "I think the plan for tomorrow has been orchestrated with military precision, sister dear. No one would dare step a toe out of line and risk crossing you."

"Not about the wedding, Laure," I pressed.

"Oh . . . do you mean the wedding night?" She sipped her tisane and tried to look nonchalant, but her voice had risen an octave.

Did she have to be so direct? The heat rose painfully in my cheeks. "Yes. I thought you might have some questions and I wanted to help."

"Do you think you're the best person to advise me on such matters?" Her tone wasn't unkind, but there was a trace of humor in it I didn't care for. My knowledge was entirely theoretical, of course, but I had asked Pauline—discreetly—to explain the goings-on between man and wife to me so I might be of some use to my sister.

"Perhaps not, but I know something about such matters. More than you should." I had personally acted as her chaperone for most of Laure and Maurice's courtship and knew the likelihood that she'd done anything untoward before her wedding was remote.

"I tried asking Tante Marie last week. She wouldn't explain much. She turned such a violent shade of crimson I was worried she was going to keel over and have an apoplexy right there in front of me."

I laughed hard enough that I felt the scalding-hot tisane threaten to spray from my nose. I struggled for a moment and regained my composure. "So if Tante Marie didn't explain things, you must still have questions."

"No. Maurice whispered a few things to me when no one could hear, and he promised he'd explain everything tomorrow night . . . before. All will be well. He's the kindest soul I know."

I set my cup down and tried to keep my expression neutral. She expected Maurice would be able to put his desires aside long enough to tell his young wife what she needed to know about the marriage bed before claiming his due. It was a staggering amount of trust.

"I'll be fine," she pressed, far too accurately judging my reticence.

I forced a smile, but I should have been the one to advise her, not Maurice.

Really, it should have been Maman, but there was nothing I could do about that. And I doubted she'd have been any more at ease than Tante Marie when faced with such a conversation.

But still, I felt I had to offer her *something*.

"Dearest, I know precious little about . . . well, you know . . . how things are to be between a husband and wife. But the advice I was given was to try to keep relaxed as much as you can. Especially at first. It will become tolerable, even pleasant, in time."

Laure leaned over and kissed my cheek, likely knowing I'd suffered more than a little embarrassment to be able to bring that fragment of advice to her ears.

"Thank you, Clarinette." She used my childhood nickname for the first time in ages. "I'll try."

And at once, I felt ridiculous. Barely a year older than Laure and trying to advise her. I had never felt so wholly inadequate in my entire life, and she deserved so much better. I pulled a parcel from the pocket of my skirt.

"I made this for you. I thought it might be of use tomorrow." I handed her the package wrapped in *peau de soie*.

She accepted it and pulled the pink ribbon until the bow came loose. She opened it to find a delicate handkerchief with a lace border I'd knit myself. The lacework was riddled with flaws, but it was my best attempt thus far.

"You don't have to use it, but I thought . . . well, you can keep it tucked away so no one will see your sister's shoddy lacework."

Laure embraced me until I felt the air protest in my lungs. "I'll have it in my reticule the whole time. It will be the most treasured item in my trousseau."

"You're an admirable liar. I hope your marriage gives you little cause to call upon your gifts."

And with this, we dissolved into fits of giggles like old times. But the hour was drawing late, and I knew I had to leave the bride to her beauty sleep.

"One more gift." I produced an even smaller parcel, this one an unwrapped jewelry box. She opened it to find Maman's favorite pearl-drop earrings and the emerald ring she'd coveted for so long.

"Oh, Claire. Does Papa mind? They'll look so lovely with my gown."

"He suggested you should have something of hers but left the choosing of it to me. I thought they would suit you tomorrow and on many occasions afterward."

"Thank you," she said, embracing me once more. "It will be like having her with us."

I cradled her in my arms a moment longer. "Indeed, sweetest girl. And one day you'll pass them down to your own daughter and tell her stories of her Mamie Eiffel and how much they would have loved each other."

LAURE LOOKED AT her reflection in the vanity mirror. Her lovely chestnut locks were pinned up in perfect curls and Maman's pearls gleamed at her ears and the emerald ring on her right hand sparkled.

"Oh, *mon lapin*. You are a dream," I breathed, kissing her cheeks. The gown, a delicate affair of the finest ivory silk from the House of Worth, boasted thousands of handsewn pearl beads. It was an extravagance, but Papa insisted she have the very best for her wedding day, and I was not one to deny Laure anything. And she was, I hated to admit it, woman enough that even a showpiece of a gown such as the one we had crafted in Worth's atelier did not overpower her. She had Bonne Maman Eiffel's gravitas in spades, though she wouldn't be twenty years old for another five months. Five months and two days, to be precise.

"You look like an angel," Valentine agreed.

"She looks like her *maman*." Papa crossed the open doorway to Laure's rooms.

"You approve, Papa?" Her dark eyes grew round as she looked to him for his benediction.

"My darling girl, I can't imagine approving of anything more. Maurice will take good care of you and you of him. What father could wish more for his daughter?"

Such a simple expectation. That Laure would be well provided for and that she might be able to find purpose in her union. It seemed so deliciously uncomplicated. But could my clever sister be happy in the office of wife, and eventually—God willing—of mother?

I stood tall and looked her straight in the eyes. "He had better, or he'll have me to answer to. If he doesn't recognize that he's the luckiest man in all of Paris, he's a fool and unworthy of you."

"Hear, hear," Valentine said with a giggle.

"Be that as it may, he might very well jilt you at the altar if we don't get you to church." Papa made an exaggerated show of looking at his pocket watch. "Let's not keep the poor boy waiting."

Papa winked roguishly at his middle daughter and offered her his arm to escort her to the gleaming carriage with four matched bay horses that awaited us in front of the house.

The wedding was to be at the Église Saint-François-de-Sales, a newer church in the arrondissement, but one whose architecture, mercifully, respected the classic styles. While I loved Papa's intricate bridges and his impressive ironwork structures, I always felt churches needed familiarity more than they needed modernity. And above all else, they needed beauty. The splendor of soaring naves so expansive the soul longed to rise to heaven, and stained-glass windows so vibrant as to delight the spirit so much it didn't mind its tenure here on earth.

I'd organized the wedding with Laure, much as any mother would have done, though without the benefit of experience. To see my darling sister married before me was no surprise at all. She had the sweetness of temperament that made her an ideal companion for an ambitious and outgoing man like Maurice LeGrain. I knew Papa's premonition, that they would support and serve each other, was bound to prove true, which pleased me beyond words. But I only wished I could have given her any sort of useful advice to take with her into the married state.

I sat in the front row on the bride's side of the church, Valentine and the boys on my left, a space left open for Papa on my right. Valentine had a new periwinkle-blue dress; the boys and even Papa had new suits of clothes for the occasion. I wore a gown of Maman's in pale rose silk that I'd had refashioned for myself and that I thought complemented my complexion, even if it was a bit out of date. I preferred the money be spent on the children since Maman's things were still serviceable.

Laure was the very vision of a perfect bride, a veritable fashion plate, but thrice as beautiful. And Maurice, tall and dark, looked fetching in his military uniform. I could see why Laure had taken an interest in him. And thankfully, after getting to know him, I could see how he was able to keep it.

The church music was familiar and comforting as hot onion soup on a cold day, though unsettling too in that the end result of this mass would be that my dearest sister and closest confidante would be lost to me.

Not really. Not in the sense that Maman was lost to us all. But Laure would leave on her wedding tour the next morning, and then would find herself more and more preoccupied with the demands of married life. She would have precious little time for her sister, especially once children came, as they inevitably would.

And this was all as it should be.

Children grew up and left their parents behind. And their mothers, I expected, mourned their leaving as I would mourn the loss of Laure's daily presence in the house. The way Maman would have mourned each of our departures as she saw us leave the nest she'd so lovingly tended, each in our turn. Édouard was busy with school and would soon find his way into the world as well. Valentine and little Albert had longer, but I knew it would all pass in the space of a hummingbird's heartbeat.

Papa presented Laure to Maurice and he joined me in the pew. He placed a hand on my knee and squeezed before threading his fingers and listening intently to the priest. Whether he was reassuring me or himself, I couldn't tell.

And in what seemed like less than a heartbeat, Laure was well and truly married. In the eyes of the state, God, and even Papa. The bride and groom took their march down the aisle to the front of the church, and we all followed back to the house, where the wedding luncheon awaited.

Pauline and the rest of the staff had worked tirelessly to create a sumptuous feast for our nearest family and friends. The staff circulated with amuse-bouches of foie gras and caviar and poured champagne generously while people arrived from the church, and we sat down to a decadent meal. Scallops, lobster, duck, lamb, perfectly sautéed vegetables, an assortment of cheese and fruits. The croquembouche towered as it was wheeled around for all to see, and the guests delighted when Maurice shattered the caramel shell that enshrouded the dozens of cream puffs with his ceremonial sword.

Laure, usually so quiet and reserved, shone as the center of attention that day, and I couldn't have been prouder of her. But soon the meal was consumed, and the happy couple was more than ready to slip away to enjoy their happily ever after. I went up the stairs with her and helped her slip into the pink dress she'd worn to the *mairie* the day before.

"Lovely," I pronounced, standing behind her as she looked in the mirror. I placed my hands on her shoulders. "Ready to face the world as a married woman."

She smiled and patted my hand.

"One fewer bird in the nest for you, Clarinette." Laure pulled me into a hug. "One less burden for you to bear."

I felt the breath lodge in my chest, painful, as though it had been caught sideways. "Laure, you have never been a burden to me. Not once. If I ever made you feel as though you were . . ." My voice quavered with emotion.

"No, not that. Never." Her voice grew thick as she searched for words. "But I know the weight you carry all the same. I hope it will be lighter for my absence."

I held her at arm's length and looked deep into her honey-brown eyes. "My *heart* is lighter for knowing you have found a good man to care for you, dearest. But there is not a moment I don't recall being glad of having you at my side or wishing you were there. If you'd wanted to grow into spinsterhood with me, I'd have gladly accepted your company in the parlor for the next fifty years."

A shadow crossed her face. "Your turn will come."

Maman's face swirled into my vision and all I felt in my soul were her wishes for the future now that Laure was well settled. Her hopes that Valentine's education would not be neglected. That Édouard's wild ways would be tempered. That Bébert would grow to be a sensible, sturdy young man.

What I could not summon was her hopes for me. Either because I was too used to thinking of the others or because she had none. But such a thing was not what Laure wanted to hear on her wedding day.

"I've no time to think of such things, darling. Three other chicks in the nest, you know."

A knock sounded at the door, causing us both to jump in our skin, invested as we were in our memories. "No doubt your dear Maurice is impatient to begin his married life. You must go to him."

She looked to the door and back to me.

"No one could have filled Maman's shoes better than you, Claire. But remember, everyone leaves behind tasks that they would have preferred to finish. Don't neglect your own for the sake of Maman's."

"Go, dearest. Don't keep him waiting."

I kissed her cheeks, and she rushed off to accept her farewells from the adoring little gathering below. I stayed behind a moment to consider her words. It was true that every life was, in some way, an incomplete tableau. But when I compared the landscape left behind by Maman and Bonne Maman Eiffel, it seemed a world of difference. Where Bonne Maman Eiffel's canvas could have benefitted from a few more brushstrokes, half or more of Maman's had been left snowy white.

Seeing the husk of her room, just yesterday the vibrant nest of a girl in the first bloom of youth, now reduced to a pleasant guest room, gnawed at my soul. But for Laure's sake, I would descend the stairs and plaster on a smile. I would let my face tell the lie that I was pleased she was leaving us for the joys of marriage and motherhood, but there was a wound in my heart too deep to be healed even by the tincture of time.

Chapter Twelve

Papa was at breakfast the following morning, spreading marmalade on his bread and drinking coffee as though Laure hadn't left a gaping hole at the table that none of his impressive designs could bridge completely. Édouard was off to school and the children were tucked away with their tutors already.

"Are you for the offices today, Papa? Or have you business in town?" I spread a thin layer of lemon curd on toasted bread and poured some coffee, hoping I could find the stomach to eat something. Pauline knew lemon curd was my especial favorite and I was certain she'd had Cook make a batch to tempt me.

"Levallois today. What about you, Cherub? Pressing social engagements now that the wedding is over?"

"No, Papa. I knew this week would be trying so I kept my diary open."

"Wise girl. But in that event, I have an errand for you." He set down his paper to look at me.

"Of course, Papa. Whatever you require." I sat straighter, ever the assistant, wishing I hadn't left my notebook on my bedside table.

"You're to go into town and have a half dozen new gowns made for yourself, along with some new skirts and blouses for daily wear too. Shoes, hats, and all the rest of it while you're at it. All in the new style. If you spend less than a king's ransom, I shall be heartily disappointed."

I set my coffee cup down with a clink. "But Papa, after the wedding, surely we must economize—"

"You will leave the worry over the household ledgers to me if you please, mademoiselle. I put enough on your shoulders without adding *that* to the pile. I admire your thrift, but your mother's things are no longer suitable, remade or otherwise."

"But Papa, it hardly seems worth—"

The sound of footsteps in the hallway interrupted my plea. Tante Marie emerged, clearly dressed for an engagement and not a visit to her brother and niece.

"Thank the heavens, my reinforcements are here. *Ma foi*, Marie. I am father to the only girl in Paris who wouldn't jump at the idea of some new dresses. Where did I come up with such a girl?" Papa looked to his sister with exaggerated exasperation.

"She is a gem, and you know it, Gustave." Tante Marie dipped to kiss my cheeks and slid into the seat beside me. "But a gem in need of some polish. We'll see to that today."

"I just don't see why when I have plenty of serviceable clothes that fit. . . ."

"Dearest, if you won't do it for yourself, think of the Compagnie Eiffel. We have an image to maintain. If the greater public sees my eldest daughter dressed in ten-year-old frocks that have been refashioned thrice, what will they think of the financial status of our company?" Papa's tone was serious. Had someone said something to him?

"People will think we're a family of great economy who will see each project built under budget and on time?" I offered.

Papa and Tante Marie chuckled in unison. "You think too well of people, child. They'll think we're in dire straits and will be apt to cut corners. I've been remiss in letting such a thing go on for so long. From today forward, your name will be whispered in the same breath as the height of Parisian fashion."

I arched a brow. I had neither the time nor the inclination to follow the caprice of fashion. That was Tante Marie's domain. Possibly Laure's too, once let loose with a proper allowance.

Tante Marie took over. "Very well, not a fashion plate; at the very least people will say that Claire Eiffel is one of the best-dressed girls of her station. For the sake of the company. And you can become more adept at it for Valentine's sake. She's nearly a woman herself and will need someone to help her with such things. She isn't as independent minded as Laure and won't take it upon herself to learn."

I sighed in defeat. Papa and Tante Marie knew they'd vanquished my final argument. Valentine was fourteen years old and would be ready for longer skirts and fuller cuts soon enough. It would be easier to teach her the proper way to dress when she came of age if I had more experience with such things myself.

"Very well," I capitulated.

"That's a good girl. Will you head to Worth like your sister?"

"Heavens no. I'll bend to your wishes, Papa, but I'm not an American heiress passing through on her way to London to marry for a title. I can find a proper modiste in the neighborhood, I'm sure."

"Go to the more fashionable part of town, at least, Cherub. There must be something more suitable near the Champs-Élysées."

"I'll defer to Tante Marie's advice."

"Hallelujah." Tante Marie rubbed her hands together. "If you remember you said that, today will be far less of a battle for your poor *tante*."

I groaned. Today was going to be torture.

"Cheer up, Cherub, and give your papa a kiss so I can head to work."

I rose from my seat and obliged. He folded his paper and hurried out the door, likely anxious to return to the workshop after taking the day off for Laure's wedding. It was only something as monumental as a daughter's wedding that would have pulled him away on a workday. I suspected he envisioned a dozen fires that could be extinguished only by him and was eager to see to it. The reality was that his staff was extremely competent and would fare quite well without him for a day or two. Of course, his vision and talent were central to the company's success, but I was convinced the day-to-day operations weren't as fragile as he seemed to think they were. While much of my time was devoted to the running of the household, I spent hours and hours in his atelier, on job sites, and in his ledger books to know the inner workings of things almost as well as he did. I didn't have the schooling for the most technical aspects of the work, but I had learned a vast deal about his trade peering over his shoulder.

"You'll need to change before we go." Tante Marie eyed the plain dress I'd worn for a day at home. "It will be a full day, so we ought to get on with it."

With a sigh, I finished my breakfast and allowed Pauline to help me change into something more suitable for the visit to the modiste. How absurd that one had to put on their best clothes to buy more clothes, but I was told several times how indispensable it was. If a modiste believed a woman was not fashionable, she wouldn't show her the best fabrics or go to as much trouble to get the cuts just right. But I wagered that with Tante Marie's keen eye and Papa's deep pockets, any modiste worth her salt would strive to do the job well to keep our custom.

The dress I wore had, of course, been one of Maman's. It was a day dress of navy-blue silk and had been the height of fashion . . . nine years before when she'd had it made. It had been remade for me at least twice and showed little sign of wear, except perhaps at the hem. The seamstress had done an adequate job of making the gown into a more current style, but it was obvious to the trained eye that the gown was past its prime. The matching hat, even if a bit dated, was jaunty and pleasing, but probably made me look ridiculous for being a decade out of fashion.

Papa was right. Tante Marie was right. It was time for new things.

"Cheer up, mademoiselle." Pauline patted my arms from behind as I took a final glance in the mirror. "It's a day of shopping with your lovely *tante*, not a hanging."

"I know, I know," I said. I crossed to the wardrobe and looked inside. Nearly every garment had been Maman's, as my own had worn out long ago. A rainbow of silks and taffetas now stitched and restitched several times over. They no longer had Maman's scent entwined in the fibers. If Maman were alive, most of these would have been replaced by now as it was. I ran a finger along a green satin that had been particularly fetching on her but did not flatter my complexion in the least. I'd worn it anyway. Papa and Tante Marie were right, and I resented them for it. I turned to Pauline. "Donate these to the poor when the parcels come in. Down to the last chemise."

Pauline worked to keep a smile from her face. "Very good."

I descended the stairs to where Tante Marie waited. Her footman and carriage would be impatient by now.

"I know just the place. The cutest modiste in the world, not far from the Boulevard Haussmann. You'll see by and by that your papa knows what's best."

"Good. Though Papa was wrong about one thing. A half dozen dresses won't be enough. I'll need an entirely new wardrobe."

Her smile grew wide as she sat back in the plush seats of her gleaming carriage. "Oh, my darling girl, you've simply made my week."

THE MODISTE, A Mademoiselle Philomène Leclerc, did indeed run a pleasing shop, just as Tante Marie promised. Better still, she moved with efficiency and insisted her staff follow suit. We began by choosing designs from sketches from her portfolio. Tante Marie chose eagerly, I chose with more selectivity, and Mademoiselle Leclerc occasionally made a suggestion or steered us away from one of ours. That process took less than a half hour, which was a relief.

An experienced modiste, nearing middle age, she was wise enough not to bog down the process by allowing the client to pore over catalogues full of fabric swatches for each gown. She presented Tante Marie and me with a few selections that would work with the cut of the gown in colors that would suit my complexion. Three to four choices for each gown, though sometimes Mademoiselle Leclerc was so enthusiastic in her recommendations that neither Tante Marie nor I had the heart to contradict her.

"This cobalt blue will be magnificent with your hair, dearest," Tante Marie said, holding a swatch of fabric up to my face.

"Indeed, Mademoiselle wants for robust colors. Ruby, emerald, sapphire. Even rich browns and blacks would suit her. A complexion such as hers cannot abide pastels and colors that lack the conviction of their courage."

"You're an artist, Mademoiselle Leclerc," I said as she bustled to and fro with bolts of fabric and ordered her assistants about.

She offered me a confident smile and unfurled a length of garnet brocade that was so beautiful it made me catch my breath. "For an evening gown, this would be too heavy. You would pass out in a ballroom from overheating. But for an afternoon dress? It would be perfection."

"Oh yes, that's just the thing. She must have it. Perhaps in this ensemble here?" Tante Marie held up the portfolio, open to a smart two-piece jacket with bustle skirt.

"Madame has a good eye. This was exactly my thought. And we have the fabric in our stocks, so we can begin this one right away." Tante Marie smiled with satisfaction. Some of the evening dresses were being made from fabrics that would be imported from goodness-knew-where and would take weeks or months to complete. Whenever possible, we tried to choose fabrics that were on hand to expedite the whole affair.

Mademoiselle Leclerc played with the fabric a few moments more and gave her own sigh of approval at long last. She had her vision for the ensemble in her head and knew how to proceed. I'd seen the same look on Papa's face when a design finally sorted itself in his mind. "Yes, this will be lovely. She will turn heads on the streets of Paris and break hearts in the most fashionable salons in the city. I suspect that if Mademoiselle wears it in the right company, she'll soon be returning to me for her trousseau."

I looked to Tante Marie, whose eyes glistened at the prospect. "Don't get your hopes up on that score. I have only the energy to run one household, and it must be my papa's."

"Your papa is a capable man. If you go off to make a life for yourself—and you should—he will find a way forward." She fussed with a fabric sample, but she was bristling underneath.

I pressed my lips into a line. Papa needed me. He depended on me in ways Tante Marie didn't recognize. When she saw me, she saw the face of the fourteen-year-old girl who had just lost her mother and was adrift without a maternal force to guide her. She wasn't capable of seeing the twenty-year-old woman who had traveled extensively and run a household. And I understood it. When I saw Laure at the altar the day before, she was just a girl in pigtails with scraped knees in my mind. But I wasn't just a child playing house; I was helping Papa build his empire.

It was work beyond what she understood, and there was no point in trying to make her see the countless things I did in order to help Papa and his work day in and day out. It went beyond just making sure the house was comfortable and that the staff had meals ready on time. It was more than making sure his favorite suit was in good repair and that his shoes were shined. It had to do with anticipating what he needed before he had to expend the energy to ask. It had to do with not only managing the house and tending to the children but also minding the workshops and his job sites.

But there was no use in trying to convince my well-meaning *tante* Marie that the work I did couldn't be delegated to staff. Even a fleet of the most attentive housekeepers and assistants could not manage all the aspects of Papa's life with the efficiency that I did. And I wouldn't waste precious breath trying.

But I would concede that I needed to look the part of the eldest Eiffel daughter and would happily spend a healthy sum at the modiste to do so. And Tante Marie didn't need to know that there were more reasons to my allowing the extravagance beyond respecting Papa's wishes. There was the benefit of, for once in my life, at least appearing to take up an interest that was typical for my age, sex, and station in life: fashion. What's more, if I dressed like a woman who took herself seriously, others might take me more seriously as well. Fewer indulgent glances from Papa's staff, who sometimes viewed me as a child playing dress-up in her mother's clothes.

And I was more than ready for that day to be upon us.

Later, once measurements were taken and a dozen gowns ordered along with an absolute embarrassment of chemises, shoes, hats, reticules, and I didn't remember what all else, Tante Marie insisted that we take luncheon in a little café only a few doors down from the modiste. I was light in the head from all the standing and fussing and pinning, and frankly dizzy at the number of fittings that would be required once the gowns were prepared, so I couldn't refuse refreshment. The café, as a consequence of being the closest establishment of its kind near one of the most up-and-coming modistes in the city, was fussy and fashionable as well. Floral motifs and soft colors to please the feminine eye. It catered to the women seeking refuge after the tedious ordeal of being poked and prodded.

"There now, it wasn't torturous, was it?" Tante Marie asked once the waiter took her order for a *filet de sole à la normande*, a dainty portion of fish made significantly less dainty with a decadent sauce of heavy cream and a generous helping of Calvados—a rich apple brandy from Normandy. She paired it with a glass of white wine and ignored my arched eyebrow. She'd been complaining about the fit of her gowns for months, and creamy sauces were certainly not helping her to maintain her stylish figure. "If a woman must endure the indignity of losing her looks as she grows older, she might as well enjoy herself along the way."

I ordered a *barigoule* of spring vegetables, but indulged in a glass of wine as well, which the waiter brought in haste.

"Very good. Drinking alone in pleasant company is an uncomfortable experience."

"I'll raise a glass to that." I clinked my glass against hers, sending the melodic tinkling of crystal floating above our heads. "And no, apart from standing stock-still for the measurements, the visit to the modiste wasn't horribly tedious. Moreover, Mademoiselle Leclerc is a master at her craft. I can respect that in any cadre of life. She constructs a gown with the same skill and care Papa constructs a bridge, and I think that's to be commended."

"Well said, my dear. I always worried you might end up with a bit of a disdainful streak when it came to the feminine arts. You spend so much time at your papa's workshops, you forget that not everything worthwhile is in the sphere of men."

I was thoughtful for a moment. Did I not tend the children? Did I not run the house with the efficiency of a naval ship? What was more aligned with the feminine arts than that? But those were things that only a handful of people saw. The greater public? They saw how I dressed and comported myself. They saw if I took an interest in charity work or the church. The less I did in that sphere, the more women like Tante Marie thought I was shunning my own sex.

"Not disdain, Tante. A lack of time is perhaps more accurate. I know you think Papa is self-sufficient, but he relies on me terribly. I can't disappoint him."

She set down her glass of wine and studied her hands for a moment. "Just promise me you won't neglect yourself in the process of caring for him. And tending to your papa's every need might not be in his best interest. If he found himself wanting for a helpmeet, he might be more inclined to go out and find one outside of his own house."

The blood drained from my face at the idea.

"Your *maman* has been gone for years, dearest. A new wife would be good for Gustave, don't you think?"

I shook my head. "Papa is married to his work. I haven't seen him so much as steal a glance at another woman in all the time Maman has been gone. Not when traveling, not here. I don't think he could bring himself to love another, Tante."

"Maybe not the way he loved your *maman*, but he could love again. Don't you think it would be better for both of you if he did?"

I loved my *tante* Marie more than I could express, but I could have screamed in the middle of the café, with all the peachy napkins and lavender flowers on the tables mocking me with their pastel insincerity. She had one idea in her head of a healthy, productive life for my father and for me, and could not be persuaded that any other paths in life could lead to happy outcomes. I set my teeth against the audacity and reined in my anger. She wasn't a visionary like Papa; she simply wasn't born with his gifts.

It was very much like when Papa's clients couldn't translate his sketches into reality in their mind's eye. You couldn't, no matter how hard you tried, induce someone without such gifts to see what the final results could be.

In the end, all you could do was persuade them to trust your vision.

Chapter Thirteen

My God, boy. How have you managed to rack up such debts at school? Are you visiting those damned clubs again? Didn't I forbid such waste?" Papa's voice carried from his library into the foyer and up the marble staircase I was descending.

"Papa, all the chaps go. What's the harm in a few hands of vingt-et-un?" a truculent voice replied.

Édouard was back from school for the summer holiday, and our peace was shattered. Usually we had a few hours of calm before he and Papa came to blows, but apparently there would be no honeymoon period on this visit. Dear Édouard continued to be an undisciplined scholar and a profligate spender, despite Papa's attempts to rein him in—and my own.

I had to meet with Pauline in the kitchens, which required passing directly in front of Papa's library. I'd hoped to swoop past undetected, but the door was ajar and Papa spotted me before I could make an escape.

"Claire" was all he needed to say, but the meaning was clear. *Get in here and support me in this.* I stifled a sigh and entered, taking a place next to Édouard in the seats across from Papa's imposing desk.

Édouard rolled his eyes. "Ever the lapdog. I'm surprised you don't roll over and beg for scraps."

"You sister has a sense of duty. To herself and this family. You could do with taking a page out of her book, young man." Papa's color was high, and I worried that his health would suffer for Édouard's antics.

"*Why must you have thoughts and opinions of your own? Why can't you be more like Claire?*" Édouard said in a mocking voice. "God, I'd rather die than be your poodle like her."

My jaw dropped. Édouard had never troubled himself to speak kindly to me—certainly not with the deference the other children did—but he had always stopped short of blatant disrespect before now. I set my teeth and glared at him. I opened my mouth to defend myself, but Papa intervened before I could form the words.

"I never asked you to be some obedient lapdog, and you know it, boy. Nor have I asked it of your sister. All I have asked is that you don't gallivant around Paris making a fool of yourself and wasting my money in gaming halls and in those godforsaken bawdy houses up on the hill. It seems precious little to require of my son."

I'd heard stories of the notorious dance halls and bordellos on Montmartre, usually in conjunction with Édouard's name or some of his friends who, like Édouard, had more spending money than good sense. I would never have been allowed anywhere near them. Even in the carriage, Papa ordered the driver to avoid the area when I was with him. Though I'd never seen the inside of such an establishment, I could imagine only too well the trouble Édouard could find in such a place.

"You never were young, were you?" Édouard spat. "You always took life so damned seriously you never took a single moment to appreciate your youth, did you?"

"Presumptuous child, you know nothing of my past. And watch your language in front of your sister, boy. I won't warn you again." Papa leaned forward and pinched the bridge of his nose. These encounters with Édouard had a way of draining him. "If this were a solitary lapse in judgment that could be excused by the folly of youth, I'd treat the matter very differently. But this has been a pattern of yours for the past two years. I worry that it demonstrates a wantonness of character that I refuse to see take root in my eldest son."

"You can't make me be like you, you know. I won't live for work as you do. I don't care that I won't leave behind a legacy like yours. I'd rather worry about the here and now." Édouard crossed his arms over his chest and proceeded to make a face that he probably thought made him look defiant but in reality made him look precisely like a four-year-old boy who had been denied a lolly. I took him just about as seriously too.

"I don't care about that. Not if it's what you don't want. What I do care about is that you lead a life that you'll be proud of in forty years' time. Twenty. Even ten. And I hope that you live to see a ripe old age like Bon Papa Eiffel. If you keep drinking, gambling, and carousing, the odds won't be in your favor."

"I've just finished my term at school—I really could be spared the lecture if you don't mind. I've had my fill." He turned his head defiantly, refusing to meet Papa's eyes.

"Based on these marks, you certainly didn't tax yourself overmuch on your professors' lectures. I think you can withstand another."

"Papa—"

"*Papa* nothing. You will go back in the fall, take your studies seriously, and stop gadding about town like a degenerate, or you won't see another sou from me. Do I make myself plain, boy?"

"Perfectly," Édouard said, finally sitting up straight in his chair. Papa had finally threatened the one thing that mattered to him: his pocket money. "It's been a long term. I'll take dinner in my rooms tonight and see you for dinner tomorrow."

I was about to object, given the strains the staff had just endured for Laure's wedding, but Papa interceded.

"You'll be at dinner tonight or go without, and you'll be up for breakfast by seven, or so help me God, I'll pull you out of bed with my own two hands. The staff will be on orders to ensure you don't leave in the night. And further, you'll find a constructive use for your summer holiday, or I'll find a use for you myself, even if it means scrubbing the floor with the housemaids."

Édouard stood and stalked out of the room without a word or backward glance and slammed the door closed behind him. Papa buried his face in his hands, then rubbed his eyes, as if trying to wipe the exhaustion from them and failing in the effort. "That boy is going to be the death of me," he finally groaned.

I felt a tightness in my chest and an overwhelming desire to beat my brother about the head. "Do you need to rest?"

"I don't mean literally, Cherub. I'm well enough. He's just the most stubborn fool to ever draw breath and cannot be made to see sense."

"So you're saying he's a teenage boy." I felt my shoulders loosen as Papa's color returned to something closer to its normal shade.

"And he's good at it. I was known to be a sot back in my time. My own dear papa likely kept hold of the apology letters I sent home when my mischief was found out. But when I did wrong, I apologized and tried to do better. Édouard takes every attempt at molding his character as a personal affront, and it's maddening. I don't know how to guide him away from this path he's on."

"I don't have any advice to offer you, Papa, other than tread gently. I think he wants to be treated like a man instead of a boy."

"Then he damned well ought to act like one." Papa tossed the report with Édouard's marks and the bills from his various accounts to the side. "Pardon my language, Cherub."

I waved the apology away. "If you treat him like one, perhaps it will inspire him to act like one? What would you do with an employee who overspent on a project or missed the mark in some other way? Would you yell and carry on?"

"No. I'd endeavor to mentor him. And if he proved teachable, I'd keep him on."

"I think Édouard *is* teachable, Papa. Truly I do."

"I hope you're right, Cherub. But I don't see your brother getting into the Polytechnic with these marks."

If Édouard didn't get into the Polytechnic, Papa's dream of passing the reins of the company to his eldest son would flicker and die. It was hard to imagine Édouard taking Papa's place, but it had always seemed the natural order of things. If Papa were forced to sell or pass the company outside of the family, it would break his heart.

"I'm sorry, Papa" was all I could think to say.

"Not to worry, Cherub." He picked up the list of Édouard's debts again and rubbed his eyes with his thumb and forefinger as he read. "My God, but I didn't think such waste was possible."

"He's impossible." I huffed a sigh and slumped in my chair. "I wish there were something I could do to make it better, Papa."

"There is one thing." He looked up from the blotted paper.

"Anything," I offered.

"Make your trips to the modiste a regular occurrence. If you spend all my money on silk and satin and ribbons and lace, your fool of a brother won't be able to gamble it away at cards."

"Tante Marie and Mademoiselle Leclerc will be thrilled."

"Better them than many others. I'm glad someone, apart from every dance hall in Paris, will be able to derive pleasure and gainful employment from my money."

I kissed Papa's head and left him to his ledger. I'd have to send Pauline with biscuits and tea when I thought he was sufficiently calm. But instead of turning to the kitchens, as had been my original destination, my feet—and my rage—led me back up the stairs.

I LEFT PAPA'S library, anger coursing in my veins. Papa might have been finished with his dressing-down of Édouard, but I hadn't yet had my turn.

I knocked on the closed door. "Go away," Édouard muttered from the other side of the door.

I opened it, to the sound of his protests. He was lying prostrate on the bed, still in his suit of clothes. His fingers were laced behind his head, and he was staring up at the heavy draped canopy over his bed.

"Get out," he barked, turning his head to look at me.

"I only knocked as a courtesy. The only rooms in this house I do not enter at will are Papa's, do you understand me?"

"Oh, shove off, you prat. You're not even three full years older than I am and you act like my nursemaid." He flipped onto his side, his back to me, pulling a pillow over his head.

"Oh, shut your insolent mouth. For better or worse, I've had to be a mother to this entire household for the last seven years, and I've done my best to do right by everyone."

He turned back and looked to me, his eyes widened in surprise at the viciousness of my tone, but he didn't relent. "You've done your best to be Papa's lapdog, you mean."

I removed my shoe, one of Maman's that was long overdue for the rag bag, and threw it directly at his idiot head. It clipped the corner of his forehead and would leave a mark. It was all I could do not to smirk with satisfaction.

"You may think taking care of this family makes me look like Papa's lapdog, but I honestly couldn't care less what you think. Perhaps I might if you showed any inclination of acting like a man, but I'm too busy to spare attention to spoiled, willful brats."

His jaw dropped in turn. Where he had previously never disrespected me so openly, I, too, had never presumed to call out his poor behavior. Today was a day for breaking down such barriers.

"How dare you—"

"Quite easily. I run this house and manage the affairs of everyone in it. I'll not hear criticism from you, do you understand me? If you want to be treated like a man, you'd do better to act like one. And until you do, I'll take Papa's side in the blood feud between the two of you."

"Like you'd ever take my side against Papa." He rubbed the lump on his forehead.

"That's where you're wrong. If I thought Papa were being unreasonable, I'd advocate for you without a moment's hesitation. I've done it before when I thought Laure deserved a new dress when he was balking. When his expectations for Albert's academics were beyond what was appropriate for his age. And I'm sure the moment will come when I have to take Valentine's corner. Not that you'd see any of that. But Papa has had the measure of you at every turn and I won't go against him in this."

He looked up to where I stood, arms akimbo and ready to take no argument from him.

"You've dared to countermand Papa?" he asked, his tone incredulous.

"I don't rail against him, no. But despite how it may seem to you, I don't blindly support Papa in all his choices. I ask myself what Maman would have done and try to honor *her* wishes." And I'd done it just as she had more times than I could remember. Maman would have never contradicted Papa in front of others, but it was clear from his occasional change of heart that she would gently influence him in private.

Papa was a man that had to be persuaded artfully, but Édouard was still a boy and required more bluntness. Sometimes in the form of the heel of an old shoe, which I retrieved from the floor by his rumpled bed and put back on my be-stockinged foot.

"So why are you here?" Édouard was no longer truculent, but weary. "Papa spoke his piece and you agree with him. What more is there to be said?"

"Your antics are killing Papa. Don't you see it? He's under enough stress with the company without you adding to it. You're nearly a man grown, but if Papa has an apoplexy from your nonsense, Valentine and Bébert will be orphaned altogether."

Édouard shook his head. "Papa is made of sterner stuff than you give him credit for. You're being dramatic."

"Perhaps I am being dramatic, but the idea of running this household without Maman's guidance *or* his is simply too much for me to contemplate. You might understand if you bothered to take up the slightest scrap of responsibility, you lout."

"Claire—"

I held up my hand. "No more from you. I know you don't give a fig about me or the rest of us, but I won't have you upsetting Papa. Just be down to dinner on time. You've done quite enough to incite Papa's ire for one holiday."

"Sister, there are nearly three months remaining in the summer. You cannot expect that Papa and I won't butt heads again."

"No, but I expect you to hold your tongue tonight unless you want another goose egg on the left side of your forehead to match the one on your right."

At this, he broke into a boyish grin. The sort he used to share with me, and that I'd come to miss desperately, in the days before I'd grown to resent his profligate nature and he my maternal chiding.

"I should think a matched set would look bully, don't you? Rather like I've got horns coming in."

"Too appropriate, Brother dear. You don't want to look too much like the devil you are. I shall reserve the other lump for when you most deserve it."

"I've no doubt, Claire." He shook his head, stood, and crossed to the mirror to admire my handiwork with a scowl. "Lord knows what I'll tell people."

"The truth, that your sister gave you a good thrashing, would be the slice of humble pie you so greatly deserve." I crossed my arms over my chest, pleased with the concern he was showing at his reflection. It would heal, of course. I didn't want to maim him. He hadn't aggravated me *quite* to that extent. Yet.

"You're ready for the Comédie-Française. Though it would be funnier if you weren't right all the damned time."

I turned on a heel, unable to persuade the smile that pulled at the corners of my lips to wait until I was in the privacy of my rooms. Papa's lectures worked well enough on the younger children, but they just served to anger Édouard. My approach, blunt though it was, just maybe got through to him.

And it might just be the making of him.

That night, as promised, Édouard came down to dinner precisely at half past seven for apéritif, dressed appropriately, and even wore a reasonably convivial expression to match his fine evening wear. We sat down to a fine meal of *sole meunière*, braised asparagus, and all manner of good things that the cook knew Édouard liked and would enjoy upon his return home.

It was a small gesture, perhaps, but showing up to dinner on time was a start. Papa looked mollified to see Édouard acting so compliant. Until he saw the goose egg on Édouard's forehead, which was swelling magnificently.

"What in the name of God and all the saints happened to your forehead, boy?" Papa asked, his eyes fairly boggling.

"Nothing to be concerned with, Papa." Édouard shot the subtlest of glances in my direction. "At least not until the matching one appears on the opposite side."

I stifled a giggle, to which Papa rolled his eyes. "I have no idea what's going on under my own roof, and for once I think I'm glad of it."

And for the first time in ages, we had a pleasant meal in Édouard's presence. I wasn't sure if he was temporarily chastened or simply worn down enough to behave for an evening, but it was wonderful to have the funny, kind young man back in our lives. But in my gut, I felt the stone of worry weighing heavy, wondering how long this improved behavior would last and how many more lumps on the forehead he'd have to endure in the process.

Chapter Fourteen

Two weeks later, Mademoiselle Leclerc delivered the first installment of my wardrobe, and Pauline was charged with emptying out my armoire of all Maman's old gowns. It was just as well that I wasn't there to watch her.

In my sitting room, I allowed Mademoiselle Leclerc to help me into the ensemble of garnet brocade she and Tante Marie had been so enthusiastic about. As I slipped into the bodice, I admired the impeccable French seams and beautiful stitching. It was a wonder to look at inside and out. She and her assistant fussed with the lay of the skirt and adjusted the ridiculous bustle until I was ready to call an end to the entire mess, but at last they were satisfied, and I was allowed to look in the expansive mirror that dominated one wall of the room.

My hair went from a flat shade of dishwater to a glistening honeyed brown all by virtue of the luscious garnet-red fabric. While brocade patterns often leaned toward the garish, the design on the fabric we chose for the dress was subtle. Little gold threads swirled in a delicate filigree that caught sunlight and candle glow and lifted the rich garnet color enough to keep it from being oppressively heavy. More important, the material had been put to good use in the hands of a master craftswoman, and

I was impressed that every cut accentuated my figure and every seam lay perfectly.

I looked in the mirror and saw a woman reflected back at me.

"Mademoiselle is displeased?" Mademoiselle Leclerc's eyes were wide with concern as she saw my somber expression.

"No, not in the least." I forced the corners of my lips upward. "I've never owned anything so lovely in all my life. You're gifted with a needle, Mademoiselle Leclerc. I hope you understand how much so."

"You are kind, my dear. Shall we help you change back into your tea gown?"

"No, thank you." Though Maman's loose gown, designed to be worn without a corset for receiving guests at home, was infinitely more comfortable than my new ensemble. "I'm going out this afternoon. I'd like to give my new finery a bit of an outing."

"Excellent." Mademoiselle Leclerc clasped her hands. "You look ready to take on Paris single-handedly. But not without your hat."

She took some pins and attached the coordinating garnet hat to my hair at an angle that was neither too staid nor too jaunty and handed me a reticule that matched the dress, though I hadn't ordered it.

"There was some remnant fabric," she explained. "Consider it a small gift of thanks from me."

"It was an embarrassingly large order, wasn't it?" My smile grew more genuine. I supposed it was akin to a grocer slipping in an extra orange or packet of sweets for the children for loyal and generous customers.

"Well, yes. But that wasn't why I made this for you. You trusted me to outfit your transition from adolescence to womanhood. This is no small thing, to move from the spring to the summer of your life. You have done me a great honor."

I looked to the floor for a moment but forced my eyes upward again. "You have my thanks and my custom, Mademoiselle Leclerc. I look forward to the rest of the order in the coming weeks."

She bade us farewell and beckoned her assistant to follow her out the door. As I turned, the swish of the bustle felt foreign and decadent. I feared I'd look a fool in the contraption as I walked down the streets or, worse, as I entered Papa's ateliers. And the latter was precisely what I planned to do.

Papa was incredibly busy with contracts for projects in the south, and I wanted to ensure he ate a proper luncheon. This would mean not only bringing a hamper full of his favorite foods but staying with him as he ate to ensure the food wasn't forgotten as he absorbed himself in schematics and ledger sheets. Papa had parted ways with Seyrig a few years prior. Papa was rewarded for his mentorship by the louse stealing a valuable Portuguese contract away from the Compagnie Eiffel, but Papa had the good grace to pretend the traitor had acted within the bounds of decency, even if it wasn't true. But since the dissolution of the partnership, Papa was forced to run the company under his own steam, and I worried the strain of it would damage his health.

Papa looked up when I knocked on the frame of his open door and his face broke into a smile.

"I've brought you a lunch to help ensure a productive afternoon, Papa." I gestured to the hamper I carried.

"Well, so much for today's output," he scoffed. "Every young man who's seen you won't be fit to work for the rest of the day. And more than half the old ones too."

I laughed and placed the hamper on his desk. I pulled out the assortment of foods and arranged them into a proper picnic. Bread, cheeses, sliced meat, fruits, chocolate, and some of Cook's famous lemon curd tarts for dessert.

"Eat, Papa." I passed him a plate with a sampling of everything. It wouldn't be as restorative as a hot meal, but it was better than not eating, which I feared had become his custom based on his exhaustion and short temper when he returned home at night. He might have had the reserves to run without sustenance when he was a young man, but he was older now and was loath to admit it.

"Kind of you, Cherub. But it's not worth going to such a fuss for me."

"Fussing over you is my greatest joy, Papa. Now regale me with news of your latest projects while we eat."

It was strategic; he would eat more if he was distracted with talk about work. Especially if things were going well, which they seemed to be.

Just as Papa was launching into an animated discussion of a new train station, a knock sounded. A tall, bespectacled man with a mustache and a rather nervous presence stood in the open doorway.

"Oh, forgive me, monsieur, it's midday and I should have known you'd be taking luncheon. I'll return this afternoon."

Papa gestured to the open seat next to mine. "Nonsense, Salles. My daughter is used to the way things are done around here. Allow me to present my daughter Claire. Claire, this is Adolphe Salles. One of our newest engineers and an exceedingly prodigious talent."

"I'm enchanted, Mademoiselle Eiffel." Adolphe took my proffered hand in his. "Though I am not sure what to say after such a compliment from your father."

"I suggest you accept it. He doesn't offer compliments lightly or insincerely."

"Then I shall be forced to accept that all your father's many accolades of you are genuine as well, and not just the boastings of a devoted parent."

"They are both in equal measure," Papa inserted. "Claire, why don't you offer Salles here a bit to eat. He's as apt to run himself to the ground with work as I am."

I offered them a theatrically put-upon sigh. "Would that you men would look after your health as much as you do the latest plans for a building or bridge that comes to your desk."

"It's an unfortunate addiction to work," Salles admitted. "But better than some alternatives."

"I cannot disagree there." Papa and I exchanged a look that made it clear Édouard's reckless habits had come to mind for both of us. I placed the plate I'd brought for myself in front of Salles, replete with a helping of all the cheeses, meats, and fruits the I'd brought along. It was just as well, as the cook had packed enough for a small army. I managed to eat a modest portion over a napkin, not wanting Salles to think I was forsaking a meal on his account.

"The Roquefort is delightful." Salles ate with such gusto that it was obvious Papa was right about his proclivity for skipping meals just as his employer did.

Papa and Salles engaged in conversation on the new train station, and it became clear that Papa's assessment of Salles's intelligence and talent weren't overstated. When he lost himself in the conversation about the project and his ideas, the charming shyness dissolved, and he was as confident and self-assured a man as I'd ever seen. He spoke of support wires and metal rivets with the same reverence as another man might speak of his lover.

"I think if we add supports to the bridge in this section, it will be stronger yet." Salles pointed to a section on the sketches he'd placed before Papa with the end of a pencil that was riddled with teeth marks. Was he a nervous man? Was it just an odd habit of his? But what fascinated me more than this quirk was that the deference he'd shown Papa on entering had dissolved into collegial respect. When they were in conversation about design, he was no longer the new boy in the office. He was in his element. "It could add twenty years of life to the other supports, saving a great deal of money in the long run."

"Sadly, those who commission us rarely think about the long term. They care about upfront costs and the look of the thing. Won't it make it a bit unsightly?"

I cleared my throat. "Not if you use some of the same techniques you used in Porto. Have you a sketch pad?" Salles, blinking, pulled out his sketch pad and passed it to me along with his pockmarked pencil. I ignored the unsightly divots his teeth had left in the soft wood when he was lost in thought, letting the pencil fly across the page as I recalled the lacelike grace of the supports on the arches of Maria Pia Bridge. Papa looked amused by my intensity, Salles almost enraptured by it. A few moments later, I passed the sketch over to Papa. "Here you are."

Both men studied my work until Papa broke the silence. "She's absolutely right. The effect will actually be quite elegant, despite the increased number of supports. Intricate and eye-catching. Almost feminine while adding strength to the structure at the same time."

Salles nodded. "The arch is one of the most stable structures in architecture, is it not? If arches and curves are graceful by definition, it would stand to reason that grace and strength aren't contradictory terms but, rather, synonymous ones."

"Amen to that. I've always thought the good Lord made woman of curves and arches rather than rigid lines like man because they are well and truly the stronger sex. It's a pity most men are too thick to see it." Papa's eyes hadn't left the sketch. "The idea is a good one, Cherub." This was the equivalent of raving praise from Papa. I didn't suppress a satisfied smile.

"Indeed it is. If Mademoiselle Eiffel had been permitted to attend the Polytechnic, she'd be on her way to becoming a great name in our circles."

"My lad, if she had been permitted to attend the Polytechnic, you'd be working elsewhere, and *she* would be my prized new protégée. But the world isn't what it should be." Papa's sigh was a heavy one. Weighed down with his disappointment that neither of his sons showed academic promise or the cruelty of nature that the one of us who would have been proud to carry the Eiffel torch forward into the twentieth century had the misfortune of being born female. Papa looked up from the sketch at long last, his keen gaze assessing us both. "We'll put it forth to the investors with my blessing at the next meeting. And Salles, you'll present it to them."

His eyes widened. "M-me, monsieur? No, I couldn't possibly. You'd be a much better advocate—"

"Salles, your skills at the drafting table will only take your career so far. You have to master the boardroom as well if you're to advance. Never refuse the opportunity to make a presentation yourself. At your stage in the career, yes, it would be customary for a senior designer to go before the investors on your behalf, but I want to see how you acquit yourself. I have a feeling that once you get over your nerves, you'll be rather persuasive."

Salles was early in his career, it was true, but Papa wanted to see him climb the ladder more expeditiously than many of the junior engineers in his employ. He didn't need the lessons in modesty that many others needed so desperately when they came out of the Polytechnic school. He was confident without being arrogant, which was a trait more valuable than gold when it came to engineers. A designer without humility was prone to getting people killed.

Papa's protégé looked pale but voiced his agreement. "I'll start preparing the presentation now." He jumped up and bounded to the door before turning back and saying, "Many thanks for the refreshment, mademoiselle. It was a pleasure to make your acquaintance."

I smiled and he lingered just a heartbeat before rushing off to his desk. Papa chuckled softly. "As bright a lad as one could hope for, and twice as eager."

"It would seem so. It's good he was available to come work for you. I would think a young man of his talent would have had many offers."

"Your papa's reputation has its advantages. Would that your brother were as conscientious as young Salles." Papa shook his head almost mournfully and returned to the last vestiges of his lunch.

"You seem distant, Papa. Are you quite all right?"

His reverie continued a moment longer before he turned his head to me and forced himself back to the here and now. "Yes, yes. Nothing for you to worry about, Cherub. Why don't you head back now? I'll be home in time for dinner."

"Very well, Papa." I rose and cleared away the dishes and the hamper and brushed a kiss against his forehead. "Don't work too hard."

"Of course not." His eyes were already back to his papers, though he paused and looked back up at me. "Perhaps you could bring in luncheon more often?"

"Any time you wish, Papa." The corners of my lips turned up; I was glad that my efforts had pleased him.

"And perhaps bring more of the Roquefort that Salles liked, if Cook can manage it?"

"Of course." My smile faltered as I made my way back to the street.

As Papa's carriage took me on the familiar route home, I allowed the sound of the hoofbeats on the cobblestones to lull me into a trance of sorts. I always knew that someone with more training than I would have to take over the company. For years I expected it would be Édouard, whom I could advise and consult as I did Papa. But Papa had welcomed an outsider. What that meant for me and the future of the company, I could not say, but none of the possibilities put my mind at ease.

The Compagnie Eiffel was new, but it had the potential to become the most influential architecture firm in France, if not the world. The sort of firm that would live on for generations if well managed. It was Papa's dream to see not just his works but the organization live on and thrive after he was gone. And there was no more pivotal moment for any company than its first transfer of power. If Papa didn't choose the proper successor, the company would falter, and I couldn't bear to see all the hard work and sacrifice come to nothing. But to see the company passed off to some promising newcomer? It was somehow worse altogether, and I could not let that happen.

Chapter Fifteen

I brought Papa his tea in the library on a Saturday afternoon in July that was so bright and sunny, he'd had to draw the window shade to keep the glare from his papers. He glanced up with an appreciative smile. "We have a guest for dinner tonight, Cherub. Be a lamb and see to it that an extra place is set, would you?"

"Of course, Papa. Is it Laure?" She'd been ensconced in married life so happily we'd hardly seen her since she returned from her honeymoon. But I realized the folly of my question as soon as it escaped my lips; if it had been Laure, Papa would have ordered a place set for Maurice as well.

"No, young Salles is coming to dine. He's rather alone in the city, you know, and we have some business to discuss."

I huffed a sigh, not bothering to conceal my annoyance. Salles had been present for every luncheon I'd brought for Papa over the past month. He was a constant topic of conversation at dinner. And now, at long last, he was going to breach that barrier of our front door too.

"Something wrong, Cherub?"

"It seems like you spend a lot of time with young Salles. Don't you think your other employees might grow resentful of such favoritism?" I used my most diplomatic tone, and Papa was already absorbed in his work so he probably couldn't detect the effort it took to make it even somewhat convincing.

"Stuff and nonsense. What's the use of founding a company if I can't run it as I please? Each and every one of them sees Salles's promise, and they won't begrudge him the chance to move up the ladder when it's offered."

"Are you so sure of that, Papa?" He looked up at me, eyes widened. "Even if they recognize his talent, that doesn't preclude that your attentions wouldn't make them jealous. Indeed, they might resent him for being favored with not only his natural gifts but your personal tutelage. It could make him unpopular with the others, and say what you will, it won't help his career path."

Papa stroked his beard, which grew whiter with each passing month. "I suppose I see your point. I don't want the boy set up to be an object of resentment."

"Precisely, Papa. It would be doing him an unkindness."

"Just as well no one will know he's coming to dinner. I'll be sure to tell him not to mention the invitation at the atelier. But I see no reason to be more circumspect with mentoring him at the office. They've seen it for weeks now, and to change course would make me look inconsistent. I don't want them thinking he's fallen out of favor either."

"Very well, Papa." I turned and headed toward the kitchens, waiting to release my sigh until I was out of Papa's earshot. Salles was an eager man, and useful to Papa in ways I wasn't trained to be. I didn't think the Polytechnic allowed women, and while I was deeply interested in all Papa did, I didn't feel compelled to complete a course of study to be another engineer in his company. But all the same, I hated the way this interloper had come to be a vital adviser to Papa in such a short time.

But if it eased Papa's burden, I couldn't contradict him. I gave the order for an extra place setting at the table and alerted the cook that there would be a guest so he would have time to add the tricks and flourishes he saved for company, knowing he'd be furious if denied the opportunity to show off a bit.

A few hours later, a knock sounded at my bedroom door, and I roused myself from my reading to answer it.

I expected Valentine or Papa with some query or another, but it was Pauline. "A bit early, aren't you?" I looked at my little clock on the mantelpiece. She usually came a half hour before dinner to help me change into a proper evening dress and to style my hair. It was a full hour before the meal was to start.

"Your father thought you might want to put forth special effort tonight, as you have company. He came to the kitchens personally to ask me to come up early." Pauline ushered me over to the vanity as she spoke, eager to get the process underway.

"Papa did?" I said, taking the seat obediently. I couldn't remember, aside from ordering me to buy new clothes, when Papa had paid the least bit of attention to my appearance, whether company was involved or not.

But Pauline was clearly chuffed to have received such attention from the master of the house, so I didn't push her away to reclaim the extra half hour of peace. We settled on a teal-blue satin evening dress with some delicate handsewn beading that had arrived in the latest installment of gowns from Mademoiselle Leclerc. Pauline deemed it elegant enough for company but not overly elaborate for a small gathering at home.

She spent an eternity weaving my hair into an elaborate confection of honey-colored curls that, though maddening while in production, was lovely in execution.

"Such a lovely young woman." Pauline placed a hand on my shoulder as I looked in the mirror to take in the effect. "Now all it wants is a necklace. What do you think? Pearls?"

Maman's rope of pearls was, to my mind, too elaborate for the evening, and was better suited for pairing with a voluminous velvet gown and an evening at the Opéra Garnier. I opened the jewel case and selected the button necklace Maman had worn so frequently and that I had reserved for myself from her treasures after she passed. Seven years that felt a lifetime ago and only yesterday all at once. It added just the right hint of sparkle and hit the gown at the perfect point on the bodice.

"Perfect, my dear." She handed me my white elbow-length gloves and opened the door for me to descend to dinner.

Salles was already in the sitting room with Papa, engrossed in conversation, as they always were once they'd been in each other's company for more than a matter of seconds. Both looked up with widened eyes.

"How enchanting you look," Salles stammered as he clambered to his feet. "I-I beg your pardon. Good evening, mademoiselle."

I offered him my gloved hand, which he kissed while I dipped into a shallow curtsy.

"Another lovely one, Cherub," Papa said, admiring my gown. I offered him a weak smile and took my place on the divan, accepting an apéritif from one of the footmen. The chilled Dubonnet was a blend of spice, blackberry, and chocolate with a bitter note that gave it a satisfying twinge on the tongue. Not unlike the Port wine we sampled on-site, but with a personality quite apart from its Portuguese cousin. Though it was pleasant enough to drink straight, especially when chilled, I preferred it mixed in a champagne cocktail, and would have to ask Pauline to remind the staff.

A footman announced dinner not long after, and the dining room looked ready to welcome the president of the republic himself. The staff, always eager to flaunt their skills, had gone to incredible measures to turn what had been intended as a simple family dinner into a grand showcase. Where I had ordered a nice beef roast, potatoes, and sautéed vegetables, as we might have for any ordinary dinner, the cook had somehow managed to concoct a seven-course meal on what must have been extremely short notice. More peculiar was that the children, usually present at family dinners, were absent. I assumed Papa had ordered that they be fed in Valentine's little sitting room.

We'd already had our apéritif in the salon, and a footman soon served a variety of canapés topped with everything from smoked salmon to caviar. The fish course was a small portion of delicate sea bass in butter sauce followed by the main course, which was lamb shank *navarin*, a dish of which our cook was particularly proud.

"Have you seen your father's designs for the cupola for the Nice Observatory? They're quite extraordinary." I swallowed a sigh and snapped my attention back to the conversation. If I were forced to sit through this dinner, I'd hoped to spend the meal lost in thought while Salles and Papa prattled on about the business. But our guest was quite determined to drag me into the conversation at random intervals, and usually when my reveries had just gotten interesting.

"Indeed I have, Monsieur Salles." I placed my fork beside my plate, careful not to thump it against the polished wood in annoyance. "And have been to the site with Papa. The structure will be a beautiful marriage of styles. Garnier's classical grace and Papa's bold innovation."

Had I seen his designs? I'd pored over the sketches for hours at Papa's side, whispering suggestions, quietly managing the workforce, and keeping an eye on the ledgers. This dolt probably thought my life was nothing more than trips to the modiste's and ordering dinners. And heaven knew those chores demanded enough of my time, but there wasn't a project that crossed his desk that I didn't know about. Especially this venture with Charles Garnier, which was an especial favorite of Papa's. Above all things, Papa was a man of science, and while bridges and railway stations were useful and worthy, this was a chance to build something that would contribute to the scientific community directly, which tugged at strings attached directly to a heart seemingly made in equal parts of warm, human flesh and efficient iron cogwheels.

"Well said." Salles's eyes glistened eagerly as he remembered I was capable of participating in the conversation more fully. "It truly is a—marriage—as you say, of form and function."

"With a dome larger than the Pantheon's that rotates to accommodate the telescopes and their view of the night sky housed atop a glorious example of classical architecture? It will be a marvel of the modern world. No one has attempted an unsupported dome of this kind before, and I suspect it will become a template for the rest of the world. Like Papa's bridges."

"You follow your father's work studiously it seems."

The fool still didn't understand. I took a steadying breath to give myself a fighting chance at keeping my temper in check.

"Monsieur Salles, I think you may be under the mistaken impression that all I do is deliver my father's luncheon and sew on the occasional wayward shirt cuff button on his way out the door. I have accompanied my father to job sites all over the continent and been a constant presence in the workshops since before you entered the Polytechnic."

"Claire," Papa warned. I was skating the line of civility and threatened to fall into the icy waters of impropriety, but I found myself not horribly concerned with winning Adolphe Salles's good opinion. Papa didn't like it, but no more did I like Salles's intrusion into our daily lives.

"No, Gustave, she is right. It was boorish of me to assume that she wouldn't be knowledgeable of your projects." *Gustave.* Since when was Papa anything other than "Monsieur Eiffel" or "*patron*" to an employee? Among people closer to him in rank, he was occasionally "Eiffel," but never, ever "*Gustave.*" My eyes flitted over to Papa, who made no sign of being affronted by this familiarity. Did Papa welcome it? Had he *invited* it?

"You'll both have to excuse me." I tossed my napkin aside on the table and pushed back my chair. "I've a sudden headache and need to lie down. I'll leave you to enjoy your dessert."

Both men stood up as I did, but I turned to leave the room before either could speak.

PAULINE, LIKELY ALERTED by Papa, showed up at my bedroom door a few minutes later.

She came with my dessert: a toothsome *tarte aux fraises* piled high with glazed strawberries and a cup of mint tea on a tray, which she set on my bedside table. "Monsieur says you're feeling peaked. I thought this might help. And I can always draw you a bath if you like. Heat and steam are good for headaches."

"No need for that." I realized my tone was harsher than I'd intended and far harsher than she deserved. I took a steadying breath and softened. "Thank you, Pauline. That was very kind of you."

She patted my shoulder and undid the never-ending column of satin-covered buttons down the back of my gown and helped me into my chemise. I sat at the vanity and allowed her to take my hair out of the elegant cliff she'd worked so hard on. With each hairpin removed, I felt the tension in my shoulders begin to ease away.

"Begging your pardon, mademoiselle, but I've been in the employ of your family longer than you've been a part of it, and I helped attend to your *maman* the day you came into this world. You don't have a headache."

I opened my mouth to say something dismissive, but there was no use trying to fool Pauline. She was too perceptive by half. "No, not really."

"Then why walk out on company and Cook's good dessert? Strawberry tart is one of your favorites. I hurried it up to you so he wouldn't think you'd turned up your nose. It would break his proud little heart." Her hands worked pulling hairpins as she spoke, never once pulling a stray hair or causing discomfort.

"Thank you for that," I said. "Papa would skin me alive if I affronted Monsieur Lebec. He'd sooner live without my company than his lamb shanks or his bouillabaisse."

At this, Pauline laughed. "Untrue, but I'll relay the message to Cook all the same. His pride enjoys a good puffing up. But lamb shanks and bouillabaisse aside, what is the matter? It isn't like you to leave the table when there's company without cause."

"Papa's 'company' irritates me." There was no use in delivering the tonic with a lump of sugar.

"Monsieur Salles seems like an affable enough young man to me, but I've hardly spent more than a few minutes in his presence. But it seems to me your father has had a bit more of a spring in his step lately. I wonder if having such a likely chap in his employ is a help to your papa."

"Of course it is. No one could find fault with him as an employee. And he's a talented engineer with a great mind for business, it seems to me. But I feel like I can't walk for tripping over him. I can't listen for hearing his name on Papa's lips. It's maddening."

Pauline's expression softened. She took the brush and began to work it through my wavy, honey-brown tresses. "I think you've been your father's shadow for so long, you don't like the idea of someone eclipsing you. But no one can, darling girl."

I thought about the lunches I'd taken to Papa where I felt invisible as a gnat. His attention was focused on Salles and their work. And I understood that Adolphe's talents were of immeasurable use to Papa and the company, but there was no part of me that liked feeling invisible. Pauline was right: Papa loved me, and nothing would change that. But it didn't signify that my opinions would still matter to the same degree if this newcomer continued to grow in Papa's esteem.

"I'm sure you're right, Pauline." I forced a weak smile. "I must be tired."

"Of course you are, my dear. I'll make sure one of the footmen takes lunch to your papa tomorrow. You should take the day to read or stroll in the park." She spoke as though she and the rest of the staff didn't work ten times harder than I did on any given day. But a day's respite from the atelier might not be the worst thing for my spirits.

"That would be a kindness, thank you, Pauline." She patted my shoulder in the way she always did when she was feeling particularly maternal, and left me to my tea and tart. I ate the dessert, out of a sense of obligation to not see food wasted and out of respect for the staff and their feelings. I took no pleasure in it, though it was usually a dish I delighted in, which made me feel all the worse. The mint tea was restorative, however, and I sent Pauline my silent thanks for her thoughtfulness.

I tried to settle in my sitting room with a book but found it impossible to keep my eyes focused on the words, though it was a well-crafted English novel, and I'd been keen to practice my skills with the language. I was about to set it aside—I realized I'd been reading the same sentence for the past half hour—when another knock sounded. I'd half expected it was Pauline come to collect the dessert tray, though it was her habit to gather them in the morning.

I slipped into my dressing gown and opened the door to find

Papa waiting at the other side. I blinked in surprise as his visits to my rooms were infrequent. More often, he summoned me to his office or one of the drawing rooms rather than coming into my little feminine enclave.

I gestured him inside and offered him a seat in the plush armchair opposite the one I favored. The room was decorated with blue velvet furniture with an Eiffel tapestry on the wall. It was a classical scene with a maiden in a forest with cherubs coming down from the heavens. Papa had gifted it to me for use in my rooms, certainly because of the nickname he used for me, but despite any childish associations I might have had with it, it was, objectively, one of the loveliest pieces in his collection.

"How is your headache?" Papa asked, taking his seat. He sounded as convinced as Pauline by my excuse for leaving the meal.

"Easing, I think. Pauline brought me tea." I settled back into my own chair and pulled a throw over my lap.

"I'm glad to hear that. Salles was worried that he offended you. I'm afraid he left the house feeling rather dejected. And I was disappointed that you left as well."

"How unfortunate. I didn't think you two were wanting for conversation. Indeed I thought my departure would go largely unremarked."

"Don't be waspish, Cherub. The two of you care about the Compagnie Eiffel almost as much as I do, and I don't want there to be discord between the two of you."

"What does it matter, Papa? He's one of your employees. I need never see him, except at official functions. I can act civil toward him when the situation calls for it."

"I'd hoped for more than civility, Claire." Papa crossed his legs, glancing to the tapestry for a moment.

"I don't see why anything more is warranted. He is a good engineer and a model employee. I won't deny this. But I don't see why any warmth of feeling is required."

"Claire, I mean to pass the Compagnie Eiffel on to him when I retire."

I felt the blood rush from my head and gripped the arms of my chair to steady myself. My lungs screamed for air, but I struggled to take any in. As much as the company was Papa's labor of love, it was mine. I knew it wasn't practical for a woman to take over the management of it. Whatever legal realities might make it difficult, the men would struggle—or refuse—to follow the orders of a woman *patronne*. That would make the endeavor impossible. But I couldn't fathom a future without the Compagnie Eiffel as a central concern in my life. I'd known Papa was toying with the idea of Salles as his successor but hadn't thought he'd settled on it so quickly. It was my own fault for confusing my hope for a certainty.

"You can't mean to let the company pass out of family hands." I stood, letting my lap blanket fall to the floor. "I know Édouard is unreliable now, but he's young. He'll learn. And what about little Bébert? What if he wants to follow in your footsteps in ten years' time?"

"And what if he doesn't? The boy is eleven years old, Claire. It's foolishness to plan on me being at the helm that long. I hope to be, certainly. But this is not a business for an old man. I need to be training my replacement *now* if I am to leave the company in good standing. It's my legacy and I can't risk it falling into the abyss the moment I step down. Watching the business decline as I slip into my dotage would be my precise definition of the ninth circle of hell. I hope you understand that."

I turned, arms folded over my chest, as though trying to keep my beating heart from escaping though my rib cage. "I *can* understand that, Papa. But certainly you know I'd never let the company falter, no matter who was in command. I may not be able to run it, but you know in your bones that I can pull the strings of the man who is. You can't mean for it to pass out of the family."

"I don't mean to, Claire. I'd hoped . . ."

Horror rose to my eyes as I realized his meaning.

"You hoped what, Papa?" I would force him to put voice to this precious hope of his. Force him to admit what he'd been plotting.

"If you married Adolphe, it wouldn't pass out of the family."

"You couldn't possibly think . . ."

"Claire, how better could I arrange for you to keep the heart of the Compagnie Eiffel beating? God willing, you'll outlast me for decades, and you'd have a far easier time influencing a husband than a brother."

"So you concocted this whole plan? Picked the likeliest of your engineers and hoped he'd take me along with the reins to the company? My God, it sounds like a livestock transaction."

"Claire, don't be cruel. I haven't spoken to him of my hopes for you two. Nor my hopes for him and the company beyond that I hope he will spend his career with us."

"I find it hard to believe that you haven't said anything. That his attentions aren't derived out of his ambitions."

"You think yourself below a young man's notice? My dear, you haven't looked in the glass lately. And more importantly, you're a woman of intelligence, poise, good birth, and better fortune. If I hadn't kept you occupied with my own affairs, I'm certain half of Paris would be lined up on the rue de Prony seeking an audience with me in hopes of securing your hand."

I scoffed. "Nonsense, Papa. You know flattery won't work on me."

"Slight hyperbole, perhaps, but not flattery. You are an extremely eligible match for any man worth having in Paris. And I've kept you locked away in my offices for so long that the fact hasn't occurred to you. Your sister's wedding was hard on you. You can deny it all you wish, but I saw the pain etched on your face when she left us. And how much longer will it be before Édouard makes his way out into the wide world? And then Valentine and Bébert before long."

"Bébert has nearly a decade left under this roof. Perhaps more," I pointed out.

"And it will pass by in the blink of an eye. You're young and think you have the luxury of time. I know you well enough to understand that if left to your own devices you'd continue in your admirable attentions to me, the children, and this house. And the next time you came up for a breath of air, you'd be thirty-seven years old, unmarried, childless, and resentful of us for all you sacrificed."

"Oh, and no doubt riddled with rheumatism in every joint at such an advanced age."

"It's five years more than your mother had." Papa arched a brow, daring me to contradict him. "Don't make the mistake of thinking you have unlimited time. We all know how short forever can be."

I sat back and looked past Papa at a flourish in the wallpaper. "I understand that, Papa."

"As fully as you can, I'm sure you do. But the passage of time, how it begins to race the older you are, you must experience yourself to fully understand. I'm not asking you to marry Salles tomorrow, or even at all if you truly dislike the boy. I'm asking you not to put me through the heartbreak of seeing all your prospects become fewer and fewer as the years march on."

"I'll try, Papa. But I can't leave you behind to fend for yourself."

"Let me build that bridge when we come to it, Cherub. And I hope you'll examine your prejudice against poor Salles. He's kind, intelligent, and ambitious. He's exactly what I'd choose for you."

"It would seem you already have, Papa."

Chapter Sixteen

I didn't sleep a wink the entire night, thinking about the exchange with Papa. There was no one, apart from Papa himself, who understood better than I how important it was to keep the Compagnie Eiffel in the family, but I had to put an end to his convoluted scheme to pass the torch to Salles. Pauline helped me dress for the day in a serviceable lavender calico day dress. It was among the plainer things I'd ordered from Mademoiselle Leclerc, as even she and Tante Marie agreed I needed a few practical dresses for ordinary occasions. They contented themselves with the fact it was of the latest style and tailored to me.

"Is Monsieur Édouard in his rooms?" I asked a footman as I descended the stairs to the foyer.

"No, mademoiselle. I don't believe he's come home." The footman looked tentative, knowing this wasn't the answer I'd wanted to hear and he wasn't keen on being the bearer of bad news to the mistress of the house. At least he didn't have to divulge where Édouard had gone. He spent his nights in the seediest clubs in Montmartre and would be all too easy to find staggering through the streets, which would, at this hour, be emptied of all but the most devout of drunkards.

It was midmorning, and despite his promises of reformed behavior, he'd taken to stumbling in around noon, waking in time for dinner, and leaving again just as soon as the dessert plates were whisked away. Papa was clearly aggravated that Édouard's habits hadn't improved, but as far as I could tell, he'd done nothing at all to rein him in.

I'm sure Papa was weary of chasing after his oldest son, and I could hardly blame him for being exasperated, but I feared that Papa's lack of interference meant that he'd given up hope in him entirely.

If that were true, there was little I could do to divert Papa from his plans.

He wouldn't force me to marry Salles. Papa wasn't brutish in the least, or small-minded like some men when it came to the business of marrying off their daughters, but if Papa did pass the company to Salles and I did not marry him, Papa's heart would break to see the company pass out of family control, and I would be responsible for that heartache.

"Prepare a carriage. I'm going out to find him."

If the footman found the request an odd one, he made no sign of it and hurried off to see to the task.

Soon after, I was scanning the streets of Montmartre from the safety of Papa's carriage. If he knew I was here, he likely would have keeled over from an aneurysm, so it was just as well the staff felt less and less compelled to report my comings and goings to Papa as I got older.

The coachman, Fabrice, was endlessly patient with me as I directed him to take the carriage up and down the streets where most of the more *colorful* nighttime establishments were located. No doubt Édouard preferred the seamiest of the lot. The streets were all but empty, as this corner of town didn't come to life until after dark.

It was perhaps half an hour before I finally spotted Édouard with a band of his miscreant friends stumbling out of a music hall, clearly still reeling from an evening of drink and debauchery.

"Stop!" I called to Fabrice, who pulled out of the main lane of traffic and over to the curb.

"That redhead of yours is delectable, Eiffel," one of the boys slurred. "I wouldn't mind sampling her charms myself."

"She's on the menu here every night, Fortescue, and the best sort of woman, if you ask me," my brother slurred in return.

"How d'you mean?" another asked.

"For a few francs, she's yours for the night and you've no obligation to listen to her nagging in the morning. And if you tire of her, you move on to the next one, and she hasn't a word to say about it."

The gaggle of schoolboys doubled over in laughter, and I felt my rage bubbling to the surface.

I didn't bother descending from the carriage, not wanting to set foot on the filthy sidewalks that reeked of vomit, urine, and wasted promise. Instead, I opened the door and leaned out and shouted Édouard's name so loudly that his entire crew turned their heads.

"Oooooh, I didn't know you had a serious girl, Édo. She looks ready to take a bite out of you." The jeer came from the tallest of the lot, a lanky boy with a particularly dim-witted expression.

"It's a million times worse. It's my sister, who has fashioned herself the worst kind of mother hen." Édouard's back was turned to me, but he spoke loudly enough it was clearly intended for my ears. His chums thought the slight was uproariously funny and they all dissolved into fits of drunken laughter.

"Édouard, get in this carriage at once!" I growled.

"Go home, Claire. I'll find my own way back before the old man even knows I'm gone."

I gritted my teeth and stepped down onto the vile sidewalk and did my best not to show my revulsion as I closed the gap between my brother and me. Without hesitation I grabbed him by the ear like the willful brat he was.

"Get in that carriage, or so help me God, I'll have Fabrice tie you to the back like a steamer trunk."

Fabrice was easily six inches taller than Édouard and outweighed him by no less than fifty pounds of solid muscle. I could actually see the blood retreat from Édouard's face as the coachman turned, poised for my command to have him do exactly as I threatened. Fabrice was more than willing to follow my orders, and I would have no compunction about issuing them.

"Fine, you damned shrew, I'll come home. It'll save me the fare for the hansom cab."

I released his ear and he clambered up into the carriage while Fabrice eyed him warily, ready to subdue him if the need arose. I turned to Édouard's "friends," who snickered derisively, and stared them down with daggers in my eyes and venom at my tongue.

"Go home to your mothers, you useless bunch of spoiled brats, and stop wasting your fathers' money. And stay the hell away from my brother, or I'll personally see to it you rue the day you ever drew breath. Do I make myself plain?"

The look of surprise was gratifying. The twinge of fear in their eyes as they mumbled their acquiescence was utterly delightful.

"Jesus, Claire. You didn't have to make a spectacle in front of the chaps like that," Édouard said in guise of a greeting as I stepped back into the carriage.

"Like hell I didn't." Temper had caused a lapse in my ladylike vocabulary. "You don't listen to our father's civilized requests for you to act your age, so I have to treat you like the willful toddler you are. You promised me you'd do better. Was that ever your intent, or were you lying to me the whole time?"

"I don't have to listen to this." He closed his eyes and turned his head to face the window.

"Yes you do." I reached over and slapped him smartly on the cheek. "I'd give you the matching lump you so well deserve, but I'm wearing boots and don't want to crush your idiot skull."

"Why not?" He sat up straighter, rubbing his cheek in shock. "It seems like your problems would be sorted if you managed to off me, doesn't it?"

"No, though it seems I make an exception for you, I don't embrace violence. And I have a use for you, so I'm choosing to spare you. For now."

"Bully for me, but what use you have for me, I can't possibly fathom."

"It shouldn't be too hard for you to fathom that I want you to start acting like the heir to the Eiffel name so Papa won't be forced to pass the company on to someone else."

"He wouldn't. Not in a million years. It means too much to him."

"It means too much to him to have it run to the ground, even if it means handing it over to someone outside the family."

"I'm not that lucky, Claire."

"What do you mean *lucky*?"

"I've no business building bridges or train stations. I have no talent for design and no brain for advanced maths. Worse, I've no passion for it. I've dreaded the idea of taking over his enterprise since I understood it was my lot in life. But there is no way on God's green earth he'd pass it on to anyone other than me or Bébert. I keep praying the boy will turn out to be some sort of design prodigy and relieve me from my role as heir apparent to the Eiffel throne."

"No luck there." I often lamented Bébert's subpar marks and willful attitude that wasn't unlike his older brother's. "But you're wrong. Papa wants to pass the company along to Adolphe Salles, the new wunderkind engineer at the company."

Édouard seemed to sober up at once. "You're serious? You heard those words from his lips?"

"Yes. You have shown yourself to be unreliable and he thinks it would be too long before Bébert would be old enough to start learning the trade at Papa's side. He thinks his replacement should be getting trained up now so he can have a hope of retirement."

He punched the air in jubilation. "My God, and I thought I'd never free myself from his yoke. It's all my birthdays, feast days, and Christmases all rolled into one with a few Easter Sundays to round it all out."

"Édouard, you can't mean that. You can't want Papa to pass it off to a total stranger."

"Why should I care what he does, so long as I am not stuck with the running of it? And why should *you*? I know you're up to your elbows in Papa's business, but you never thought he could pass it on to you. You know he'll see you taken care of for the rest of your days. Married to the wealthiest eligible landowner in France in a fortnight if you signaled your desire for it, with an independence all your own. And you'd have earned it for all you've done for him."

I raised a brow. "That's the first kind word you've ever spoken to me since we were in the nursery."

"It's the first time I didn't have the weight of the Compagnie Eiffel and Papa's expectations on my shoulders since I was old enough to know what they meant. I'm feeling charitable."

"How novel. But I don't think you realize the full implications of what Papa wants. He doesn't want for the company to pass out of family hands. He means to make Salles a part of it."

"How could that possibly work? It's not customary, even for someone of Papa's situation, to adopt a grown man."

I stared at him, willing his remaining brain cells to catch up. It was a few moments before his face lit up with comprehension. "So he doesn't intend you for the richest landowner in all of France, then?"

"No. He'd have me down the aisle and pronounced Madame Salles as soon as the banns were read."

"And you dislike the chap?"

I shrugged. "I hardly know him, despite Papa flinging him at my head at every turn. He means no more or less to me than any other engineer at Papa's company. But just because he's the best qualified man to take over the reins for Papa doesn't mean I want him for a husband."

"So tell the old man no." Édouard opened his cigarette case and lit one, defying Papa's orders against smoking in the carriage. I didn't bother trying to dissuade him. He offered me one and I waved it away. His expression was indignant as he looked out the carriage window, and I liked to think it was in my defense.

"So easy for you to say. I've spent every waking moment since Maman died in service to Papa and his company. I can't see the needs of either discarded so lightly."

"If it were true, then you would have never come to plead with me to take my place at Papa's side. You know in your heart of hearts I'd be rubbish at running the business and, even at my best, would be of far less use to Papa than this Salles fellow. You didn't come to me to save our birthright. You came to me to save your own neck."

I opened my mouth to protest but he held up a hand to silence me.

"I don't blame you, Claire. In fact, I rather respect you for it. I thought all this time you lived only for Papa and that you'd effaced yourself completely for his benefit. It was awful to watch too. You were such a vibrant girl when we were young, but you let yourself be swallowed up by Papa and his work. I thought you'd do *something* with all your wit and charm, more than just be a helpmeet to a man, Papa or any other."

I sought words to rebuke him but found none.

"Listen, I can't be the one to help you, Claire. Either you stand up to Papa and refuse the match or face the alternative. The choice, for once, is yours. For what it's worth, I will defend you if you defy the old man."

I snorted at the irony as I turned my head to look out the window. The streets were becoming more familiar as we approached the rue de Prony. Back to Papa's house and the duty it represented. "You don't understand, Édouard. You've left me with no choice at all."

Fabrice stopped the carriage in front of the house so Édouard and I could enter. My brother hopped down first and stumbled in the door, his misspent evening catching back up with him. He didn't offer a hand down from the carriage or hold the door, but ambled up the steps, likely in search of his bed and a tray with toast and tea.

I felt a pain in my chest, knowing that Papa was right. Édouard could never be trusted to run the Compagnie Eiffel, and I would be the one to pay the price.

"YOUR BROTHER ISN'T up?" Papa asked a week later at breakfast from behind his curtain of newspaper.

"No, Papa. If you haven't noticed, he hasn't been down to breakfast but a single morning since you issued your directive." Édouard continued his dissolute habits, though he was less surly than he'd been before. Likely relieved that the birthright he'd viewed as his yoke—or perhaps his noose—was now removed from his neck.

Papa shrugged. "He's at least been a bit more affable at dinner; perhaps he's coming around."

"It's an improvement, I suppose, but I find little comfort in it.

He's unmoored, Papa. He needs a direction. If it isn't the company, he must find something."

"Indeed he must, but I can't find it for him, Cherub. He must do it on his own."

I set a knife down with a *thunk* on the wooden table. "He needs your guidance, Papa, now more than ever."

Papa peered over his paper. "He has to grow up on his own terms. I can't force it."

My teeth were ready to grind into powder. While he directed every element of my life as well as Laure's and Valentine's, Édouard somehow had to be left with the freedom to make his own mistakes. "You're making a grave error, Papa."

He set down the newspaper, eyes widened at my rebuke. "Since when do you speak like this to your own papa?"

"I am two years older than Édouard and yet I'm not allowed the freedom to go for a stroll without a maid or a footman to attend me. All the while, Édouard is free to drink and carouse all over Paris and make a fool of all of us and you do nothing to stop him. Not even curtailing his pocket money."

"If I cut off his funds entirely, he might fall into a worse crowd altogether. There is nothing for it but time. Eventually he'll grow up and realize the folly of his ways." He returned to his newspaper, a signal that he was ready for the conversation to cease.

"If he lives that long. I saw the club he stumbled out from. It was the worst sort of dank cesspool you can imagine. You can't let this continue."

He sat straighter, color draining from his face."You had no business going into that part of town. Even with Fabrice, something might have happened."

"Do you not hear yourself? Édouard is in that club, or one just like it, every night when they're full of the worst sort of degenerates, yet you dress me down for going by in a carriage when the streets are all but empty in the company of the most fearsome coachman in Paris? Heaven knows what might happen to Édouard when he's out all night, but you seem completely unperturbed by any of it. Well, if he ends up shot, dead in a ditch, or riddled with some whore's pox, it'll be on your head, not mine. I've tried to warn you."

"Don't you use that language, Claire. And you wouldn't understand. Boys cannot be raised the same as girls."

"Perhaps if you tried to keep the boys on as short of a leash as you did the girls and me, Édouard and Bébert would be better off for it, and you'd have an heir in the family and wouldn't have to bequeath your life's work to some junior engineer."

"Claire, I won't hear this. Not from you." Papa stood, most of his breakfast left untouched. "I expect better from you."

"No. You should have expected better from Édouard," I countered. "But it's too late for that now, and Salles will be the beneficiary of all your hard work."

"At least you've come to understand the necessity of that." Papa tossed his paper on the table and rested his palms on the polished surface. He looked weary; bone weary. The sort of exhaustion that permeates one's soul and cannot be eased with sleep, but only with peace.

"Yes. There is nothing for it. Salles is the brightest you have and the logical successor, though it pains me to say it. At least he's of use to you in ways I cannot be and where Édouard refuses."

Papa cast his eyes downward. "I hope you'll consider the other element of my plan for succession."

"For someone who is a staunch anti-royalist, I certainly feel like you're a king marrying off a princess for the sake of political advantage."

"I may be a republican, but I'm a pragmatist first and foremost.

I won't force you into a marriage that will make you miserable, but I want you to consider Salles as a worthy choice. More than just a good engineer, he's a good man. He'd treat you with the same care he would my company, and leaving you both in good hands is all I could ever wish for."

He spoke of the company as if it were a person. A sixth child, perhaps. His second wife, certainly. And one that stood to outlive him, if handled with care. And he was depending on me to ensure it stayed within family hands.

Tears pricked at my eyes, and I wanted to hurl the priceless vase at the center of the table against the wall. It wasn't fair. I'd given so much of my life for this family, for this company. And I was being called on to sacrifice the one thing I thought I'd have a measure of control over: my marriage. But there was no use in tears and fits of rage. My shoulders sagged as defeat penetrated my soul.

"Invite him to dinner again this coming Saturday, but I warn you, I make no promises."

"Of course not. This isn't the twelfth century, after all. You have to come to an understanding on your own."

"I do make one condition."

Papa said nothing but waited expectantly.

"You cannot leave Édouard to his own devices as you have done. It will lead to his ruin."

Papa exhaled slowly, reminding me of a balloon with a slow leak. "I'll do what I can there, Cherub. I know you worry about him."

"Of course I do, Papa. As Maman would have done. And as you should too."

Papa crossed to my side of the table and kissed my forehead, leaving wordlessly for his atelier. I hoped it meant he was taking my words seriously, but I had more room for doubt in my heart than I liked.

Chapter Seventeen

I was dressed in an evening gown the same shade of garnet as the afternoon dress that Mademoiselle Leclerc had fashioned for me. It was a bold color for an unmarried woman, but I enjoyed the afternoon dress so much, I entreated her to find a lighter material in the same color for evening wear. She'd risen to the occasion with magnificence, and I was now swathed in featherlight gossamer dyed in such a vibrant hue of garnet red that it seemed positively ethereal.

I chose a heavy ruby necklace from Maman's collection to wear that night. It was the most elaborate, most dear piece she'd owned. She brought it out for only the grandest of occasions, and I had not yet dared to wear it. But tonight I would use every weapon in my arsenal.

Pauline took especial care with styling my hair, and I managed to still my impatience. Every lock was placed with precision, and the effect, as she pinned it up with garnet-encrusted hairpins, was breathtaking. I realized I'd been wrong to dismiss the importance of my clothing choices. This gown, though made of whisper-thin fabric, was my armor; the jewels at my neck were my shield. I felt poised. Beautiful. Confident.

Ready for battle.

Though all that awaited me below stairs was a dinner with Papa and Salles, it might as well have been a reliving of Waterloo, and I felt far too much like the ill-fated Napoleon for comfort.

As I descended the main staircase, I saw Papa and Salles in the foyer, rather than settled in the drawing room with apéritifs as I would have expected.

"You look enchanting, Mademoiselle Eiffel." Salles took my gloved hand and kissed the air above it in a practiced display of polished manners. "As always."

"Ravishing," Papa agreed. "And it's a lucky thing too, as it seems Salles has a surprise for us."

I felt my breath catch, turned to Salles, and hoped my expression was one of cautious curiosity and not the grimace I feared was marring my face.

"I hope you won't object, but I have secured tickets and hoped you and your father would accompany me to the opera after we dine this evening. It seems a fitting apology for my blunder the last time we dined together, to see a production at the Palais Garnier in person."

I glanced at Papa, who discreetly nodded his approval.

"Very well, Monsieur Salles. I should be happy to accompany you." It had been ages since I'd had an evening's entertainment, and never in the presence of a suitor. Of course he'd had to include Papa in the outing for propriety's sake, but as was the grand tradition with chaperones, he would endeavor to make himself as invisible as he could so that we might get to know each other, all the while keeping a watchful eye for the sake of my reputation.

A reputation that had to be guarded like some sort of precious treasure, while Édouard was free to cavort all over town like a randy tomcat.

The footmen and kitchen staff, clearly alerted to our after-dinner plans by Papa, served the meal with more alacrity than was customary. The staff usually took their time between courses, especially if conversation remained lively and the company seemed to be enjoying themselves. I found the quicker pace gratifying, as even the best dinners grew tedious as they spilled into their third hour.

I studied Salles closely as he dined. His manners were impeccable, practiced from youth and not a recent acquisition of someone who was a newer member of the *grande bourgeoisie*. He made a point, as always, to include me in the conversation, though it was plain that he could have spoken to Papa about their business affairs until the morning light. It no doubt delighted Papa to have the company of someone he could speak to as an equal in terms of both design skill and business acumen.

This was the man Papa wanted for me, and I had to concede that he could have made a worse choice. Salles was intelligent, to be sure—and kind, which mattered far more in a world where kindness was a commodity in short supply.

But when I looked at him, there was no divine spark. No longing to spend every moment in his company. Nothing beyond recognition that he was, fundamentally, a man of the first order.

Would that be enough?

I wished I knew. And more than anything else in the world, I wished I had Maman to discuss the matter with. Papa had made all the rational arguments for Salles as my suitor. Logically, there was very little I could object to concerning the match. But Maman knew better the inner workings of the heart, especially those of her children. She would have been able to counsel me in ways Papa could not, no matter how much he might wish to.

I took Salles's arm. The Opéra, which I had yet to visit since it opened almost ten years before, was a magnificent building that filled my soul with wonder every time I rode past. Garnier's style was so unlike Papa's: classic, almost doggedly so, and opulent to a degree that made me feel like I was in a cathedral rather than a theater. I loved Papa's clean lines and modern vision but thought there was room for the gracious classical styles as well. That the two great men had collaborated on a project as impressive as the Nice Observatory despite their disparate styles was remarkable. That they'd gained respect for each other was nothing short of miraculous in my eyes.

Salles had paid for the best available seats in the house, a box with an incomparable view of the stage. The opera was *Henry VIII* by Saint-Saëns, and my stomach tightened into a ball of ice as I read the libretto. Henry's desire to divorce the loyal Catherine of Aragon in favor of the witty and alluring Anne Boleyn. I knew British history well enough, and knowing both Catherine's and Anne's fates—and that of their four successors—gave me no sense of ease as I considered the future my father wished for me.

Salles sat immersed in the opera, while Papa looked ready to fidget out of his skin. He enjoyed music well enough but was not one for sitting captive in a theater for almost four hours. He'd have been happier at home with a book, though I myself was happy to be out in the city and taking part in all it had to offer. But I did not have an occupation like Papa's that provided such enrichment for the mind and soul; I had to find mine in diversions like these.

As the drama unfolded and Henry's affections for Anne began to unravel his two-decades-long heirless union to Catherine, I wondered how the woman herself had felt about her husband's change of heart. . . . Had she, like Henry, believed her marriage to be cursed by God because she was his brother's widow? Had she expected the betrayal? Henry was, after all, the spoiled younger brother of the rightful King Arthur, who had died far too young and before his marriage to Catherine could result in a little prince.

Or had she truly loved him and been heartbroken when he left her to waste away in a nunnery, casting her aside in favor of an ambitious young courtier who cared for nothing beyond herself?

Was *any* marriage impervious to such caprices?

I, as surreptitiously as I could, studied Salles's profile. He was serious and well-mannered. He was kind in all his interactions with me. But how long would that last? How tight a rein would he hope to hold over the household? Would he want to have his fingers in every pie when it came to the running of the house? Or would he, like Papa, give me great latitude to manage things as I saw fit?

I had no way of knowing.

But would assurances be better with any other man? It was unlikely. And Salles was in Papa's employ. As long as Papa lived, Salles could not mistreat me, or his career would pay the price. It was the ultimate leverage against a man who loved his work above all things, including, I suspected, any family he might have.

I forced myself to listen to the strains of the orchestra and ignore the actors on the stage. I couldn't bear to see more of the familiar marital disaster unfold before me, when my own marital fate was a question that bubbled so close to the surface.

I'd never been more grateful when the lights rose at intermission, and we assembled in the vestibules behind the boxes. Salles dashed off in search of champagne for the three of us, and Papa stretched, finally able to yawn without giving offense.

"How are you enjoying the opera, Cherub? I thought you'd take to it, but never seemed to have the time to bring you before now."

I offered him an indulgent smile. He had found the time to take me on any number of outings, but it was clear he was never going to be a patron of the Palais Garnier.

"It's enchanting," I said truthfully. I could imagine spending many pleasant evenings at the Opéra in good company. "Though I confess the topic of tonight's spectacle isn't to my liking."

Papa looked sheepish. "It's an unfortunate subject, to be sure. But at least we have the benefit of knowing how it all turns out."

"I don't think that's making it any easier for me."

"Salles isn't an egomaniacal monster like Henry. I wouldn't nudge you in his direction if he were. But there can be joy found even in marriages made for pragmatic reasons, my darling girl." His face grew wistful, and it was clear he wasn't thinking in hypothetical terms.

I arched a brow, an invitation for him to elaborate.

He grinned ruefully for a moment and turned his gaze to meet mine. "After three failed proposals to other women, your *bonne maman* wrote to your mother and made the match. And I was beholden to her for it from the moment she took pen to paper."

The look on my face must have been one of utter bewilderment because Papa chuckled and patted my arm. "I knew your mother for years before your grandmother intervened. She just gave us the nudge we needed to see each other . . . differently. That is all I'm trying to do for you and Salles. And I assure you, the years I spent with your *maman* were the happiest of my life, even if they didn't begin like something from a fairy story."

I couldn't find a reply but was grateful for Salles's reappearance with a waiter bearing flutes of champagne. I sipped the golden elixir slowly, appreciating the burst of every bubble on the tongue, and the notes of tart cherry and cassis that finished with a hint of toasted bread. Would that I could be carried away on one of the little bubbles, even for a short while, so I wouldn't have to worry about the weighty concerns of the present moment.

Salles was attentive, asking my thoughts on the performance, to which I gave answers that I hoped sounded intelligent enough, given my general ignorance on the subject of the theater. When he offered his own thoughts, it was clear that he hadn't just come to the opera to be seen; he wasn't an expert, perhaps, but when he did attend, he paid attention to the spectacle on the stage and not the social climbers in the boxes.

I tried to breathe easier as the second half of the show unfolded and met with some success. I wasn't the long-suffering Catherine, who had been forced to endure the indignities of her husband's infidelities and callousness. Nor was I the cold and calculating Anne Boleyn.

And Salles, thank God and all the saints, wasn't Henry.

And this gave me some solace. I mulled over Papa's revelation about how his engagement to Maman came about. One could never know the inner workings of a marriage from the outside, though I'd been present for the lion's share of theirs; they had always seemed so happy in their choice of spouse. It wasn't the bland civility that some couples had for each other. When Papa came into the drawing room after a day at the atelier, Maman's face lit up. On special occasions, Papa endeavored to find Maman gifts that weren't just costly and extravagant but truly meaningful to her. The sort of gifts that showed not only how well he knew her but how much he loved her.

When the opera finally reached its conclusion, we found our way to the lobby, where Papa was hailed by a man roughly his age—Garnier himself.

"My goodness, Eiffel. I never thought to see you here. I pictured you holed up in your office until bedtime."

"I am, most nights." Papa gestured to Salles and me. "I was called upon to act as chaperone, and not sorry to have performed the office. A good show in a glorious theater, old friend."

"And I like her all the better for having your approval," Garnier said with a bow. "I hope to see you here again."

Papa returned the bow and pivoted to me with a smile. "The man himself. Quite the treat."

I smiled back though momentarily distracted by a face that looked too much like Édouard's slipping into a side room. The one where the ballet dancers greeted male visitors after the show. The rumors of how they entertained those guests had reached even my sheltered ears.

"Are you well, Claire?" Papa looked suddenly concerned at my ill-concealed expression.

"Overheated, I think. Can we get to the carriage?" As much as I wanted to grab Édouard by the nape of the neck away from those poor girls, the scene that would have arisen if Papa saw him wasn't worth the risk.

I felt my shoulders lower by inches as the carriage pulled away, leaving the theater behind.

"I hope you enjoyed the evening, mademoiselle. I certainly did." Salles looked at me with his earnest brown eyes, eager for my approval.

The image of Édouard back at the theater popped into my head, and there was no denying that Papa was right. Salles was the only way forward for the company. And it was within my power to keep that company in the family.

"Very much, Monsieur Salles." I forced a smile. "I hope it will be a pleasure often repeated."

And with those words, my fate was sealed.

Chapter Eighteen

December 1884

"Why the delay?" Tante Marie looked over the fabrics in Mademoiselle Leclerc's collection. The wedding wouldn't be until late February, but already my trousseau was underway. This would be my last series of fittings until after the holiday season, and I was grateful beyond words for the impending respite. Laure, who had accompanied us despite her uncomfortable condition, let out a tiny groan as she sat in a nearby chair to ease the pain in her swelling ankles. She and Maurice had come back from their wedding tour with a precious little surprise that would arrive just before my own wedding.

"Why rush things? Adolphe doesn't seem the sort to grow cold feet." My betrothed's first name still felt foreign on my tongue, but I was adjusting to it over time. "And I couldn't bear if my own dear sister couldn't attend in case the little one decides to make an early entrance. Besides, isn't it essential that Mademoiselle Leclerc have adequate time to work her magic?"

"Hear, hear," the modiste chimed in, teeth clenched around pins as she fitted me into one of the many traveling gowns I'd commissioned. It was a fetching shade of emerald green I rather liked and was happy to add to my ever-increasing wardrobe. Of all the dresses I'd commissioned, the one I cared for least was the creamy confection of heavy satin that was to be my wedding gown, which we'd ordered the very day after Adolphe had proposed. I felt drawn and peaked in such pale fabric, but there was no convincing Laure and Tante Marie that I could be married in anything other than some variant of white. In addition to the gown, my sister and aunt had ordered any number of garments for me, as though their plan was to ensure I'd have a wardrobe vast enough I'd never need so much as another stocking for the rest of my married life.

The truth was that Papa and Adolphe were now so busy with their proposal for the Exposition Universelle that an extended engagement suited all involved. Papa and Adolphe because of their work, and I because of my nerves.

In the best of times, my new engagement ring, a large oval amethyst encircled in diamonds, was uncomfortably heavy, as I had yet to adjust to the unfamiliar weight. When I was at the modiste, with so little to distract me, it might as well have been a cannonball chained to my left hand.

"You are happy, aren't you?" Laure's hand absently rubbed her distended abdomen.

"What a ridiculous question," Tante Marie interjected. "Her young man is a kind and serious one, hand selected by her papa. How could she be anything less than thrilled?"

"Come now, Tante Marie. Just because he is a logical choice doesn't mean he's the choice of her heart," Laure chided. Mademoiselle Leclerc scuttled off for more fabric, giving Tante Marie leave to speak more openly.

"Thank God you have many years before you have to worry about matches for your own children. I hope you understand better by then that following the heart is rarely prudent. You were simply one of the lucky ones to find love and a smart match in the same package."

A shadow crossed her face. Tante Marie rarely spoke of her first husband, and I knew only fragments of the story, but by all accounts he'd been a scoundrel and a cheat. It wasn't a source of much grief when he died when I was a small girl, and no one thought less of Tante Marie for marrying dear Oncle Albert less than a year later. But I suspected, though I'd never ask, that Tante Marie had fallen riotously in love with her first husband, only to be all the more heartbroken for being deceived by his duplicitous nature.

"Indeed I'm the luckiest bride and future *maman* in all of Paris, but why can't we wish the same for our dear Claire?" Laure pressed.

Tante Marie heaved a sigh that spoke volumes.

I hoped Laure would never come to understand Tante Marie's wariness firsthand, but there was a part of me that was happy to be going into my marriage with no delusions that ours was a love match.

I was sure there would be twinges of regret sometime down the road, where I was sad to have not experienced a great love story. That I never knew what it was to be swept up in the fervor of new love, but I would much rather forgo all that excitement and spare myself pain like Tante Marie's.

Mademoiselle Leclerc reemerged from the back rooms of her shop, her arms draped in familiar cream-colored slipper satin.

"My seamstress Babette informs me your wedding gown is ready for a fitting, mademoiselle. Do you have the time for it now?"

"Oh yes," Laure interjected, answering for me. "Luncheon can wait. It was a great cruelty indeed that I wasn't with you to select your gown."

"You were in Italy with your husband, dearest. I think that's consolation enough, don't you?" I reminded her.

A smirk appeared at the corner of her lips.

"Perhaps a little. But all will be forgiven if I can see you in it now."

I shot her an exasperated, if slightly indulgent, look and gestured to the seamstress that she could proceed.

The gown, which I had seen only in sketches and fabric samples before now, was more terrifying for being real. It fit exquisitely, given that Mademoiselle Leclerc and her staff had sewn so much for me in the past months and had my measurements down with precision. The cut of the bodice accentuated my corseted waist and made my bosom look more ample than it was. The skirt flowed gracefully to the floor, catching the light at all the right angles, while the bustle gave the silhouette definition. The pearl beading was masterfully done; eye-catching without being overdone. The gown was the picture of elegance, and I felt absolutely out of place in it.

I'd heard of women feeling a sort of giddiness when they first tried on their wedding gowns. A delight in knowing that this all-important milestone in life was going to come to pass. All I felt was a rock in my gut.

Tante Marie dabbed at her eyes with tissue and Laure clasped her hands in delight. "You're the most beautiful bride I've ever laid eyes on."

I felt a smile tug at my lips and was glad I could at least feign some excitement. The gown *was* enchanting, and I was grateful the cream fabric didn't wash me out entirely, but the enormity of the commitment I was to make in a few short months was a leaden mantle on my shoulders.

I let my mind wander to happier thoughts as I endured Mademoiselle Leclerc's fussing as she pinned the hem. Travels with Papa and quiet evenings at home reading by the fire. But soon those moments would be at an end and Papa would be left to fend for himself and the children as I set up housekeeping for Adolphe. He'd yet to show me his home, nor had I asked to see it. The day would come soon enough that it would be either my haven or my prison, for I didn't think there could be middle ground in such things, and I was in no hurry to turn my imaginings into a reality.

I had not the least idea how much time had eclipsed before Mademoiselle Leclerc pronounced that the hem was marked, and she was ready to free me from my satin cage.

"Your gown will be finished the first week after the Christmas holiday." She noted my new purchases in her account ledger. "A full month ahead of schedule. We'll do our level best to make sure the rest of your trousseau will be ready with ample time for alterations as needed."

"My papa ought to hire you on as chief engineer. Not a single project would come in late or over budget."

"Your papa knows my address well enough by now, prompt as he is with settling his accounts. You tell him I'm ready and willing to serve." She made a mock salute that caused us all to chuckle.

"Never in this world," Tante Marie said, throwing her head back in a laugh. "I'd sooner do without my brother's bridges than your gowns."

"Don't you dare let him hear you say that," I replied. "His heart couldn't bear to hear such disloyalty, even if it's true."

In a fit of girlish giggles, we found our way to the tearoom and enjoyed a sumptuous luncheon. Though I eyed the dishes smothered in rich cream sauces, I abstained, thinking of the gown that Mademoiselle Leclerc was likely handling with utmost care at that very moment. It wasn't that I was vain; it was that I couldn't support the idea of standing for more fittings to let it out.

"Are things winding down at the atelier for the season?" Tante Marie asked.

"Not in the slightest. They've put in a bid to build the showpiece for the Exposition Universelle. It's all Papa and Adolphe can speak of."

"Do you think it's likely they'll get the commission?" Laure asked. "There must be dozens of applications for such an honor."

"But only one from the Compagnie Eiffel. They seem confident. They've proposed a massive tower at the entrance to the fair, near the Champs de Mars. Quite a lovely thing if the sketches can be trusted."

"But the fair isn't for another four years or more; isn't it rather early for such things?" Tante Marie beamed a smile at the waiter who arrived with generous glasses of Bordeaux. I accepted mine almost as readily as she did.

"It's supposed to be an expo of special magnificence. If they win the contract, they hope to begin work in just a few months."

Laure slapped a hand down on the table in mock exasperation.

"I swear before God and man, the very best part of having been married and moving away is no talk of whatever building project Papa has going on over the dinner table. Let's have no more of it and speak of more amusing things. Have you got everything ready for the Christmas celebrations?" Laure asked.

"Nearly," I said, unable to contain an indulgent smile. It would be the eighth year I'd taken on the preparations for the holiday celebrations, and I tried to make each year grander than the last.

"It won't feel like Christmas when you move out," Laure said. "We'll have to reinvent our traditions."

"Nonsense," I said. "Things will go on exactly as they have. Papa will want all his chicks come home to roost, and I can't imagine we'll live so far from Papa's house that I can't go over to plan the festivities for us."

Laure looked mollified. "That makes sense, though I imagine the holidays will run you ragged, managing two houses."

"I don't know how Papa will do without me. I suspect I'll spend my time shuttling between two houses to ensure Papa is tended to."

Tante Marie clicked her tongue but said nothing. I think, in her heart of hearts, she thought that my coddling Papa was keeping him from moving on. It wasn't for me to push Papa back onto the marriage market. If he wished to find a lady to take Maman's place, he'd have to do it under his own steam. But if he needed my help, who was I to refuse him?

"You don't know where you'll settle?" Tante Marie asked. "With less than two months before the wedding?"

"No," I admitted, and realized that it was perhaps a bit strange I hadn't thought to question him. He was a man of means and in no way averse to creature comforts, so I didn't fear that he'd move me to a hovel in some remote backwater. "He'll need to be close enough to Papa's atelier for work, so it must be reasonably close to Papa's house, I should think. Otherwise, it would be impractical for all of us."

Tante Marie nodded. "True enough. I just hope not *too* close. You need to stretch your wings and run your own home."

"But it won't be *my* home, will it? It will be Adolphe's. I don't see how running his home will be much different than Papa's."

Tante Marie took a sip of her wine, her eyes turning to the other side of the room. "The expectations will be different when it's Adolphe and not your papa."

"Oh, I am sure Adolphe will have differences of opinion on certain things, but whether dinner is at seven or eight or how to tell the cook to prepare his eggs can't matter all that much."

"More than that, darling. Since your Maman died you've been trying, with every fiber of your being, to do everything as she would have done. Don't you think it will be good for you to run a house without her specter looking over your shoulder?"

Laure looked to me. "I think there is some truth to what Tante Marie says, Claire. You've been trying to make up for Maman's absence for so long, you might be happier figuring out how to do things as they please *you* and not Maman and Papa."

I took a sip of my own wine. "I know you both mean well, but I don't do things as Maman would have done them. She didn't have time to teach me everything. I've simply asked myself what she would do and have tried to keep things running the best I can."

"Dearest, neither of us meant to criticize you. You've done a marvelous job rising to the occasion. You've done more than any girl your age should have been asked to do." Tante Marie reached across the table and clasped my hand. "And it's precisely for this reason we worry about you."

"Don't spend your concern on me," I said, perhaps more forcefully than needed. "If you find yourself needing to fret, you can direct your attentions to Édouard. He's far more in need than I am."

Since school had resumed in the autumn, the same stream of letters from creditors and the same reports with abysmally poor marks arrived in the post with tedious regularity. With each missive, Papa would growl and threaten, but nothing ever came of it.

The color drained from Tante Marie's and Laure's faces at the reprisal. They had to know I was right and likely felt just as helpless as me to do anything about it. I wanted to soften and apologize but found I desperately needed the solace of my rooms and my own company.

I rose, leaving my meal largely untouched. "I'll take a hired carriage home."

"Claire, we're so sorry. Today was meant to be fun—" Laure began.

I raised a hand to silence her. "I know. And I know you both mean well. But if you think I can keep a house—any house—and not constantly feel like Maman is looking over my shoulder, you're both greatly mistaken. There won't be a day when she doesn't guide every decision I make, big or small. Until you come to understand this, you won't understand me."

With every clop of the horses' hooves on the way back to the rue de Prony, I felt them tap out the words *you're a fool, you're a fool* as the cobblestoned roads wended to the north part of town. I'd been waspish to my sister and my aunt, who had been my dearest companions and who had supported me through all manner of troubles, both girlish and serious. They deserved better from me, and I would have to apologize.

But there was something even further to the lump of ice in my gut. I recalled my indifference toward the gown that should have delighted me; my utter disdain for being trussed into it. I could, intellectually, acknowledge how exquisite a creation Mademoiselle Leclerc had fashioned for me. But no wedding gown, no matter how lovely, would be right because my mother hadn't been there to select it with me.

Chapter Nineteen

December 24, 1884

The air was laced with pine boughs, fresh oranges, and warm sugared pralines and highlighted with an undercurrent of mulled wine steeped in a blend of cinnamon, nutmeg, and star anise. As fond as I was of purchased scent, and I'd acquired quite the collection ranging from delicate jasmine to more daring blends of musk and sandalwood, there was no perfumer in the world proficient enough to bottle the scent of Christmas. Perhaps it was the infrequency of the season that made the particular scent so alluring.

The kitchen was a flurry of activity as the staff prepared for the grandest meal of the year. The advent wreaths with their pink and purple candles were in place, and Papa's magnificent crèche had been set up in the largest drawing room, where we would gather to celebrate until we left for midnight mass. Every staircase was festooned with green garlands and red bows to commemorate the festive season. Every detail was perfect. I insisted on it.

The preparations were immense, but I looked forward to it every year. From the dusting off of the Holy Family to selecting gifts, it was a flurry of activity I anticipated as soon as the autumn chill hit the air. And the family had come to love my celebrations. Even foul-tempered Édouard, who normally loathed family dinners, looked forward to the roasted goose and whipped potatoes and the *bûche de Noël*: a rolled spice cake perfectly frosted in dark chocolate and sprinkled with icing sugar to resemble a log dusted in snow and decorated with moss and mushrooms made of marzipan and meringue.

Laure had come early to help with the last of the preparations, dragging dear Maurice along. She installed him on the sofa with a newspaper and set about fussing with every bit of the decor until it was all letter perfect. She reminded me very much of a mother bird feathering her nest before her chicks were set to hatch. She put the finishing touches on an evergreen arrangement on one of the side tables and breathed a contented sigh. I'd asked for her forgiveness, and Tante Marie's as well, and it was gratefully bestowed. They likely attributed my churlish behavior to pre-wedding jitters, and I wouldn't go to the effort to correct them. Their explanation was easier for them to understand and easier for them to forgive.

But the very thought of someone else tending to Papa and the younger children sent ice in my veins. How could staff, even the most dutiful of housekeepers, possibly hope to put the same love into their care as I did?

In leaving Papa's home, and in marrying Adolphe, I was obeying the fondest wish of his heart. He was choosing to proceed in the next chapter of his life without my help, and I should not feel any guilt about it, but controlling the sensation that I was abandoning Papa, Valentine, little Bébert, and even Édouard was as likely as a snowstorm over the Sahara.

The younger children were escorted in by the nanny, Édouard following on his own a few minutes later. Valentine peered over the lavish gifts discreetly. She locked eyes with me for a moment and heaved a sigh and moved to chat with Laure. I pulled her away before she reached her objective.

"What's the matter, dearest? You know I can't bear to see a long face on Christmas Eve." I moved to wrap an arm around her, but she dodged my attempt.

"You're making me wait to open gifts with Bébert in the morning like a toddler. I'm fourteen."

I shut my eyes and tried not to groan in frustration at my own stupidity. It was the custom in many homes for children to open offerings from Papa Noël on Christmas morning, while the Christmas Eve celebrations were centered around the adult members of the family. Maman had told us it was to teach us the virtue of patience and sacrifice. And because adults had to exercise those talents throughout the year, their reward was opening gifts a day early.

But I knew Valentine. She wasn't cross because I was forcing her to wait an extra half a day to open her gifts. She was cross with me for lumping her in as a child with Bébert. Eleven-year-old Bébert still loved the childish trappings of the holiday, while at the age of fourteen, Valentine was beginning to think of such things as beneath her.

And I couldn't fault her. At her age, I was running Papa's household.

"I was thoughtless, Valentine, and I apologize." I turned her to look at me. "I thought about how Bébert might feel being the only one to wait until morning. I didn't pause to consider *your* feelings on the matter."

And at this, her face brightened. She responded to my logic with the calm of any young adult . . . and it made me feel all the worse. She *was* mature enough to be counted among the adults, at least in matters like this, and I had done her a great disservice.

I muttered a silent prayer of thanksgiving that I'd at least selected gifts suited to a girl on the cusp of womanhood. She'd be greeted with a new silver vanity set for her room—that ought to please her given that her lovely head of mahogany hair was a source of pride for her. It was an extravagance, but I hoped the set would last for years and perhaps be an heirloom she could pass along to a daughter, if she were ever blessed with one. She was also getting a lovely bottle of scent, a pair of good kid gloves, and several books she'd been keen to read. The most precious of the offerings was a pair of Maman's pearl ear bobs. They were dainty and sweet; appropriate for a young lady ready to bloom into adulthood.

And I was grateful her transition from childhood to the vast world beyond would be more gradual than my own had been.

"You'll indulge your sister in one last Christmas morning with Bébert? Next year it might be time to dispense with Papa Noël entirely, I believe."

She nodded. "Papa Noël won't have much of a respite. Laure's little one will be here and crawling on the rugs at our feet by next Christmas. And before long, you'll have your own little ones to spoil."

I tried to force my lips into a smile and to postpone consideration of all manner of duties that would lay before me in the coming months.

"I'm sure you're right, darling. I know dear Maurice is so keen on being a papa, he'll convince her to have a dozen." She allowed me to wrap an arm around her shoulder and I placed my lips against her temple. If she'd noticed my deflection on the conversation, she was kind enough not to chastise me in public for it.

Papa bounded into the drawing room, his smile broad to see his brood reunited. He was spry for any age, but having his children all under the same roof and in good spirits had him as buoyant as a school lad home for the summer holidays. Tante Marie and Oncle Albert arrived just as the canapés were being circulated, and Adolphe was shown to the room by a footman shortly thereafter, looking dapper in his black tails and a green waistcoat.

I tried not to let my face fall when I saw him. It was to have been my last Christmas at home with my papa, siblings, and aunt and uncle before my marriage and I had been looking forward to this last special celebration alone with them. I wanted to shoot Papa a withering look but held it at bay. It was Christmas, after all, and the dressing-down could wait until the doldrums between our yuletide festivities and the new year.

"Adolphe, I hadn't realized you were coming. I thought certainly your family would have claims on your time." I accepted the kisses on the cheeks that he offered with nervous enthusiasm.

"Nonsense, we are his family now, Cherub. Or very soon will be." Papa's smile radiated warmth from his mirthful blue eyes.

I looked to a nearby footman and caught his eye. "Monsieur Salles will be joining us for dinner. Please ensure a place is set for him."

"I didn't realize I wasn't expected. I thought certainly your father would have alerted you to the invitation. I wouldn't have dreamed of—" Adolphe's face had drained entirely of color.

"Nonsense, Salles. Of course you'll celebrate with us if your employer is too much of a tyrant to give you the time necessary to make a journey to Marseille worthwhile." Papa winked at me. "And if I know my daughter, she wouldn't want her fiancé spending the holiday alone, now would she?"

"Of course not." I forced a smile. Marseille. I should have remembered that his parents lived so very far. And with all the high-profile projects Papa and Adolphe were tending, there was some veracity to the claim that Adolphe couldn't be spared. Their time was filled with not only the bridges that were being installed the world over but also the copula for the Nice Observatory, the interior structure for a massive statue destined for New York Harbor, and submitting the proposal for the expo. The winning design had yet to be selected, and the anticipation had been grating on the nerves of all involved.

Papa had been right to invite him, but I couldn't help feeling a bit peevish at the missed opportunity to have my last Christmas at home alone with my family.

I tried not to consider what it meant that Adolphe's presence felt like an intrusion. Laure certainly never felt that way about her Maurice, nor had any of us. When they were courting she'd contrived every scheme known to God and man to get him invited to every family gathering and social function we attended. And shouldn't it be that way? Shouldn't I *want* Adolphe to be included?

Perhaps it was because he spent so much time with Papa at the atelier. Perhaps it was the very fact that Papa had pushed for this union at all. But I couldn't shake the feeling that Adolphe had wormed his way into my family and there would be no extricating him from it. He was bonded to Papa through their work. That Adolphe would be his successor was all but carved into the cinder-block walls of the Compagnie Eiffel's atelier. It was the sort of bond that rivaled only marriage for its scope and duration of commitment. And it made my engagement to Adolphe all the more irrevocable. It wasn't just about him and me and our lives together. The company was bigger than that.

Especially to Papa. And to Adolphe.

It wasn't long before a footman ushered us into the dining room, which shone with candlelight and fairly sparkled with anticipation of the holiday meal. Papa was seated at the head of the table, as was his right as head of the house. Adolphe was seated to his right, which had been my place since I was old enough to be allowed the privilege of dining in adult company.

He couldn't have known how Papa's change to the seating arrangement would have affected me, nor why his inoffensive smile felt like a rusted horse rasp being dragged over the very last of my nerves. It wasn't his fault.

But he was the only one I could bear to hold responsible.

My gloomy thoughts, pervasive as they were, could not withstand the splendor of the decadent meal that the staff had worked so hard to prepare. As the soup course gave way to fish, Laure, who was seated to my left, leaned back in her chair with a contented sigh.

"Exquisite, Claire. Every detail is simply perfect for your last Christmas living in Papa's house. How exciting will that be for you. You'll have your own home and your own set of traditions so very soon." Laure looked gratified, as though she were reminding me of something so pleasant, I couldn't help but be delighted.

"What's this?" Papa asked, peering over to his second daughter. "Where do you have her running off to?"

"Well, dear Adolphe's home, of course. And he couldn't dream of a more charming chatelaine for his chateau," Laure said, beaming a smile at her future brother-in-law. "Though I'm sure it will be a hardship for you at first, Papa, I'm certain you'll learn to manage without our Claire in time."

"No indeed, I will not," Papa said. "Salles knows I can't do without her. It makes more sense for him to set up residence here, where Claire can tend to us both. I can't think two cantankerous men will be that much more of a hardship to care for than one. Furthermore, there's no need for Adolphe to spend his hard-earned money on a home in Paris that befits his station—and Claire's—when there is ample room here. I can rent them rooms far more cheaply here than anywhere half as comfortable. We settled the matter weeks ago."

My voice was low and at the point of seething. "And you didn't think to inform me?"

Papa and Adolphe had the good graces to look sheepish as they exchanged glances before turning their eyes to me. "I suppose we didn't think you'd mind," Adolphe said. "In fact, the notion that this would be the least disruptive living situation for you was among its chief virtues."

"A young lady like Claire needs disruption from time to time," Tante Marie interjected. "Don't you think she deserves the chance to run her own home, Brother?"

"And so she shall continue to do as she's done for the better part of a decade. It just so happens that it will be this one," Papa said, placing his napkin next to his plate. It was one of his signals that his patience was wearing thin.

"But Gustave—"

"No more, Marie. It's Christmas Eve and the matter is settled."

Laure looked just as crestfallen as Tante Marie but swallowed back her commentary. She was more easily cowed by Papa, which stood to reason. Though she was grown and married, she was still his daughter.

But despite all the cross looks on Papa's, Tante Marie's, and Laure's faces, I felt a leaden mantle lift from my shoulders.

"If anyone is interested in what I have to say on the matter, I think it's a brilliant solution to what has been my greatest concern since the engagement was formed. I was loath to leave Papa, Valentine, and Bébert to their own devices after depending upon me for so long. Indeed, I should much rather stay on here than have Versailles itself at my disposal."

Adolphe smiled, truly smiled, for the first time since I'd made his acquaintance. "I'm so happy you're pleased with our solution."

"There would have been one simple way to find out for certain." I set my fork down after a bite of sole. "You could have asked me. And you too, Papa. I cannot express how pleased I am to stay on here, but it won't be without conditions."

"And what, pray, are those?" Papa asked, looking wary.

"If you expect me to take up the responsibility of running a dual household under one roof you will no longer make decisions for me as you would for a dependent child. You will—both of you—consult me in all things concerning the running of this house, and certainly my own welfare, from this moment forward. You will afford me the respect to which I am entitled as lady of this house."

Papa blinked, surprised at my forceful comment, and looked at a loss for words.

I met his eyes. "You consulted Maman in all things. If you wish me to continue with her duties, I must be afforded the same regard as you offered her. If you refuse, then this whole arrangement, all of it, is for naught."

The very engagement itself if I was pressed. I didn't have to speak the words, but the meaning was clear.

Tante Marie's scowl turned into an impish grin. "What argument can you offer against that, Gustave?" She turned to me. "This plan might not be quite so disastrous after all. A bit of backbone suits you marvelously, dearest."

Chapter Twenty

Though Christmas Eve was the grand affair, I always preferred Christmas luncheon after the children opened their gifts. It was the moment, after weeks of toil, I felt like I could breathe. I likened it to the delicious rush of air I felt when Pauline helped me out of my stays at the end of the day but multiplied many times over. The luncheon consisted of any leftovers from the previous night's feast that were fit to eat, though artfully presented on trays that we passed ourselves, allowing the staff a bit of respite at midday. In addition to the remainder of the evening meal, Cook would prepare a hearty soup and delicious little sandwiches to supplement. It was simple fare but nourishing and restorative. And though I'd been raised to appreciate the elegance of a formal dinner, I vastly preferred the warmth of Cook's Christmas feast to the perfectly sculpted bite-sized canapés with caviar and foie gras that looked straight from Carême's *Le Cuisinier parisien*.

The meal was complete, and we were now settled in the drawing room, drowsy from attending midnight mass and having enjoyed several sumptuous meals in the last two days. Bébert played on the rug with his new collection of tin soldiers and fine carved horses he'd opened earlier that morning. I was disappointed he didn't show more interest in the books I'd procured for him, but Valentine read one of her books with great interest in one of the plump armchairs. I was pleased beyond measure that she'd deemed the rest of her gifts sufficiently adult for a young lady of fourteen. Papa seemed thrilled with the prayer book I'd had made for him and the embroidered handkerchiefs I'd toiled over that looked far less of a mess than my efforts at Valentine's age, though I'd never have Maman's or Tante Marie's skill.

As for myself, I wore the cameo that Adolphe had given me the night before, pinned to my blouse at the hollow of my throat. It wasn't made of agate or conch as was the tradition of most cameos I'd seen, but rather it depicted the profile of a young woman carved into deep blue lapis lazuli and had been mounted in an intricate gold setting that allowed it to be worn as a brooch or pendant. It was as fine as any piece in Maman's collection, and indeed was a piece that she herself would have been proud to wear.

"It belonged to my grandmother, and she was very fond of it. My grandparents were not wealthy when they married, but Papi managed to make a success of himself after many years of hard work. He bought this for her when the tide finally turned for them. She gave it to me before she died to remind me of the importance of hard work and persistence."

"You've taken those lessons to heart. You're a credit to her memory and the rest of your family." That praise cost me nothing to offer. If I could name only one of Adolphe's virtues, it would have to be his work ethic. I was certain it was the quality that had first caught Papa's attention. Like recognized like, after all.

"It means more than I can express to have you bestow such a generous compliment. I shall strive to be worthy of it." The color had risen in his cheeks.

I handed him the gift I'd selected for him weeks ago, though I had thought it would be a token for the new year instead of yuletide. "It's nothing extravagant," I said dismissively as he tucked his forefinger under the flap of wrapping paper. Inside was a set with a gold fountain pen and drafting pencil, engraved with his initials and nestled in a carved rosewood box. They were store-bought less than a month before the holiday, between a fitting at the modiste and luncheon at Tante Marie's, and now seemed rather pathetic when compared with the significance of the gift Adolphe had offered me.

"Not sentimental, but useful, I should think." I hated the heat I felt threatening to burn at my cheeks.

"Not sentimental, Claire? This is the first gift I have ever received from my beautiful bride. To my mind, it isn't the object that makes a gift sentimental. In most cases, it is the person offering it. But these are truly lovely."

He'd been welcome to use my name, especially when not out among the wider public, but it still sounded unfamiliar, almost forbidden, on his tongue. I exhaled, unaware I'd been holding a nervous breath that had caught in my throat. "I'm glad you enjoy them."

He kissed my cheeks in thanks. "I will carry them with me for the rest of my days."

A frisson went down my spine as his breath tickled my ear.

He absolutely meant it. He had loved the gift, and largely because it was *me* who gave it. Whatever practical influences there might have been over our betrothal, there was a part of him that cared for *me*. That was delighted it was *me* attached to the end of the strings that came with inheriting the Compagnie Eiffel.

God how I envied him.

I wanted so much to feel a spark of affection for him. There was warmth, and I was ever so grateful for it. But there was no burning flame of passion that I'd read about in the romantic novels Papa didn't fully approve of, but that I occasionally read in the privacy of my rooms.

And there would never be a flame without a spark, no matter how much warmth there was.

And because of this, as I sat next to him on the divan, the lovely lapis cameo at my neck seemed to grow exponentially heavier under the weight of expectation. I busied my hands with some embroidery, which left me more open to conversation than reading, and found some comfort in the deep blues, vibrant greens, and rich purples of the threads.

Our butler, Deschamps, entered the drawing room carrying a newspaper on a silver tray.

"My dear man, you shouldn't trouble yourself with the paper on Christmas Day," Papa chastened. "Certainly there isn't any horrible news going on in the world that won't wait until tomorrow."

Deschamps gave Papa a rare smile. "I wouldn't normally, monsieur. In fact, I confess I took the opportunity to read it myself before bringing it up for once."

"Good man."

"But indeed there was an article that concerns you, so I ironed the pages straightaway and brought it to you."

One of the many tasks that fell to the butler, often before we were awake and ready to take our breakfast, was using a hot iron to set the ink on the newsprint so it wouldn't rub off on our fingers.

"Not bad news, I hope." I placed my embroidery on a side table. All we needed was a workplace incident or—God forbid—a bridge collapse on this of all days. There wasn't an engineer that didn't fear such things after the horrible disaster at the Tay Bridge. It had been five years, almost to the day, since the bridge failed and killed sixty people or more in Scotland. To all of us attached to the industry, it seemed like it was yesterday, and in our own backyard.

"No, no, mademoiselle. Quite the contrary. I thought it would serve to brighten your celebrations even more," Deschamps said, immediately dispensing the tension in the room.

"It's an article advocating for our proposal for the expo." Papa's face split into a wide smile. He scanned the article for several moments, nodding occasionally as though the author could see his approval. "They assert the Eiffel plan will provide Paris with a tower that is both beautiful and useful for scientific experimentation. There is at least one person in this city who understands what we're trying to do. Hallelujah for that."

Beautiful *and* useful. The marriage of those virtues was the hallmark of good architecture.

Papa passed the paper to Adolphe, who angled the article so I could read alongside him. Papa stood and, breaking our usual protocol, offered Deschamps a brandy and a chair with the rest of us to celebrate our victory in public opinion, and to thank him for being the messenger of good news. Deschamps accepted the former but could not bring himself to sit in our presence. Papa remained standing with him, engaging him in idle conversation for the length of time it took them to enjoy their brandy.

The article, though it could judge the merits of Papa's project only from the official sketches that had been submitted to the committee, seemed wholly in favor of the massive three-hundred-meter tower that Papa and Adolphe planned to construct at the Champs de Mars, which was in sharp contrast with the general public sentiment up to this point. It wasn't the first time Papa had met with opposition, to be sure, but the utility of his projects brought people around in the end. If people saw the tower as merely an imposing architectural parlor trick, it would have been next to impossible to persuade people it was worth the expense and inconvenience, even if there were those who saw beauty in the modern design. This was the first time anyone had seen the potential of the tower as a tool for scientific advancement.

There were always detractors in matters of taste. Some claimed that Garnier's Opéra looked like a mausoleum. But it didn't stop anyone from attending the performances, for it was the shows they wanted to see. The building itself, while lovely in my view, was really just a showcase for the musicians and dancers it housed. Aesthetic preferences could be overcome if the public could be convinced there was a greater purpose. And for the first time, this article made that claim. As Papa had said, *hallelujah*.

"What do you think of the design?" Adolphe asked me, setting the paper aside and angling toward me.

"From the sketches I've seen, it looks like it will manage to be graceful, despite the immense size," I said, accepting a brandy from Papa, who had come to rejoin us.

"I sense some hesitance," Adolphe prodded. "What worries you?"

"I try to think about how I would feel if it were in my own neighborhood. I can hardly fathom exactly how large a three-hundred-meter tower will be. Will the people in those lovely neighborhoods be forced to live in shadow for the next two decades? Would they have to worry that a few faulty rivets might send huge lengths of iron flying onto the roofs of their buildings? I can imagine their concerns are not trivial."

"Some of them are ridiculous." Papa leaned back in his fauteuil and threaded his fingers. "One man wrote, concerned it would change the weather patterns in Paris and we couldn't know if it would see the city transformed into a desert, or under a thick billow of rain clouds the whole year long."

"But it will serve as a lightning rod, will it not?"

"The tallest structure in the city always does. And a tallest structure there must be. But we have the benefits of modern engineering on our side. We can ensure the lightning will have minimal effect on the structure. Or indeed we may learn how to better harness its power."

"I am sure you're right. But people are more concerned with their own day-to-day affairs. Construction will disrupt the lives of countless Parisians for two years while it's being built. Not to mention the twenty years following as it dominates the skyline and attracts hordes of ill-mannered tourists. The people who live near the Champs de Mars are monied and are not likely to support you. Many of the residents are of a certain age, and they see the tower as a permanent imposition on their lives."

"I thought we were to be celebrating," Papa said with a guffaw. "We've had a victory today."

"Indeed we have, Papa, but we will need many more of these victories if we're to have wide support—and financing—for the tower. We want people to know, not just believe, that the tower will be a boon to their daily lives for as long as it stands."

"Hear, hear," Adolphe said. "We need you on the board of the Compagnie Eiffel as our chief officer of public relations."

"Oh, Adolphe. If you don't think I'm already on the board, you're greatly mistaken. I'm just clever enough to do it in such a way that doesn't require me to attend all those tedious meetings."

At this, Papa and Adolphe laughed in unison. I took the copy of the paper Deschamps had so proudly presented to Papa. The sketches of the tower the paper had shared showed a structure that was, despite being massive and made of iron, almost feminine in its grace. Convincing the people of Paris, especially those whose opinions mattered most, would be a battle, but as I looked at the design and I thought of Papa's aspirations in the scientific domain, I genuinely hoped it was a battle they would win.

Not just because it would be a boon to Papa and the company but because I truly believed Paris would be the better for it.

Chapter Twenty-One

February 26, 1885

I stood in the vestibule of the church, dressed in the cream confection Mademoiselle Leclerc had concocted for me, and a small nosegay of blush-pink roses and myrtle trembled in my hands. An altar boy, dressed in his black-and-white vestments, opened the door to the nave of the church and nodded to Papa.

The priest was ready.

Adolphe was ready.

I was anything but.

"I think it's time, Cherub." Papa proffered his arm.

Less than a year after we'd gathered to join our dear Laure and her Maurice in marriage, our family and friends again gathered at the Saint-François-de-Sales church, where we attended mass every Sunday and holy day of obligation. Where we feted every major family milestone, both joyous and somber.

This particular occasion, when I rolled it around on my tongue, tasted of both the sweet and the bitter moments of life. There were dozens of faces, most of them dear to me; the rest were dear to Adolphe and I hoped to befriend them all in time. But the one face I needed to see most of all in the front row, Maman's, was painfully absent. Tante Marie's smile helped. Papa's arm was steadying. But nothing could replace Maman. There were so many vital moments she'd missed. So many times I'd longed to rest my head on her shoulder and ask for her advice. So many times I simply wanted to feel her hand around mine, reassuring me that all was well. But none of them more than today.

I'd come to the conclusion that she would have loved Adolphe, just as Papa did, and became more certain of this with each encounter. He would have charmed her with his quiet intelligence and flawless, unaffected manners. She would have encouraged the match in her own way. Gently, and with an awareness of the importance of romance. I could envision her discreetly slipping Adolphe hints about my preferences and guiding him to a better understanding of me. Not just to aid in our courtship, but to help make him a better husband in the years that followed.

And I ached for that loss.

Papa nudged me forward and we left behind the safety of the vestibule for the open expanse of the nave. This time it was me in the gleaming silk gown with all eyes keenly focused on each cautious step I took down the impossibly long aisle. I found that I preferred the role of stand-in mother of the bride to being the center of attention, but there was no way to swap places now.

With a kiss on the cheek, Papa handed me off to Adolphe, already my husband according to the state after our brief ceremony at the *mairie* the day before. This was just for show. The *spectacle familial* as Édouard called it with his signature disdain. But it mattered. It mattered to Papa, who believed in the sanctity of Catholic marriage. It would have mattered to Maman, and therefore, it mattered to me.

"Man's soul awakens little by little. It has, like the earth, seasons, and divine seeds which are planted and grow there . . ."

The priest, Père Didon, was a friend of Papa's. He spoke in a soaring oratory, offering a long sermon that spoke of both love and duty, which I appreciated. I thought so many priests fought too hard to scare the bride and groom with tiresome lectures about how hard married life would be once the bloom of first love had quite gone off the rose.

But why dismiss those early days of joy, fleeting though they may be? Why not marvel that we as human beings are capable of such all-encompassing devotion to another? Just because the early days of a besotted couple might seem easy doesn't mean they shouldn't be treasured.

Laure and Maurice had deserved those halcyon days. I suspected they were succor to help them through the trials of the past few weeks. The young couple sat in the first row, next to Papa. Her complexion was wan from her travails just two weeks before, though there had been no persuading her to stay at home. Maurice, though he tried to keep his eyes respectfully on the priest, could hardly take his eyes off his frail bride. The last days of her pregnancy, and the resulting labors, had been arduous for her. I was with her through her ordeal, praying all the while that she would not be taken from her loving husband so soon.

Thankfully, we were convinced she would recover, given enough time and rest. Little Margueritte was the worry now. Laure named the little one for Maman, making a slight change to the spelling to set them apart. The babe was incredibly small, even for a newborn, and was so pale she seemed not of this earth. We prayed that she wouldn't rush off too soon to be with her namesake.

The one small blessing in all of this was that Laure's struggles had put my own worries about marriage to Adolphe into perspective. Compared to Laure agonizing over the fate of her fragile daughter, my own lot in life seemed a relatively easy burden to bear.

Père Didon was a commanding speaker, and I could see that Adolphe was taking the priest's directives about the importance of hard work and providing for and protecting his family to heart. Then the priest turned to me:

"Your mother bestowed upon you a maternal heart, and when death took her from you, you came to know the place of the woman in the family. You will know it once more, by observing your husband's mother. Taught by such examples, you will never forget that duty of sacrifice, which is the honor of marriage, comes to rest first and in largest measure on the shoulders of the woman, the wife, and most of all, the mother."

This priest had not known my mother, as we joined the parish after we moved from Levallois, but he'd known our family since she'd died. He could not have helped but see the gaping hole she'd left in our hearts. Especially Papa's. Though I wouldn't consider myself friendly with the priest, my heart twinged with gratitude that he knew the words to speak.

I felt a tingle in my spine, followed by a warmth and the sensation of a hand being placed on my back, between my shoulder blades. The logical side of my brain, the one so nurtured by Papa, knew that this was a manifestation of what I wanted to feel: the comforting presence of my mother.

But the part of me that wished upon shooting stars, that delighted in blowing the fluff from dandelions, and that secretly believed in miracles, knew she was there.

I spoke my vows with a clear voice and met Adolphe's and Père Didon's eyes in turn. I pushed my reservations aside and resolved that I would make this commitment with all that I had to offer. I thought of the maxim Papa often spoke, that any task worth undertaking was worthy of excellence, and my marriage would be no exception to that credo.

Tante Marie had seen to most of the preparations for the reception, with Valentine serving as her faithful assistant. Though Papa had wanted a full seated luncheon, I'd managed to persuade everyone that champagne, canapés, and the traditional croquembouche—a tower of caramel-shrouded cream puffs—would suffice. And I was never more thrilled that I'd prevailed. The thought of taking more than a few polite bites of smoked salmon or the decadent cream puffs was beyond comprehension as the excitement of the day twinged at my nerves, and anticipation for all that lay beyond caused my gut to churn.

Laure, who would have normally been at Tante Marie's side for the preparations, was far too preoccupied with her tumultuous transition to motherhood to expend much energy on the task. Seeing her slouched shoulders and the dark circles under her eyes, I thought it just as well she'd not taken part. Though I did my best to be a lively and engaging hostess to our guests, I kept a watchful eye on the new mother to make sure she wasn't exhausting herself. Unsurprisingly, she began to look restive about an hour into the gathering, her eyes flickering to the massive grandfather clock that dominated one wall of the drawing room. I begged indulgence from the friend of Papa's who had cornered Adolphe and me in conversation and crossed the room to her.

"You seem tired, darling." Her fatigue concerned me less than the worry that was laced in the wrinkles of her furrowed brow. "If you want to go home to Margueritte, I'm sure Maurice will be happy to take you."

Laure blanched, almost imperceptibly, likely disappointed she'd not been able to keep up her facade as a joyful and energetic new mother, and forced a smile. "Nonsense, I want to celebrate your day with you. I'm perfectly well."

She was pulling a trick out of the pages of my own book and

putting my needs before her own. I stepped closer and rubbed her arm. "You've had some cake and champagne, have you not? You gave Papa a kiss on the cheek and congratulated the lucky groom? No one will mind if you slip away and look after yourself."

"Claire, you'll only be married once. I don't want to let you down." She spoke sternly, but I suspected it was an attempt within herself to buoy her reserves of energy.

Though she was an adult, and no longer under my purview, I gave her the best *no nonsense* look I'd mastered in my tenure as stand-in mother to my siblings. "You haven't, dearest. The job is done. You saw me wed and you've blessed me with your well wishes. I'll carry those happy thoughts with me all the way to Sèvres."

Laure smiled. "I'm glad they're strong enough to travel the enormous thirteen-kilometer distance to the countryside. But it's a shame you won't take a proper wedding tour."

"Travel in February sounds abysmal to me. I'd rather wait so that the train ride won't feel like ten hours sitting in an ice truck. We'll take a proper trip later. We can't all be as clever as you, marrying in May."

"I can't argue with you there." She mustered a fatigued smile. "I am the cleverest of us."

"And Valentine is the sweetest, Édouard is the funniest, and Bébert is the strongest."

"And you, my dearest sister, are the bravest. You always have been." She kissed my cheek.

God, how I wished that were true. But that she believed that falsehood in any small measure meant that some shred of her childhood had been left unmarred. A better wedding gift I couldn't have asked for.

I took her in my arms and whispered in her ear, "Go home. Rest and cuddle my niece, will you? Nothing would make me happier."

"Well, it's bad form to cross a bride on her wedding day. I'll tell her you're coming to see her soon. Tatie Claire will need the practice for when her own little ones arrive."

"Don't be saucy, young lady." I kissed her cheeks. She rewarded me with a girlish giggle, and it was good to hear her sounding mirthful after the last three arduous weeks. I shot a meaningful look at Maurice, who, like me, had been watching Laure closely all afternoon, but doing his best to keep it from being patently obvious to the rest of the assembly.

Maurice glided across the room and whisked Laure away with a hasty kiss to my cheek and a nod to Adolphe, who was still trapped in conversation. Maurice's military training was evident to anyone paying attention: he'd clearly mapped out an exit plan to get Laure back home as soon as she showed the first sign of willingness, and I was glad he'd found a use for his strategic talents in the domestic sphere.

Few seemed to register when the door clicked behind them, but I realized that my greatest ally had left. Tante Marie swooped in and linked her arm in mine.

"I think you need to freshen up, don't you?" She all but dragged me to my rooms and closed the door behind me.

"People will wonder where I've gone. Is something the matter?"

"People will think you need air. Or the privy. It's no matter," Tante Marie said dismissively. "I should have pulled you aside yesterday, but I hadn't the nerve. But so it is. We have a few minutes to talk now and I wanted to see if you have any questions about . . ." Her face flushed a violent shade of crimson.

"The marriage act?"

"Yes. As your aunt, the responsibility falls to me to ensure you're prepared for your marital duties—"

"You make it sound like I'll be signing proclamations and christening ships," I said with an ill-concealed snort.

"If only it were so simple. Now, when a man and woman truly love each other—"

I held up a hand. "Peace, Tante. Laure told me she approached you when she was to be married, and it was an ordeal for you. I thought to spare you the discomfort and do some reading on the subject."

Tante Marie rose a hand to her mouth, though I couldn't be sure if it was to cover her dismay or a grin. "Oh Lord, don't tell me you found some salacious tract on married love. What will Adolphe think?"

"No, I found a well-regarded book by a proper physician written for mothers to advise their daughters," I explained. "It wasn't quite as detailed as I might have liked, but I can at least go into married life knowing a bit more than nothing."

"I'm shocked that a reputable *bouquiniste* would have allowed you to purchase such a title without your mother in tow." Heat rose in her cheeks. "I hope at least you went to a shop where we aren't known."

"Quite the contrary. I went to Papa's very favorite. They would know full well why I'd need such a tome and why my mother wasn't the one to purchase it for me. They know enough about our family to know there was nothing untoward about it."

"Oh Claire, how mortifying. You ought to have been more circumspect."

"Why ever should I be? I'm a motherless woman who was about to be wed. Does the world expect me to proceed in utter ignorance? How is it different than any other medical book I might purchase?"

"It just is, Claire. And if the book didn't make you realize as much, I doubt it was worth the paper it was printed on."

I couldn't help but roll my eyes at her. "Consider this: you've been spared the embarrassment of a lecture you don't want to give. And by the time Valentine's time comes, she won't have to rely on you."

"That was unkind, Claire." She took a step back as if I'd slapped her.

"It wasn't meant to be, Tante. But if imparting this necessary knowledge is too painful for you, then I will not accept any criticism for seeking it out on my own."

Tante Marie's eyes widened. "Girls are supposed to—"

"But I am not a girl, am I? I've been forced to be a woman since I was fourteen. Do you know how horrified I was the first time I bled? The woman who housed us in Portugal had to explain to me what was going on . . . in the most absurd blend of broken French and idiot-level Portuguese you can imagine. I had to endure that mortification, so you'll excuse me if buying a simple book to avoid *more* humiliation doesn't give me pause."

Tante Marie lowered her eyes for a moment. "Very well," she said, looking up again. "I wish you well, my dear."

She turned and closed the door behind her. I would soon be missed, and couldn't linger long, but I couldn't resist sitting on my green tufted chair and absorbing the silence for just a few moments. I had been harsh with Tante Marie, but this time I would offer no apology. She had been an excellent source of strength and support to me, to all of us, since Maman died, but she had failed in her duty to Laure and me in this one area, and I wouldn't be censured for preparing myself for what was to come.

I clasped my head in my hands and felt a hot band around my chest. I looked over at my bed longingly, and though it was only afternoon, I would have gladly divested myself of my wedding gown and corset and slid into the comfort of its covers. I would have reveled in the freedom of wearing naught but my loose chemise and being able to breathe unrestricted. In normal times, I loved the support my corsets offered. The strength I felt being encased in steel boning, which I often delighted in picturing like the scaffolding of one of Papa's buildings. Or perhaps more accurately, like the framework he was building for the statue being sent to New York. I wasn't as vain as some women, lacing themselves to the point of vapors. I had always shut down Tante Marie's suggestions to "try to whittle off another inch" and had forbidden Laure and Valentine from going to extremes either.

But now my beloved second skin was betraying me. I struggled to take a breath and worried I'd be found on the floor in a dead faint. At least Tante Marie would know where to look when people became concerned. The room was becoming fuzzy, but I had the presence of mind to ring the bellpull and hoped that Pauline or one of the maids could be spared from the festivities to come attend me.

It was a mercifully short time before Pauline arrived, and I felt my pulse slow measurably in her comforting presence.

"What are you doing up here, Mademoiselle Eiffel . . . *mon Dieu,* Madame Salles. You must forgive me as I adjust to your new name. But you are missing your own reception."

"I can't breathe. Help me out of my corset, please."

She looked ready to object but followed my orders without complaint. The first rush of air into my lungs burned like raging wildfire, but relief soon followed. I stood, gripping one of the bedposts like a life preserver, and continued to take in giant gulps of air.

"Let me get you some tea, my dear. It will set you to rights."

I nodded. "If you see Papa or Monsieur Salles while you're downstairs, tell them I won't be long."

She offered me a reassuring smile.

Knowing Pauline's habit of keeping a pot of water boiling at all times in case tea or coffee was ever needed at a moment's notice, I had less than five minutes to myself in the freedom of my billowing chemise. Rather than mess the bed Pauline had so carefully made, I lay down atop the plush damask bedding and allowed myself to take in the sensation of sinking into the layers of feathers, cotton fluff, and silken bedding. I imagined myself sinking into a cloud of cotton and floating in the warmth of a late-spring day.

And by the time Pauline returned with the tea, I could breathe normally once more.

I finished the restorative beverage and ate three biscuits at her behest before she agreed to lace me up again and help me back into my gown.

"Your color is better," Pauline admitted as she smoothed my hair and arranged my skirt.

I thanked her and descended the staircase to where the guests were still milling about cheerfully. Hopefully my absence hadn't been remarked by too many.

But of course Papa's keen blue eyes settled on me when I entered the drawing room and he made a beeline for where I stood.

"Everything all right, my dear? You've been gone an age."

"I have a new project for you, Papa." I lowered my voice so he would step closer. "Next time you're at the atelier, you must devise a contraption for a lady to enable her to use the privy when she's strapped into enough fabric to see the entire French navy outfitted in sails. It's a feat that calls for expert engineering if ever there was one."

Papa threw his head back in laughter. "I'll see to it, Cherub. You have my word."

I laughed in return, hoping mine sounded as earnest as his. "Every fashionable woman in Paris will speak the name Eiffel with reverence if you do."

I saw Pauline peering into the drawing room, ostensibly to ensure that the footmen were not short on food and drink, but I knew she was chiefly looking in to assure herself that I was well again. I caught her eye and flashed a smile to assuage her worry.

But she had voiced a truth earlier in my rooms that would take me a long while to accept. I was "Madame Salles" now, and it was my responsibility to learn how to be that woman.

And all the while, I remained, and always would be, Mademoiselle Eiffel as long as my father lived.

Chapter Twenty-Two

As the last guests departed several hours after the festivities had begun, I began to see the wisdom in brides and grooms immediately leaving for a wedding tour, or at least the privacy of a hotel or country cottage, rather than staying in the family home on the wedding night. We could have absented ourselves hours before, with peals of good wishes from all our nearest and dearest, and left them to their merrymaking. But instead we waited for the door to close behind the last of the guests, whom Papa had been gradually inching toward the door for the past quarter of an hour, and were ready to faint from exhaustion when the latch clicked shut.

"A successful endeavor indeed," Papa announced as he flopped unceremoniously and uncharacteristically onto the divan. He pulled a cigar from his coat pocket and lit it, despite his usual tendency to avoid this naughty habit of his in my presence. He offered one to Adolphe, who accepted it readily. Both looked worn from the exertions of the day, nor could I blame them.

"Successful enough, as we ended up well and truly married by the end of it." I poured us each a brandy, with an extra half inch in mine since I wasn't about to indulge in a cigar. I passed them each an etched-crystal goblet full of the topaz-hued liquid that glowed warm in the candlelight. Adolphe sat on the divan across from Papa's and patted the velvet cushion next to him in invitation.

"My eldest child, my dearest girl, is married." Papa took a slow drag from his cigar and lazily exhaled the smoke in neat rings. "It's a grand day indeed."

"I'll drink to that." Adolphe raised his glass in Papa's direction and then clinked the edge of mine. The chime of the crystal rose over our heads like church bells.

Papa finished his brandy, not lingering over it as was his custom. "I suppose the two of you will be wanting some rest. I trust Claire will orient you to the ways of the house with her usual cordiality."

I ignored the sweat pricking at my palms and nodded my assent. Most of Adolphe's things had been moved over the past week, and the rest would come shortly as the lease on his apartment extended another two weeks. Most of his furniture would be sold, as little of his could compare with the rich furnishings Papa had inherited or acquired. For his rooms, Adolphe would keep his carved walnut writing desk, which was one of his prized possessions, and a couple of comfortable chairs he'd been given from his parents. Papa had assured Adolphe he wouldn't need a thing, but I intervened on Adolphe's behalf and insisted that he retain a few pieces that would make his rooms feel like his own.

The rooms that had once been Laure's. They had an adjoining door to my own, designed for easy passage between the two spaces.

Adolphe finished his own brandy, stood, and offered me a hand to assist me to my feet. Rather than awkwardly wishing us a pleasant evening, Papa simply squeezed my arm as he left for his own suite of rooms, which were, mercifully, on the opposite end of the house from ours.

I allowed Adolphe to escort me to my door, and he looked anxious as we reached the corridor that led to our rooms. He didn't speak a word, but the expression on his face was clear enough. *What do we do next?*

He was likely far more informed than I was about the goings-on between a husband and wife. He didn't strike me as the sort to frequent the kind of establishments that Édouard did, but it didn't mean he hadn't had youthful dalliances. I didn't feel a twinge of jealousy at the idea, and wondered if I should. The rational side of me reasoned that it was just as well one of us would have some practical experience. The passionate side of me seemed to be huddled in a corner hiding under a quilt.

Despite this, he seemed frozen to the spot and waiting for me to make the first move in this horribly unfamiliar, uncomfortable dance.

"I should like to freshen up. If you need anything at all, the bell-pull will summon a footman. I'm sure someone's in the kitchens quite late tonight just in case."

He cleared his throat and looked as though he wished to say something, but seemingly thought the better of it. He turned and padded down the hallway until I heard the click of the door to his rooms.

I felt my shoulders drop by a number of inches as I entered the familiar solace of my rooms, as though I hadn't seen them just a few hours prior. The sight of my books, my sorry attempts at knitting, my knickknacks from travels with Papa, was as comforting as *chocolat chaud* on a cold morning. I could have delayed. I considered sitting down with a book for a few moments, but knew the words would simply swirl on the page.

And the duty would remain, no matter how long I stalled, and it would only grow in its enormity in my mind. I crossed to my bedroom and rang the bellpull for Pauline. She arrived within minutes, armed with more tea and biscuits, bless her, and saw me disrobed and de-coiffed and then left with an affectionate pat on the shoulder. She was far less chatty than usual, and I knew she probably thought she was doing me a favor by performing my toilette expeditiously on such a momentous night. I would have gladly discussed poetry and horticulture and cabbages and kings with her for an hour or two, but she spirited out of the room with fewer than a dozen words spoken.

I stood before the long mirror in my room. My golden-brown hair was brushed to gleaming in ripples down my back. My face was plain but pleasing enough. I wasn't vain enough to begrudge that I didn't have Valentine's beauty or Laure's elegance, but I wouldn't have minded borrowing them for an evening. I would have to cover my doubts in a cloud of ethereal white muslin and intricate lace. My nightgown, made by the expert hands of Mademoiselle Leclerc, had been her wedding gift to me in thanks for the voluminous business I'd brought her in the past months. I wasn't beautiful, but I hoped at least I was pleasing enough.

I felt my throat constrict and took a sip from the tea Pauline had brought, though the biscuits were as appealing as sawdust. I felt a tremor in my hands and wished that the book that had so scandalized Tante Marie had explained better what I needed to do in this moment. Did I go to his room? Open the door to my own?

No, both were too forward and felt ridiculous.

But I could unlatch the door that separated his rooms from mine and let him make of it what he would.

I made sure to rattle the latch just a bit, so he might hear my subtle invitation, then found my way under the bedcovers, unsure of what to hope for next.

Would it be awful if he came to collect his due . . .

Or worse if he showed no interest in me.

I counted my breaths and listened to the ticking of the clock.

I don't know how many minutes passed before I heard the click of the door and the muffled sounds of Adolphe's slippered feet on the carpets, but I fought to keep my heart from beating straight through my rib cage.

He went to the opposite side of the bed, untied the knot at the waist of his robe, and placed it on a chair before climbing into bed next to me.

"A-are you well?" he stammered after a few moments.

"As well as I can be after the excitement of the day," I replied, then hastened to add, "And you?"

He paused. "It feels as though I've been watching my own life from the outside for the past twelve hours. Floating around and observing myself like a spirit. *Surreal* is perhaps the best way to describe it."

"I'm not sure I have a response equal to that." I pulled the covers up to my chin.

"What an idiotic thing for me to say." He squirmed in his place, settling his thoughts as much as his person. "I suppose what I mean to say is that today was such a momentous one, it was hard to take it all in."

I found myself glad to hear this. It had been more than just a business transaction for him. I was certain that the weight of the day was different for each of us, but at least he'd felt it too.

"I understand what you mean. I didn't experience it in the way you did, but the commitment we made was larger than ourselves. It seems sensible that a person would have to take it all in from the outside."

"I thought you'd think I was daft for a moment there. I-I'm glad you were able to parse meaning from my babbling."

"Of course." I mumbled my words, wishing I'd found something cleverer to say.

There was a long enough pause, I wasn't certain that he hadn't fallen asleep. I tried to think of something to break the silence, but each idea that came to mind was more vapid than the last.

"I do mean to try to make you happy. Inasmuch as I am able."

I opened my mouth to echo the promise, but could not. My happiness was inextricably linked to his whims, while he could pursue contentment in his profession or in any other number of pursuits. He didn't need me to make him happy. If I failed in that regard, he had ample outlets to find it elsewhere.

"I believe you," I finally said.

"And to that end I trust you will never be afraid to tell me what you think and how you feel. Without that as my guide, I have little hope to secure you happiness."

"That's very forward-thinking of you." I turned to my side to look at his profile while he stared up at the canopy.

"I have seen what happens when a man pays too little heed to his wife's happiness. I don't wish it for us, nor any children we might have."

"Oh?"

"My mother and father are excellent people. And loving parents. But Papa's views of the woman's place in the home did not serve to make her happy." Adolphe's tone was distant as he seemed to recall tarnished memories from his youth.

"They seemed jolly enough today. And in the times I've observed them together."

"You have not seen them at home in Marseille. In the comfort of their own domain. Papa fancies himself a lord with the duty to rule with an iron fist. Maman is a woman of intelligence and fine sensibilities. She'd be an asset as the wife of a leading politician, but Papa is too provincial to believe that a woman can possess such qualities. Or if she does, it's more seemly for her to conceal them so she never runs the risk of outshining her husband."

Images of Bon Papa and Bonne Maman rose in my mind, and I snorted in derision despite myself. "My own *maman* had a docile temperament, rest her soul. But Papa knew where her gifts lay: in charming people who were convinced they could not be charmed. In creating a lavish banquet on precious little notice when there were important people to woo in the professional sense. He was too wise to hide Maman away just to preserve some ridiculous belief in his own superiority."

"Your papa is a man of discernment and vast intelligence. I cannot say the same for my own. He's a man of small mind and little information."

"Oh, I hope he had the chance to converse with Édouard. They would get on famously."

At this, Adolphe laughed. It was the first time I'd heard him offer more than the polite social chuckle, and there was a pleasing, almost musical lilt when he laughed in earnest.

And it emboldened him.

He rolled to his side so that we were looking eye to eye. He raised a hand and smoothed a tendril of hair from my forehead. "We can take all the time we need for . . . well . . . Nothing need happen until you're ready."

It was a generous offer. From the look in his deep brown eyes, I recognized a trace of desire despite knowing only in the most rudimentary way what was expected of me. I imagined many men would have simply claimed their due without regard for their brides' misgivings.

It was a tempting offer too. I could defer my duty and face it later. Perhaps tomorrow. A week from now. Months even. But the day would come, whether I felt prepared for it or not.

And as I had reasoned when I unlatched my door, the anticipation would only make it worse.

I didn't speak, but tentatively took my hand and rubbed the outline of his clean-shaven jaw with the back of my forefinger.

He inched closer, gently caressing me, then finally placing his lips on mine.

Before long, he held me tight against his chest as his kisses deepened and his fingers grew bolder in their exploration. I wasn't sure if I was meant to match his embraces or simply allow his, so I compromised by gently rubbing his back while I took in the new sensations his embraces evoked.

He was as tender and thoughtful in his movements as he was in every other aspect of our courtship. Quietly asking my permission before touching areas of my body that I'd never dared to explore myself. He murmured reassurances and sweet words as he finally gave in to his desires, trying so desperately to avoid causing me any more discomfort than was necessary. And when he cradled me in his arms when he found release, I felt as cherished as a fragile china doll.

Aside from allowing Laure or Valentine to share my bed after a particularly disturbing nightmare from time to time, I'd never slept in the same bed with anyone in the course of my life. Certainly never a man. As Adolphe drifted off, I found sleep eluded me. I watched the rise and fall of his chest and listened to the cadence of his even breathing as I tried to ignore the discomfort between my legs. This was to be the symphony of my sleep for the next fifty, sixty, or even seventy years. In ten years' time, would he grow plump and develop a snore that would drive me mad? Or, in time, would the sound of his slumber and the warmth of his body next to mine be what coaxed me into sleep?

With every slight movement, the dull aches and new sensations in my body reminded me that I had irrevocably crossed the threshold from girlhood to womanhood, but I wasn't overwhelmed by this truth. I had been filling the office of a grown woman for so long, this milestone perhaps felt less significant than it might to a girl whose wedding night would correspond with her taking over the role of mistress of a home. I was neither repulsed by the act nor as driven by it as my brother seemed to be.

But it had certainly given Adolphe pleasure, which felt right and good. Natural even.

I wasn't sure how long it was before the hazy lines of his profile blurred into the fog of dreams, but I felt safe and warm in his presence; and hoped that would be enough of a foundation on which to construct a life together.

Chapter Twenty-Three

April 1886

"You mustn't strain yourself, sweetling." Adolphe rushed into my suite of rooms, where he saw me packing a few items in a case. I was enormously pregnant with our first child, though I found my impending motherhood was less arduous than poor Laure's experience had been. She was only a few months away from the arrival of her second child, and her travails were no less with this child than with her first.

"I'm not, Adolphe. I can lift a hairbrush and a novel," I replied, trying not to sound more cross than I felt. I *was* exhausted, as any mother would be within weeks of delivering her first child, but the constant coddling from Adolphe—and Papa as well—only added to my fatigue. I tried to explain to them that whiling away the day in a chaise longue with a book, as enticing as it might sound, would leave me weak when my time arrived.

I'd read every tome on the subject of childbirth that I'd been able to procure, not wanting to leave everything to the explanations of gossipy old midwives, harried doctors who had no time for the questions of young mothers, or Tante Marie's blushed explanations. And bothering dearest Laure with my queries seemed cruel when she was facing it again so soon and with little Margueritte's health so perilous.

"I really don't think you should be going," Adolphe insisted. "What if something should happen?"

"I'll be in the next arrondissement over," I replied. "And the baby isn't due for several weeks. If I feel the slightest twinge that the child has decided to make an early arrival, I'll have the carriage bring me home. And if things inexplicably turn dire, the hospital is closer to Laure's home than ours."

I shoved a few more small items in my bag. I wouldn't need much as I was only planning to spend a couple of nights, but Laure's pleas for me to join her had been impossible to resist. Given my condition, she wouldn't have asked if it weren't vital.

"I don't see why the three of them can't come here. There's ample room," Adolphe pointed out. "And you know your father would insist on the best possible care for the little one. And Laure too, when the time comes."

"Margueritte is too frail to be moved." I looked up from the contents of my valise and met his gaze. "And Laure needs me. I cannot refuse her."

Adolphe pinched the bridge of his nose and exhaled in exasperation. "I don't see why—"

"No, you don't," I retorted, more harshly than was necessary. "Who else would sit with her? Her mother-in-law is unwell and I'm all she has in the way of a mother. Valentine is too young and inexperienced to help in the way she needs."

"Claire, I know you fancy yourself the Queen Mother around here, but it's high time you looked after the welfare of your own child. Rushing to all corners of the city in your state is the opposite of prudent."

I set the valise down with a *thump* on my vanity. "Fancy myself?"

I folded my arms across my chest. "So the love and care I've given my siblings is somehow a child's game?"

"You know that's not what I mean."

"Do I?"

"I just think our child should take precedence over rushing off to hold your sister's hand." Adolphe's voice grew smaller.

"After all this time, you still don't understand, do you?" I rarely showed my temper to Adolphe, knowing it usually served no purpose, but the discomfort of my pregnancy and Margueritte's fragile state had frayed my last nerve. "Laure *has* no other mother but me. On my day of judgment, how could I face God—or more important, my mother—if I did not go to her side today?"

"And who is there to hold yours? You spread yourself thin rushing to Laure's side. Preparing Valentine for her entrée into society. Coddling Bébert. Cleaning up Édouard's messes. None of them do a thing for you in return."

I felt the heat rise in my face but tried to force myself to calm for the sake of the baby. "You think that because I don't have a mother to support me, that Laure should be denied that comfort when I can so easily provide it?"

"I'm not saying that precisely—"

I slammed a book loudly on my bedside table. "Oh, I think you are saying that almost word for word. Since when do children worry about repaying their parents?" I placed a hand to my stomach. "By the time this little one makes his or her appearance, I hope you'll realize the constant practice of parenthood is giving without expectation."

"I just thought by the time you were with child, you'd shift your priorities." He crossed his arms. "I understand that Bébert needs some looking after, and Valentine will need your guidance, but shouldn't Laure and Édouard be managing themselves by now?"

"And I thought you understood that by marrying me and moving into this house that I would be managing two households under one roof. And just because Laure is grown and married doesn't mean my obligation to her has ended. If this child is a girl, would you have me indifferent to her transition to motherhood and the fate of our grandchildren?"

"Of course not, but—"

"But nothing. Margueritte is my niece and granddaughter both. She needs me, as does Laure. I will not brook any further conversation on the topic now or ever again. I am not a child and have sense enough to know my own limits. And I'll thank you not to enter my rooms again without invitation."

Blinking, he stepped back out into the hallway, and I heard the sound of his footfall leading off to the direction of the room he'd claimed as his study.

All the better. Get your mind on something other than me. Adolphe had taken to working from his study at home in the last several weeks, rather than going into the office with Papa. He said it was because his work on the proposal for the tower for the world's fair, which was becoming a pet project of his and Papa's, needed his undivided attention. He claimed the quiet of the house was more conducive to his work than the lively bustle of the office, but I knew it was because he wanted to keep an eye on me and to be on hand when my travails began.

Which was all well enough. He was acting out of kindness and concern, which I ought to have appreciated more than I did in that moment, but his constant hovering was driving me mad. He cared for me and was anxious to see me safely delivered of our first child, but the tension he caused by his incessant worrying was only making the ordeal more arduous and unpleasant than it needed to be. I set down the valise I'd been filling with a few necessities and sat heavily in my plush chair, forcing in deep breaths. The baby deserved a calm mother, and I was determined that was what the little one would have.

The child was not small. I had precious little lap left when I sat upright and was just as eager as Adolphe to see the baby born and to reclaim my body for myself again. I wasn't as eager to relive this experience as Laure had seemed to be, though I knew persuading Adolphe to wait some time for any subsequent children would be difficult.

Once I felt less agitated, I stood and gathered my things and descended to where the carriage was already waiting to drive me to Laure's. I felt the tension ease in my shoulders as we left the rue de Prony, but I felt the unsettling fear in my gut as we continued to Laure and Maurice's little town house.

I was shown in by a maid, who accepted my valise with a curtsy, and waddled my way up the stairs until I found Margueritte's bedroom. Laure was in a chair, holding her daughter's hand, looking white as a sheet when she should have been the picture of health and radiance with her upcoming arrival.

"Thank God you've come," she said, not looking up from Margueritte's face.

"What do the doctors say?" Papa had sent over one of the best physicians in town to examine the baby that very morning, and I was clinging to the hope he'd found some room for optimism.

She shook her head, and though she fought valiantly to restrain her tears in front of Margueritte, a high-pitched squeak escaped her pressed lips, and her shoulders began to shake. "He says there's nothing to be done. Some children are born with a weak constitution and simply waste away, and this is to be Margueritte's fate as well."

I crossed over to her and wrapped her in my arms in such a way she didn't have to release Margueritte's hand. The darling girl looked as fragile as a china doll against the white bedsheets. Though she was a year in age, she weighed the same as a healthy infant of eight or nine months. Though she was born when expected, she had been unusually small at birth and had been reluctant to suckle at her mother's bosom or, later, that of her wet nurse. She didn't develop as other babies seemed to, grabbing their *maman*'s finger, making eye contact, and offering gummy smiles. She was a calm, sweet baby—but somehow too calm to be a comfort to any of us.

Babies were meant to wail and fuss, and our little Margueritte did none of those things.

I pulled a chair to the opposite side of Margueritte's bed and held her free hand. "I was so pleased to name her for Maman," Laure said, brushing a tendril of downy hair from Margueritte's forehead.

I pushed past the lump in my throat to find my words. "She would have been her first grandchild, and I knew she'd have been tickled at the honor, especially since you changed the spelling to make it her own."

"She would have been," Laure agreed. "She rarely thought of herself but was thrilled when *we* did."

"Perhaps . . ." I drew in a breath, giving myself a moment to gather my words. "Perhaps Maman decided this little one is needed more in heaven than here with us."

As much as I'd tried to ignore the truth over the past weeks, Margueritte's fate seemed inevitable. All Laure could do was sob, as silently as she could, and hold her daughter's hand. We sat in vigil for hours. How many, I couldn't be sure. Maurice stopped in once but couldn't bear the sight of his firstborn fading away. He sent up trays of food. I ate so that Maurice wouldn't have cause to send a report to Adolphe that I was being cavalier with my health and was able to persuade Laure to do the same for the sake of her unborn child.

The sun was setting when Margueritte's breath grew shallow and eventually stopped. When the moment happened, Laure had already wrung herself dry of tears. She sat, pale and motionless, unable to look away from her beautiful daughter's face.

I rang the bellpull so the staff could be alerted and Maurice summoned to say his goodbyes. When he arrived, he rushed to Laure and held her in his arms. I left the room so the family could be alone one last time but rested with my back against the wall in the hallway, ready in case I was needed.

Some time later, Maurice emerged from Margueritte's room. "Laure won't be equal to company, even yours, for a while. I'll have your carriage brought round."

I nodded and glanced to the door, behind which Laure sat in her darkest moment. I longed to hold her in my arms. But there was nothing I could do for her. The carriage ride home seemed, by turns, interminable and far too short. I wasn't ready to face Papa and Adolphe with the terrible news, but it was better than leaving the task to Laure.

Dinner was being served as I arrived, and though I had no appetite, I joined Papa, Adolphe, and Valentine. Seeing my face, they guessed the awful truth.

"My first grandchild," Papa lamented. "It doesn't seem quite just."

"It isn't, but as you've told us all countless times, fairness is only a fable we tell to console ourselves."

He took a sip from his wineglass. "I rarely loathe being right. . . ."

"At least she'll have the new baby to cheer her up," Valentine suggested from her end of the table. I offered her a weak smile. It had to be a comfort to be young enough not to fully understand.

"We can hope it will soften the blow," I said. And there was no doubt in my mind that the arrival of the new baby would, at the very least, provide the grieving parents with a distraction from their sorrows, though it would rob them of the time they needed to grieve. But their love for this child would never take the place of the one they'd lost.

And because they had known loss, their love for this new child would be forever bittersweet. Tainted with worry that was born from experience. I wished more than anything I could make it all well for Laure and Maurice but was helpless to do anything about it.

Later that evening, Adolphe followed me up the stairs as he'd taken to doing each night, I suspected to safeguard against a fall.

"Would you like company?" he asked when we reached the door to my rooms. He'd had no expectation of intimacy over the past few months but had occasionally joined me for the simple pleasure of sharing a bed. I was tempted to agree. To cry on his shoulder and mourn for little Margueritte. To ache for Laure and Maurice. But I couldn't find it within myself to nod.

"No, but thank you," I was able to mumble, and escaped to my private sanctuary. The clothes I wore at this stage of my pregnancy didn't require Pauline's assistance, so I was able to slip into a nightdress in quiet. I poured myself into bed and felt the exhaustion in every bone I possessed. I could hear Adolphe preparing for bed on the opposite side of the bedroom wall, and knew I'd hurt him, first this morning and again just now.

I ached for the release of sleep, but it proved elusive. Some time later, the ache I'd been feeling began to sear like a firebrand across my lower back, and it had me clutching at my bed coverings. I buried my face in my pillow to muffle my cries. I'd read that the body often experienced phantom labor pains as it prepared for birth, and prayed this was the case now. I'd counted on two weeks or more to prepare myself for the child, but the pains became more insistent as the night grew on. At last, I gave in to the reality that my child would be born so soon after little Margueritte had been taken from us, and yanked the bellpull in defeat.

Chapter Twenty-Four

The baby was born as the sun rose with a gentle midwife in attendance. Laure had originally planned to be with me for support, as I had been for her, but she wasn't equal to leaving the house. I didn't think it right for Valentine to experience such things at her age, so she slept undisturbed as I labored. Adolphe and Papa paced in the drawing room below stairs, smoking cigars and nursing brandies as sunlight timidly spilled in through the easterly windows. No doubt Adolphe was worried, but I was grateful convention barred him from the bedroom during my travails. It was better he expend his nervous energy with Papa instead of irritating me with it while I was in need of tranquility.

As I understood things, the baby arrived quickly for a firstborn, though the midwife suspected I'd been in labor for quite some time and dismissed the contractions as the back pain that was ever present in the final months of pregnancy. Likely I was too absorbed in Laure's anguish to pay my paltry physical discomfort any mind. The midwife washed the baby while Pauline and the maids attended to me and the horrifying state of my bedsheets. As minutes elapsed, a sense of relief lapped stronger and stronger as my body recognized that the ordeal was behind me. Clean sheets and a fresh nightdress felt like the height of luxury.

As the midwife handed me the swaddled baby and sent a maid to inform the men that all was well, I took advantage of the few moments alone with my baby before the others swooped in.

A boy. Round, pudgy, and the picture of health.

The difference between him and little Margueritte was astounding. Where she had been alabaster and solemn as a newborn, he was rosy-pink and capable of lustful cries that could wake the dead. Though he was only minutes old, his eyes were open and he seemed to be scanning the room and taking in his new surroundings. He seemed particularly taken with the oil lamp beside my bed.

He clung to my finger with an incredible strength and made cooing sounds as he calmed from the excitement of his own birth and slowly began to make sense of the world. I looked at him in wonder. Like all mothers, I thought he was the most beautiful, most perfect baby that had ever been born. But I was also filled with heartache and grief for the cousin he'd never meet and who should have been just as robust and healthy as he was. I grieved for Laure, whose entrée into motherhood should not have been plagued with a year of fear and worry only to end in heartbreak.

I was glad that the little one had chosen to make his arrival after midnight, so that the day of his birth wouldn't be forever entwined with the anniversary of Margueritte's passing. Soon I heard the hurried *clack-clack-clack* of leather soles up the marble stairs, then muffled by the hall carpets. The midwife opened to the firm rapping at the door.

Adolphe rushed in, Papa a couple of respectful paces behind him.

I held him up for the men to see. "A boy. A handsome addition to the Salles family, I should think."

"And the Eiffel family as well," Papa interjected.

"Indeed," Adolphe said, accepting the baby into his arms and admiring his son. "As hale and hearty a babe as I've ever seen."

He looked down to where I rested in the bed, worry furrowing in his brow, though not as deeply as it had been in the last months of my pregnancy. "And you, my darling? You're well?"

"I can't say that bringing your son into the world was the most enjoyable experience of my life, and I'll be happy to stay in this bed a few days, but I'm better than I feared I'd be." I'd learned he would be more assured by the truth than an exaggeration of my well-being.

"Madame Salles acquitted herself marvelously," the midwife interjected. She'd been so soft-spoken during my labors that the sound of her voice now was almost jarring. "I've rarely seen a new mother with such sangfroid despite the fact that the lad is not a small baby."

"Our Claire is made of stern stuff," Papa said, his chest actually puffing with pride.

"I've been trying to convince your son-in-law of this for months now," I said to Papa with mock indignation. "Perhaps now he'll believe me."

"The first babe is always the most worrisome," the midwife agreed. "But I think Monsieur Salles can rest safely now."

"Thank heaven." Adolphe's eyes never left his son's face. "I don't think I've had more than a two-hour stretch of sleep in the last three months."

"Well, you and the little one can share sleep habits for a few days. Eighteen hours a day ought to do it," I chided.

Adolphe smiled. "What shall we call him?"

We hadn't discussed names before now, thinking it was bad luck to speak of such things before our proverbial chick was hatched. I'd thought of a dozen family names: Jean for his paternal grandfather, François for my own grandfather. There had been several Alexandres and Renés, but as I looked at the miraculous little man, I knew he deserved a moniker of his own that wasn't too steeped in family history. "What do you say to Robert?"

Adolphe looked down at the bundle in his arms. "I think it suits him marvelously. Robert Salles." The words were tinged with pride on his tongue.

"A fine name," Papa agreed, finally angling to hold his grandson in his arms. The pride he felt was as clearly etched on his face as his laugh lines. "We'll get you a drafting table and some pencils as soon as you're big enough to hold them."

I chuckled. "A fine way to ensure the boy never becomes an engineer, Papa."

"Perhaps. But whatever path he chooses in life, I'm sure he'll make a success of it. He has a determined face, and determination is half the battle."

"I do believe that determination you see means that young Master Robert is hungry," the midwife suggested. "Have you engaged a wet nurse?"

"No, I shall feed him myself. I've read that it's best for the mother to do it herself if she's able." I'd also read horrific accounts of what happened to the infants of wet nurses who couldn't supply enough milk for her charge and her own babe. Not to mention bloodcurdling stories of wet nurses who were cruel to their charges, sometimes in retribution for the loss of their babies when they couldn't nourish both.

"Cherub, you'd do better to bring on a hardy farm girl to feed the boy. It's not a job for a lady."

"Two of Queen Victoria's daughters nursed their own babies and they're far grander ladies than I ever aspire to be."

"Claire—" Papa began.

"I am sure Claire is wise enough to know when the endeavor is beyond her," Adolphe interjected. "And I'm certain she'll enlist help at the first sign that little Robert is not getting what he needs." Adolphe's words were addressed to Papa, but he was looking at me. It was him gently making a condition of his support of this endeavor. A reasonable one I couldn't fault.

"Naturally. His welfare is my main concern. If I find the enterprise isn't serving him or is too taxing for me, I'll have Pauline engage a wet nurse within the hour. I've already instructed her to have candidates in mind that she can contact at a moment's notice."

Papa looked mollified, knowing I wouldn't take chances with the baby's health, nor was I foolish enough to run myself into exhaustion. I'd learned in the past nine years that one cannot give to others from an empty basket. I was entering motherhood with that lesson learned, which was, to my mind, a great advantage that many new mothers could not boast.

"Then perhaps it is best we leave mother and child to have some privacy." The midwife gestured meaningfully toward the door.

Papa passed the baby to me, and he and the midwife turned to leave. Adolphe lingered just a moment to stroke the downy tufts of brown hair on Robert's head.

"Thank you for trusting me."

Adolphe swooped to kiss my brow. "I endeavor to, always. Sometimes my worry just gets the better of me."

With another stroke of Robert's head and a brush of his finger against my cheek, he left me in peace to nurse our baby. Adolphe *did* try to treat my opinions with consideration, while other men barked orders and expected to be obeyed without question. I was lucky in that and knew it full well. I knew he'd been acting from concern, and that future children might not elicit the same worry that the first had done. I was sure that Laure's troubles had exacerbated it all, and prayed she was coping with her grief as well as she could. As little Robert suckled contentedly, I hoped that the little one Laure was expecting would be just as robust as my own. She deserved to know motherhood as it should be—not totally free from worry, for such a thing was impossible, but not defined by it either.

Robert, finally fed and sleeping, was placed in his bassinet the midwife had wheeled to my bedside, which was where he would sleep until I thought him old enough for the nursery and to be in the charge of a nanny. Six months, perhaps? A year? That decision could be made later. For now I could enjoy every moment where he could be at my side, our bond uninterrupted.

I gingerly leaned over to my bedside table to retrieve some writing paper. I would have to send word to Laure that the baby had been born but could not imagine finding the words to break the news gently enough. How would her heart not rend in two to know that just as her precious girl was leaving the world my son had made his way into it, and was the very picture of health besides? But if I waited to tell her of her nephew's arrival, it would make the blow even worse.

I tried a half dozen times to write the note, searching the deep, dark crevasses of my vocabulary to find the words that could convey the message in the right way. One draft, so laden with condolences, barely mentioned little Robert's birth at all. The next was as terse as the newspaper announcement we'd need to make in a few days' time. As I tried, and failed, to find a middle ground, I finally gave in to the wave of exhaustion that had been threatening to lap over me and pull me out to sea.

When I woke, I found my failed attempts at correspondence had all been for naught. While I had sought to send word in the most delicate way possible, Papa had sent his carriage over midmorning with a simple missive that her presence would be welcomed at my bedside.

Laure was there, looking wan in a black dress, but gazing down lovingly at Robert as she rocked his bassinet with her foot. "Oh, I hope I didn't wake you," she said, noticing my stirring.

"No, no." I sat up and reached for her hand. "The baby will be needing to eat again soon. It's better I'm awake."

"He's magnificent, Claire. The perfect blend of you and Adolphe. You're well enough?" She stared at the baby lovingly. Desperately, as if he were the first food she'd come across after weeks of starvation.

"Fine, fine," I said, though the exhilaration of childbirth was beginning to fade, and as I transitioned more fully from sleeping to wakefulness, I realized how much trauma the birth had inflicted upon my body. There hardly seemed to be a muscle that hadn't been pushed to exhaustion in bringing Robert into the world. "You didn't have to come, Laure. I know you have your own burdens to bear at home."

"Margueritte doesn't need me now. She's where nothing can harm her any longer. I'm trying to take some comfort in that. But if you don't want me here, I understand. Some women don't want their babies around mothers who have lost a child. Bad luck and what have you. I can leave if you wish."

Her face fell as she pondered the possibility that I might not want her near the baby—or me—out of some foolish superstition or fear.

"Stuff and nonsense. I simply thought it might be too painful for you." I reached for her hand. "I only thought of you."

She brightened a bit, and I showed her the drafts of the message I'd tried to send to her before I'd fallen asleep. For the first time in ages, I saw a glimmer of laughter in her eyes as she scanned the overwrought message of condolence followed by the terse one that came after.

"Papa merely said, 'Claire is safely delivered of a healthy boy. Come when you can to see them both,'" Laure said with an affectionate roll of her eyes in response to Papa's economy of words. At times it was as if every message he scribbled down was as costly as a telegraph and he was determined to trim every unnecessary letter from the note he was drafting.

"Well, it was far more effective than my failed letters. And it got you here. But I don't want you to exert yourself too much."

"Claire, you've been by my side through everything these past years. I only wish I'd been here to hold your hand as your gorgeous boy was born as you were there for me when Margueritte was born. It's only right that I should do my part for you as you have done for us."

"I know you would have been if circumstances had been different. And I'll be there for you when your time comes again. You have my word."

Laure set the letters that she was still holding down on my bedside table and peered into the bassinet. "He truly is a marvelous little chap. May I hold him?"

"Of course. You know how it's done better than I do."

She picked up the swaddled infant, rosy and plump, not quite roused from his sleep. The look on Laure's face was delight as she held him close and felt the warmth of him against her bosom. If he could help her forget her pain for just a few moments, he was already as dutiful a nephew as one could hope for at just a few hours old.

"In moments like these, I'm glad for one of Maman's best lessons." Laure reached for my hand while she held Robert close with the other.

"Which one is that, dearest?"

"That it is a testament of true character when one can grieve for one's own losses while being delighted for the blessings bestowed upon another," Laure said, squeezing my hand.

"That sounds so very much like her. But I think the same logic can be applied to greater effect in reverse. I can still hold grief in my heart for you and dear Margueritte, while appreciating my own joy just the same. I think we must do our best to make room for both."

Laure handed me the baby, who was beginning to fuss for another meal, and kissed my forehead. "She would be so proud of you."

"I've only tried to finish the work she started." I lifted Robert to my breast.

"No, Claire. You've gone far beyond what she or anyone else would have asked of you. And I know she's watching down and knows that you will be an even better mother to this little one than even she was to us."

I cast my eyes downward, unable to meet her gaze. "That isn't true, Laure."

"It is, but I don't mean it as a slight to her. She was too sickly to raise us as she would have wanted. She would tell you the same right now if she were here with us. I just think it's high time someone told you that you've not just filled Maman's shoes, you walked, ran, and danced a flawless waltz in them for years. You deserve to hear that."

And then, for the first time since we were children, she crawled into bed next to me and wrapped an arm around me and Robert alike and promptly fell asleep, brought to exhaustion by her grief. I placed a kiss on her forehead and hoped that a few hours' rest would help her face the mountain of grief she had before her. The grief others would expect her to push past once the new baby was born. The grief she would carry more than any other and from which she would never truly be unburdened.

Chapter Twenty-Five

June 12, 1886

At the city hall, champagne flowed like the Seine as Papa received word that the plans for the tower had been accepted. I'd been summoned to be on hand when the announcement was made, and the cases of Moët & Chandon I'd been charged with seeing chilled in the back rooms betrayed that Papa knew full well the Compagnie Eiffel would win the coveted contract. He'd been working every connection he had for months to jockey his reputation and the company's resources to the front of the competition. I'd learned in the past nine years, or perhaps more accurately, since I'd been able to parse intelligible speech, that if Papa set his mind to something, there was little that could deter him.

As maddening as that habit could be, that tenacity was the reason a three-hundred-meter tower would be built in the very beating heart of Paris.

The gathering for the announcement, which had the air of a solemn proclamation at first, quickly transformed into an impromptu cocktail party. With ample champagne and not a scrap of food to dampen its effects.

"Papa, did you think about more—substantial—refreshment beyond champagne?" I spoke in a low hiss that I tried to hide with a demure smile.

"No, Cherub. I hadn't spared it a thought. Ought I have done?"

"Well, Papa, it all depends on if you planned on setting every one of your closest professional contacts drunk this afternoon and finding them scattered throughout the dance halls of Paris without a clue how they got there come morning." I held a less-than-charitable thought for Édouard for the briefest of moments before looking expectantly at Papa.

He looked suitably horrified, which gratified me in no small measure. Of course, I spoke in hyperbole. There were any number of the guests present who would have the sense to indulge in moderation. But for every one of those sensible persons, there were likely two who would happily drink themselves to the point of public humiliation and influence the others to drink more than they might have done otherwise. And no matter who it was, Papa would share in the embarrassment.

I sighed for dramatic effect, hoping Papa and Adolphe realized the position they'd put us in. "I'll manage something. Whiskey may be stronger stuff, but I'd swear on Maman's grave there is nothing to make a person act like three kinds of fool faster than champagne on an empty stomach."

Papa nodded, though I saw his ebullience become tempered when he returned to the crowd. He took only occasional sips from the flute, perhaps helping to subtly convey a message of restraint.

So, as none of us wished the assembly to spend the rest of the afternoon with their heads lost in a cloud of foamy champagne bubbles, I begged our chauffeur Fabrice to arrange for the restaurant just a few doors down to prepare as many canapés as they could and as quickly as possible. I gave him orders to give Papa's name to the proprietor and offer them an ungodly sum of money for the task if they could round up a server—or better still, four of them—as there were hours yet until the dinner service, and even the most devoted conversationalists would have finished their luncheon by now. Any Parisian restaurant worth the cost of laundering its table linens would be able to toss together a few platters, even on a moment's notice. And within twenty minutes, Fabrice returned with generous platters and several eager waiters. I'd line their pockets at the end of the evening and thank the heavens for them when I offered up my prayers that night.

With the amuse-bouches now in circulation to help moderate the effects of the champagne, I could breathe freely. Papa and Adolphe, too, seemed to have lowered their shoulders by a number of inches, now able to give their conversations the attention they deserved and to soak in the admiration they'd worked so hard for. The admiration they, undeniably, craved.

Stopping every few feet to speak to various colleagues and city functionaries to whom I'd been introduced over the course of the past decade or so, I crossed the room to claim a view of the plans that Papa and Adolphe's men Koechlin and Nouguier had designed for the tower and that Papa and a host of others had collaborated to perfect over the course of the past months. It was rare when Papa was so personally invested in a project that the process had come to this point without me seeing the plans.

Certainly, my value to Papa's endeavors didn't lay in design, but he had always made a point of including me and asking my opinion on a topic, even when he knew full well that in certain cases it wasn't appropriate for me to have an opinion. But to not be included at all—to see the final designs along with the rest of the Parisian elite, especially on a project of such a grand scale—pained me in a way I was too proud to admit to anyone. Including myself. I tried to remember that these designs had been shrouded in a veil of secrecy more than any other project on which the Compagnie Eiffel had previously worked.

That isn't to say I hadn't seen some preliminary sketches and hadn't heard so much about the thing that I wasn't equipped to draw a reasonable likeness from those details alone, but it was the first time seeing polished drawings of the tower as it would be built. The way Papa envisioned it. My eyes scanned over the graceful arches and the intricate web of iron that would dominate the face of Paris for the next twenty years.

"What do you think?" Adolphe sidled up next to me on my right and offered me a flute of champagne as I took in the months of hard work the plans represented. I'd been so concerned with people getting tipsy that I hadn't thought to take a glass for myself. Papa joined to my left, equally keen to hear my response.

I paused a moment longer, considering the juxtaposition of the arches and rigid lines, trying to envision the impact of the structure on the city's skyline. There were elements of it, certainly with the supports and beams, that called to mind any number of his famous bridge projects. But at the same time, the design of the tower evoked something more personal, unique, than what I'd seen in any of his previous work.

I stumbled searching for words. "It reminds me of Maman's lace." The spindly web of the tower's support beam, if made from thread instead of iron, would have been a remarkable replica of the patterns Maman crocheted and knitted for our collars. Adolphe cocked his head, examining the drawing carefully. Perhaps he was unable to see it as I did. But Papa squeezed my elbow, shot me a wink that was almost mournful. I'd hit the mark precisely. I realized he was hoping to surprise me with this tribute. He brushed a kiss against my cheek and left my side to mingle in the crowd and enjoy his triumph.

His meaning was clear: *I'm glad you see it too.*

It was a subtle tribute to Maman, not meant for the larger public. But he and I would know. Laure, Édouard, Valentine, and I would know. We'd be able to explain it to Bébert, whose memories of Maman were as faded around the edges as old photographs. We would know that Papa had found a way to have one small piece of her live on. It was a testament to how much he had loved her, and how he loved her still despite the passing of time.

I, very discreetly, put my hand in Adolphe's for just a moment. He lingered, giving me a gentle squeeze, brief enough no one would notice. I didn't know if we would ever share the same level of affection that Papa and Maman had for each other, but I found myself unconcerned with such sentimental, overly romantic thoughts. I'd never doubted he would be devoted to the family and the company, but there was more to the way he performed his duties to us all than a sense of obligation. Papa depended on his advice, which was invariably sound. He was a kind and generous sibling to the younger children. I hoped he would continue to be a stabilizing influence for Édouard, but I feared *that* was a hopeless case. He adored little Robert and was convinced he was the most brilliant baby to ever bless the city of Paris with his presence. I was certain Adolphe hoped we'd be in the family way again before long, though I was more hesitant about supplanting Robert as the baby of the family. I wanted just a bit longer to dote on him as my only child before splitting my heart in two to love another child as much as I loved my darling boy.

Yes, Adolphe was a model father. Not falling short even when compared to my own. And I could never say that my husband was anything but attentive and kind in all things when it came to me as well.

Adolphe released my hand, though it seemed tinged with a bit of regret that he couldn't prolong the subtle embrace. But we were in public, and while some people might be able to get away with overt displays of affection in public, our lot could not.

He was soon pulled away by some important dignitary I'd never met, and Papa was similarly engaged on the opposite end of the room. I found myself at a loss. The waiters bustled about with efficiency, the crowd seemed happy enough to congratulate Papa and Adolphe for their successes. There was nothing for me to do, and it felt intolerable. I longed to call for the carriage and return home to little Robert. It would be time for his afternoon walk when I got home, which sounded like heaven itself on a glorious June day. But I had to remain. I had to stand in solidarity with my husband and father, no matter what else I might wish to do.

I screwed a smile to my face, hoping it was secure as a rivet in the tower, and circulated about the room. I made small talk and spoke with breathy admiration for the design that had won Papa and the company the contract. At least I could speak honestly, for I thought the design was a brilliant one. The tower would be Papa's triumph. His chance to make his mark on the cityscape of Paris, even if the contract stipulated it was only to stand as a temporary exhibit for twenty years. But that was still a great deal of time, and there would be photos and paintings and the like to serve as a memory when, in the early days of the twentieth century, it would be torn down. In that way, the impermanence of the tower was quite different from Papa's previous projects that were meant to stand potentially for a century or more. But Papa, Adolphe, and the Compagnie Eiffel would soon have their moment of great victory.

And I wondered when, if ever, I might know mine.

Chapter Twenty-Six

December 23, 1886

"Damn it all and blast it to hell," Papa said by way of greeting as he entered the drawing room. For the past month, his greetings had become increasingly curt, but had, until today, stopped just short of profanity. Adolphe followed him in, looking pale and drawn, and not just because of the especially frigid winter we were having.

"Nothing from the city?" The question didn't need to be asked. I could see the answer carved into their faces, as immutable as if they'd been cast in stone by a master carver. I hoped that eventually news would come that would give their faces cause to break free from their perpetual scowls.

"Not a word," Adolphe said in more measured tones than Papa was capable of in recent days. "More stalling, more objections. To the tower, to the location—to the entire project."

It was the last workday before they shuttered for Christmas, and precious little could be done before the new year. The tower was stalled and was likely to remain so for the foreseeable future. The city had yet to present Papa with a contract, and without it, nothing could be done.

Though it shouldn't have lessened the thrill of Papa's victory, the inevitable delays and backlash against the tower since the fall had served to dampen spirits that holiday season. Though the drawing room was festooned with greens and garlands, the spirit in the room that evening was anything but merry. Though the timing of the complaints against the tower were not a surprise to me or anyone else in the company who was paying attention.

With the announcement of the tower having been so close to the grand exodus from the city, away from the summer heat, the previous August, we'd had a reprieve from the naysayers who hadn't time to lodge any motions against the project before the annual retreat to the countryside or the mountains. During those quiet weeks, Papa's lawyers planned their defense against the complaints that would come rolling in as soon as the city repopulated in September. Even projects with obvious, tangible benefits to the common man, such as a railway station, met with some measure of consternation from the people. There was no way that something that, at least to many eyes, appeared only ornamental would pass through its construction without serious opposition.

The complaints of one Comtesse de Poix and her well-heeled neighbors argued that the fine neighborhoods near the Champs de Mars where she lived would be barricaded for months during construction, and then by tourist traffic and the tower itself for another twenty years. That it would impede her ability to take her daily promenade in the charming areas she preferred were the sort of arguments Papa and the rest had expected. They sought to convince the people that, while some blockages could not be avoided, the disruptions to their daily lives would not be permanent. He would not only have to promise that safety would be of central importance to the project; he would personally have to see that it was. Thankfully the project was just a few kilometers to the rue de Prony and he could be on-site in the Champs de Mars or in the atelier in Levallois as often as he was needed—and could go between the two even several times in a day if the situation called for it.

I shook my head in sympathy. It was true that a number of the concerns about the tower were ridiculous—the infamous one about changing the weather patterns in Paris had become a household joke. Other concerns were harder to argue against. There was no denying it would be loud, dirty, and disruptive while it was being built. Once completed, it would bring throngs of visitors to the neighborhoods nearby. It might be a blessing for the cafés and shops, but a curse for the residents. The aesthetic argument was too subjective to counter, but it seemed to be the argument that was having the most sway.

"This great city is a bunch of cowards," Papa grunted into his glass of Armagnac. "The building should have commenced months ago. If we don't break ground as soon as the new year is rung in, there is no way we shall finish in time for the exposition. It will be a debacle if we don't."

"What are the things holding it back?"

"Shortsighted fools," Adolphe quipped.

I shot him a testy look. "That's usually the case, but pointing that out isn't particularly helpful. What specifically is holding the city back from making a contract?"

"Money," Papa answered succinctly. "They're worried about the liability if the *comtesse* or one of her cronies sues for damages if a windowpane gets broken or an ankle is twisted. They're also worried that the project will go over budget and will end up costing them more than the value it will bring into the city."

"So we sign a pledge to hold the city harmless in the event of any damages or injury caused by the tower. It wouldn't be the first time a company has agreed to such things. It rarely comes to much value. As you say, a broken windowpane, a shopkeeper's cart left too close to the site. We already know we must be extraordinarily careful in all things concerning this project. I have confidence enough in the Compagnie Eiffel to think we can complete the project with no damage to private property whatsoever."

Adolphe and Papa looked favorably enough on this pronouncement. They were men of safety, after all. "But what about the errant fool who wanders into the site and breaks his fool head?"

"Guards and signs everywhere. We can ask the lawyers what measures must be taken to ensure the company isn't held liable if someone trespasses. Of course the workers will have to be meticulous, but we knew this from the start."

"This doesn't answer the larger question, the one that I am certain is the driving force behind why no contract has crossed my desk: the city is only willing to pay one and a half million francs. Not even a quarter of what the tower was likely to cost."

"So we raise funds. For every cantankerous poet who doesn't want to see the tower built, there are dozens of others who know what this tower could mean for Paris. We ask them to invest."

"And if we cannot raise the funds?" Adolphe asked. He was deep in thought, forefinger to his upper lip and pacing as he often did when solving one of the many riddles that crossed his desk in a day. He wasn't being churlish with his question; he legitimately wanted to know what I envisioned our prospects might be.

"We could front the money ourselves if we had to." I kept a close enough eye on Papa's books to know he could make a tremendous dent in the cost of the tower if he had to. It wasn't an ideal situation, to be sure, but it was better than scrapping the project altogether. Papa would never recover from such a humiliation.

"That is an incredible risk." Adolphe's eyes went wide at my suggestion. "A tremendous sum we would stand to lose."

"We would have to hedge our bets, so to speak. Insist on the lion's share of the income from the tower for a period of time. But reserving a percentage for charitable acts. It will make the company look magnanimous."

"Shrewd." Adolphe crossed his arms over his chest as he did when lost in thought. "It makes the risk a bit more palatable."

"Unless the whole damned thing flops," Papa said.

Adolphe and I both looked to him. It was the first time in my life I ever heard Papa voice doubt about a project. Of course he debated about the best supplier for iron beams and wire rope or wondered if there were ways to improve upon the efficacy and elegance of a truss design. That was the hallmark of a wise man who continually wanted to improve upon his craft. But never once had he considered that one of his projects would—or even could—be a failure.

But this tower was different from all of them. Even the great statue that had gone up in New York was different: it was out on an island where no one's daily lives would be disrupted. Even in a catastrophic failure, the thing would fall out to sea, and it wouldn't take down a city block's worth of expensive townhomes with it.

I looked him straight in the eye. "Papa, the Compagnie Eiffel does not fail. It never has accepted failure, and it won't start today. Not when so much is at stake."

"You'll forgive me, but I hope that you're not speaking with false bravado." Papa refilled his glass and offered one to Adolphe and me as well. "Your pride in the company is admirable, but no institution, no matter how deftly run, is infallible."

"Of course not, but we can't dwell on the possibility of failure, or we're certain to do just that." I accepted the glass and stood by the mantel, idly running my finger along the ribbon laced in a garland I'd placed for the holiday that had gone unnoticed.

Papa rubbed his temples. "I began writing a letter last night. Telling the city that if they do not come forward with a contract in the first week of the new year that the Compagnie Eiffel will withdraw from the project altogether, leaving the expo without a centerpiece."

Adolphe and I froze in place, mouths agape. If Papa was issuing an ultimatum, he was prepared for them to turn him down. There would be any number of architects willing to design a showpiece for the expo. It might be less grand, given the time constraints the new designer would be under, but there was also every chance it would be cheaper, less disruptive to the daily life of the people in the Marais, and unequivocally less controversial.

If Papa offered to bow out of the project, the city would likely jump to accept a more modest proposal.

"You can't mean that, Papa."

"No. You've convinced me I have the means to fund the endeavor, risky though it might be." He crossed to the small secretary desk in the corner of the drawing room that he used for correspondence when he didn't feel like holing away in his library. He took a scrap of paper from one of the pigeonholes, tore it into quarters twice over, and tossed it in the bin. "I'll write them tonight and tell them of our new position. If that won't appease them, the contract will never materialize, but I'll know I've done everything in my power. We can just pray that we can complete the blasted thing in time or this will all be for naught."

I breathed a sigh of relief audible to all in the room to hear Papa talking like himself again. "Try to keep a positive outlook. Construction in winter is rife with weather delays and frustration anyway. You might not be losing that much time in the grand scheme of things."

"You're right, Cherub. We'll find a way. We always do." Papa kissed my cheek and left the majority of his second Armagnac untouched, which was a good sign that he was feeling optimistic enough not to need it.

ADOLPHE'S EYES WERE hollow with fatigue so I suggested retiring early. There would be a constant wave of activity over the next few days as we celebrated the holidays, and if my instincts were correct, they would be in up to their necks with the tower as soon as the holidays were over. As always, we stopped by the nursery on our way to our rooms to look in on little Robert.

I looked down at the sleeping babe. His brown curls framed his porcelain face, and I was daily convinced it was long since time that I passed along the nickname Papa had bestowed upon me to this little one, though it would be precious few years before he resented such a syrupy nursery nickname. He was the embodiment of all that was pure, beautiful, and innocent in this world; to my mind at least. I rubbed his plump cheek with the back of my forefinger and held a hand to my heart when he cooed a contented sigh of dreams. He'd left behind the mewling redness and curled-up body of a newborn, and his features were, day by day, becoming more like those of a toddler.

"It's a marvel we made such a beautiful little one," I breathed, barely a whisper.

"A miracle indeed," Adolphe agreed. It was the same refrain every night, but it never ceased to be true. And every time we made the exchange, I offered up a prayer for little Margueritte, who was too delicate for this world, and her hardy sister, Thérèse, who—blessedly—seemed determined to stay in it.

I could have stayed in the nursery for hours, but knew that our presence wasn't likely to help his sleep. We retreated into the hallway, and I paused, placing my hand on the door, clinging to the fleeting moments of his babyhood.

"I wouldn't countermand you in front of him, but I hope you're right to encourage your father so." Adolphe spoke in low tones as we left the nursery behind us. "For all your optimism, I can still envision a million scenarios where things could go poorly. Your father investing such a massive sum in the project terrifies me and I'm not ashamed to say it."

"The blow to the company would be substantial even if we stopped immediately. We stand to lose even more if we do *not* invest and save the project. By continuing as planned and giving the outward appearance of confidence we may be materially increasing our chances at victory. Don't you see?"

"I think your papa will have to learn what it is to live within his means if he invests and loses millions in this project. And it will impact all of us. Including little Robert's prospects." We stopped in front of my bedroom door.

"The boy is eight months old. I refuse to worry about whether we will be able to afford the finest schools and to surround him with the best society before he's even *in* leading strings let alone out of them. Even if Papa paid for the tower down to the last girder and rivet, we wouldn't be paupers."

"By God, I hope you're right, Claire. Sometimes you have more confidence in the company than either your father or I do."

"I don't have the luxury of choice. I have to be calm and rational at all times, or you and Papa will think me shrill and alarmist. Or worse, hysterical. If I didn't choose to consider the ways things could go right, I'd run mad. I'll leave the doomsaying to you and Papa since you are allowed to express your anger and frustration whenever you choose."

I made the gesture to Adolphe, opening the door wide enough that he could pass through if he desired, that he was welcome to enter my rooms if he wished. It was rare that I entered his, preferring to leave him a small corner of the house that was entirely his own. I had commandeered a study for myself, and in a way, I felt an ownership over the place that even Papa didn't feel, because it was I who had the running of it.

He accepted the wordless invitation, and I closed the door behind us. He turned to me and brushed a tendril of hair from my face. "Are we really such brutes?"

"Not intentionally, but yes. As soon as my voice becomes strident, you and Papa dismiss every word that comes from my mouth. If I were a man, you would call me a passionate defender of my cause. But as I am a woman, I am not afforded such grace."

"I truly am sorry, for the entirety of my sex." He pulled me into his arms and kissed me at the hollow of my neck as he liked to do. "It's a wonder women haven't risen up and stuck us all behind bars where we belong."

"You're less offensive than most. And Papa, too, when he isn't in one of his moods." And it was true. Papa was traditional in many of his views, but Adolphe had read some of the treatises of the American suffragists and found them compelling. It was more than most women could boast of their husbands.

"You do handle him marvelously. It's a delight to watch."

"I'm glad I meet with your approval in some respects." I nuzzled his neck playfully.

"Claire, you meet with my approval in a great many things. I hope you know that." He lowered his lips to mine, still gentle, even tentative after all this time. We fell into our comfortable pattern, and I curled up, sated in his arms. He fell into an easy sleep soon after, but it was in these dark moments that I was able to indulge in my worst fears.

What if the tower were a failure?

What if the company took a financial hit from which it could not recover?

What if Adolphe were right and I was foolish to goad Papa into pressing on past the point of no return?

I did all I could not to toss and turn and spoil Adolphe's sleep, but the visions of that future plagued me. I kept coming to the vision of a room, though none in this house, with papers strewn about every surface. I had a vision of Papa, his face ashen, proclaiming that his career was finished.

It was more vibrant than any nightmare I'd ever endured, though I never really drifted off to sleep. It was simply my mind running amok and rending my heart into shreds in the process. I forced myself, for the sake of tomorrow, to take even breaths, and eventually sleep washed over me. I would be no use to anyone if I indulged in these thoughts and emerged from my room in the morning, haggard and surly from lack of sleep.

For in the morning, I would have to don my mask of bravery in optimism, no matter how tightly it pinched.

Chapter Twenty-Seven

January 28, 1887

It was a bitter-cold January morning. The winter was one of the most frigid in my memory, but we would not be delayed any longer. Despite the bite in the air, the Compagnie Eiffel broke ground on the tower at the Champs de Mars with a modest crowd to commemorate the event. I stood by Adolphe's and Papa's side, bundled in layers of wool, warmed with not just pride but relief that the project was underway.

Papa looked out at the site, where not one but four massive foundations were being dug by scores of workers. The warmth of their breath as they toiled created an eerie fog that rose a few inches and dissipated into the morning air. In the first week of the new year, Papa had made his offer to the city. He would indemnify them from any damages caused by the construction of the tower to the surrounding area and would finance the rest of the project beyond the one and a half million francs the city had allotted for it. Five million francs he would have to raise from investors, loans, and our own coffers. This was an offer too great for them to cast aside, so the contract was on his desk within days.

"This is a fine day, Cherub." Papa squeezed my elbow. "A bit too long in coming for my liking, but it's grand to see all the same."

"It is, Papa." I planted a kiss on his whiskered cheek and turned back to marvel at the workers who attacked the soil with their spades. "The people of Paris will love it. And everyone will come too see it as a beacon of science and industry as well as beauty."

"Well said," Adolphe chimed in, touching two fingers to the brim of his hat and bowing his head in a little salute.

"I hope you're right about all that, darling girl. But even if it misses the mark to some degree, to see the men at work is a joy to my old heart."

I knew what he meant. At long last the project was underway. Never before, at least not in my lifetime, had Papa driven a project with such undivided attention. Papa was usually the sort who thrived when he had a dozen concerns going at once. He delighted in the juggle as others might delight in a tango or a waltz. Indeed, dealing with a number of pending projects all at the same time *was* a sort of dance for Papa, and there were few who could claim to be able to dance it with even a fraction of his dexterity. But the tower was different. He personally oversaw elements that usually junior engineers would have seen to.

But no project had ever mattered so much, for it was the one that would lord over the city. The project that wouldn't bear the name of the ruler who commissioned it or the businessman who financed it. It would bear his name for as long as it stood. And there was no room for error in calculation or execution, or the tower would fail, potentially with disastrous results to the nearby homes and businesses. Certainly to the company's name and reputation, not to mention Papa's. There was no room for accidents either, for the public would be merciless.

This was the element that worried me the most. Laborers got hurt. Most of the men we employed went into their line of work with the expectation that building structures on such a grand scale came with an enormous risk to personal safety. Injuries, and even deaths, were factored into the cost of most projects of this magnitude. How one could devise a sum equal to a human life, I didn't want to speculate. In that rare instance, I preferred ignorance to in-depth knowledge and wouldn't apologize for it.

But the reality we faced was that not all men on the project could be skilled veterans in the field who had worked on structures of tremendous size for the span of a storied career. No, there would be novices and unskilled men aplenty. Day laborers, even, though I hoped we'd be able to keep steady crews who would learn the art of constructing this massive structure from—quite literally—the ground up. And one slip of a foot would be a disaster in the press.

But the day we broke ground, I was able to banish those thoughts from my mind, at least for a short while. Today, the work was as safe as it would ever be, and the press would have little to report on apart from a small battalion of men with their shovels making headway at the site. It was a day of victory for all of us.

But it would last for only two weeks.

A petition to halt the construction of the tower had been formed and it was growing massive in scale. A scathing report printed in *Le Temps* said the design of the tower was downright vulgar and contrary to the ideals of French beauty and the gracious style of architecture the city sought to embrace.

Adolphe skimmed the article and let out a grunt of disgust. "It's just a pack of blowhards trying to puff themselves up." Adolphe tossed the paper aside and poured generous measures of liquor in cut-crystal glasses for the three of us. Far more than our usual after-dinner apéritif. "They see the modern design of the tower as a threat to their so-called aesthetic genius. They're afraid *real* genius will make them look shoddy in comparison."

Papa laughed into his Armagnac in response. "Thank you for the compliment, I suppose."

"I mean it as one to yourself and all who had a hand in the design. And it's not flattery; it's merely a statement of truth. The tower will be a marvel and they're jealous."

I opened my mouth, tempted to play devil's advocate, but thought better of it. These artists and writers and men of influence likely *were* jealous—Adolphe hadn't missed the mark entirely—but there was a real concern that the temporary tower would signal an irrevocable change in the direction of art and architecture in Paris. A revolution for the entire artistic community. The people of Paris were likely willing to embrace change, but the old guard was not willing to give up their control of the city without a fight.

And they mounted an impressive one.

"Do we have a list of signatories?" I asked.

"I don't see what difference it makes," Papa said. "It's the sheer number of them that matters."

Adolphe nodded his agreement.

I turned to them. "The names on that list matter immensely. Don't let the fervor surrounding the centennial of the revolution dazzle you out of reality. Some names matter far more than others."

Adolphe pulled a paper from his breast pocket. *Le Temps* hadn't printed the entire list of names, but as the subject concerned the company, they were able to procure it from the paper. "They call themselves 'The Three Hundred.' One for every meter of the tower."

I couldn't restrain an eye roll of my own at the pretension they donned as easily as a rakish hat as I scanned the columns of signatories. Composers, artists, writers; a selection of the very biggest names in their fields. A list of the cultural elite, a long one, who were happy to thwart Papa's vision for the tower. And I had no doubt Papa would remember the name of every single person who had stood up against him. He wasn't a man for grudges, but he wasn't precisely one to forget a slight either. Papa joined me at my elbow and peered over my right shoulder.

"Et tu, Garnier?" Papa muttered, downing his glass. "I worked with him on a project we both loved, and the bastard does this? We were nothing but cordial to each other. I'd never stand in the way of one of his projects as a matter of professional courtesy." Even worse than publicly voicing his animosity toward the project, rumor had it Garnier had even attended a dinner that some awful man had organized to raise opposition to the tower, but this I kept to myself for now. To know that Papa's onetime friend was dining and watching malicious skits that painted Papa a fool—or worse, participating in them himself—was too great a burden to foist on Papa. He would find out; no secrets in Paris were held for long, but I couldn't bear to be the one to tell him.

"None of his projects are three hundred meters tall," I pointed out. "An ugly building is usually of no consequence, but one that is visible from nearly every corner of the city is another matter. People won't be able to escape it." And this was one of Garnier's chief arguments . . . his Opéra didn't tower over the buildings in the avenue where it resided. Quite the inverse: despite its massive size, it was a squat building nestled among much taller buildings on either side of it.

"Whose side are you on?" Papa challenged. His tone was sharper than what he'd ever dared to use with me before, but he had rarely felt such professional pressure before either. He ran his fingers through his black hair and his shoulders slumped. I'd never seen him quite so exhausted. But such was the price of changing the face of Paris.

"The Compagnie Eiffel's side. Always." I kept my tone measured. Papa and Adolphe were emotional enough they needed the temperate influence of a cool head. "And if what the company needs is me telling the two of you the hard truths you don't want to hear, then so be it. You both need to understand the arguments being made, not just pretend they don't exist or are without merit just because you wish it to be true. That's how arguments—and court cases—are lost."

The men were silent for a moment. Adolphe shook his head, discouraged. Papa set his glass down with a *thunk* on the wooden sideboard and rubbed his temples. "It's awfully rich for Garnier to criticize the project. His opera house looks like a gargantuan tomb. He has no room to make aesthetic judgments when he inflicted that dead stone box on the landscape of Paris."

"Whatever you do, don't malign Garnier or his opera house like that in front of the press. People love the Opéra. More than a few consider it a masterpiece of Parisian architecture, if not the very pinnacle of it. We won't win hearts by disparaging it."

Papa scoffed but Adolphe crossed his arms over his chest and expelled a breath slowly, brooding as he was wont to do. "Claire is right. We won't garner anyone's support by responding to bullies with more bullying. We must take the high road; especially you, as his peer. Express concern about the dissent from such prominent names in architecture, even if Garnier is the lowest of the low to stoop to such a public display. But be the model of restraint and professionalism."

"You two even deny an old man the fun of abusing the blackguard in the privacy of his own drawing room?" Papa asked, leaning back in his chair.

"Oh, delight in it now," I said, finally able to smile. "Call him every name in the book and immerse yourself in rage like a swimming pool three meters deep if you like. Just not a word when anyone from the general public—or God forbid the press—can overhear. Not at the office, not in the street. Definitely not at the building site."

"Your wife is free with her orders, Adolphe. I wish you much patience." Papa rested his head against the back of the chair.

Adolphe barked a laugh. "I've found, in several years of careful study, it's a sound practice to follow those orders."

"Well then, Son. You've learned the most important lesson in the pursuit of a happy marriage. I knew you were a canny one the first time I set eyes on you. Many a man takes far longer to take that lesson to heart."

I crossed my arms in mock indignation. "You two paint me as a shrew. The next thing you know, you'll be telling me Maman was just as domineering and hid it under a thin veneer of sweetness for the public."

"Nearly," Papa said, rising and kissing my cheek before retiring. "Less exasperating, perhaps, but not nearly as skilled in keeping me from running my mouth."

"Well, it's nice to have a life which holds some distinction, but you mustn't worry about these fools. I'd wager a year's dress allowance they'll come to regret speaking against you by the time the tower is open."

"From your lips to God's ears, darling girl. I've never wanted you to be more right in all my life."

Chapter Twenty-Eight

July 14, 1888

"It's remarkable, isn't it?" I whispered to no one in particular. As Paris commemorated the centennial of the liberation of the Bastille, a crowd had gathered at Papa's tower for a display of fireworks he had organized to celebrate the halfway point of the construction of the tower. But even without the dazzling display to come, the tower was an incredible sight, even as it stood incomplete. It was hard to imagine that the immense thing would stretch twice its height farther into the heavens when it was blessedly finished.

"Papi's tower!" Robert exclaimed from my arms, pointing at the four pillars.

"Yes, darling. That's Papi's tower. It's beautiful, isn't it?" His face split into a resplendent toddler grin as he reached for his cousin, Thérèse, who slept on her papa's shoulders before the excitement of the fireworks got underway. I pulled his hand back to me before he could disturb her slumber. She could be a holy terror if she were denied her sleep. Though Laure might not agree with me, seeing the vibrant little Thérèse in mid-tantrum gave me a secret delight. Every fit she threw was a sign that she was thriving and healthy.

And even better, she and Robert were inseparable, and I loved the bond they shared.

"Claire," a voice called through the crowd. "It *is* you."

The voice was a more mature version of the one I'd known, but it was attached to the same frizzy mop of hair that still couldn't decide if it was blond or brown. "Ursule!" I exclaimed, causing Robert to blink in surprise.

She closed the gap between us, earning a few nasty looks from those in the crowd who she jostled as she tried to make her way to my side.

"I haven't seen you in ages!" She threw her arms around me, despite the child in my arms, like we were girls again. "I almost didn't recognize you. You've stayed a girl of fourteen in my memory these ten years and more. But look at you, grown and so ladylike."

"And you look so very well." Ursule's complexion looked fresh, if a bit freckled, as though she'd been spending plenty of her time out of doors with her canvas and easel. Her clothes were a bit bohemian in style, but in good repair. More important, she had the glow of a woman who looked well and truly happy.

Her eyes diverted to the baby wriggling in my arms. "This little one is yours? I must have missed the announcement in the papers."

"Yes, this is our little Robert." I angled him so she could get a better view. He rewarded her interest with a winning smile. I introduced Ursule to Adolphe and Maurice, and she exchanged warm greetings with Laure, with whom she'd always been friendly but never really friends. She fussed appropriately over the babies, at which Laure beamed. She was, as most mothers were, extremely susceptible to any flattery pertaining to her children.

"How about you?" Laure asked. "Have you started a family?"

"Oh . . . no. I've been terribly busy with my studies. And truth be told, not much on the market for a husband, much to Maman's chagrin."

"Plenty of time yet," Laure said with a demure smile, and turned her eyes back to the tower. Ursule and I locked eyes for a moment and exchanged a silent understanding. Laure was more traditional than Ursule and I were. Or at least more traditional than I had once been. Laure couldn't quite imagine a life for a woman that didn't eventually end up nestled in the comforts of home with a husband, children, and perhaps a fluffy white dog. At least she had imagination enough to believe a woman could find some amusement before she settled there.

"Your art? You've kept it up, then?"

"Yes, I'm studying at the Académie Julian. I haven't quite succeeded in my mission to force the point of women's admittance to the École des Beaux-Arts, but the *académie* is a good one. Students from all over the world, and many just as talented as those from the *grande école*, and I like the instructors very much, but it's challenging work. There isn't a soft touch among them."

"I well believe that." I'd heard of the Académie Julian by reputation. It prided itself on accepting women as well as the foreign applicants who couldn't pass the rigorous French exam the École des Beaux-Arts insisted on. It was, naturally, a device to keep the institution as French as the baguette and "La Marseillaise." I tended to believe a more open-minded admissions policy would have led to a wider range of artistic talent, but of course the École des Beaux-Arts had its philosophies about what art should be, and nothing, including—or perhaps especially—the experience and perspective of other peoples would change their minds.

"You'd love it." The familiar sparkle glowed in her eyes that she used to get when speaking passionately about her art. "It's everything we always talked about. Living for our art and really being part of the artistic world."

"I'm sure I would have." I was careful to use the past tense, as much for me as for her. "I'm so very glad you honored your promises to yourself. You had talent in spades and I'm sure that serious instruction has done nothing but elevate your work. I'd love to see it."

"I hope to display a piece at the expo next year. Clearly it will be a small offering to the proceedings compared to your papa's," she said, gesturing to the tower. "But it will be nice to make my mark all the same."

I couldn't deny there was a twinge of jealousy in my heart at the realization that, despite all the challenges she must have faced from her parents, Ursule had managed to make her dreams come true. Even if she never became a famous artist—and the odds had always been against that—she had done what she set out to do. She studied art with the masters and would have the chance to share her art with the world. If she hung up her brush for a husband and children the following day, at least she'd made the most of her opportunity to follow her passion. And I was *happy* for her. Far more than I was jealous on my own account. More than my fourteen-year-old self would have thought possible.

I put an arm around her, awkwardly thanks to Robert's squirming. "I'm so proud of you, Ursule. Promise me you'll let me know where I can see your work?"

She returned the embrace and looked in my face tentatively. "Do you think I could write to you sometimes? I often think about the way we parted, and I'd always hoped to mend it."

"Of course. We were children then. We both said things we didn't really mean. Especially me."

"I was cruel. I can't think about what I said without loathing myself for it."

"And I was brokenhearted over Maman and unable to respond the way I should have. I was brutishly unfair to you."

Amid the sea of people assembled for the fireworks display, a small group of women called out Ursule's name. She waved to them and looked back to me. "I've got to run, but I'll write to you soon. I do hope we can meet up for a coffee sometime soon and talk about the old days."

"And the new ones too," I promised. "I'd like that."

She kissed my cheek and dashed off into the bustling crowd that was anxious for the festivities to begin. Adolphe arched a brow in question.

"Our neighbor in Levallois. We were chums for ages. We spent hours in the garden with our paints and canvas. We drifted apart after Maman died and I haven't seen her since we moved to town."

"You haven't pulled out your easel in a long time. It's a shame. You're quite good."

"Not quite as good as Ursule, but better than mediocre. We dreamed of studying art seriously before settling down. She at least made good on it."

He wrapped an arm around me and Robert and placed a kiss on my forehead. "I hope the sacrifice was worth it."

Adolphe spoke as if I'd given up an evening at the opera I'd been looking forward to, and not the vocation I'd spent years dreaming of. The precious dream of my youth that I'd had to sacrifice on the altar of familial duty before it had even had the time to truly take root.

But I didn't blame him. He'd had no way of knowing. In his mind, he probably thought it was a childish fantasy I'd long since forgotten. If it were otherwise, wouldn't I have clung harder to it? Certainly that was what he thought.

And perhaps he was right. Maybe art had simply been a beloved pastime of my youth but was never more than that for me. But as red, blue, and white sparkles left their traces on the summer night sky, I found myself cradling a feeling of loss that felt as palpable as the sturdy child in my arms.

That Ursule had been granted the opportunity to continue her studies was truly marvelous. She was talented and deserved all the numerous accolades I was sure she would rake in over the course of her career.

In a way, she was like Papa; she was passionate about her work and driven to excel. She didn't just make art; she ate it, breathed it, lived it. It was just the same for Papa and Adolphe with their architecture. Ursule was able to pursue her career with abandon because she had the support of her parents. Papa and Adolphe were able to pursue theirs . . . because of me.

And I knew I lived a life of immense privilege and comfort. I lived in a world of beauty and grace. But the sacrifices I'd been forced to make meant I would never leave my mark on it. I cast another glance up at Papa's magnificent tower and wondered if it would be enough to have been a part of this dream, far grander than any I'd have the chance to realize on my own.

Chapter Twenty-Nine

March 1889

I awoke to Adolphe gently shaking me awake. I was usually the first to awaken and dreadfully unused to the sensation of being roused from my sleep by anything apart from the sun cresting over the horizon each morning.

"What is it?" I sat bolt upright; a million horrible scenarios crossed my mind in the briefest flash. Papa taken ill, Édouard in trouble, something wrong with Laure or the baby or—God forbid—both of them.

"An accident at the tower." His face was drained of color. "I don't know anything beyond that. Your father is being briefed in the drawing room now."

"My God." I jumped from the bed, slipped my feet in my bedroom slippers, and wrapped my dressing gown around my body before rushing down to Papa, praying fervently with every step that whatever it was, it wasn't as catastrophic as the images I was able to conjure. It was in the wee small hours of Monday morning, so I couldn't imagine it was anything to do with the workers. Was something wrong with the structure itself? I tried to push the thought of a thousand feet's worth of iron and rivets capsized on the Champs de Mars. The destruction would be devastating.

We'd taken every precaution against accidents and injury we could contrive, and several others for good measure too. Aside from the usual bruises and scrapes that were the province of hard manual labor, there had been no serious injuries. It had been nothing short of miraculous given the height and complexity of the structure. We had scaffolding with wide edges to prevent construction debris or errant tools from falling on workers below, which was the biggest danger, with netting as an added safeguard. The men were not novice construction workers, and their pay increased as the tower stretched to the heavens.

The sounds of footsteps in the foyer suggested the police were leaving, and I quickened my pace to the drawing room. Papa was sitting, head in hands, on the settee. "A man died," he said when the footman closed the door behind the officers. "The thing is all but done and a man died."

In my haze, I hadn't registered the time before then. My eyes flitted to the clock on the mantelpiece, which read two in the morning. "It can't have been a worker. Surely there wasn't an accident on the job site on Saturday and you're just now hearing of it."

"No. It happened an hour ago. But indeed it was one of my employees. One of our finest riveters on the construction crew." Papa looked at Adolphe. "An Italian, Ange Scagliotti. Did you know him?"

Adolphe paused to reflect, stroking the stubble on his chin. "Just well enough to be able to put a face with the name, but not much more than that. Affable sort, if memory serves me, and experienced too. What was he doing on-site?"

"He took his wife there to show it off. From all accounts, he was proud of his part in the tower, bless him."

"But what happened *exactly*?" I pressed. I stood to pour the men a small measure of sherry before they could indulge in anything stronger and procured a tin of butter biscuits that I kept hidden from the others. I'd learned to stash these little indulgences of mine or risk doing without. I took an obliging saucer from the sideboard and offered each of them a serving.

Papa arched a brow but didn't voice his question about the biscuits. We were all permitted our little secrets, and mine happened to be made of flour, sugar, and butter.

"The police don't like to speculate at this juncture. And you can imagine the wife is too distraught to speak much. But it isn't too hard to parse out what happened. They snuck in after dark because security would be less. It might be he was showboating a bit for his sweetheart. Maybe he simply couldn't see the ledge well enough. But the material point is that he slipped and fell and didn't survive the fall."

"Oh, Papa," I said, wrapping an arm around him.

"What of the wife? Is she unharmed?" Adolphe asked. I looked to him, pleased he'd spared a thought for the poor woman.

"I should think she is well and truly damaged in a manner so profound she will never fully recover. But physically, I don't think she sustained any injuries."

"That's a mercy," I replied. "We can take some solace in that much at least."

"Not to sound too cruel," Adolphe interjected, his eyes focused on the rug beneath his feet as he paced, "but if she's alive, she'll be able to recount her side of the story. And there's nothing we can do to control that narrative. Worse, there are no witnesses to refute anything she says if she tries to lay blame at our feet. True or false, there is no one to contradict her."

I felt the air release from my lungs as though I'd been kicked in the chest by an irate donkey. This unfortunate woman's existence was a liability. "What can we do about it?"

"Precious little," Papa said. "Once she speaks to the press, it will be a feeding frenzy. Each exaggeration, each small embroidery of the tale becomes a tapestry."

Adolphe gave Papa a wary nod. "If the press catches wind of this, it could raise questions about the safety of the tower. The city could close us down. And even if they don't, the press could deter people from visiting."

There were unspoken words that hung over the room. *You invested everything in this. You didn't mortgage just your own future but that of the entire family. If this enterprise fails, we're sunk. And work will become scarce if it does, so recovering the losses will be even harder.*

Adolphe, as much as he probably wished to, didn't voice his words aloud, for which I was grateful. Papa didn't need the added stress of a reminder of what was at stake. It wouldn't take much for the city government to halt the project and force an investigation. Even if they found nothing, public trust would be shaken, and the delay would be costly. If they did find that we were—in some backward way of thinking—at fault, it could mean the tower would be condemned before a single visitor took admittance. It would be ruinous to the company. Ruinous for the family fortune. Ruinous for Papa.

And it was a blow from which I was certain he wouldn't recover.

"We must find this woman," I said. "Logically, how could we be responsible when they were trespassing? We must find a way to convince her to not hold us liable for the accident."

"Easier said than done, Cherub. She's grieving the loss of the man she pledged to spend her life with. I would think she's not in the best frame of mind for considering the logic of anything. Quite the contrary, our efforts to indemnify ourselves may embolden her desire to speak out where once she might not."

"There was nothing we could have done to stop this," I said, knowing as soon as the words escaped my mouth that the truth of the thing didn't really matter. It was appearances that counted. And because of the actions of one man—foolish at best, selfish at worst—all our efforts to keep our workers safe would be ignored by the press and used against us. I could see the story, ink drying on newsprint before my very eyes. *Despite extraordinary safety precautions, the tower still led to one man's death. How many are sure to follow if this monstrosity of a tower is left standing. . . .*

I felt my intestines coil into a knot. Adolphe had been right to question my encouragement of Papa risking so much of his own fortune in this endeavor. I had thought Adolphe was being shortsighted, but tonight proved that his caution was warranted. We were flying perilously close to the sun, and we were about to test the mettle of our wings over a churning sea of vicious press and vindictive detractors. If I were a stronger woman, I would have told him he was right. I might have even made a plea for forgiveness. But I was equal to no words. I was paralyzed with the fear that this simple act of carelessness would be our undoing.

There would be no sleep for us that night. Adolphe finally gave up his pacing and sat next to me on the settee. At one point, I offered him my hand. He took it in his and held it until the weak March sunshine began to creep in the windows and we were called to break our fast. Our bodies were hungry, but the food seemed as appealing as wet sawdust. Robert had his breakfast in the nursery, and I was grateful I could delay putting on a facade of cheerfulness for just a bit longer. The mask I was forced to wear grew chafing, and the reprieve from wearing it was a blessed relief.

"I'm going out," Adolphe announced almost the moment the

clock struck eight in the morning. It was, as I referred to it, the first civilized hour of the day.

Papa had already declared his intent to go to Levallois to boost morale as much as he was able, which was the best use of his energies that morning. I would be left at loose ends, and though my body ached from lack of sleep and my head felt thick, as though my thoughts were wading through a soupy fog, the idea of trying to sleep was laughable.

"Where?" It was unlike me to pry into the workings of his daily life, but today, with all that was going on, I felt the need to know.

"I was going to see if I can talk to the wife of our falling victim. The police were good enough to provide me with an address."

"Do you know if they have children?" I pushed my toast aside, unable to play at eating it any longer.

"I can't say for sure. But I would assume so. The man was about forty years old and in good health."

"I should come with you. I could be of some use."

"You ought to stay and rest." The familiar glint of worry shone in his eye. "You got less than three hours of sleep."

"You got even less. And besides, Madame Scagliotti may respond better to a fellow wife and mother than to a businessman."

He looked pensive for a moment, then exhaled. "Get your coat and let's pray you're right."

MÉLIE-THÉRÈSE SCAGLIOTTI OPENED the door to us and, miraculously, didn't throw us back out when she learned who we were. She had to have been more than ten years her husband's junior and was a classic Italian beauty with glossy black hair, olive skin, and soulful brown eyes that looked haunted after the events of the previous evening.

The Scagliotti family lived in a modest apartment on the Quai d'Orsay, right in the heart of the city. It would have been a quick bicycle ride to the building site, and a wonderful opportunity for a family whose opportunities in Italy were limited due to the economic problems the country faced. Madame Scagliotti showed us to the parlor, little bigger than a shoebox from our perspective, but it was lovingly furnished and impeccably cared for. The room was clearly a source of pride for the young widow, who offered us both coffee, though her hands shook with exhaustion and grief.

"I don't know why you've come." Her words were in impeccable French, but the music behind them was Italian. "I've told the authorities all I know." She bowed her head and stared at her hands, the effort of recounting the worst moments of her life having taken their toll.

"Madame Scagliotti—" Adolphe began. I hushed him with a hand on the knee.

"We've come to inquire after *you*, Madame Scagliotti. You suffered a horrible shock last night and I was concerned that, in their efficiency, the police were more concerned with their investigation of the circumstances leading to the dreadful accident rather than tending to you."

She looked up. "Th-that is very kind of you." Just as I suspected, once they'd assessed that she was physically unharmed, they'd ignored her well-being entirely. No one thought to ask how she was doing or what help she might require. "I can't seem to make my brain understand that my Angelo is gone."

I reached across the little parlor table and offered her my hand. "It is a cruel deprivation, Madame Scagliotti. I can't begin to comprehend what you might be suffering."

The widow's face looked on the verge of crumpling when an earsplitting cry emerged, not from the depths of her wounded bosom, but from a room off the side of the parlor. She mumbled her apologies and dashed to the source of the sound. She emerged a few moments later with a newborn baby in her arms and two tiny children in her wake. The oldest looked to be just over three years old, almost exactly our dear Robert's age, and the other was perhaps a year and a half old and still toddling behind his brother.

"What a beautiful family." It wasn't a rapturous compliment, but indeed a lament, that the father of these darling children should have been taken from them. Whether by an unlucky stumble in the dark or a foolish moment of bravado, fate had done a grave disservice to these innocent babes, who would likely have no memory of the father who had come so far to give them a better life.

The color rose in her cheeks. "Thank you. My boys are Pierre and Emile." She gestured first to the older boy, then the younger. "And this is my little Ernestine." She looked down at her daughter's face, the love she felt tinged with creases of exhaustion and worry on her own.

"Good French names," Adolphe observed.

"They have Italian names as well. Pierrino, Mauro, and Maria-Theresa Ernesta. And mine is Amalia back at home. At the job site, Angelo became Ange." Her voice caught as she mentioned her husband's name, perhaps thinking of its now all-too-appropriate meaning. "We wanted to have French names so we'd get along better among the people of your country."

"Have you been here long?" Adolphe asked.

"Two years, or nearly. We came to this country when Emile was no bigger than Ernestine." She cradled the baby close to her breast.

I felt the ache in my heart twinge again. This country was the only one the younger two had ever really known, and little Pierre wasn't likely to have memories of his native Italy, if any.

"Have you any family here?" I asked, to which she shook her head.

"No, my people are from Bressana. In the north. Not far from Verona."

"You must be very homesick," Adolphe interjected. "Especially now in light of the tragedy."

My eyes slid to him, and I prayed he would not overplay his hand. If she were to leave Paris and, better still, to leave France entirely, it would be the answer to our prayers.

"I am," she admitted.

"You will certainly need help with the children," Adolphe pressed. "Your mother, sisters, aunts? It would lessen your burden quite considerably, would it not?"

She remained silent. Of course the notion of returning home had likely occurred to her within an hour of the accident. And though Ange's wages had been very good for his line of work, it would likely take every penny she had to transport herself, the children, and any of her belongings of value back to Italy.

"If you want to go home, we will help you with expenses," Adolphe said, gleaning the same information from her pause. "We will ensure that your journey isn't onerous in the least. Five hundred francs will see to it that you travel in comfort."

"That is generous . . ." she said, not meeting his eyes.

"And some money besides," I said, with a sideways glance to Adolphe. "To help you begin afresh and to shore up the children's futures."

Adolphe grimaced but said nothing. Papa's coffers were deep, and I was perfectly content to see them raided for this cause.

Adolphe quickly followed my offer with a stipulation. "We would require that you sign a paper releasing Monsieur Eiffel from responsibility for the accident. I'm sure you agree that it was not the fault of the company that your husband chose to make an unauthorized visit. We're only too grateful that harm didn't befall you as well. Think of what that might have meant for the children."

She clutched the baby tighter to her bosom. I placed my hand on Adolphe's knee to silence him once more.

"Ange would rest easier knowing you and the children are cared for." I took her hand in mine. "He was proud of the work he did on the tower. He wouldn't want the project to suffer, nor for the labors of his fellow workers to go to waste."

"I will go to Italy," she declared. "And I will take your money. This way I will never have to see your father's awful tower ever again."

She stood, and it was our signal to leave. Pierre, the oldest, offered me a timid wave from behind his mother's skirts. I knelt before him, and it might as well have been my little Robert. A memory of Adolphe and Robert's horseplay in the gardens flashed before me. The way his little face lit up when his papa entered the nursery. Pierre would never again see his dear papa, and I couldn't bear that reality for him. He came closer and kissed my cheek. I returned the gesture and held him in my arms for just a moment. From that position, I looked up at Mélie-Thérèse Scagliotti—Amalia—and peered into her anguished eyes.

"I am so truly sorry," I said, the words ashes on my tongue.

"Not as sorry as I am." Her eyes flashed with a grief I knew all too well. I'd seen it in Laure's eyes and Papa's. There was nothing to be done to soothe her apart from leaving her in peace.

I stood, shaking as Adolphe led me back to the carriage.

"Well done," he said as the carriage lurched forward. "You were right about the approach with her. Masterful, indeed."

"Masterful? It was horrific. We bought her silence."

"But necessary for the tower's success. You said it yourself: if the tower is condemned, Scagliotti's work, and that of his brethren, will go to waste."

"We're giving her blood money, Adolphe. It's abhorrent."

"It is," he agreed. "But it's not the first time such a thing has been necessary. And it's far better than leaving her to her wits and hoping she doesn't speak."

"I can't argue with the last part. If you give her less than a thousand francs, for her *and* each of the children in addition to her travel expenses, I will make your life well and truly difficult."

"Almost five thousand francs? That's quite a lot of money."

"It will seem like a bargain if she speaks out. And consider it an investment in domestic bliss. It's not like the company couldn't afford many times that sum."

"Very well, but she doesn't see anything beyond the five hundred francs for travel until she's settled in Italy. We'll insist on wiring the money to an Italian bank."

I assented. There was no use in hoping Adolphe would ever put his pragmatism and business acumen aside in favor of more sentimental interests, but at least he was doing the right thing in this case.

And even then, the right thing seemed woefully inadequate. I could only hope Papa's money would help seed prosperous lives for Amalia and her brood. They'd come to France hopeful for a bountiful new life and found themselves impoverished in a way they never imagined. As we drove by the tower, gleaming red in the sun, I prayed it would all be worthwhile.

Chapter Thirty

March 31, 1889

"Whatever happens now, you're a success," I whispered to Adolphe. He took my hand in his and gave it an affectionate squeeze. He said nothing, too nervous to speak.

Papa's name was on the tower, but Adolphe had headed up so much of the effort, it might as well have been his. His reputation didn't hang in the balance quite like Papa's, but his pride certainly did. Forty-nine guests would accompany Papa to the top of the tower, and Adolphe and I were among the lucky group who would be the first to ascend to its summit, aside from the brave workmen who built it. The lifts were not yet operational, and wouldn't be for weeks yet, so we would have to climb the more than seventeen hundred steps on our own steam.

As I made my way, I scanned the vast crowd awaiting the opening of the tower. It seemed to spread for miles, like a human tapestry carpeting the entire city. After I climbed the equivalent of a few flights of stairs, which I did often enough in the course of a day, the effort grew considerably. With each step I found myself winded and struggling, though I always prided myself on regular exercise and not overindulging at mealtimes.

I forced my face to remain neutral, not wanting a photographer to catch me mid-grimace and create bad press for the company. Somewhere around the midpoint, my hand fluttered to my stomach when the reason for my fatigue dawned on me. My cycles were never regular, but as I counted the weeks in my head, I realized it had been at least two months since I had bled. The house had been in such turmoil with the completion of the tower and keeping Papa and Adolphe from running mad with overwork, I'd had precious little time to draw breath, let alone track the regularity of my cycle. Every day I didn't have to contend with the nuisance was a blessing, and I had just been grateful to not have another worry.

I shoved the tender thought from my head. I was months away from being assured the safe delivery of my second child, and Papa and Adolphe needed me present in both body and mind on this momentous occasion. I would find an appropriate moment in the next few days to whisper my suspicion to Adolphe and then do my best to ignore it until my stays required me to acknowledge the truth and I'd be forced to have dear Pauline unearth my maternity dresses from the back of my closet.

But until then I had to remain focused on the task at hand. Charming the guests and being a witness to Papa and Adolphe's greatest triumph.

It seemed like hours later, but we finally arrived at the summit of the tower. Even the fittest among us was damp with perspiration from the effort, which made me feel somewhat less aggrieved that the three-hundred-meter trek had been so arduous for me. Once there, Papa hoisted a tricolor French flag up the pole, one hundred years after it had been a symbol of revolution and progress, to commemorate the most progressive structure of its kind.

"That, my dear ladies and gentlemen, is the first French flag with a three-hundred-meter flagpole. Will it do?"

The crowd went mad with applause, both the modest crowd that had been admitted with us and the massive throng of onlookers below who hadn't heard Papa's words but had seen that the blue-white-and-red flag now flapped proudly in the stubborn March winds.

Papa first shook Adolphe's hand, and rightly so, for he knew full well there would have been no tower without Adolphe's untiring support. There were financiers and government officials he had to greet and charm, but eventually he made his way to me. He kissed my cheeks and held my face in his hands.

"Thank you, Cherub. For all you've done. For Adolphe and me both."

I returned his kisses. "It's a marvel, Papa. You must be so proud."

He looked rueful. "You know, I've been waiting for this day for so long it doesn't seem quite real now that it's here. It's not like one of my bridges that I see with pride when I have the chance to pass by. I could never surpass this tower."

"Well, no matter, Papa. I think three hundred meters is quite tall enough, don't you?"

Papa chuckled and linked his arm in mine. "It's a queer feeling to know when one has reached the pinnacle of one's career."

"Most people only realize their pinnacle in retrospect. I hope knowing it in the moment helps you to appreciate it."

"I think so. I suppose it's hard to take it all in." His eyes scanned the horizon. Wistfulness wasn't an expression that looked at home on his face, and I felt unsettled by it. "But it will soon be time to slow down."

I took in a shaky breath as I looked over the marvelous city below. The thought of Papa not working on some far-flung bridge or railroad station was as disquieting as a river running a vibrant shade of daisy yellow. But lines in his face had grown deeper over the past two years. He was grayed and carried himself in a way that betrayed the sort of bone-weary fatigue that sleep couldn't cure. No, the only elixir for Papa was rest and time. He *should* retire, but could a mind as active as his truly find rest? "I'll believe you when I see the pipe between your lips, your feet propped on a pouf, and your nose in a thrilling mystery by Arthur Conan Doyle."

"Good God, child, I'm retiring, not entering my dotage just yet. I've a mess to clean up in Panama, but when that's all sorted, I want to enjoy this magnificent tower of mine and see what I can make of her." He gestured to the small apartment that he'd built at the top of the tower. It wasn't an apartment in the true sense; it didn't house a bedroom or a real place to sleep. But it did contain a comfortable sitting room, three offices, and even a small kitchen.

"I wondered why you wanted to carve out your own space here. I couldn't imagine a purpose for it beyond entertaining a few dignitaries."

"Oh, there will be plenty of that, I'm sure."

I rolled my eyes in a show of being put out. It was true that we already had an impressive list of guests scheduled to visit the tower, and a number were prominent enough that Papa really was obliged to meet them and shake their hands. Which meant I had to be on hand to organize refreshment and look pleasant and cheerful for all the guests.

"No, there will be no finer place to study, say, meteorology, than the tower. Radio too. And that's only the technology we know about. Who knows what the human mind will come up with next. And while all the other eccentric madmen of the world have their laboratories and offices on the ground, mine will be a thousand feet up in the air. I think that's rather remarkable, don't you?"

"Most assuredly, Papa." I kissed his cheek. "This will be an exciting new chapter for you."

He patted my hand and excused himself to visit with the other guests.

My services unneeded for the moment, I was finally free to wander the observation area for the first time and marveled at the city below. The city seemed to span forever, giving way to fields and pastures only at the farthest reaches of my view. Had the tower been built a few decades earlier, the city would have looked much more like a medieval hodgepodge, but the influence of Haussmann and his penchant for orderly streets and elegant design was evident in so much of what I took in. But from this height, Haussmann's wrought iron trellises, Garnier's Opéra, and even the mighty Notre-Dame seemed small. Instead of feeling insignificant in the presence of the massive tower hulking over the city, for a fleeting moment I felt like an all-powerful goddess looking over her dominion. For the first time in ages, I felt not just competent but commanding. And it felt so incredibly . . . good.

And perhaps that was—at least in part—what attracted people to the tower. Not to be humbled by its magnificence, but to be elevated into greatness along with it, if only for an hour or two. I expected most would feel it was worth the five-franc ticket to experience such a sensation.

And Papa had known this. Despite all the bleak moments in the past two years, he knew he would succeed, and this grand tower would enchant even our most illustrious guests. The visitors on the platform, now increasing in number as the second wave of first-day guests had been admitted up the stairs, seemed to be elated with the view and no one seemed to grumble about the unending stairs to scale it. Adolphe and Papa circulated among the guests like debutantes at a ball and looked as merry as the prize catch of the season.

And so it would be from this moment until the expo wound down in the autumn. I would be on hand when we had important guests to charm and serve lemonade and shake hands and smile. Hours of adulation for Papa and Adolphe's hard work, which was so well deserved. This was the crown jewel in Papa's career, and even Adolphe would likely never have the opportunity to work on such an illustrious project again though he had many working years ahead of him. And I was so happy for them both to have their hard-earned moment of triumph. And though they both insisted, almost on a daily basis, that they couldn't have done the work without my support, it did not, in any way, feel like my accomplishment.

I was able to marvel at the beauty of the tower and the breathtaking views she afforded the guests. But in truth, I felt the old tug of longing—the one I'd tried desperately to keep buried in my chest for ages.

Chapter Thirty-One

May 1889

"Maman! Look!" Robert pointed at the horses in the Buffalo Bill Cody act, which was, even more than Papa's tower, the most popular attraction at the expo and was now underway. "Look how they prance!"

"I see them, darling. They're remarkable, aren't they?"

He nodded enthusiastically from his father's lap.

The American performers seemed downright exotic compared to the displays of classic art and architecture in other parts of the expo, and somehow equally belonging to a life that was disappearing when compared to the exhibits in the Gallery of Machines. How long before the horse and carriage would disappear from everyday life and be replaced by the mechanized contraptions we'd heard were being produced in Germany by some man named Benz? Twenty years? Thirty? At the moment, they were objects of curiosity and toys for the wealthy, but it would certainly happen in Robert's lifetime, if not my own, that they would become commonplace.

Annie Oakley regaled the crowd with her sharpshooting and fantastic costumes she stitched herself. She was a charming guest at the tower, and we'd held a pleasant conversation over lemonade when she'd made her way to the top. Thankfully the elevators were now operational, so the trek to the top was far less arduous, though I confess I didn't fully trust the confounded metal boxes that whisked us up to the heavens.

The arena held thousands of visitors, and there wasn't an open seat in the place. Among the throng of people assembled, not one of them looked bored by the antics on the stage below. Robert was particularly enthralled, thrilled to be included in an event where his toddler energy didn't bar him from attending. My own energy had been flagging as the reality of a second child was now impossible to ignore. Adolphe had guessed the truth a few weeks ago, before I'd had the chance to tell him. He was thrilled at the news, as was Papa. My own excitement was tempered by the reality of another birth and another child to care for, but I knew all would be well once the little one was safely arrived.

As was my custom, I tried to camouflage any flaws behind fashionable clothes. I was dressed in a smart blue day dress that would soon pull too tight around the middle and a rather fetching white hat with matching plumes and a red ribbon. It gave the effect of the French *tricolor* in honor of the occasion, and the bold ensemble proved an effective distraction from the bags under my eyes and my wan skin.

Despite the theatrics and the cheers from the crowd, Robert had fallen asleep in Adolphe's lap. "Quite the spectacle." Adolphe raised his voice to be heard over all the commotion from the show. "I imagine you're just as tired as this chap. Why don't we go home and come back another day? You can both take a rest."

I was tired, but I was leaving the worst of the fatigue that plagued the first few months of pregnancy behind me. We'd been at the expo only a few hours, and I knew there would be dozens of household tasks that would keep me from touring the exhibits over the coming months, dozens of important occasions at the tower, and my condition would grow burdensome before long. We'd seen only a small portion of the exhibits, though it would likely take us days to see them all. The chance that I'd get to see them all at my leisure was nonexistent.

"Would you mind taking him home? I'd like to see more of the expo while I have the chance."

"Are you sure?" He adjusted Robert on his lap. "We could go and settle him with the nanny and come back together."

I swallowed a sigh. "You know that once I cross the threshold, I'll get swept up in a hundred things. It will be weeks before we have enough free time to explore. You could come back in a few hours to collect me after you pass Robert off to the nanny and put your feet up or catch up on correspondence for a bit."

And, astute man that he was, he understood my meaning. *I want some time for myself without the responsibilities of the house and the company.* He rubbed my upper arm and leaned in to kiss my cheek.

"I'll take you to dinner at the tower. I hear they have a good restaurant," he said with a wink.

"The very best. That sounds lovely."

We made plans to meet at the Palais des Beaux-Arts, the one exhibit I couldn't bear to miss, and the one I most wanted to visit alone. As dear as Adolphe was, his appreciation of art was one that came from practical need for his work, not creative expression. At least, not quite in the same way. His intentions were good, but I couldn't help noticing the glazed look in his eyes or the impatient way he bounced on the balls of his feet when I lingered too long at a painting. It was one thing to hurry through a wing of the Louvre when I knew Adolphe was growing tired of it. The Louvre, monolith that it was, would always be there. It was like Ursule's chestnut tree. But this exhibit was fleeting, more like the flowers I'd once rushed to capture before they faded from glory.

Adolphe and the sleeping Robert deposited me at the doors to the Palais des Beaux-Arts. I felt myself in awe of the cavernous rooms brimming with the works of the living French masters: Manet, Corot, Delacroix. Names I knew as well as my own. These masters, these great men of Paris, all had many paintings on display. A dozen for Manet, at least. Nearly four times as many for Corot. But I was looking for an artist who had one single tableau among the sea of oils and watercolors.

Rosa Bonheur, whom Ursule and I had revered, had one painting selected for exhibition: *Labourage nivernais*. It was an exceedingly realistic depiction of a dozen oxen plowing a field with four men guiding them with wooden rods. These were simple farm men, faces obscured, having endured hours of labor with more hours before them. The oxen were massive with rippling muscles, the hard earth being upturned into arable land beneath their hooves.

It wasn't a posed portrait of a rich woman dripping in her family's jewels. It wasn't a grand representation of the Madonna or the crucifixion. It was a field being tamed by beasts of burden in order to be cultivated. To provide a living for the farmers. To provide sustenance for them and many others. It was the struggle, the reality, and yes—the beauty—of life the way most people lived it.

The colors were breathtaking in their restraint. The sky was not the shade of bluebird feathers, nor was the grass the hue of emeralds. Even the whites and blacks in the cattle's coats were muted as if with the dust from the fields they plowed.

"It's magnificent, isn't it?" a voice beside me said, shattering my reverie. I turned my head and saw Ursule's profile. Her eyes fixed on the canvas as they always were when she worked on her own. Her attention so rarely divided.

"Incredible. You can almost breathe in the dust. It reminds me so greatly of how I imagine the American West looks."

Ursule nodded. "It would be a muse for her if she were to go. She should."

"Where does your muse lead you?" I didn't ask why the letters she'd promised never showed. She was too busy painting. Chasing her dreams. Living them. Just as I was busy tending to Papa's and Adolphe's.

"Indochina," she answered without hesitation. "East, anyway."

The response didn't surprise me. All things from the Asian continent were the rage these days. *La chinoiserie,* they called it. And I admitted a fondness for the delicate flowers and stylized designs.

"Do you have work on display?" I remembered her hope from our encounter the previous July. I felt a tingle of excitement for my old friend, who would have seen a place here as a coup for her career.

She shook her head. "Close, but not quite. But I was proud of my efforts."

"Then I am too." I took her hand in mine. "And I bet Rosa would be too."

"Oh, I am miles beneath her notice." I heard a small lump of emotion in her voice. "But maybe if I keep working, I will be worthy of it."

"You are now, Ursule. You were twelve years ago in the gardens of Levallois. You always will be as far as I'm concerned."

"You're a good friend. I wish I'd been a better one."

"Me too, for what it's worth." I swallowed back my own tears. "I wish so many times I had listened to you and not forsaken our grand plans."

"And there were countless nights when I was convinced you were the smart one. To give it all up and devote your time to a family and something real. I've been grasping at this dream for years now, and half the time, I feel like a damned fool for pressing on." She discreetly wiped her eyes. "Only a handful of us will find a level of success like Rosa."

"But you're giving it an honest chance and I didn't. You won't have to live with that regret."

"And you won't have to live with the regret of wasting a life if it all comes to nothing. You have a family to show for yours."

"And you have a body of work to show for yours. I don't think there's such thing as a life free of regrets. But let's make a pact not to dwell on ours, shall we?"

She squeezed the hand she still held in hers. "You have an accord, Madame Salles. And so long as you promise to dote on your family for me, I'll do my best to succeed with my artwork."

"Between the two of us, we have it all, don't we? That's pretty good, isn't it?"

"Marvelous, even," she agreed.

A few minutes later, she excused herself to rejoin some friends from the Julian Academy. They were dressed as bohemian as Ursule and looked at my prim blue dress with suspicion. I returned their curious gazes with a warm smile that baffled them. I knew no letters from Ursule would ever come, though I wished they would. I wished, more than anything, that in a year or two's time, I'd find an engraved invitation from her parents for a reception in honor of her acceptance to the Salon or something equally as prestigious. I wanted her art to soar for her sake, as well as for the memory of the dreams I'd long since put to rest.

The rest of my free afternoon slipped away in half a blink, and I met Adolphe, who was waiting eagerly for me to join him at the doors of the Palais des Beaux-Arts. We walked to the base of the tower and were passed to the front of the queue and shown to the lift to the first platform.

We dined on a fine meal of *confit de canard*—slow-roasted duck in a delicious marinade—served with fresh spring vegetables and crusty roasted potatoes, followed by a decadent cheese course, and looked out over the city. Adolphe reached across the table to take my hand in his as the waiter came with an airy lemon soufflé for dessert. It felt warm and familiar, like slipping into my own bed at the end of a very long day. I felt the stirrings of the baby growing within, a reminder of the happiness that awaited us in the months to come.

No, there was no such thing as a life without regrets, and mine would always sting. There was no use pretending that there wouldn't be a part of me that wondered what my life might have been like if I'd somehow managed to put my artistic pursuits at least occasionally ahead of running a household for Papa. But I would honor my pact to Ursule and do my best not to dwell on those thoughts. I'd made my choices—and they were my choices, no matter how I allowed my guilt and sense of obligation to guide them. And if I accepted that truth, I stood a far better chance of finding my own version of happiness.

Chapter Thirty-Two

September 10, 1889

"There's a smudge on the glass. Fetch a clean one, will you?" I whispered to one of the waiters I'd hired for this, the most important reception we'd ever host at the tower. The waiter, unable to conceal his annoyance, ran off to do as I asked before I had a chance to scold him. Papa, Adolphe, and the Edison family would soon be joining us for an elaborate luncheon in the apartment Papa kept in the tower. My ankles had swollen to three times their natural size and every part of me ached as the tiny life inside me sapped my energy, and I offered up a prayer that the little one would stay put for the duration of the meal.

Mademoiselle Leclerc had come to the rescue with an afternoon dress in a rich shade of crimson that resembled a good Bordeaux wine. It would have taken more than Leclerc's skill with a needle to hide the bulge at my middle—witchcraft more like—but she'd done magic enough in making my graceless form look a little more svelte for the occasion.

Papa had told me countless times that Tante Marie, Laure, or even Valentine could be charged with organizing the meal, but I knew Papa would rest easier knowing I was at the helm. And indeed, a luncheon for a medium-sized party was no great trial any longer. I knew the right chefs, hired enough staff, and chose a menu that would be sure to please a variety of palates.

The so-called Wizard of Menlo Park was to be our guest, and though countless princes, dukes, sheiks, and premiers had come to view Papa's marvel, no guest had Papa so thrilled as this one. Edison was an inventor and an innovator, if not exactly of the same bent as Papa, close enough that he felt a sort of kinship. He was exactly the sort of man Papa respected because his notoriety didn't come from the happenstance of a fortunate birth but rather the workings of his mind.

From what I'd read of him, Edison was of humble origins, but evolved to become a shrewd businessman and rather obsessed with money—all in the pursuit of funding more of his work, of course, but I found this made me dubious of him. I'd come to believe that a pursuit of money for its own sake led a man to be ruthless. And ruthless men were not to be trusted. But Papa was delighted to welcome the American to his tower, and so a feast had to be prepared.

Papa's apartment in the tower, though small, was as cozy and welcoming as I could make it. Papa had equipped the little apartment with a small kitchen, but most of the food was prepared in the grander kitchens on the second floor and transported up via elevator—the metal contraptions of which Papa was so proud. At least the modest kitchen would be able to keep the dishes warm as we awaited Edison's arrival. Tante Marie had been invited to attend, and the master hostess herself gave the arrangements a nod of approval. That she didn't fiddle with the centerpiece on the table or the place settings was a silent vote of confidence that spoke volumes.

I'd been told to prepare a feast as opulent as ever I'd orchestrated. I thought of the first time I'd planned a meal, for the workers in

Portugal. The simple fare and lively music to please a crowd of hundreds, a stark juxtaposition to this meal for fewer than fifteen guests that had to be the grandest of the grand. There would be caviar and foie gras, duck and lobster, an array of vegetables, bread and cheeses, and a host of desserts. Champagne would flow abundantly, and everything had to be flawless, from the white linens embroidered with the likeness of the tower to the polished silver, right down to the smudged water glass that was, as the table cards indicated, at Edison's daughter's seat.

The clamoring sound of the elevator preceded the boisterous arrival of our guests.

"This really is incredible, Eiffel." Edison bounded to the windows with the giddy energy of a schoolboy and peered out over the city. "One would swear they were on top of the world but feel as stable as if they were on solid ground. Well done, my good man."

"Thank you, thank you. The work of an army, of course, but it was my pleasure to have been part of it," Papa said with his usual dismissive tone when he was faced with praise. Secretly, I believed he lived for the ebullient words honoring his accomplishments and the crowds cheering "*Gloire à Eiffel!*" when the tower opened to the public, but to show that outwardly would have been the height of vulgarity in Papa's eyes.

Papa made rather a business of introducing me to the Edison family. The man himself shook my hand with the brand of enthusiasm that Americans had patented. "I spent the entire elevator ride in anticipation of the chance to meet you. Your father and husband spoke your praises practically within their first breath of our meeting."

"Like many men, they know flattery will get them far when applied liberally and frequently," I said, accepting his enthusiastic handshake. He stood perhaps half a foot taller than Papa, and an inch taller than Adolphe, and was a reasonably attractive fellow, though his keen sense of curiosity was more captivating than his physical person.

The Edison women were beauties, impeccably dressed and coiffed, making me feel cloddish in comparison, given my condition. Edison's wife, Mina, a dark-haired and astute-looking woman, appeared to be nearly twenty years his junior. She had polished manners and a soft voice compared to many of the brash Americans we'd met, but the sweet smile that seemed always close to her lips was a trademark of her open and friendly people. It was inviting when compared to the neutral mien of the Frenchwoman or the perpetual scowl that seemed to linger on the faces of the British aristocracy, but I found myself wondering how sincere it was.

Edison's daughter Dot, a young lady of sixteen, seemed like an affable enough girl, though the coldness she felt toward her stepmother was plain. Dot's mother had died only five years before, and he waited just two years to remarry a woman not ten years Dot's senior. I somehow doubted the relationship Mina had with the rest of her stepchildren was any more cordial, and found myself remembering the fears Laure and I had shared soon after Maman's death. On the rare occasions I'd considered Papa remarrying, I envisioned a respectable widow. Not old and dowdy, for I couldn't imagine that sort tempting Papa, but approaching middle age with a dash of matronly sophistication.

Over the years, I wrestled with my fear that one day he would find a suitable woman and my role in the household would be supplanted, all the while wondering what it might be like to have a maternal influence once again. The prospect of having my responsibilities shared with another woman both set my teeth on edge and filled me with a peculiar sense of longing. There was no doubt I would have experienced the jealousy and animosity Dot seemed to be feeling toward Mina, but in time, would those feelings have tempered to a warm affection? Or at least a quiet cordiality built on a foundation of mutual benefit?

But Papa had remained unmarried these twelve years, and that seemed unlikely to change. And with Adolphe and Robert now in my life, and the new little one that was due to arrive in the coming weeks, Papa's remarriage wouldn't have the same relief of burden it might have done once upon a time. I just hoped that this devotion to his work was enough that he didn't feel lonely. Night after night, climbing the stairs to his rooms alone, it had to be painful. My eyes drifted to Adolphe of their own volition. Where once I viewed him as my nemesis, the one who would usurp my place in Papa's heart, I now felt only warmth. I found the even rise and fall of his breath in bed next to me was the metronome that regulated my sleep, and his moods were often the barometer for my own.

"Let's have some music," a male voice declared. On the way to greet Edison, Papa had passed by a friend, the composer Charles Gounod, and invited him to our luncheon at the last moment. He sat at the little spinet that Papa had placed in the tower apartment. The composer played marvelously, and I was grateful that the musical interlude gave the staff the chance to ensure everything was perfect before serving the meal.

I was on the point of whispering to one of the footmen to set an extra place at the table for him as discreetly as possible, and preferably while he was invested in playing the piano, so he wouldn't notice that he was a late addition to the party, when Papa slipped away from the little gaggle of guests.

"Where is your brother Édouard?" he whispered.

"I thought he was meant to come with you," I replied, and realized as I quickly counted the heads of the guests, places enough had been set for all in attendance. Adolphe looked back at us, a brow arched. I offered him a smile to allay concern, but he could read it well enough. *There is a problem, but one we will have to concern ourselves with in private.*

Papa heaved a sigh, and it was clear that even though he had just taken waters in Évian-les-bains, the exertions of the past two years were taking a toll. With the Panama project apparently at an end, an unmitigated disaster from what I understood, I would have to urge him to consider the tower his chef d'oeuvre. At fifty-six years of age, he wasn't a young man, and I worried the stress of the tower and the troubles in Panama had aged him further still.

"We'll deal with him later." Papa shook his head. I felt the heat rise in my cheeks when I thought of Édouard and his selfishness. Papa wanted nothing more than to have something to take pride in where his son was concerned, but he willfully and joyfully disobeyed every decree, no matter how reasonable.

"I don't know how Mina and I will go back to plain American fare after such treatment as we've known in Paris," Edison declared. "I've never had such sumptuous food in all my life."

"I shall miss France a great deal, but I do believe my corsets will approve of our return home to lighter cuisine," Mina added with a tinkling laugh. Dot shot her daggers for the somewhat-daring reference to ladies' undergarments, but the rest of us chuckled good-naturedly at her joke.

Papa beamed at me. "Our Claire is a magnificent hostess."

"I'll drink to that." Edison lifted a glass of champagne in my direction. The rest of the assembly followed suit.

I turned to Edison's daughter, who had been a bit neglected in conversation. "Your name, Dot, is adorable. I assume it's short for Dorothy?"

"No, my Christian name is Marion," she replied.

"Perhaps my English fails me, but how does one derive Dot from Marion?"

"They don't," she said, heaving a much-put-upon sigh. "It makes more sense when you understand that my brother Thomas Junior's nickname is Dash."

"Dot and Dash?" Papa said, his face splitting into a grin. "Like a telegraph."

"Precisely," Edison said between enthusiastic bites of his meal. "I thought the nicknames were becoming."

"Absolutely charming," I said, though the expression on Dot's face betrayed that she found it less so. "I understand you're off to Germany in the morning, Mister Edison?"

"You understand correctly. Off to visit some contacts that will help bring my inventions over here across the pond. Should be quite an interesting visit, I expect."

"Oh, how fascinating," Papa interjected. And the two great men of invention were lost in the mire of discussing their work. I exhaled to know they were diverted for a few moments at least, and could let my mind wander. I wondered what it might be like to bring an easel up here and paint the clouds with watercolor or to re-create the Paris skyline in charcoals. Of course these offices were to be a hub of scientific experiment and discovery, but I wondered if I could persuade Papa to let me cramp the small space for a few hours from time to time.

Just then the baby kicked. A reminder that I would be occupied rather intensely for months to come. There would be no more time for sketches and painting in the future than there had been in the past twelve years. I shoved the perfectly prepared peas off to a corner of my plate with my fork, pretending to eat as the others chatted companionably. Adolphe squeezed my knee discreetly under the table, his little show of support when he knew I had to be uncomfortable, and my discomfort was only thinly veiled from a very important public.

The Edisons begged off after another hour. Their tickets to Germany were on the early morning train and they had another engagement still that evening. And by the time I reached the rue de Prony, I was grateful for the comfort of my rooms and the hot bath Pauline had prepared for me. I was about to slip into the warm, perfumed waters with Pauline's assistance, given the awkwardness of my condition, when one of the other maids knocked at the door. Pauline went to answer it and returned with a missive.

I recognized Édouard's hasty scrawl with my name on the envelope. The stationery was ivory and heavy, the sort I kept for important correspondence, but I wasn't familiar with the monogram on the top of the single page: CZ. On it, Édouard had scribbled a curt message:

I need you urgently. Don't tell Papa. Bring your pocketbook.

~É.

Below his message was scrawled an address on the Boulevard de Clichy, in the heart of Montmartre, only a mile or so from the house. If he could not come such a short distance, something truly was wrong. If he didn't want Papa to know, it was not mere boyish antics from which he needed rescue; he was usually all too happy to risk Papa's displeasure with such nonsense.

I cast a split-second look of regret back at the perfectly prepared bath, then ordered the messenger-bearing maid to have a carriage readied and Pauline to help me back into my clothes. Each step was a momentous effort, but I couldn't let Édouard fall to harm.

At the bottom of the stairs, I was greeted by the sight of Adolphe in the foyer handing his hat and overcoat to the footman as the maid was handing me mine.

"I thought after the exertions of this morning, you'd be taking the afternoon to rest." Adolphe's mien betrayed concern as I stood before the entryway mirror pinning on my hat.

"So did I." I was unable to keep the annoyance from my voice. Édouard had asked me not to tell Papa but had not sworn me to secrecy from Adolphe. "It seems Édouard is in trouble and he's sent for me to help him out of it."

I handed Adolphe the note to read as I readied myself to leave. Remembering the request in Édouard's missive, I checked the contents of my pocketbook. A fair amount of cash, but I had no way of knowing if it was enough.

"I'm coming with you." It was not a question. "I won't bother trying to convince you to let me go in your stead. I know that would be a waste of breath. But you're not going alone."

I felt the tension in my shoulders release just a bit. "I won't argue with you on that score. I've no desire to go into Montmartre alone if I don't have to." Memories of my last trip into the butte to find him had not endeared the place to me.

Adolphe's eyes widened. "I'll recover from that shock once we've found your fool brother."

Chapter Thirty-Three

The address Édouard provided was to a music hall not far from the one where I'd found him before. It was a new building, still in the final stages of construction, it would seem. Though for all the gleam and polish of its newness, it was destined to become as seedy as all the other clubs, dance halls, and thinly veiled brothels that permeated the arrondissement.

Adolphe helped me from the carriage, which was no easy feat in my state. When we approached the door to the cabaret, a hulking guard greeted us and opened the door. Clearly, we were expected. I shot a meaningful look back at Fabrice, a plea to intervene if things got out of hand before we entered the dark expanse of the club.

The main showroom was a tangle of chairs and tables, yet to be put in order for the patrons. At first glance, the club looked elegant and inviting, the sort of gentleman's club that respectable men might have enjoyed. But where a fine cabaret might have gilded candelabra, the ones here were simply painted to resemble it. The fabrics that looked like rich, red velvet from a distance were cheap and unappealing at closer proximity. It was the illusion of wealth without the expense; elegance and refinement without the bother of acquiring taste.

We were shown to an office in the bowels of the place. The hulking man opened the door and closed it behind us.

"Oh my God, Édouard!" His face was a bloody mess, and I couldn't tell how much was injury and how much of it was merely residual blood that would wipe away. "He's hurt—why have you not summoned help?"

"Calm yourself, good lady. He'll be perfectly well." A great walrus of a man had answered. He was dressed in a garish green suit with an impressively bushy beard and eyebrows, sitting calmly behind a gleaming walnut desk that looked to be one of the few genuine pieces of decent furniture in the place. Where Papa's office in the tower was understated and carefully curated, this man's office was a temple to all things tawdry. As experienced as I was at keeping a guarded expression, I was certain my disdain was written plainly in every line on my face, and this seemed to amuse the showman to no end. "Tell her."

"I'll be fine, Claire. It looks worse than it is." Édouard's voice was strained, but strong enough that I believed him. I pulled a handkerchief from my handbag and passed it to him to staunch the bleeding.

Adolphe cleared his throat. "We haven't had the pleasure of an introduction, but perhaps you would be good enough to begin by explaining to me why my wife has been summoned to this . . . place . . . in her delicate state and why my brother-in-law looks like he's lost a prize fight, and badly too."

"Where are my manners? I'm Charles Zidler, proprietor of this fine establishment." He gestured for me to take the open chair next to Édouard, which left Adolphe standing. "I understand you're young Édouard's elder sister, yes? I'd been so hoping to meet with your father, Madame Salles."

"If you buy a ticket to the top of his tower, you may find yourself lucky enough to shake his hand." My tone was crisp as Édouard held my handkerchief to a nasty gash on his forehead.

"I meant in a more businesslike capacity." He leaned back in his chair with the sort of self-assurance of a man who had leverage. His fingers were arched in a lazy pyramid as he spoke, calculated and precise.

"I told you I wasn't going to bring my father into any of this," Édouard interjected. "This isn't the sort of enterprise of which he approves."

"And yet his oldest son is one of my best patrons and has been for years. How curious." Zidler's smile was positively feline as he looked at us like so many mice.

"My brother has a fondness for unseemly environs. Much to his detriment." I shot Édouard a hard look and he had the good grace to bow his head in embarrassment.

"So many of your lot do," Zidler said. "And so many of the petit bourgeois wish they could pretend to the same level of class and distinction as your family can lay claim to. This is what we seek to do here at the Moulin Rouge. To create a place where men of great birth and men of more humble means can spend an evening commingled in affordable elegance and glamour. And of course the pleasure of seeing the most beautiful women in Paris."

"You mean a place where the rich can enjoy a bit of 'slum tourism,' in which poor and desperate women with pretty faces can be exploited for *your* gain?"

"You insult me, madam. This will be a veritable sanctuary where women are paid homage. A palace of women. The first of its kind. Oh, I rather like that. I shall have to jot it down, so I don't forget it."

I exhaled, exasperated, as he scratched his own words into a notebook on his desk. "Let us out with it, Monsieur Zidler. I find myself lacking my usual patience. What has my brother done and what can we do to make it right?"

"As you can see, the Moulin Rouge is not yet open for business, though we hope to be in a few weeks' time. Before the end of the expo, you see. But it seems that your brother has run up quite a tab at one of my other establishments. The funds he owes will be indispensable in getting the Moulin Rouge opened on schedule."

"How much?" The sum in my pocketbook would never match the figure if it were considerable enough to delay the operations of the cabaret.

He wrote a sum on a sheet of paper and passed it across to my side of the desk. I gasped at the amount. I hadn't a fraction of the sum at my disposal. Adolphe took the sheet and shot a withering glare at Édouard. "You absolute imbecile."

"I had no idea that the tally had grown so high," Édouard finally interjected. "Every time I tried to pay, Monsieur Zidler told me to put my billfold away and we'd settle another time."

"And you charged him interest on his bill for months and months to garner a profit off a drunken fool with a rich father," I supplied.

"My dear, you make it sound quite uncivilized when you put it that way."

"Then how would you put it?"

"I merely charged your brother a fee for the convenience and safety of not having to settle his accounts each night. Removing one's billfold in such places can be a risky endeavor."

"I'm sure," Adolphe scoffed. "I want to see his ledger."

"Naturally. I expected as much." Zidler produced a packet of papers—a thick one. Adolphe looked it over, shaking his head while Édouard shrank smaller and smaller in his seat.

"Wine, spirits, food, lodging . . ." Adolphe's omission of the last line was telling. Édouard had obviously availed himself of the hospitality of the dancing girls whose acts, as I understood, were merely advertisements for the services they offered after the show for the highest bidder. “Two years’ worth of it, and everything charged at ten percent compound interest. It’s a damned fortune.”

“I had no idea about the interest,” Édouard managed to squeak. “I told him I wouldn’t pay it.”

“Many of my patrons consider the fee quite modest when compared to the potential risk to their person. Which is why my man, unfortunately, had to remind young Monsieur Édouard of his fiduciary obligations.”

“Are most of your patrons in the habit of waiting two years to settle their accounts, or is that a special privilege for my brother?”

“I admit it is an extreme case,” Zidler said. “But your brother is such a devoted guest, I felt it was my sacred duty to ensure he get the finest service in all things.”

“Is it your usual practice to hoodwink your best clients, Monsieur Zidler? How is it you’re able to charge such exorbitant rates of interest without his knowledge?” I pressed.

He opened the folder to show Édouard’s signature. It was his, if sloppy. “Every bill of sale Monsieur Édouard signed included a legal binding statement of the terms of credit. I cannot help if he chose not to read the terms despite being presented with the notice hundreds of times in the past two years.”

“Because he was dead drunk every time he was presented with his tab at the end of the night.” Adolphe pinched the bridge of his nose in exasperation.

“My establishments provide some of the best refreshment in the city, and it is not my position to nudge my patrons into moderation. I’d never presume such impertinence.”

I felt the air whistle through my teeth as I fought to keep control of my temper. Heaven knew if I indulged the fervent desire that was building in my breast to throw the crystal paperweight on his desk at his fat head, he'd press every charge he could reasonably throw at me, and a few more besides. "I think you ensured he was never shown a bill when he was sober to lure him into this very position. Édouard has his faults, but he certainly would have settled his bill before it came to this if he'd known how dire the circumstances were. He's done it before."

"That is a very serious accusation, Madame Salles. But you'll find there's very little legal recourse for your brother, even if your claims are justified. If I were forced to only present bills of sale to sober customers, I'd have a terrific time collecting what I am owed, would I not?"

"At any point over the past two years, did you confront my brother-in-law about settling his account? Certainly he's not the first of your patrons to need a reminder," Adolphe asked. He sounded like an attorney cross-examining a witness and I found his quick wit stirred the strings of devotion in my heart.

"Naturally, any number of them do," Zidler said.

"Édouard, has he asked to collect money before now?" I turned to my brother, though he'd been trying his best to shrink away from the interview altogether.

Édouard found a bit of courage to shore up his words. "No. This was the first time I'd been presented with the full record of things. I was heading back home when his goon pulled me from the street into a carriage and brought me here. I'd been planning to wash up and rest a bit before the luncheon today—oh, damn and blast it all, the luncheon—he's going to murder me, isn't he?"

"It seems there's quite a list of people in this city willing to perform that office," I said without humor. "But we'll worry about that later."

"Easy for you to say—it isn't your neck on the line."

"I've never had the opportunity, much less the inclination, to make such a mess of things, Brother."

"As charming as family squabbles may be, I'm afraid I haven't much time for them this afternoon," Zidler interjected. "I must insist on the account being settled in full before the end of the day, or things may continue to get . . . awkward."

Adolphe pulled his billfold from his breast pocket and threw a tremendous pile of bills on Zidler's desk. "That is about a quarter of Monsieur Eiffel's debt before the interest charges. I'll have the rest of the original sum brought to you within the next two hours. I shall be in contact with our legal counsel to determine whether the interest charges are indeed within the scope of the law."

"You'll find that the best lawyers in Paris have devised the verbiage we use on all our bills of sale, and everything is quite in order, but I certainly welcome you to verify this with your own people if it will give you solace. But I hope they're able to perform the job with some haste. It won't extend the deadline for payment."

"What are you threatening us with, Zidler? Are you going to send your thugs after the rest of the family as well?" Adolphe leaned over Zidler's desk and was only a few inches from his red, bulbous face.

"No, no. I'm not a man who embraces violence, whatever you may think of me. I am a ruthlessly efficient man, and I find resorting to such measures rarely derives the best outcomes, and often creates unnecessary delays. A man rendered unconscious cannot run to the bank to make a withdrawal, can he?"

"How forward-thinking of you," I said, unable to control my sneer.

"I like to think so," he replied as though my tone had been admiring. Oh, but he was smoother than Mademoiselle Leclerc's best silk. As much as I loathed the man, I was taking notes for my own social encounters. "I will be glad to accept the payment for the rest of Monsieur Édouard's bill by the end of the day. However, I might be able to come to an arrangement when it comes to the interest charges."

"What sort of arrangement?" Adolphe asked.

"The establishment would be willing to overlook the considerable interest charges if Monsieur Eiffel would consider investing in our enterprises here. His patronage would be an immeasurable asset to the Moulin Rouge. Like your father's tower, we hope to create a space that will draw Frenchmen from all walks of life, and guests from abroad as well, to gaze in wonder at what our fine country has to offer. It's why our little rendezvous is here, despite the commotion of our preparations for opening. I'd hoped to show your father the premises."

"My father offers the people a panorama of the greatest city on earth. You offer them cheap champagne and loose women. It's hardly the same thing, Monsieur Zidler." I was seething at the audacity of his comparison. My father's masterpiece compared to this vulgar imitation of elegance.

"Though I would never wish to contradict a lady, both are marvels in their own right, Madame Salles."

"My father would never invest a single sou in a place like this. He'd sooner pay the interest than have his name intertwined with yours," I replied.

"That may, regrettably, be unavoidable. The debt your brother has accumulated in my other cabaret is large enough that it might be of interest to the press." Zidler's eyes glistened, anticipating our panic at his thinly veiled threat.

"And it might not," Adolphe said, his tone almost bored. "Really, Zidler, do you think the Eiffel family is really naive enough to fall for your blackmail?"

"*Blackmail* is such an ugly word—" Zidler began.

"Because it's an act performed by ugly souls," I interjected. "Leak whatever you wish to the press. Édouard's antics haven't interested them in the past. I don't see why they would now."

"Your father has grown in notoriety, Madame Salles. I would think the press would be far more interested than they were, even a few years ago," he said, his voice going low and sinister.

"And that well may be, but a few reports of errant behavior on the part of my brother won't have the impact you fear, Monsieur Zidler. Don't overplay your hand," I warned, pushing myself up from the chair with what small modicum of grace I was able.

Édouard and Adolphe followed me out of the office, and I was able to get another glimpse of the music hall. It was vast, and the seating area was open to the sky above. At night, the stars would serve as stage lights. The wooden dance floor shone under the afternoon sun, and various plants and greenery filled open spaces. A veritable Garden of Eden. And with a glance back to Zidler's office, I knew there was no question the snake was at the helm of the whole affair.

Chapter Thirty-Four

"Give me one good reason why I shouldn't cast you out of my front door and never have another thing to do with you. One reason, boy." Papa was home by the time we arrived, and when he learned the nature of our errand, his buoyant mood at meeting the Edisons had dissipated.

"I was a fool, Papa" was all Édouard offered by way of defense as Pauline fussed over the cut over his brow with a wet cloth.

"At least on that, we can agree." Papa crossed his arms over his chest. "What do you mean calling your sister into that godforsaken hovel? And in her condition too? Why didn't you send for me?"

"Adolphe was there, Papa, I was fine." I wasn't trying to excuse Édouard's behavior, but I didn't want to deal with the awkward mess if Papa killed him. The press might ignore Zidler and his stories, but this would be harder to keep quiet.

"Lucky for your brother's neck," Papa growled. "Now, boy, explain to me how all this came to be."

Édouard launched into an explanation of the events that had transpired, with the occasional interjection from Adolphe to supply information. I sat back on the settee, my feet perched on a pouf that Pauline had fetched for me, and let them hash it out. There wasn't a part of my body that didn't ache, and I was afraid I wouldn't be able to restrain my temper if I joined in the conversation.

Papa was more furious than I'd ever seen him by the time the explanation had been offered, and I felt all the more weary for having to relive the events.

"I plan to take this to the attorneys and make sure the charges are legal." Adolphe handed Édouard's considerable dossier from Zidler to Papa, who grew a worrisome shade of purple as he flipped through the pages.

I cleared my throat and the men turned to look at me. "I trust Zidler as far as little Robert can throw an anvil, but if one thing can be believed, it's that his paperwork is in order and legally watertight. It would be a waste of time and lawyer fees."

"So we're to pay him off and pray he doesn't leak to the press?" Adolphe took a seat across from me and rubbed his eyes in exasperation. "Zidler wasn't wrong that we'll be more of an object of interest now than we ever have been."

"It won't be that easy. We need to speak to the editors of all the papers that foul man might contact and make sure they don't print a word he has to say."

Papa paused in his pacing. "That sounds expensive."

"It will be. We can't let Zidler win, or we'll never be free of him. We have to beat him at his own revolting game. We'll have to get the press on our side preemptively. *Le Figaro* is indebted to you as you've leased them space on the tower. We have influence at some of the others. In addition to getting them not to run a story about Édouard, we need to persuade them not to accept advertisement fees from Zidler, which would be ruinous for his new cabaret."

Édouard looked over at me and grimaced in pain from the effort. "He'll be furious. Nothing matters to him more than that club."

"Which is why, when he finds out it was our family who placed the embargo on his advertisements, he'll be easily persuaded to destroy all the records of your visits to any of his clubs and will never again dream of going to the press in any matter concerning this family. We have to show him our strength."

"It's so diabolical, it just might work," Papa said. "But we must settle the bill as soon as the funds can be withdrawn from the bank. I won't be indebted to that swine a moment longer than I must."

"I'll deliver the funds myself." Adolphe moved to his feet. "On the condition that my wife and her diabolical schemes get some rest before she keels over."

"No arguments here."

"If only we had one of Edison's contraptions here to capture that on record," Papa said with a dry laugh.

Adolphe's eyes danced, likely remembering my easy acquiescence to his accompanying me to the Moulin Rouge. "It's a day for astonishment on that front, I assure you, Gustave." He hurried off to the bank, no doubt hoping he could make a withdrawal before it closed for the night.

"I'm sorry," Édouard said at length. To me or to Papa, to the room in general, I couldn't be sure.

"No more than I am," Papa replied. "I've been so damned busy trying to build every bridge in Christendom I didn't have time to give you the lashing you so clearly needed. I was never a man who believed in the 'spare the rod, spoil the child' claptrap, but it's the only thing I can think of that might have gotten through your thick skull."

"I've been daft," Édouard admitted. "I'm done with Zidler and his clubs. But I hope you'll believe I had no idea what he was doing."

Papa's look was hard, and I felt I had to defend Édouard on at least one score. "Zidler's a confidence man of the first order. I'm sure other young men like Édouard, and cleverer too, have fallen victim to his ploys before. He was played like a fiddle in the hands of a master, there's no denying it."

"Thank you . . . I think," Édouard said, gently removing the cloth from his forehead. The gash where, as his story went, his forehead hit the jamb of Zidler's office door had bled profusely as head wounds were wont to do, but fell just short of needing stitches, which was a relief. The last thing any of us wanted to do was fetch the doctor and have to relive the story once more.

"You're welcome . . . I think," I offered in return. Papa let out a loud sigh and turned to us.

"I need to lie down before supper." Papa looked more peaked than I'd seen him in months, which was quite remarkable given the constant demands of the tower. "Claire, I believe you made your husband a promise to do the same. Édouard, I'll deal with you later. In the meantime, you will escort your sister to her rooms, where she should have been resting herself these three hours or more."

Édouard nodded his assent and stood gingerly from his chair.

"Thank you for today. I swear if there was ever a match for the likes of Charles Zidler, it's you. You really were a wonder." He allowed me to lean heavily on him as we ascended the grand staircase that seemed impossibly long after the trying events of the afternoon.

"I suppose that's a compliment, but I'd rather not have the occasion to best a smarmy man like him in a battle of wits again if you please. And especially not while I'm ready to pop like a circus balloon," I grumbled.

"A fair request. I'll do my best to honor it."

"But what I want to know is when you will learn your lesson. You've made promises of reform before now. Will it take you getting killed to make you see sense? Or someone you care about? If I had come to the Moulin Rouge alone, what might the outcome have been? I couldn't have prevented Zidler from harming either of us. Did you ever stop to consider that?"

Édouard stayed mute.

"I know that you find me an irritating and interfering older sister, but mothering you is the duty I was charged with when Maman passed. You may resent me, but Valentine, Bébert, Robert, and this new little one need me, and you thought nothing of putting me in danger to save face with Papa."

"And to save him from being seen there. Whatever I do, or even you or Adolphe, it won't matter to the press nearly as much as what Papa does."

"A convenient excuse that serves your purposes, Brother," I retorted.

"I know," he said, his eyes fixed ahead on the corridor. "It was the act of a coward."

"No, it was the act of a child. Just like the time you broke Maman's vase, and instead of telling anyone, you tried to hide it. Do you remember what happened then?"

"Laure cut her foot on one of the shards that I missed."

"And the thing you fail to learn is that you always forget shards, Édouard. We all do. Sometimes we have to ask for help cleaning up our messes to avoid hurting other people. This could have been much worse, Édouard, and not just for you."

"I know, Claire. And I'm so sorry. I'll do better from now on."

"I don't want to hear that from you ever again. You've spoken those words a million times and a week later, you're back doing the same selfish things that you did before. Don't make promises anymore. Change your behavior or do what you can to minimize the damage to the rest of us. I won't bail you out again."

"I'm done with clubs. Especially anything to do with Zidler."

I knew full well this was likely another one of his empty promises but couldn't help but respond. "I hope that's true."

"I confess, I would have loved to see the Moulin Rouge in all its glory. I do think it will be a remarkable place when it's all said and done. But Zidler won't stop. I see that now. Even if I paid for every drink in cash before it was poured, he'd find a way to gain leverage over me to get to Papa."

"You have the measure of the man. I hope you remember this for more than a few days."

"I wish I could promise you that I won't do more stupid things in the future, but I don't think I can," Édouard said. "It seems to be my talent and my one true calling."

I threw my head back in a genuine laugh. "You really are a horse's ass; do you know that? Édouard, you're a smart and capable man. You have talents. You just need to find them and cultivate them. Just like Papa and his designs. He wasn't born with a sketch pad and pencil in hand."

"All the better for poor Bonne Maman," Édouard said, to which I jostled him in the ribs with my elbow. "But I think you're right."

"Find your skills, Brother. Or find a purpose to keep you out of trouble until you do."

He looked thoughtful for a moment. "You're right."

"I usually am."

"What about you and your art? What happened to all your grand plans to attend art school with Ursule?"

I paused as we reached the door to my rooms and was relieved to hear Pauline bustling about on the other side of them, refreshing the forgotten bath. "Some of us don't have the privilege to follow our passions, Édouard."

"That doesn't seem fair. You should have been able to paint and scribble away instead of trying to civilize the pack of us and following Papa around all over the place."

I could have cast it in his face that had he not wasted his youth, he could have taken a meaningful place in the company at Papa's side. At any point, he could have stepped up and relieved me of some of the burden of responsibility. But it would have served no purpose. "Thank you for that. But as the saying goes, life isn't fair, and I've found that anyone who tries to claim otherwise is usually stupid or up to no good. But you can make it up to me by making something of yours before it's too late."

Chapter Thirty-Five

September 1, 1891
1, rue Rabelais

Where does this set go, madame?" One of our new footmen, Thierry, stood before me, a massive rosewood footstool with an elaborately embroidered cushion top braced in his arms. A line of footmen, most of them new to our household, stood in line behind Thierry awaiting my orders.

I inspected the motif on the upholstery more carefully and consulted the page in my notebook where I'd catalogued all our purchases. "Cream with the floral spray goes in the second drawing room." I gestured down the hall. "The third door on the right."

All looked relieved that the heavy stuff wasn't bound for one of the bedrooms on the third floor. Poor lads. I shook my head as more rich tapestries, not from our family collections, gilded mirrors, furniture crafted of exotic woods, and rich fabrics made their way to the room in the arms of beleaguered footmen who had been at the exercise all day. Once one room was filled, another was waiting.

The contents of our home on the rue de Prony would never have stretched to adequately furnish this enormous home Papa had purchased, and the acquisition of new furniture fell to me, whether I wanted the job or not. But as the task was under my purview, I had the liberty to procure what pieces I wanted from the brokers of my choice. Largely, I opted for solid secondhand items I'd sourced from reputable dealers who helped to liquidate estates that had fallen on hard times or whose family line had died out. To Papa's mind, the chief virtue of buying the sturdy antique stuff was that it allowed us to take up residence here all that much sooner. To me, it seemed less vulgar than commissioning all new things. Less wasteful too.

Of course, there was the added benefit that if the furnishings had come from old monied families, the hope was that, by using their things, our own home would take on the look of those fine old chateaux whose trappings had been collected over numerous generations. A new wardrobe gifted to the mistress of the house by a doting aunt in the seventeenth century. A dining table commissioned in the eighteenth century to allow the family to host even grander suppers, and so on. If any of it looked imperfect or a bit mismatched, all the better. There was cohesiveness in the rooms of an old estate, but there wasn't the artificial uniformity that came from buying a houseful of new pieces. That look was the hallmark of "new money" and I would avoid that taint at all cost.

I ordered the broker to search widely and purchase from numerous estates so that none of our well-connected guests would step into a drawing room and instantly recognize that every stick had come from one of their old friends' homes. They wouldn't say a word, of course, but I'd see the light of recognition in their eyes and would know my efforts had been uncovered. I kept matching chairs and sofas together, but never too many pieces of the same provenance in one room, and never paired with any paintings or tapestries from their house of origin.

It was a complex game of cards that required thorough shuffling. But I'd devised detailed charts with the source and eventual destination of each piece, complete with sketches of how I envisioned the rooms might look when fully furnished. It had been far too long since I'd taken pencil to paper, and I lamented the skill I'd lost. Not all, but the atrophy was noticeable. I found it was much like horseback riding. Even after a long absence from the stables, one would still know how to handle a horse, but would grow stiff until reaccustomed to the practice. The trick was, quite literally, getting back in the saddle.

And so must I. The more I sketched, the faster my skill would return. Perhaps to its former level of proficiency; perhaps even better. Or not. Perhaps the spark of talent had flickered and died from years of disuse. But there was no harm in seeing what might come of it. There would never be the time to take things as seriously as Ursule had, and did, but it would give me some pleasure. And after all this time, I felt entitled to some of my own making.

"This all looks splendid, Cherub." Papa's voice boomed from the foyer. I looked over the railing to see the army of footmen swirling around him like so many spokes on a bicycle spinning around their axle: Papa himself.

I swept downstairs to greet him with a kiss on his cheek, and Adolphe too, who entered three steps behind him, as always.

"I'm glad you approve, Papa. It's been quite a project." I beamed, for even now his approval meant the world to me.

"Quite a statement, given the other project you just completed," Adolphe chimed in, his eyes glancing upward in the direction of the nursery. Our precious little Geneviève, or "Ninette" as we called her, had arrived just a few months before. The girl I'd quietly hoped for after two strapping sons, and just in time for the move to rue Rabelais and a rather chaotic few months that surrounded it. Papa was determined to have everything as perfect as a postcard before Christmas, and there was only so much I was willing to delegate. If

I were dead on my feet and still healing from the birth of my third child in five years—the last two delivered in closer proximity than I would have chosen if I were fully mistress of my own destiny—it mattered not.

"I hope you have it in you to manage a bit more furniture. I've been making inquiries about a chateau in Sèvres and a villa near Vevey. With my retirement soon upon us, we might as well have a few comfortable spots to land when the opportunities to travel present themselves." His chest was puffed out in pride. He'd probably dreamed of such luxuries when his well-heeled classmates boasted wealth that was both greater and older than his own.

But I felt a stone in the pit of my stomach. "Is this wise, Papa? Wouldn't hotel stays be more economical?"

"Perhaps, but I can't deed you a rented property after I am gone. It will all be part of your inheritance." He squeezed my arm, turning to leave for his study, his way of saying the conversation was concluded.

"I don't need villas, Papa." My voice carried in the great foyer, far more than I expected, as there were no carpets to dampen the sound.

He turned to look at me. "No, but you shall have them all the same." He continued to his private sanctuary without another backward glance or word in my direction.

Adolphe remained by my side, wrapping an arm around me. I melted into him for just a moment. Not too long, or I would remember how weary I was. "You ought to indulge him, dearest. Men of his age begin to worry about what they will have to leave behind for their children. I do believe it's his way of thanking you for everything you've done for him and for the company."

"If he truly wishes to thank me, he'll spend his precious resources prudently. Perhaps I haven't been enough in the ledgers of late, but it seems a tremendous amount of expense in such a short period." I rubbed my eyes with my hands and tried to ignore the heavy sensation in my arms and legs that beckoned for me to sit.

"He has the reserves, my sweet. The Panama blunder may have been a failure, but your father was at least able to turn a profit." His face was impassive as he studied mine.

"How can that be?" Papa had been commissioned to build the locks as a last-ditch effort to save the doomed project, but he had been enlisted too late. Even with an army of men and Papa's best designers on the job, he hadn't been able to save the endeavor despite several new subscription efforts to infuse more cash into the project. More people who would lose the savings they depended upon to see them through their old age.

"It's a complicated business, but your papa technically met the demands of his contract for the locks. He was able to more than recoup what he invested. It's just a shame the project didn't come to fruition."

The canal was to open the seaway from Europe and the east to the western coast of the Americas by allowing passage in the narrow gap between Central and South America. It would have been a boon to commerce, but the jungle was an inhospitable environment. We lost hundreds of men to yellow fever alone, not to mention accidents and other bouts of misfortune. The tower had been Papa's riskiest undertaking when it all began, but I was beginning to fear the Panama Canal had long since eclipsed it.

"If that's the case, shouldn't Papa be all the more circumspect in his expenditures? Out of deference to those who are to lose everything?"

"Perhaps, but your papa wants to see the funds from this, and more substantially the revenue from the tower visits, invested in real estate for the family's use. And once he has an idea in mind, there is little to be done to dissuade him."

"As I know all too well. But do answer me this: How much profit did Papa earn from this?"

Adolphe's color drained and his mouth opened and closed a few times, adjusting itself around the right words. "Six million or so."

I exhaled slowly. "So much? Surely he should give some back to help the investors recoup their losses?"

"Dearest, the whole of your papa's fortune wouldn't stretch far enough to help them in any substantial way. The losses were too great."

"God above, how much was lost, Adolphe?"

He couldn't meet my eyes. "Over a billion francs."

I regretted the lack of a sturdy chair back on which to steady myself. The blood pounded in my ears and my knees felt weak.

"It can't be so much. How many investors were there?"

"Over eight hundred thousand."

My arm involuntarily circled my waist, as if trying to keep my organs from spilling onto the foyer floor. I better understood the term *gutted* in that moment. In moments of panic, my ability to perform calculations became frighteningly quick and precise. "Twelve hundred and fifty francs per investor, on average." It was a small sum for Papa or Adolphe, but it was a tremendous sum for a person of the working class.

Adolphe nodded. "Some of the poorer ones invested less, hoping to make what little they had stretch further. Others invested quite a bit more. So many of them saw it as a sure opportunity to shore up their futures that they rushed to invest in the beginning. Loads of widows hoping to make their late husbands' pensions extend to see them settled for the rest of their days."

"What can we do?" I asked after a long pause. "Surely *something* can be done."

"There is. See your father's homes furnished. Wear pretty dresses. Smile as he offers you a new bauble. We cannot do anything of worth for the poor souls whose money was sunk in that blasted jungle, but you can lift your father's spirits by enjoying the fruits of his labors. You bear no guilt in this. I was the one who encouraged his involvement, so if anyone should feel some guilt about all this, it's me."

He kissed my brow and turned to join Papa in the study, where they would no doubt prattle about the events of the workday over a brandy as I saw that the preparations for supper were well underway as the kitchen staff found their rhythm in their new space.

As he left the room, I bowed my shaking head. It seemed like a small thing to ask, but it felt Herculean on my shoulders. Papa had overcome so many setbacks in his projects, so many attempts at slander in the press, but I couldn't imagine a scenario where he came out of this unscathed.

One week later, when we returned from the Opéra and a sumptuous dinner at the Café de la Paix to find Papa's study in disarray, the subject of a surprise search from the police, I knew the moment of Papa's triumph for his glorious tower was over all too soon.

Chapter Thirty-Six

November 1892
1, rue Rabelais

"They have ruined me." Papa sat in his favorite fauteuil near the window that looked onto the courtyard of his stately home—our home—in the very heart of the city Papa loved, throughout which he'd placed his indelible marks. The butler had looked terrified to deliver the paper to the sitting room as though we might revive the old tradition of shooting messengers, but I'd thanked him with a smile that radiated sincerity but contained none—the mastery of which had taken me years.

Papa looked small, impossibly small, that evening. The plush chair looked as though it might swallow him whole as the evening paper was spread across his knees. No doubt he wished it would. "They have ruined me and there is nothing to be done for it." He tossed the paper, headline upward, onto his side table so I could read the headline:

EIFFEL TO FACE TRIAL FOR PANAMA SCANDAL

I tossed the paper back onto the table and swallowed a sigh of annoyance that would have set the men on edge. We'd known this was coming in the year since the raid on our home, but to see it in print was a blow. All the same, I stifled the desire to wail and shout that prickled far too close to the surface and turned to my father and husband.

"Nothing about this is shocking. Thousands of people have lost their life savings. The only provisions they had for when old age would make employment impossible. You cannot expect our countrymen to let such a thing go unpunished. They demand that heads roll, and you know full well the powers that be will see they get their wish."

Papa blanched. "You seem to forget, Cherub, the head they're asking for is mine."

"I have not in the least. We do ourselves no favors by pretending the situation is any less grave than it is. Since the Panama endeavor folded, we moved into this massive house. We bought several others. We're seen at the opera. The people assume we eat off golden plates and that I have an entire suite of rooms dedicated to my wardrobe. That their image of us might be hyperbolic doesn't make it any less real to them. If we're to survive this scandal, it will be because we know exactly how dire the situation is."

The men exchanged glances, as they often did when I pointed out an uncomfortable truth. But coddling them wouldn't serve to make the outcome any brighter. Adolphe claimed the paper and read the article for himself, though he apparently found his own sighs of exasperation harder to restrain.

Of course we'd known Papa was going to trial long before the filthy reporters sullied his name with ink and grimy newsprint filled with lies and half-truths. We always knew before they did.

And it was fortunate too, as it gave us time to prepare, to minimize damage, to launch our counterattacks when necessary. But those disgusting prevarications printed for the world to see were breaking Papa's heart. I worried that if the scandal grew any larger, his heartbreak would become all too literal.

Barely grown, Valentine and Albert were too young to be orphans. Even at the age of thirty, I felt too young to claim that title myself. Losing Maman had been devastating, but losing Papa too would leave me unmoored. Perhaps it was an odd thing for a married woman with three children to think, but it was no less true. Papa and the company had been my life for more than a decade and a half—more than half my life's purchase—and to lose him would mean the loss of the very ground under my silk slippers.

Adolphe removed his spectacles and rubbed the bridge of his nose, taking his own opportunity to toss the paper aside. But he seemed to rally his resolve. "It won't be as bad as all that. The press love to destroy their own heroes, but the courts won't fall for it. It's a smear campaign through and through. You'll come out the other side of this looking better than you ever have," Adolphe assured him, going to the sideboard and pouring Papa a healthy measure of cognac. Papa accepted it but did not drink. He swirled the rich honey-colored liquid and stared at it, perhaps hoping it might contain the answer to the debacle before us. The crystal snifter bounced the flickering light from the fire onto the thick Turkish carpets.

"My God, but I envy your confidence, *mon garçon*, but today I cannot share in it. The press will make sure my reputation never recovers."

I drew a breath and smoothed my skirts. I had to do as I'd always done and make things right for Papa. It wasn't good for him to drink cognac on an empty stomach, so wordlessly I set a plate of his favorite biscuits on the small round mahogany table next to his chair. I never prodded, but he knew my meaning.

He always did.

He took a biscuit from the plate and took a few obliging bites as I went to stand by the fire. It was one of those bitter days in Paris where the cold went bone deep despite the warmth of the hearthstones and the heavy emerald velvet of my gown. But it wasn't just the weather. The papers were intent on making Papa a pariah. After all he'd done for Paris, it seemed like poor recompense for his work.

"We shouldn't waste time pretending this news isn't catastrophic for our public image. Because it is." Their heads turned. It was a rare moment when I broke the silence.

I heard the click of Adolphe's teeth. He had started to contradict me, but he knew better. When I chose to make my opinions known, they were worth hearing. He hadn't needed seven years of marriage to learn this, though occasionally he forgot.

"What would you have us do, dearest? How would you move forward?"

I didn't hesitate. "With our heads held high and the best lawyers in Paris at the ready. There is no escaping the trial now. You've made every appeal that you can to have the case thrown out and they failed. So we must look on this as a chance to prove your innocence so thoroughly that the public will have no doubt of it. In some ways it's better that we go to trial. No one will be able to say you bought your way out of this when they find you innocent."

I broke my rule of speaking wishes as though they were certainties, but Papa did require a glimmer of optimism. If he went to trial thinking the cause was already lost, it would simply expedite that very verdict.

"My reputation, my legacy will never recover. No matter what the outcome." Papa's face grew gray, and I felt my heart clench in my chest. Only the three babes sleeping above stairs could induce me to the same state of concern. Little Geneviève was barely a year old and deserved more of my attention than I'd been able to give her of late. I'd have to arrange a time with Nanny to take her to the park. Unlike Papa, I could go out in public and not be recognized.

"Papa, your legacy will survive as long as your buildings and bridges stand. Even longer. We will convene with your counsel in the morning to strategize, so rather than fret, you'd do better to sleep so you'll meet them ready to fight. We need you in top form."

Papa downed the cognac and stood, looking a bit wobbly at first, but steadied himself. "I can't imagine my brain will quieten enough for me to rest, but you're right that I should at least try."

"I'll ask Pauline to send you warm milk. Pair that with one of your engineering texts from the Polytechnic and you'll be asleep in minutes."

Adolphe and Papa had the good grace to look affronted at my abuse of their beloved tomes. "Careful, Madame Salles. The press I will learn to handle, but such an insult is too much for my old heart to bear."

"Well, if you have a cardiac incident, it might mean some sympathy from the jury. Don't rule it out as a strategy."

Papa turned to Adolphe. "I believe that Englishwoman Mary Shelley wrote of such monsters, my boy. I wish you all the best of luck with this one."

Adolphe snorted at Papa's rebuke. "If she is a monster, she is one of your making, Gustave." Papa chortled on his way out of the room, but I couldn't bring myself to laugh. They spoke an uncomfortable truth I wasn't equal to pondering just then.

Adolphe placed his snifter on the sideboard and offered me an arm to head upstairs. Rather than retreat into his own rooms to change, he entered mine without invitation. He was world-weary and didn't want to bother with the illusion that we didn't share a room.

"I am a fool," he muttered as he undid the buttons on his boots and kicked them off under our bed. "I should never have persuaded him to take on the project. Lesseps assured me the only thing wanting with the endeavor was good craftsmen, which I knew we could provide. Your father kept the company's involvement limited to the locks on the canal because he thought he could manage it without overpromising. I'd hoped to ensure the comfortable retirement of those investors, not see it lost in the bottom of the damned canal."

"And it will be on your shoulders to speak so passionately to the judge, my love. You'll have to convince them that your intentions were good, no matter what misfortune befell the project later. The company worked on the locks until they were ordered to stop. That must be the very thing the judges are told over and over."

It would be the best—perhaps only—defense that might move the hearts of those who wanted blood for the wealth that was lost. Those who sought justice for the lifetimes of savings that had vaporized seemingly overnight. Eight hundred thousand people left depleted with no recourse other than vengeance. Papa had been paid for his work, but he had endeavored to complete it within the scope of his contract.

And I didn't blame them. The healthy Eiffel coffers hadn't suffered as the company had been able to liquidate the equipment onsite. Our lovely homes, of which there were now several, were not at risk. We left the project richer, and while I was certain Lesseps had been, and his cronies still were, far more to blame than Papa, it didn't improve the look of the thing.

Instead of ringing for dear Pauline, Adolphe unfastened my dress and loosened my corset so I could slip into a cool chemise and into bed. Though adrenaline had been coursing in my veins for the last hour or more, the moment I lay down, I felt the weight of the day settle into my arms and legs. I felt as though my muscle and bone were made of the same iron as the tower that loomed over the Champs de Mars.

"What if he's found guilty, Claire? What will happen to the company? Our livelihood?" He spoke the words like a plaintive prayer. It reminded me more than a little of Laure's pleas for God to return Maman to us all those years before.

"We'll soldier on," I said, though the thought of a life without Papa at the center of it made my core turn to ice. "We Eiffels always do, and I'm convinced the Salles are made of stuff just as stern as ours. If you hadn't convinced me of that, little Robert would have."

Adolphe chortled, no doubt thinking of our young son's daredevil antics that had caused some of my hairs to go prematurely white. "I hope you're right, dear."

I wanted to offer him more reassurance. That all would be well and that we'd come out smelling of jasmine and honeysuckle as we always did. But this wasn't a quandary with a building that needed to be overcome. We couldn't simply engineer our way out of this issue, no matter how clever Papa and Adolphe were. No matter how I managed gossip in the back channels, the damage wouldn't be entirely contained. And though Adolphe and I had faced our challenges over the course of our marriage, I loved and respected him too much to fill his ear with the beautiful lies he so desperately wished to be true.

Chapter Thirty-Seven

February 9, 1893

The trial aged Papa worse than the tragedy of Maman's death or the stress of any of his projects; even the tower. I wanted nothing more than to bear the strain for him, but permission had been denied. No matter how much I protested, Papa argued that women of my station did not appear in courtrooms unless bidden by court itself. And so I was forced to send Papa and Adolphe to the Palais de Justice to face the wrath of the jury without my support. It felt like a betrayal of all the vows I ever made—to both of them—but I would do no one any favors by flaunting convention and drawing more unwanted attention to the proceedings.

I was left at home to learn his fate after it was all decided. The house felt empty, though the children were snug in the nursery, blissfully unaware of their beloved *papi*'s travails. The staff scurried about, largely unnoticed, though I knew they were there, efficiently keeping this behemoth of a house running. Papa had been so proud after the money from the tower had begun rolling in. He built this house as a tribute to that success. And though every inch of it was lovely, today it felt like a gilded prison as I was left to imagine the worst outcomes for Papa, the company, and this family.

Papa loved this house and all it represented, but now as we faced the reality of his ruin, I wondered if we hadn't overstepped our mark. Had we offended the natural order of things by not being contented with our stately home on the rue de Prony? If we'd lived a more modest existence, would the investors have come after Papa with such ardor? If we had been humbler people, would we never have gotten ourselves involved in the Panama mess in the first place? Papa's genius was so rarely challenged, except perhaps in matters of aesthetics, that he thought he was capable of building anything. Worse, the rest of the world had agreed with him.

Until it didn't.

I paced the drawing room, feeling much like the unfortunate tigers I'd seen circling in their small cages when we'd taken the children to the circus last fall. I wondered if my eyes were any less wild, any less terrifying than those magnificent beasts who had been reduced to mere playthings for the amusement of a capricious public. In moments like this, I understood why men pursued violent sports like boxing, rugby, and polo. It allowed them to let off the aggressions that life in the modern world couldn't help but excite even in the most forbearing of souls. But women? We were permitted no such outlet for our anger. We were forced to stopper it in like a cork in a wine bottle and hope it wouldn't explode.

Whether it was a reminder born from one of the antiques that had passed to us from the Eiffel family, or strain from the ordeal we were all under, Bonne Maman Eiffel's face sprang to my mind. She had been a bitter, nasty old woman, and no one of her acquaintance could claim otherwise. But had she always been so, or had a lifetime of suppressing her anger, her frustrations, and the myriad disappointments simply caused her hopes and dreams to fester into a poison dart in her bosom, setting her against those whom she should love, and who would have loved her in return?

I thought of my darling children above stairs and knew that regardless of the result of this trial, the one thing I could maintain control over was how I responded to it. It could break me, or I could rise. It would be easy to say I would choose the latter without hesitation, but it wasn't just a simple choice I could make once and be done with it. It would be a choice I would be forced to make day after day. And there would be times it would be so tempting to let the darkness have me. To wallow in the injustice of the sacrifices I was forced to make at an age when no child should have been forced to make them.

And maybe that's why Bonne Maman had been so against the idea of me taking such an integral role in Papa's life and with the business. It would remove any pretense that the choices in my life were my own. Perhaps if she had argued with more delicacy. Perhaps if she hadn't belittled me so much that I couldn't help but go on the offensive, I might have listened.

But I shook the errant thought from the cobwebs in my brain. It wasn't that she wanted me to have choices in my life; it was that she didn't want me to deviate from the plan she thought was the only one available to a girl of good standing. Whether that path was just a road to misery for her didn't matter . . . it was what society expected of us, and she was perfectly willing to sacrifice my happiness on the altar of respectability.

And if she saw how successfully I'd managed Papa, Adolphe, the children, and all the company affairs too, she wouldn't have a word of praise for me. She'd find things to criticize at every turn. Likely because no one in the whole city of Paris would dare reproach me for the role I played in my father's life and work, and she'd never recover from her jealousy.

I would never be able to do the job well enough to have pleased her. But Maman? She would see what I'd done to finish what she'd started, to raise her family and care for Papa. And she would be proud.

Even if today was a failure, she couldn't have expected more from me.

I couldn't please everyone, so it had to be enough to please her.

I heard footsteps leading into the drawing room, and though I felt scarcely equal to company, I felt lighter at the prospect of not bearing the wait alone. Valentine, Laure, and Tante Marie were shown in by Denis, one of the new footmen, and I threw myself into their arms as if I were two decades younger and not a woman of thirty with a family and a sense of decorum. The latter, I was finding, mattered less and less as Papa's trial drew on.

"We thought we'd come to cheer you up," Valentine said, looking every bit the stylish young matron since her wedding to her darling Camille, an up-and-coming statesman, almost three years before. It seemed impossible that she was grown, married, and the mother of two children already, but time never ceased to be a thief. She looked scarcely older than she had the year Father Christmas made his last appearance, but my eyes were just as biased as a mother's when it came to her and Bébert in particular.

"You've already succeeded marvelously." I pressed a kiss against her cheek. She was still recovering from her last travails but looked healthy enough even to satisfy me.

Tante Marie discreetly gave orders for some refreshment to the footman and took her own embraces in good humor. She was growing a little more frail with age, just like Papa, but her posture was still ramrod straight as the day she'd completed finishing school. "Be honest with us, darling, while the staff can't overhear. How are you holding up?"

"I haven't keeled over weeping. I eat when I can. I manage a few hours of sleep most nights." My voice was cheerier than I felt, but the pretense of holding up was less exhausting than the reality that my spirits were frayed like a fifteen-year-old corset after years of too-tight cinching. I could unravel at any moment, and I preferred that these three women I loved so dearly not bear witness to it.

Laure looked deep in my eyes, and I could see she was unconvinced. But she didn't try to needle me for the truth. What would it serve to admit that with every tick of the minute hand on the clock, my heart stopped, wondering if it was the moment that Papa's verdict had been read to the people. How many minutes would it be before the carriage came with Adolphe bearing the news? I squeezed Laure's hand, appreciative that she didn't press further.

Yves, pushing a cart with fresh-brewed coffee and all manner of baked goods, arrived, rescuing me from my aunt and sisters' questioning.

"Mille-feuilles, even? My, but Cook has been busy," Valentine noted. "He usually saves the pastry baking for Easter."

"Cook always spends his worry in the kitchen," I reminded her. "And a better use of nervous energy I can't imagine."

"Amen to that." Laure helped herself to one of his famous mille-feuilles, her special favorite, and a cup of coffee with a generous measure of cream. Tante Marie widened her eyes at Laure's unabashed helping.

"Stow your questioning brow, Tante. I haven't eaten a thing today, and I won't do Papa any good if I pass out," Laure said. Her voice had found a bit of authority in the past years and it suited her well. Tante Marie didn't look chastened, but she perhaps realized that her niece's appetite wasn't a battle worth picking. We were, for some unexpected reason, expected to sip the coffee and perhaps nibble at a pastry, but leave the lion's share behind. But the days might soon come where we'd regret every crumb wasted.

Laure and Valentine would be fine. Their husbands had made good careers. Tante Marie was even more comfortably settled than they . . . but Adolphe's and my future was tied inextricably to Papa's. If today went badly, I would bear the consequences just as surely as if I'd bribed half of the Assemblée nationale myself. It sure seemed Lesseps and his cronies had. And the newspapers too. The project couldn't afford bad press—but we'd long crossed that point now.

I helped myself to a *canelé*—a lovely custardy cinnamon tart—as well, though I didn't bother with cream in my coffee. I wanted the bitter brew to keep me in the present and keep me sharp in case I was needed. I didn't want to dilute it in the least. I ate, though my stomach wasn't keen on the idea until the rich pastry reminded me of how long it had been since I'd eaten a bit of toast and jam with my morning coffee.

Valentine, not being one to be left out, took a few madeleines for herself, though she was more reserved than we were. Still early days in her marriage, and she was determined to close her stays to the same measurements she'd worn before Marcel and Jean were born.

"Well, what updates do you have for us?" Tante Marie pressed. She hadn't been by since last week, busy as she was with her own affairs.

Adolphe had sworn to recount the events of the day to me without regard for my sensibilities—either feminine or filial—and did so every night once we were out of Papa's earshot. It was bad enough to ask Adolphe to relive the events of the day, but it would have been even crueler to subject Papa to it. I filled in Tante Marie and the girls with exacting detail. I'd learned that skill in Papa's offices, taking notes in meetings and dictation for correspondence. I'd been called on less and less to use those skills as my role in the house grew weightier, but I was pleased to know I had them all the same.

"It will all be over soon." Laure spoke with a certainty based on wishes, rather than facts. "Papa will be acquitted, and it will all be as it was before."

I shook my head. "Even if he's declared innocent, and that still remains to be seen, and even if every newspaper from Paris to Panama that has been calling for his head apologized in the morning edition—which they won't—nothing will change the fact that Papa's name is tarnished by association with this whole sordid affair."

The slurs they'd used against Papa had become bolder as time went on. The rising tinge of anti-Semitism in the press hinted at whether the Bonickhausen-Eiffel family hadn't been very strategic in dropping the old German surname when the family had crossed over to France generations before. There were implications about our religious affiliations, though Papa attended mass regularly, as all our family had done for generations. To call Papa out for wrongdoing where there was cause, I was prepared to bear. The risk of lawsuits was never absent in the construction business. But to imply that said wrongdoing was due to some cultural or genetic predisposition made me uncomfortable on an entirely new level—and not just for Papa but for everyone who didn't fit into the traditional French Catholic mold.

Tante Marie looked sober. "I'm afraid Claire is right. You will face some scrutiny yourselves, and I urge you to brace for it. Some doors will close to you, perhaps permanently. But we'll be given a priceless gift: knowing who our true friends are."

"And when Papa is proven innocent and builds another marvel to outstrip even the tower, the rats will all come scurrying back." Laure had gained some knowledge of society since her marriage and particularly the loss of little Margueritte. As she'd predicted, some young mothers simply let their acquaintance fade without regard for Laure or her feelings.

"You'll have to decide how you'll act when they do," Tante Marie replied. "It will be up to you to welcome them back into your life or to shun them altogether. Though you'll find that carrying a grudge becomes a heavy burden. I think it's better to pretend as if the unpleasantness never happened, but remember well who slighted you. Forgiveness is a virtue, but naïveté is not."

"Well said," a voice said from the doorway.

"Papa!" I found my voice, but it was a husk of itself. The four of us bounded from our seats, temporarily forgetting our decorum, to embrace Papa.

"Home triumphant!" Laure declared. "I knew the judges couldn't possibly take the charges seriously."

I let my aunt and sisters go first, which gave me a chance to see my husband's expression as he followed Papa into the room. To see storm clouds in his velvety brown eyes.

He nodded once in response to the question I'd not yet put to words.

Papa claimed his favorite seat by the window, looking well beyond his sixty years. He looked in my direction, but his eyes never met mine.

"Tell us the good news, Papa," Valentine pressed, sitting on the settee nearest him and leaning over to take his hand.

"The good news is that I have been acquitted of swindling. It was the most serious charge leveled at me."

"Marvelous," said Tante Marie. "Whatever you paid your counsel, he deserves a bonus."

"What aren't you saying?" I interjected, eliciting incredulous looks from my sisters and my aunt, who were used to my tone remaining calm long after they had gone shrill with frustration.

"I was found guilty of breach of trust." He choked on the words like fetid meat. They poisoned him just as surely.

I turned my gaze to Adolphe, who looked scarcely less pained than Papa. "A fine of twenty thousand francs and two years in prison."

"Two years?!" The blood drained from Tante Marie's face. "Surely there has been a misunderstanding. Surely something can be done."

Adolphe spoke in low tones. "We can appeal, and we will. But Rousseau seems to think it won't be won overnight. The judges were benevolent and allowed him several months to set his affairs in order. He's to report in June to serve out his sentence. The best we can hope for is that we can win the appeal before then."

"Does he think it likely?" I asked.

"You know lawyers, Clarinette. They never like to raise hopes. They'd rather their clients be pleasantly surprised than gravely disappointed." Papa tried to inject his words with some levity but wasn't equal to it.

I closed my eyes, willing the maelstrom of thoughts in my brain to quieten. "We have time. We'll rally all our resources and set this thing to rights. Beginning with the press—"

"No, Cherub. We'll leave Rousseau to his work and hope for the best. At this point an aggressive campaign in the press would look tawdry. The best we can do is hope to minimize the damage."

"What will you have me do?" Adolphe looked to Papa directly for the first time since their return. "Name it and I'll see to it."

"Tomorrow," I insisted. "Or next week. Papa needs to rest."

In his own bed. While he can. I didn't dare utter those last words aloud.

"Yes, Claire is right. Tomorrow you will send word to the board of the Compagnie Eiffel that you will convene at their earliest convenience."

"You wish to address the directors to give them your directives for your absence? You'll need weeks to prepare." Adolphe began pacing as he always did when he was formulating a to-do list in his mind.

"No, Son. You will take to them my resignation and my last decree as its president. You will change the name of the company to whatever you see fit, so long as it does not bear my name."

The gasp from Valentine was audible, and I doubt my own reaction was any more composed.

I fumbled for words adequate for the enormity of what he'd just declared. "Are you sure about this, Papa? It's your life's work."

"And it's the only way to protect it. I would rather see the company continue the way I began it without me at the helm and without my name on the atelier than see it dragged into infamy with me. It will be the only thing that could give me solace when I'm in that . . . place."

He spoke with a certitude I did not like, but I could not bring myself to rebuke him for it. Better that we all expect the worst would yet happen so we would be braced for it.

"Of course, Gustave. I will put before them that the company be called the Levallois-Perret Construction Company and will nominate Koechlin as its president. It will look better than me taking over for you."

Papa nodded. Clearly, Adolphe had expected this. And though it pained me, he was right. Koechlin had designed the tower that bore Papa's name—and that always would bear it as long as there was a breath in my body. He was a talented architect and truly understood Papa's vision in a way few did, apart from Adolphe.

And me.

Papa looked satisfied at Adolphe's promise and rose from his fauteuil. "See to it, lad. Knowing you and Koechlin are managing everything is as much as a man could hope for." His eyes turned to me. "And knowing you will keep things going here means just as much. I'm just so sorry to have disappointed you all."

I opened my mouth to contradict him. A better daughter would have assured him that she loved him so well that there was no room in her heart for disappointment. But the words would not come.

The Compagnie Eiffel was no more, at least in name. Papa was removed from the presidency of the enterprise he'd loved as a sixth child. Our family legacy was inexorably stained by the blood of those who had perished in the futile attempt to build the canal and that we'd been engaged too late to salvage from ruin.

And though I wished I could silence it, there was a whisper in my head that wondered what purpose all the sacrifices I'd made in the past fifteen years would serve now that those things were lost.

Chapter Thirty-Eight

June 8, 1893

For four months, we were certain that every week would be the week that Papa's verdict was overturned. We prayed for a telephone call or a telegram from Rousseau letting us know he'd been successful in his endeavors, but no such call or telegram arrived. So on a sunny Thursday morning in June, Papa readied himself to report to the Conciergerie at the Palais de Justice.

And the sight of his small frame and eyes that had long since surrendered to exhaustion as he carried his valise down to the foyer broke my heart.

He was allowed to bring personal effects. He was permitted daily visitors. We were able to provide him with proper meals. He would not freeze to death while he was forced to endure two winters as a prisoner. It was more reassurance than most families would get when sending their loved one off to such a fate, but it didn't soothe me much.

It wasn't his physical well-being that concerned me as much as his spirit. He might be putting on a brave face for us all, but I knew better. Once he entered the jail cell, he would be forever changed. I felt iron bars clench around my heart so that it could scarcely beat; I could only endeavor to imagine how much worse it was for Papa.

"I'll visit you every day," I promised, kissing his cheeks. I forced myself to swallow back the tears. I'd be brave for Papa so he could make his exit from the house with dignity.

"You should attend to the house and the children instead. Go to Sèvres and paint. Busy yourself in charity work if that keen mind of yours needs a bit of exercise. Don't waste your precious time on me, whatever you do."

"Papa." I placed my hands on his biceps and met his eyes.

"I had to try, Cherub. You know that."

"I do. But you won't succeed. Not in this." I'd conceded when it came to the trial because it might have materially damaged his chances, but there would be no keeping me from him as long as the guards would allow me entry.

Two weeks prior, Papa had insisted that none of us would go with him as he reported to serve his sentence. By then, we'd come to terms with the reality that we were out of time for an appeal to go through and Papa would indeed have to serve his sentence. We'd conceded this, for the sake of his pride. As a footman took his one valise and escorted Papa to the waiting carriage that would be back without him within the hour, it took every bit of my resolve not to dissolve into sobs.

But I would remain calm for Papa. And I would ensure that everything would run smoothly at home until he came back.

Two years from now.

The door clicked shut behind Papa and I felt the air squeeze from my lungs. I reached for the back of a chair to steady myself and I felt betrayed by my own body. I needed to be strong, but as soon as Papa was out of sight, my knees reacted as if given permission to collapse. My empty stomach churned, and I wondered if, for the first time in my life, I might faint like one of the leading ladies in an opera. My younger self would have thought it terribly romantic and rife with drama. Now it was just maddening.

Adolphe placed his hands on mine, but wisely offered no platitudes. There were no suitable words of comfort, even for the most eloquent of men. I felt the iron grip on my stomach lessen minutely. It was enough.

"He is equal to this," I said, more to convince myself than anything.

"He is the bravest person I know." Adolphe kissed my temple and pulled me into his arms. "Present company being the only exception."

I chortled into his chest, taking a moment to breathe in the scent of him. All cloves, cinnamon, and sandalwood. The scent of home.

"I can stay home if you don't want to be alone," he murmured into my hair. "We could go for a stroll. Take the children to the park. Whatever you need. I am yours."

I tightened my grip around him. "Tomorrow. I want to do all those things and visit Papa too. I'll take him luncheon every day and letters from Robert. Doodles from Georges and kisses from Geneviève. But today, I think my mind would be easier knowing you were at the atelier. Papa's would be too."

He sighed. "Wise. It will be good for morale too. But I'll skip off Friday as the brass are entitled to do in summer."

"You clearly didn't take every lesson out of Papa's books. Though he was more likely to work from home when the weather got too warm."

"Your father has been my role model in many things, but you and the children will always come before my work. I will never be the great man your father is and make a name that will forever be linked with Paris, so I see no reason to make the same sacrifices he was forced to."

"Papa was an attentive and loving father and we all understood how important his work was."

"I'm not talking about the sacrifices he made on his own behalf. I'm talking about the ones he required of you." Adolphe kissed me again. This time he kissed my lips, slowly, tenderly, tinged with the hint of regret that he couldn't linger.

"You'll be all right?" His eyes searched mine for doubt as he pulled away.

I forced a smile. Papa wasn't the only one who needed my strength. "I always am, my love."

The solitude in the house was now as profound as any I'd known. Papa had taken his essence with him to prison instead of being good enough to leave a bit behind for me. I waffled about the house, unable to find useful occupation that I could stand for more than a few moments. Knitting was hopeless; though I'd become better at the skill, I needed the pleasure of company to make it less tedious. Robert was engaged with his lessons with his tutor, and the nanny wouldn't appreciate my interference with the routine of the younger two.

Reprieve was found when a footman delivered the post to the drawing room, where I tried and failed to read a novel Tante Marie had recommended. There were the usual bills from the grocer, butcher, and bakery. A letter to Adolphe from family in Marseille. No invitations of any kind. Of course no one had come to pay calls this morning. People were well-enough informed to know we wouldn't be at home to visitors on such a day . . . but it was a rare summer day when there wasn't at least one invitation extended for some event or other. This was undoubtedly a portent of things to come, but I couldn't dwell on it.

A yellow envelope with familiar scrawl caught my eye. Ursule. I'd not received a letter from her in months, but the return address showed she was back in town.

Ma chère amie,

You won't be surprised to know that news of your papa's troubles has reached me, even in my studio. I can only imagine how your heart must be breaking. Of course the lion's share of my sympathy goes to those poor souls who find themselves without the reserves so desperately needed, but I remain convinced that your dear papa is an honorable man who thought he could complete the work to his exacting standards. Even great men make mistakes, and usually to scale with the proportion of their greatness. And the women in their lives must pay the price along with them. I know none of this will change what you are going through but know that I am now and always have been your friend. All you need do is send the word, and I shall be at your stoop with canvas and easel in hand.

~Ursule

I pressed the letter to my bosom, grateful for the friendship it extended, though I'd done precious little to deserve it over the past fifteen years. Could I drop her a line and resume our friendship where it had left off so abruptly? Unlikely. But perhaps we could develop a new friendship based on who we had become as women. We'd led incredibly different lives up to this point, but a common ground could always be found beneath the feet of an easel.

Chapter Thirty-Nine

A knock sounded at the door before dawn. I sat bolt upright and tossed the covers onto Adolphe's sleeping frame. Pauline was at the door, fully dressed, but her hair still in the braids she wore for sleeping. I guessed the hour to be near five, given that she looked fully awake, though not entirely ready for the day.

"The children? Is something wrong?"

"No, madame. There is a telephone call for Monsieur Salles. I wouldn't have disturbed you, but it sounded very urgent." Little wisps of hair that had escaped her braids, illuminated by the kerosene lamp she'd carried to light her way to our rooms, gave her a frazzled appearance. She mistrusted the telephone in the best of circumstances, but being forced to field a call so early had left her especially rattled.

Adolphe was already half out of bed, wiping the sleep from his eyes. "The atelier?"

"I don't like to stoop to conjecture, monsieur, but it was none of the voices I know from the office. The man refused to give his name but said it was an urgent matter of business."

Adolphe grabbed his dressing gown from the chair where it lay draped and rushed past Pauline in the doorway and down the stairs.

"Shall I leave you to rest longer, madame?"

"No, that's all right, Pauline. I couldn't hope to sleep after all that." And if the call was as important as Pauline seemed to think it was, I'd do better to be dressed to face the day.

"I wouldn't expect so. How would you like to dress this morning?"

Not knowing what news the phone call might bring, I scarcely felt prepared to make an informed decision. "For a morning at home, but something smart. The white tea gown with the Brussels lace and amethyst redingote will do well enough."

"Very good, madame." It was a lovely gown for receiving anyone at home, loose enough to allow me to bustle about the house, and the flowing redingote could be exchanged for a fitted overdress if I had to leave. Pauline took extra pains with my hair and even suggested I wear my mother's amethysts that she'd loved so dearly. If nothing else, the cold gems might serve as a talisman for good luck. Maman would have liked it that way.

Pauline rushed off to finish her own morning toilette and I promised to linger above stairs for another quarter of an hour before descending for breakfast to allow the staff a moment to collect themselves. I stared at the door, hoping Adolphe would reemerge to inform me of what merited a phone call before dawn, but the quarter hour came and went, and he did not return.

"Monsieur Salles ordered the carriage around." Pauline looked less disheveled as I entered the dining room. The table was set with coffee, pastries, bread, jam, and butter. Nothing complicated on such short notice, and I was grateful for it. "He's already changed and gone."

I blinked. "In such a hurry. Did he say why?"

"No, madame. He just asked that you stay at home this morning and wait for him here."

I stopped myself from rolling my eyes in front of Pauline, no matter how exasperating Adolphe was being. "Did Monsieur Salles leave any other instructions?"

"Only that we might have company later." At this, she looked as exasperated as I. Company? Was it to be one guest for luncheon at midday? A dozen for a cocktail reception after dinner this evening? How could one prepare?

"Take stock of the pantry to see what Cook can make in a hurry. We should be prepared for anything."

"Very well." She bowed her head and scurried off to the kitchens with a slew of orders for the staff on the tip of her tongue, no doubt.

I forced myself to eat, though the coffee was the only offering that appealed. If Adolphe flew off in such a hurry, the day might quickly devolve into the sort of mess where I'd be grateful to have had some sustenance to get through it.

Breakfast was cleared away almost two full hours before I usually rose for the day at seven. The staff was barely stirring in the moments before dawn. The stillness of the hour didn't bring me peace. The eerie silence ushered in only disquiet. I wanted to write notes to Tante Marie and the girls. Édouard too. Bébert was home from university but could be left to sleep until there was news to share with him. But what would I tell them? There was something wrong with either the company or Papa, I'd convinced myself of that much, but what use would it be to bother anyone until I knew what to prepare them for?

Pauline entered the drawing room, where I paced, no longer pretending that I was equal to any occupation more than wearing a trench in Papa's expensive Turkish rugs and staring at the tapestries that Papa's grandfather had made all those years ago. For the first time in perhaps ten years, I found the space to admire the attention to detail. The subtle variations of the colors in the shepherdess's gown. The precision of the thousands of stitches. Their craft was different, but this was the gift of the Eiffel family. A genius for detail. An eye for beauty. An insistence upon perfection.

"I envied her, you know."

Pauline took her place at my side, looking up at the tapestry with admiring eyes of her own. "She is quite lovely, though I don't think she outstrips your beauty in any meaningful way."

"How diplomatic of you, dear Pauline. But no, not her looks. I envy her the simplicity of her life. She has but one responsibility: to guard her sheep."

"You think that's so easy, madame? She has quite the flock. And you might not think the task so easy when the wolves came to the hills looking for their supper."

I chuckled. "I suppose that's a fair point."

"That's precisely what's happened to you, if I may be so bold. You've been a shepherdess of this flock for fifteen years now. A fine one. But the wolves have come to the hills to test your mettle, just as it's been tested a hundred times before now. And I've no doubt you will rise to the challenges before you with the same grace as you've done before."

"I always appreciate when you speak plainly to me, Pauline. You've been a rock to me all these years."

"It's what your dear mother would have wanted, and I could ask for no higher calling than that. I've only come to ask if I can fetch anything for you that might bring you a bit of comfort."

"You've already been a wonder, Pauline." I took her hands in mine and squeezed them. "I'll be fine. If not now, I will be when Adolphe finds his way home to explain what the trouble is."

Uncharacteristically, she patted my cheek as she used to do when I was a child. Remembering the halcyon days when things were as they should be, with Maman alive and well.

"They're lucky to have you, you know. The lot of them."

She padded from the room with her quiet efficiency, and I watched her shut the door behind her. It was another hour before I heard voices in the hallway and footsteps on the marble tile leading to the drawing room. Adolphe entered, not looking as though he'd spent a harried morning at the offices as I expected.

"I've brought you a surprise, my darling," he said, and opened the door a bit wider.

"Papa!" I dashed to my father and wrapped my arms around him, pelting his cheeks with kisses.

"That Rousseau is a clever chap," Papa said as I walked him to his favorite chair.

"The statute of limitations had lapsed," Adolphe added. "If they'd succeeded in getting a court date sooner, Gustave would never have seen a day in jail."

I gaped at him, probably looking a fool. "Why did it take so long?"

"They wanted to make an example of me." Papa eased into his chair with a groan. He looked whiter and more frail, even in the week since he'd gone to prison.

Édouard and dear Marie Louise entered, their one carriage having been just behind Papa's, looking as relieved as the rest of us. There was a healthy glow to Édouard's skin and a brightness in his eyes that too many nights of drinking and carousing had robbed from him, but Marie Louise had brought it back. I kissed both their cheeks, gestured for them to sit, and sent a footman off to rouse Bébert and to give word to the kitchens that we would need refreshment.

Pauline had anticipated my request and came followed by a footman pushing a cart laden with coffee and all manner of pastries. They all tucked in, having been denied their breakfast before now.

"Pauline, please ring the girls and Tante Marie to join us at once. They'll want to see your return with their own eyes."

"And I them. I should very much like to have all my chicks in the nest tonight." He turned to Pauline. "Tell them to bring their things and stay the night. Husbands and babies too."

She hurried out to follow the order, unable to conceal a smile of relief.

"It will be the merriest house party Paris has ever seen." I bent and kissed his cheek before pouring his coffee.

"Not a house party. Just a family gathered under one roof for a pleasant meal and good company. And I hope you're all amenable to doing it often. I've been given a second chance at life and I'm going to foist myself on all of you at every opportunity." Though he'd been imprisoned only a week, his expression made it clear he was eager to make up for lost time. Not only those horrible days behind bars, but also the countless hours he'd spent at his atelier instead of at home with us.

Adolphe rested a hand on Papa's shoulder. "I bet ten francs that you'll be back in the offices of the Compagnie Eiffel by Monday morning, ready to take back the helm from Koechlin."

"No indeed, Son. The Levallois-Perret Construction Company will retain that name and Koechlin's job is safe. I am finished with building bridges and towers. It's time to let younger men take over." There was resignation but no melancholy in his words.

"What will you do to keep yourself busy, Papa?" asked Édouard. "You're not one to sit idle or putter about the garden."

"No, you know well my views on indolence, and you seem to have finally taken a lesson or two to heart, and thank God for it. But as for me, I'll move on from the company and finally devote myself to my research. New technologies, radio, weather. Whatever captures my fancy. I think I've earned the right to become the mad scientist in my old age, don't you?"

"We'll clear the attics for a laboratory. No doubt fine enough to make the universities envious," I said. I likely would have swept the cobwebs from the rafters myself, so glad was I to have him home.

"Oh, I have a space already, Cherub." He gestured to the window in the direction of his tower. "How many can study the world and how it works from a bird's-eye view?"

"Not many," I admitted. "I think it's marvelous, Papa."

It wasn't long before the entire family had assembled and was gathered around Papa to hear of his ordeal and to regale him with stories of what he'd missed during his short incarceration. And beyond that, what he'd missed when he was preoccupied with his trial. Preoccupied with salvaging the Panama project. Preoccupied with the tower. That he realized he'd been given a second chance to be truly present in the lives of his family was the biggest blessing I could have ever imagined.

While Valentine entertained everyone by letting little Jean grip her fingers and attempt to walk across the drawing room floor, I quietly stole to the little secretary desk I kept in the corner for my correspondence. Ursule's yellow stationery was calling me like a beacon. I pulled out a piece of my own stationery, a more sedate shade of cream with my monogram in crimson embossed at the top.

Ma très chère Ursule,

If you are free tomorrow in the afternoon, bring your case. Mine has been collecting dust in a closet for far too long, but perhaps we can find an obliging chestnut tree to pose for us once again.

In friendship,
~Claire

Chapter Forty

August 10, 1933

"Mamie, do you think we can have ice cream when we get to the top?" asked my granddaughter Solange, her large brown eyes, so much like her mother's, pleading. Her ladylike hand fit neatly into mine, which was once smooth like fine porcelain, now a bit bony with age and showing a few spots from too many hours in the sun without gloves. Perhaps Bonne Maman had been right, and I should have taken care to cover my skin in the out-of-doors, but every blemish on my hands revealed a blessed memory.

"It's been quite some time since your old *mamie* made it to the top, but I think the ice cream will be on one of the lower floors. I am sure there is some to be had, and I've no doubt you can persuade me. It isn't every day my granddaughter celebrates her tenth birthday."

"Very true, Mamie," she said sagely. It would seem that her entry into the world of double digits had convinced her that she was now quite grown up and must act the part. Perhaps that was her mother's well-intended influence, but I'd do what I could to counter it. Childhood was far too short and there was no sense rushing this darling child, my great joy, into adulthood before it was truly necessary.

She lived with me on the rue Rabelais with her parents and younger brother, Bernard. The four of them had been my greatest comfort since Papa and Adolphe passed just a few days apart from each other. It seemed that one could not bear to be long without the other, and I was grateful they had each other in the great beyond. It was still hard to believe they'd been gone these ten years. Some days, the pain was as fresh as the days after Papa suffered his first aneurysm. He ended up enduring a series of them before he finally went to his rest. Adolphe passed suddenly just three days later, the day before Papa's funeral, and I was left to enter the year 1924 alone.

Had it not been for Ninette and her dear family, surviving the months that followed would have been a hardship indeed.

Solange and I took the elevator to the very top of Papa's tower, which had been slated for demolition two decades before, but whose utility in technology had spared it from the wrecking crew. Papa had fitted the tower for radio during the Great War and made advances in aviation while I ran a hospital in Switzerland. I was awarded a Medal of Honor for my work there and found it some of the most rewarding work of my life.

Every so often, there were renewed attempts to take down the tower to make room for some building or other in the city that never ceased to grow, but it showed its resiliency more with each passing year. I knew that would have made Papa proud, and it was one of my great comforts that the tower had not been demolished in his lifetime. Though it had to be said that Papa sometimes felt the tower eclipsed his own legacy. Probably due to the unpleasantness in Panama, Papa's funeral was quieter than that of other great men of France. There was no send-off for Papa like there had been for, say, Victor Hugo. But in the end, I thought the solemn church funeral was better suited to Papa's quiet dignity. And in truth, the pomp of a state funeral would have been an ordeal I would have had to overcome. Far better to have a moment to grieve and reflect on a life well lived.

We joined the queue for the lift, and Solange's face lit up with anticipation. It wasn't her first trip to the tower, but we did try to make these excursions rare enough to be memorable. The ride to the top was smoother now than it had been forty years before, but so it always was; progress had a way of creeping into all things. And I had to admit it was usually—but not always—for the better. Rather than going to the top, I herded Solange out on the first platform.

"Let's make a proper day of this, shall we? Not just ice cream, but luncheon too."

Solange's lovely face split into a grin. The tower's restaurant was a special treat for a child her age. Heaven knew I was never permitted to eat in public, except when traveling, at such a tender age, but things had changed. Especially since the war.

We were escorted to a table with a fine view of the city. After a few moments a waiter appeared, looking to us expectantly. I placed my order for *sole meunière,* then looked to Solange, who remained mute, expecting me to choose a dish for her. Her eyes were wide, and I could practically see her thoughts telegraphed across her dear forehead: *Please remember I don't like fish.*

"You may order. You're quite old enough to make such decisions for yourself, I should think."

This directive might have seemed in contradiction to my idea that Solange ought to be permitted to cling to her childhood as long as she was able, but in my view, childhood was meant to be a training ground. Children needed guidance, of course, but little by little, they must learn to make decisions for themselves. Growing up wasn't just about learning to act ladylike; it was about becoming a lady with a mind of her own.

She placed her order, selecting braised chicken over the fish, and sighed contentedly as she looked out over the cityscape.

"It is so beautiful, isn't it, Mamie?"

"The most beautiful city in the world, darling. I'm glad you don't take it for granted." I took a sip from the glass of crisp sauvignon blanc the waiter had brought and leaned back in my chair to enjoy the bustling scene before me.

"Not at all. I wish I could memorize every corner of it." Her eyes were transfixed on the city below, just as my dear friend Ursule used to focus on her canvases.

Ursule and I had resumed our old friendship, though she was rarely in town anymore. It was a thrill to get postcards from far-flung places like Indochina, Algeria, and Tahiti. We had luncheon together whenever she was back in Paris, which was becoming more frequent as she began to slow down in her sunset years. She'd married a painter, Rémy, and they had a daughter: Amélie Claire. She'd never succeeded in getting her art into the Salon but found acclaim elsewhere. And from what I could tell, it seemed to be enough for her. And that, too, was one of my great comforts.

"I'm sure you will, darling girl. This city will have to brace itself for your brilliance."

She giggled at my grandmotherly enthusiasm, but I wasn't speaking in jest. She was an incredible girl, and the city was lucky to have her.

I produced a parcel from my large handbag. "I know most of your gifts will be after dinner tonight, but I wanted you to have this one while I had you all to myself."

Indeed, her "official" gift was a lovely party dress I'd had made for her, and she could open it with all the others when we gathered for dinner that night. But this was to be something special between the two of us.

She daintily unwrapped the box and found a Leica camera, small enough to fit easily in a handbag. It was incredible to me how quickly the devices had shrunk from the unwieldy boxes we'd had to pose in front of when the tower was in its infancy. I'd included some film and all the other accoutrements she'd need to be able to snap photos. She was simply mad about her father's camera, but he claimed it was too dear to let her "play" with. So I'd taken it upon myself to get her one of her own. With the help of a competent shop clerk, I'd selected the smallest model available, and one that should be simple enough for her to master easily. If her interest continued, she could procure more elaborate equipment when the time was right.

I'd been about her age when I got my first easel, canvas, and paints, and I wanted to be the one to give her the same gift. Even if it was only a pleasant amusement for her, it would be well worth the investment.

"Oh, Mamie! This is incredible! No one in my class has a camera. I can't wait to show them my photos!"

"I hope you'll have fun with it. Just remember that photography is an art form. Think about how you spend your film as carefully as you spend your pocket money. A few snaps of your school chums will be a lovely souvenir, but think carefully about what you want to preserve."

"Of course, Mamie. I'll look for the most beautiful things and help them last forever."

"Not just beautiful. Sometimes things that are worth saving aren't beautiful. They're real. They're meaningful. But they're not always beautiful." The painting of Rosa Bonheur's with the oxen sprang to mind. It was captivating, but I wouldn't call it beautiful. Not in the conventional sense.

"How will I know, Mamie?" she asked intently, though her eyes were fixed on the booklet of instructions for the camera.

"You'll learn to pay attention. Your eye will develop over time."

"You sound like an artist," she said, looking up. "Did you study?"

A small smile tugged at my lips. "A bit when I was about your age. I wanted to be a painter."

"Why didn't you, Mamie?"

It was a natural question, especially coming from a curious and intelligent child, but one I was loath to answer. I took another sip of the chilled wine as I considered my response. "I was called to different things," I said. "And I was willing to sacrifice my art before I was willing to let down my family."

Solange looked out at the skyline, taking in my answer.

"That must have been a hard choice."

"It was. And it was one I had to make a thousand times over. Every day, I had to choose between my duty and my art. And it was rare that the art prevailed. But it is my hope and my prayer that you won't have to make such a choice. And certainly not when you're as young as I was."

And I looked at this darling child, only four years younger than I was when my life was irrevocably sent on a new course. I couldn't imagine her being charged with such weighty responsibilities at so young an age. And I'd do everything possible to ensure that would never happen. She should be free to pursue her passions and discover her own path, not have one chosen for her.

And blessedly, the world was becoming more friendly to that reality.

"May I take some photos while we wait for our luncheon, Mamie?"

"Of course, darling. It's your camera, and I want you to have fun with it."

She hopped up from her seat and kissed my cheek before dashing to the edge of the platform to capture the skyline. Her photos would be the same as millions of others taken from the same vantage point, but as she grew, she would find subjects that were more uniquely her own. But I had to admit, for a first subject, the city of Paris would never be a poor choice.

I smiled as I watched her flit along the observation area, as intent as a trained professional as she chose her perspective. It was, perhaps, a lavish gift for one so young, but what good was money if it couldn't be used to encourage the dreams of children? And I knew she'd be asking for a darkroom next, but her father would have to help in that endeavor a few years down the road. I didn't know one of the chemicals from the other and was too late in life to be fussed with learning them now. No, I'd slip a few francs into her pocket for film and professional developing fees until she was old enough to do it herself.

Her chestnut hair glinted in the August sun as she judiciously captured the city below, considering the light and angles with a cautious eye.

I hoped Papa and Adolphe could see this precocious, darling girl standing on the tower they built and studying the city they loved with such serious intent. They would have been just as proud of her as I was.

And though there was no such thing as a life lived without regrets, this tower in all its monstrous beauty helped to make them feel insignificant in comparison with all the incredible things I'd seen and done in the course of one short human life.

Author's Note

I visited Paris for the first time when I was eighteen. I was studying in Avignon, and during the summer break I spent six weeks traveling with a shoddy backpack, a Eurail Pass, my meager savings, and the good graces of my hardworking parents (thank you again). I visited the major capitals of western Europe, ate amazing food, and saw sights that my small-town-girl heart had only dreamed of. And the last stop before heading back to Avignon before fall term was Paris. The city I'd dreamed of visiting from the time I was in third grade. I'd already had my breath taken away by the splendor of Rome's ancient architecture, the quiet dignity of Vienna's enchanting coffee shops, the friendly charms of Dublin's bed-and-breakfasts, and the vibrancy of London's West End theaters. But Paris was . . . Paris.

It seemed like every corner held significance from a book I'd read, a tidbit of history I'd loved, or a new delight altogether. I knew it was overdone and clichéd, but a full tour of the Eiffel Tower was toward the top of my to-see list. I remembered feeling awed at the view and, for once, not too annoyed with the ever-present crowds. After all, visiting the tower is a top-tier bucket-list item for people all over the world. People flock to it out of admiration for its beauty or out of respect for the feat of architecture that it is.

Of course there are those who scoff and say it's merely "a lamppost with a publicist" (thank you to Hannah Waddingham and the writers of *Ted Lasso* for that laugh while I was working on this manuscript), but their censure pales in comparison to the controversy the tower stirred in the late 1880s when it was proposed and built. Despite the criticism then and now, there's no denying that this massive structure, originally painted red to attract attention and designed to be removed after twenty years, has become the symbol for this remarkable city, and France as a whole.

For those of you who read *A Bakery in Paris* (and if you haven't, you should!), Claire Eiffel's story takes place roughly ten to twenty years after Lisette's timeline, in the period known in French history as *la Belle Époque*: the beautiful era. After the calamity of the Franco-Prussian War and the massacre following the Paris Commune, France enjoyed forty-odd years of unprecedented prosperity. Paris was the cultural hub of the world, and men like Gustave Eiffel ruled the growing elite class of cognoscenti in the city.

Eiffel succeeded in building the most recognizable monument, not just in France, but in the entire world. That he designed the internal workings of America's iconic monument, the Statue of Liberty, was just one mote accolade on an impressive résumé. Yet, despite decades of studying French history and culture, I'd known little about Gustave Eiffel's story. There is no place for him in the Panthéon. There is no wide, glistening Boulevard Eiffel as there is for the famous Prefect Haussmann. His funeral rites were subdued compared to those for a favored son of Paris like Victor Hugo. He was Icarus, and the Panama Canal was the sun that tarnished what had otherwise been a career almost entirely without blemish, especially by the standards of the nineteenth century. His services were enlisted too late to save the project, which was no fault of his own. But that he was paid well for his work when more than eight hundred thousand people lost all they had invested in the gargantuan project was enough to condemn him in the court of public opinion, even after the success of the tower. The result was that Gustave's role in the history books has been minimized compared to other men of similar significance.

If Gustave's role has been minimized, the contributions of his daughter Claire have been almost entirely lost from the historical record altogether. I had the privilege of two research visits to the Eiffel archives, housed at the Musée d'Orsay, where I was able to pore over family correspondence, photographs, and other memorabilia. Claire's correspondence showed an indefatigable devotion to her family—especially her father—and a keen intellect. Had she been given the same opportunities that her father made use of and that her brothers (at least in their youth) squandered, she might have been the talent to outshine them all. But as so many of the details of her life have been lost to time, I have had to rely on the "fiction" half of "historical fiction" rather heavily to bring this narrative to life by extrapolating from the better-documented elements of Gustave's life.

The timeline of events is largely unaltered and respects the known dates of building projects, pregnancies, births, deaths, press releases, and so on. Nearly every detail included in this book to do with the tower is pulled from documented history. On a more personal level, Claire's concern for her overbearing grandmother's influence on Laure was included in a letter to her beloved aunt Marie from her stay in Portugal just two months after Claire's mother had died. From the tone of her letter, she had already taken on the role of surrogate mother to her siblings. I expect she'd come to occupy that space gradually over the course of her mother's long bouts of illness, and it could be why it was so natural for her to take over officially as the female head of the household after Marguerite's passing.

By all accounts, Bonne Maman Eiffel was a formidable woman. She was the driving force behind her husband's success, and later her son's to a somewhat lesser degree. Whether she was quite as domineering as I have depicted her, we cannot be certain, but I am confident that she was a woman of strong opinions who was not to be crossed. It is true that Gustave had several failed proposals to young women whose parents objected to the newness of his fortune (one of those stories is depicted in the largely fictional but well-crafted film *Eiffel*, which I highly recommend). Gustave did enlist his mother's help in securing an engagement to Marie "Marguerite" Gaudelet. She was only seventeen years old to Gustave's thirty-one when they married in 1862, but despite the businesslike beginning of their courtship, they appear to have been deeply devoted to each other.

What is less certain is the nature of Claire and Adolphe's courtship and marriage. Given that neither of Claire's brothers had the skill set or the drive to run the Compagnie Eiffel, it was logical that Gustave would have looked within the company to find his replacement. Marriage to his eldest daughter would have ensured it stay under family influence, so to assume there was a bit of nudging on Gustave's part to see the couple wed seems within the scope of plausibility. Whether Claire was willing or reluctant, we cannot be entirely sure. Given that she was a young woman of learning and intellect, I felt very comfortable giving her some doubts about the union.

I found no correspondence between the couple in the archives, which leads me to believe they were not often separated, despite having the financial means to travel apart. There aren't many candid photos of the couple together to judge the warmth of their union, as I suspect Adolphe himself took many of the more casual family photos in the early twentieth century when personal cameras became more readily available. However, the photos of Claire with her children, especially her daughter, Ninette, display a warmth that cannot be fabricated. It was plain to my eyes that Claire adored her children.

Gustave insisted the young couple live with him for the rest of his life, and it seems, despite what modern sensibilities would expect, the trio got on famously. It likely helped that their residences on the rue de Prony (now converted to office buildings) and later the rue Rabelais (sadly demolished and now a modern embassy building) were spacious enough to allow for the size of their personalities. After his retirement from the Compagnie Eiffel, Claire and her father did spend time separately at the various homes they owned in France and Switzerland, but the correspondence during those times was frequent and affectionate.

Perhaps the biggest creative license I took was Claire's penchant for art. While there are numerous sketches from Gustave and simply *stunning* notebooks from Adolphe preserved in the archives, that Claire herself had artistic talent was an invention of my own. It was a point for her to bond with her father as well as Adolphe, and a link between Claire and the world of design. Unlike her contemporary, the illustrious Emily Roebling of Brooklyn Bridge fame, I don't believe Claire possessed the engineering knowledge that her father and husband did but would have had her opinions on aesthetics and design. Likewise, Ursule is a fabrication of my own, crafted to be a doppelgänger for Claire herself. Had Claire's mother lived, and she'd not been roped into becoming her father's confidante, house manager, and crisis coordinator, would she have pursued her art in a serious way, or taken a more conventional path for a nineteenth-century woman?

I think many of us get caught up in the "what if" question about pivotal moments in our past. *What if I'd chosen a different college?*

What if I'd said yes to the date with that guy from philosophy? What if I'd taught English in Martinique instead of going to grad school right away? We like to think about how making opposite choices of the ones we made in our past would have somehow magically come to perfect, or at least better, outcomes. For Claire, the biggest of those obviously would have been: *What if my mother had lived?* In my heart, I do think Claire, my version of her, would have chosen to pursue art and had a measure of success at it. But in the nineteenth century, it would have been an incredibly difficult slog for a woman in a field that is already difficult enough without additional obstacles. The Eiffel name might have helped to leverage her way into the art world, but it would have likely become a liability in the days after the Panama Canal scandal.

The truth that mattered to me is that, had Claire Eiffel been given a fraction of the opportunities that modern women of similar circumstances in the western world are afforded, she would have been a brilliant addition to whatever field she chose to pursue. But like so many women of her time, she was shunted out of the spotlight and into the service of great men who were able to achieve greatness only by dint of the support the women in their lives provided.

Claire's granddaughter Solange did indeed pursue photography and has at least one book published of her work. That Claire gave her beloved Solange her first camera was an invention of mine, but symbolically true. Claire sacrificed so that her daughter and granddaughters would have infinitely more choices than she ever had.

Today, Claire's likeness is preserved in the display in Gustave's apartment on the top story of the Eiffel Tower in the form of a wax figurine à la Madame Tussauds, standing ready to serve her father and Thomas Edison, whose figures appear deep in conversation. No doubt about serious matters of great men. I spent more than a few minutes staring not at the two great men of science but at the likeness of the brilliant, capable woman who selflessly supported her father throughout the course of his storied career. I'm profoundly glad that she is remembered there—I think she'd be glad of it.

I am writing this note on the one hundredth anniversary of Gustave Eiffel's passing and just a few days shy of the centennial of Adolphe's, and I lift a metaphorical glass of champagne (not on an empty stomach!) in their honor. But most of all, I toast to Claire and the remarkable woman she was. I hope you'll join me in celebrating her story.

Fondly,
~Aimie

Reading Group Guide

1. Bonne Maman Eiffel proves a formidable opponent to Claire in the early chapters. Why do you think she is so hard on her granddaughter? Do you think her actions are in any way justified? What do you think is the significance of the corset scene?

2. Claire, almost immediately after the death of her mother, ascends from peer to mother figure to her siblings. How does she seem to feel about this? How do the others react to her assuming this role?

3. Claire, early in the novel, is forced to leave a painting session she desperately needed after her mother's funeral. What does this symbolize in a larger sense, and what does it foreshadow for her?

4. Gustave trusts Claire with more and more responsibility as time goes on. How does Claire react to these added burdens? Do you feel he was wrong to put such pressure on an adolescent girl?

5. Discuss the evolution of Claire's relationship with Adolphe. What are some pivotal moments as their relationship matures?

Do you feel their marriage was a happy one? Was Gustave right to encourage the union?

6. Claire's mother, while never present on the page, looms large over the narrative. How do you feel losing her mother impacted Claire? Her siblings? What are some instances in the story that illustrate this?

7. Claire has, out of obligation to her family, abandoned her pursuit of the arts. Usrule, on the other hand, has been given full rein to study and paint as much as she likes. Both lives have their advantages and disadvantages. What do you feel the author was trying to illustrate with Ursule as a foil?

8. How do the various "catastrophes" surrounding the tower and the Panama Canal affect Claire? How does she respond to the assorted obstacles that fall in the path of her father's and husband's careers? What do you think this tells us about her character?

9. In the final chapter, we see Claire and her granddaughter enjoying a special birthday outing. What is the significance of the gift Claire offers Solange? Why do you think she chooses to give such an extravagant gift to a young child?

10. Ultimately, do you think Claire was fulfilled? What do you think she would have changed about her life? What do you think was a driving question in her life?

For more book club resources, for further reading, or to book me for a virtual visit to your book club, please visit www.aimiekrunyan.com.

Acknowledgments

I wish to express my humble thanks to all those who helped bring this story into the world, including:

- My incredible agent, Kevan Lyon, for being a devoted champion to my work and historical fiction in general. I'm so grateful to have you in my corner.

- My talented editor, Tessa Woodward, whose enthusiasm for this project was a beacon of light when I needed it.

- Mary Interdonati, Madelyn Blaney, and the whole team at William Morrow and HarperCollins for the long hours helping bring Claire's story into the world. You are the unsung heroes of the publishing world.

- Caroline Hewitt, audiobook narrator extraordinaire. Thank you for giving Claire her voice. (Also, Micheline and Tempèsta too!)

- Claire Guitton and Fabrice Golec of the archives department of the Musée d'Orsay for their help and hospitality during my research. The days I spent in the archives truly helped bring Claire to life, and I am so thankful.

- Savin Yeatman-Eiffel (Claire's great-grandson!) and the Association of the Descendants of Gustave Eiffel for directing me to the archives and for keeping Gustave's work preserved for generations to come. I hope you will see the love in this tribute to your ancestors.

- My dear writing community, not limited to: Kimberly Brock, Andrea Catalano, Kate Quinn, Janie Chang, Heather Webb, Eliza Knight, J'nell Ciesielski, Rachel McMillan, the Lyonesses, the Tall Poppies, the Business Hat ladies . . . you're all amazing and I appreciate you more than I can say.

- Reader groups like Bloom with Tall Poppy Writers, Friends and Fiction, the Romance of Reading, Great Thoughts Great Readers, Readers Coffeehouse, Bookworms Anonymous, A Novel Bee, Blue Sky Book Chat, and so many others—you help keep us authors going. Many thanks to you and to your hardworking leaders.

- Independent booksellers, especially Macdonald Book Shop in my beloved Estes Park, my hometown bookshop, Face in a Book, The King's English, The Poisoned Pen, The Ripped Bodice, FoxTale Book Shoppe, Litchfield Books, Cleary's Bookstore, and every other indie bookshop here and abroad for being the beating heart of the book world. I love you all.

- Stephanie, Todd, Carol, Danielle, Julie, Jim, and all the rest of my wonderful friends for all your support.

- The Trumbly and Vetter families for their unflagging support. Especially my mother-in-law, Maureen, who holds the land speed record for liking and sharing every bookish post I put on social media.

- Jiji for being a patient and understanding Editor Cat. I'm sorry I went to France (okay, not really). And Zuri for keeping him on his toes.

And my foremost thanks to:

- My darling children, Aria and Ciaran, for putting up with their mother's bookish nonsense. I love you more than I can put into words. Now please stop squabbling and clean your rooms.

- As always, my incredible husband, Jeremy. I am so grateful for the life we continue to build together and I'm looking forward to decades more of shared adventures. (And thank you for being brave enough to drive in Paris.)

About the Author

AIMIE K. RUNYAN is a multipublished and bestselling author of historical and contemporary fiction. She was nominated for the Rocky Mountain Fiction Writers' Writer of the Year Award, named as a Historical Novel Society Editors' Choice selection, and chosen as a five-time finalist for the Colorado Book Awards. She is an adjunct instructor for the Drexel University MFA in Creative Writing program and endeavors to be active in the literary community in Colorado and beyond. She lives in the Rocky Mountains with her wonderful husband, two (usually) adorable children, two (always) adorable cats, and a dragon.

READ MORE BY
AIMIE K. RUNYAN

"Aimie K. Runyan whips up a feast of a novel, full of the warmth and heart characters give each other during two despairing periods of French history. Recipes for boulangerie classics remind us of the power of simple ingredients, artfully assembled. Lisette and Micheline walk their own unique paths to happiness, fighting for their independence and finding loves that support their true selves. As delicious and satisfying as a perfect cup of *chocolat chaud*."
— KERRI MAHER, internationally bestselling author of *The Paris Bookseller*

"Equal parts fascinating and horrifying, *The School for German Brides* is a riveting tale of love, loss, and survival, not only of life but of the human spirit. Readers are dipped into a genteel world of young ladies, wooing suitors, satin dresses, and proper etiquette, but this world is a thin veneer for hatred and intolerance for anything less than perfect. Compelling from start to finish, this is Runyan's finest work yet."
— J'NELL CIESIELSKI, author of *The Ice Swan*

DISCOVER GREAT AUTHORS, EXCLUSIVE OFFERS, AND MORE AT HC.COM.
Available wherever books are sold.